The House by Princes Park

The House by Princes Park

Maureen Lee

ORION

First published in Great Britain in 2002
by Orion
an imprint of the Orion Publishing Group Ltd.

Copyright © 2002 Maureen Lee

A CIP catalogue record for this book
is available from the British Library.

ISBN 0 75 283803 2

Typeset by Deltatype Ltd, Birkenhead, Merseyside

Set in Monotype Bembo

Printed in Great Britain by Clays Ltd, St Ives plc

The Orion Publishing Group Ltd
Orion House
5 Upper Saint Martin's Lane
London, WC2H 9EA

For Patrick

Olivia

Chapter 1

1918–1919

Olivia had only been to London once before, on her way to France, and she'd liked the busy, bustling atmosphere. But now, she hated it. She hated everyone looking happy because the war was over. Surely there must be people around who'd had relatives killed? And women who felt as empty and desolate as she did.

There might even be women, single women, single *pregnant* women, who could advise her, tell her what to do, how to cope, where to go.

Because Olivia didn't know. She didn't know anything except that she couldn't look for work in her condition. She'd always planned on going straight from France to Cardiff when the fighting ended. Matron had promised to take her back at the hospital where she'd been a nurse. But she'd got off the train in London and there seemed no point in going further. Matron wouldn't want her now. She was ashamed of feeling so helpless when, since leaving home, she'd thought of herself as strong.

Never before had she had to think about money or somewhere to live or where the next meal would come from. The small amount of money she'd earned was more than enough to buy occasional clothes and over the years she'd managed to save a few pounds. Now, the savings had almost gone on accommodation in a small hotel in Islington. She was eking it out, eating only breakfast which, as a nurse, she knew wasn't enough for a pregnant woman.

Despite this, she felt well and had never had a moment's sickness. It was one of the reasons she hadn't suspected she was pregnant when she missed her August period. She'd thought it was because she was upset over Tom. It could happen to women; their periods ceased when they were faced with tragedy. For the same reason, she wasn't bothered when there was still no period in September, but by October, she had started to feel thick around the waist, and the terrifying realisation dawned that she was expecting a child. At that point, her brain seemed to freeze. She became incapable of thought.

With November came the Armistice. Olivia was glad, of course, but instead of rejoicing, she felt only despair.

She still despaired, weeks later. New clothes were needed because she could hardly fasten the ones she had. Soon, she wouldn't be able to go out, and the proprietor of the hotel, a woman, was looking at her oddly because she was in her fifth month and seemed to be growing bigger by the day.

It was strange, but she rarely thought about Tom. If it hadn't been for the baby squirming lazily in her womb, she wondered if she would have thought of him at all. The ring he'd given her that had belonged to his grandfather was in her suitcase. It wasn't that the memory of him hurt, but it was impossible to believe the night had actually happened. It seemed more like a dream. She couldn't remember what he looked like or the words he'd said or the things they'd done.

Mrs Thomas O'Hagan! She recalled whispering the words to herself the day he'd left.

'What was that?'

Olivia was eating breakfast in the dingy dining room of the hotel. She looked up to find the proprietor glaring down at her. 'Sorry, I must have been talking to myself.'

'I've been meaning to have a word with you, Miss Jones,' the woman said officiously. 'I'll be needing your room from Saturday on. I've got regulars coming, salesmen.'

'I see. Thank you for telling me. I'll find somewhere else.'

'Not in a respectable place you won't,' the woman sniffed as she went away.

It had been bound to happen; either she'd run out of money or be asked to leave. Olivia's thoughts were like a knot in her head as she walked towards the city centre. She preferred the noise of the traffic to the quiet streets, even if the West End clatter was horrendous. There were homes for women in her condition. They were terrible places, so she'd heard, but better than wandering the streets, penniless. But how did you find where they were? Who did you ask?

If only she didn't feel so cold! Specks of ice were being blown crazily about by the bitter wind. She turned up the collar of her thin coat, pulled her felt hat further down on her head, but felt no warmer.

On Oxford Street, one of Selfridge's windows had a display of warm, tweed coats, very smart. Olivia stopped and eyed them longingly. Even if she'd been working, they would have been way beyond her means, but she hadn't enough to buy a coat for a quarter of the price from a cheaper shop.

She could, however, afford a cup of tea. She made her way towards Lyons' Corner House, noting all the shops were decorated for Christmas – only a few weeks away – and trying not to think where she would be when it came.

A large black car driven by a man in uniform drew alongside the pavement in front of her. Two young women got out the back, wrapped in furs, silk stockings gleaming. Their matching handbags, gloves and shoes were black suede. They swept across the pavement into a jeweller's shop in a cloud of fragrant scent.

Olivia had always been perfectly content to be a nurse, earning a pittance. She'd never envied other women their clothes or their position in life. But now, standing shivering outside the jeweller's, watching the two expensively-dressed women seat themselves in front of a counter, the assistant bow obsequiously, a feeling of hot, raw jealousy seered through her body. At the same moment, the baby inside her decided to deliver its first lusty kick.

'Are you all right, darlin'?'

A man had stopped and was looking at her with concern as she bent double clutching her stomach with both arms.

'I'm all right, thanks.' She forced herself upright.

He nodded at her bulging stomach. 'You'd be best at home in a nice warm bed.'

'You're right.' She appreciated his kindness. Perhaps he wouldn't be so kind if he knew that beneath her summer gloves she wasn't wearing a wedding ring.

She recovered enough to make her way to Lyons. As she drank the tea, Olivia realised with a sinking heart that there was only one way out of her predicament. She would have to ask her parents for help.

★

She couldn't just turn up, not in her condition. Mr and Mrs Daffydd Jones could never hold up their heads in public again if it got out that their unmarried daughter was having a baby. Her father was a town councillor, her mother given to good works which she carried out with a stern, disapproving expression on her cold features. Olivia, an only child, was already in disgrace. There'd been a row when she gave up her job in the local library to take up nursing in Cardiff, and an even bigger one when she announced her decision to nurse in France. She daren't go near the place where she was born, let alone the house in which she'd lived.

A letter would have to be sent, throwing herself on their mercy, and it would have to be sent today, so there would be time for a reply before Saturday when she left the hotel.

The tea finished, she searched the side streets for a shop that sold inexpensive stationery, then went to the Post Office and wrote to her mother and father, explaining her plight. She didn't plead or try to invoke their sympathy. She knew her parents well. They would either help, or they wouldn't, no matter how the letter was framed.

The reply came on Friday morning. She recognised her father's writing on the envelope. Although he wrote neatly, he had managed to make the 'Miss' look as if it might be 'Mrs' – or the other way round. The proprietor didn't look impressed when she handed the letter over. It crossed Olivia's mind that she could have bought a brass wedding ring and signed the register as Mrs O'Hagan, claiming to be a widow if anyone asked, but she'd been so confused it hadn't crossed her mind. Still, all it would have avoided was the indignity of, in effect, being thrown out. She would have had to leave in another few days when she came to the end of her savings.

The envelope contained a rail ticket and a curt note.

'Catch the 6.30 train from Paddington Station to Bristol on Saturday night. I will meet you. Father.'

Bristol wasn't far from where she'd lived in Wales. Relief was mixed with a sense of sadness as she re-read her father's note. No, 'Dear Olivia.' He hadn't signed, 'Love, Father'.

At least now she was leaving she could treat herself to a decent meal with what was left of the money.

Her father was waiting under the clock at Temple Meads Station, legs apart, hands clasped behind his back, glowering. He was rocking back and forth on his heels, a big, broadshouldered man, in an ankle-length tweed overcoat and a wide-brimmed hat that made him look rather louche, though he would have been horrified had he realised. His coat hung open, revealing a pinstriped waistcoat and a gold watch and chain.

There was something forbidding about the way he waited, as if his thoughts were very dark. Olivia had always been frightened of him, although he'd never laid a hand on her, either in anger or affection.

He nodded grimly at her approach and had the grace to take her suitcase. He made no attempt to kiss the daughter he hadn't seen for two and a half years. Even if she hadn't been returning home under a cloud, Olivia wouldn't have found this surprising.

She followed him outside and he stowed the case in the boot of the little Ford Eight car that was the only thing she'd known him show fondness for. He would pat it lovingly when it had completed a journey and murmer, 'Clever little thing!'

'Where's Mother?' Olivia asked as they drove out of the station.

'Home,' he said brusquely.

There was a long silence. The gaslit streets of Bristol were mainly deserted at such a late hour. They passed a few pubs that had recently emptied and where customers still hung noisily around outside.

'Where are we going?' Olivia asked when the silence began to grate. She wondered if she was being taken to a home for fallen women. It would be horrid, but she'd put herself in a position where she had no choice.

'A Mrs Cookson, who lives near the docks, will look after you until . . . until your time comes.' His voice was grudging. 'It's most unlikely anyone we know will visit the area, but I would be obliged if you would stay indoors during daylight hours in case you're recognised. Mrs Cookson has been given money to buy you the appropriate garments. You'll be comfortable there. When everything is over, you will leave. I'll make arrangements for the child to be taken care of, if that is your wish. If you decide to keep it, don't expect your mother and me to help. We never want to see you again.'

Although she'd had no wish to see them, either, the bluntness of his words upset her. They made her feel dirty. She opened her mouth to tell him about Tom, but before she could say a word, her father said tonelessly, 'You're disgusting.'

She didn't speak to him again, nor he to her. Shortly afterwards, he turned into a little street of terraced houses, and stopped outside the end one. He got out, leaving the engine running, and knocked on the door.

It was opened by a gaunt woman in her fifties with hennaed hair and a vivid crimson mouth. She had on a scarlet satin dress and a black stole. Long jet earrings dangled on to her shoulders and she wore a three-strand necklace to match. Her long fingers were full of rings – if the stones were real, she must be worth a fortune, Olivia thought.

Her father grunted an introduction, almost threw his daughter's suitcase into the hall, and left. The Ford was already in motion by the time Mrs Cookson closed the door. She folded her arms and looked Olivia up and down.

'Well, who's been a naughty girl?' she said archly.

Olivia couldn't remember the last time she'd smiled. She'd been expecting to be treated like a wanton woman over the next few months and, although Mrs Cookson wasn't quite her cup of tea, it was a pleasant surprise to be greeted with a joke.

'Come along, dearie,' the woman seized her arm, winking lewdly, 'Come and tell us all about it. Would you like a cuppa? Or something stronger? I've got some nice cherry wine. I'm about to have a bottle of milk stout, myself. Oh, and by the way, call me Madge.'

Madge Cookson was the unofficial midwife in the area of Bristol known as Little Italy because of the street names. Her own house was in Capri Street, and there were other similar streets of tiny houses: Naples, Turin and Venice, as well as a small cul-de-sac called Milan Way, all off Florence Road. She had a weakness for milk stout and a rather brittle manner that hid a soft, generous heart. Olivia was to grow quite fond of her over the next few months.

'How did my father know about you?' she enquired after she'd been living in Madge's house for a week.

'He must have asked around. You're not the first well-bred young lady I've had under similar circumstances to your own.'

As a young woman, Madge had been a singer on the music halls and there was a poster in her bedroom listing Magda Starr fourth on the bill at the London Hippodrome.

'That was the highest I ever got,' she told Olivia sadly. 'I always wanted to be top, but it wasn't to be. I got married soon afterwards and had our Des.' Her husband had died years ago, but Desmond had followed in his mother's footsteps and was a ventriloquist on the halls, although he had never reached such an exalted position as fourth on the bill. Desmond Starr's name was usually in small print at the bottom.

'Was your name really Starr?' Olivia asked. She would never cease to be intrigued by Madge's fascinating and varied life.

'No, my maiden name was Bailey, but Magda Starr looked better on posters than Madge Bailey.'

'How did you become a midwife?'

'I'm not a proper midwife, am I, dearie? I worked in a hospital for a while after my husband died and saw how it was done. I helped deliver a couple of babies and word got round, that's all.'

The house was comfortable, as her father had promised. Madge's exotic taste in clothes was reflected in the furnishings. Instead of a conventional runner, a garish shawl covered the sideboard on which stood a vase of enormous paper flowers. A bead curtain separated the kitchen from the living room, and there were numerous satin cushions embroidered with silver and gold thread scattered around. The covers had come from India, said Madge, as had the big tapestry over the mantelpiece in the parlour and the black and gold tea service with fluted rims that was brought out for best.

A fire crackled in the living room from early morning till late at night. On Sundays, a fire was also lit in the parlour for Madge's visitors; women about her own age, who came in the afternoon to play whist and drink milk stout.

Olivia stayed in the other room on these occasions reading one of Madge's collection of well-thumbed romantic novels. Sometimes she went upstairs for a nap in her room at the back with its lovely springy double bed.

She was as happy as anyone could be in her position. It would have been nice to have gone for a walk in the bright winter sunshine, or even the winter fog, wearing the new, warm coat, bought by Madge with money provided by her father but Madge, usually very easygoing, was strict about her staying indoors while it remained light outside.

'I promised your father you wouldn't go out until it was dark. It's what he's paying me for. I can't force you to stay in, but I'd feel obliged to let him know if you didn't.'

'I'm not likely to meet anyone I know round here,' Olivia said sulkily.

'The world is made up of coincidences,' Madge said. 'You could walk out and come face to face with the sister of your mother's best friend.'

'My mother doesn't have friends.'

'Well, her next-door neighbour, then.'

'Has my father given you his address?'

''Course. I'm to send him a telegram when the baby's born, aren't I? "Package Delivered" I've to put, case anyone reads it. Unless you decide to keep the baby, that is, in which case he doesn't want to know.'

'I wouldn't dream of keeping it.' Olivia shuddered. Once it arrived, she intended putting the whole episode behind her and finishing her training, to become a State Registered Nurse.

Madge looked at her thoughtfully. 'You might feel different when it's born.'

'If I do,' Olivia said harshly. 'I want you to tear it out of my arms and let my father have it.'

'Your father can do the tearing, dearie. Not me.'

The baby seemed even less real than Tom. It might well be in her womb, but it had nothing to do with her. She didn't care what happened to it as long as it didn't come to any harm.

Christmas came and went, and soon it was 1919, the first New Year in half a decade with Europe at peace with itself, celebrated with a joy and enthusiasm that was infectious. Madge and Olivia watched fireworks on the River Avon and sang 'Auld Lang Syne' at midnight in Victoria Park.

January became February, and February turned into March. The baby was due at the beginning of April.

Desmond Starr, Madge's ventriloquist son, came home for Easter, a cheerful, outgoing young man, just like his mother. He was booked to appear all summer at a theatre in Felixstowe and invited Madge and her guest. He could get free tickets.

'Well, I'll try,' Olivia lied. By summer, she would have started afresh. She was fond of Madge, but never wanted to see her or her son again.

She knew she had become very hard, very selfish. In days gone by, she'd been regarded as a soft old thing, too sympathetic for her own good. But now, there seemed to be a barrier in her brain, stopping all thoughts from entering that weren't concerned solely with herself.

The baby signalled it was on its way one lovely sunny Sunday afternoon in April, dead on time. Olivia was reading one of Madge's torrid romances when she had the first contraction, a strong one. It wasn't long before she had another, stronger and more painful. She'd spent time on a maternity ward during her training and recognised it was going to be a quick birth.

Madge was playing whist with her friends in the parlour. Olivia calmly made a cup of tea and waited for the friends to leave. She boiled two large pans of water and laid a rubber sheet on the bed. The worn sheets Madge had boiled to use as rags she put ready on a chair.

She gritted her teeth when another contraction came, worse than the others, but was reluctant to disturb Madge while her friends were there. Not that Madge could do anything, but she wouldn't have minded the company. The contractions were coming every ten minutes by the time the visitors were shown out.

'By, God! You're a cool customer,' Madge gasped when Olivia called her upstairs where she was lying on the bed, already in her nightdress.

'I've got a couple of hours to go yet.'

'You're too cool, d'you know that?' She sat on the bed and took Olivia's hand. 'My other young ladies have cried themselves silly during the entire confinement, but there hasn't been a peep out of you.'

'I haven't felt much like crying,' Olivia confessed, wincing when another contraction gripped her stomach like a wrench.

'It's time you did. Didn't you cry when your young man was killed? What was his name? Tom! You hardly ever talk about him.'

Olivia permitted herself a wry smile. 'I slept in a dormitory with the other nurses. There was no place where I could cry in private. And I don't talk about Tom because he doesn't seem real. I can't even remember what he looked like.'

Madge sniggered. 'Well, the baby's real enough. You can have a good old yell, you know,' she said when Olivia winced again. 'Let yourself go. Next door's deaf as a post and the street won't mind.'

'I'd sooner not. And I don't feel all that bad. Most of the births that I remember were much worse than this.'

The time passed slowly. Children could be heard playing in the street outside. Someone knocked on the door but Madge ignored it. A woman in a house behind was singing, her voice carrying clearly in the still, evening air. 'Keep the home fires burning . . .'

It was the song the men used to sing in France, Olivia remembered. It could be heard late at night, from miles away across the fields, when the fighting had finished for the day. Some nights, the nurses and the patients joined in. They'd been singing it the night when she and Tom had made love . . .

. . . the sky had been spectacular, she recalled; deep, sapphire blue, as lustrous as the jewel, and powdered with a myriad glittering stars. The waning moon was a delicate lemon curve.

Although not yet completely dark, it was dark enough to disguise the fact that the French landscape was a battlefield on which more than a million men had died. In daylight, the flat ground was a sea of dried mud, a jigsaw of trenches, empty now that the fighting had moved on.

Spurts of white smoke could be seen on the horizon, where the battle now was, where shells were landing, killing yet more men. The smoke occasionally turned to flames, indicating a building had been hit. On such a night, the flames even added something to the splendour of the view, flickering as they did like giant candles at the furthest edge of the world. A few broken trees were silhouetted like crazy dancing figures against the lucid blueness of the sky.

People had come outside the hospital to marvel at the magnificent sight amidst so much mayhem; staff, a few of the walking wounded. There was the faint murmur of voices, the occasional glimmer of a cigarette.

'Olivia! I've been looking everywhere for you.'

'Tom!' Olivia turned and instinctively lifted her arms to embrace the man limping towards her. She dropped them as he came nearer and hoped he hadn't noticed. He was her patient. He mustn't know how she felt, though she sensed he had already guessed. After all, she had a strong suspicion he felt the same, something of a miracle when he was so attractive and she so plain.

'Great night,' he said, panting slightly. The walk had been an effort.

'Beautiful,' she breathed. She nodded towards the smoke and the flames in the distance. 'That spoils it rather. And there's something sinister about not being able to hear the explosions.'

'Or the screams,' Tom said drily. He took her hand, his fingers curling warmly inside her own. She made no attempt to pull away. 'So, this is it! Our last night together.' He gave the glimmer of a smile. 'Or should I say, our last night in the near vicinity of each other. I'm sorry my leg is better. I feel tempted to take off my clothes, wander into the darkness, and pray I catch pneumonia again.'

'Not if I have anything to do with it!' She pretended to be outraged. He was joking. He was American, and the Americans joked all the time. They seemed exceptionally good-humoured. 'I'm a nurse. I want my patients to get better, not worse.'

'Don't be so practical.'

'Nurses are always practical, they have to be.' She didn't feel practical, not now, with her hand held so tightly in his.

He gave another tiny smile. 'Couldn't you be impractical just for tonight?'

'Not if it means you catching pneumonia, no. Anyway, it's exceptionally warm. You're not likely to catch anything except a few insect bites. Mind you, they can be nasty.'

'In that case,' he said lightly, 'Maybe we could forget about war, explosions in the distance, illnesses, hospitals, doctors and nurses, and just talk about each other?'

She should really say no, that's impractical too. Instead, she murmured, 'There's nothing much to say.' She already knew quite a lot about him. He came from Boston. His parents – he called them 'folks' – were Irish. He was twenty-three, worked in a bookshop owned by his father, and had volunteered to fight when America joined the war in 1917. His full name was Thomas Gerald O'Hagan and he had two sisters and five brothers of which he was the youngest. She also knew she wasn't the only nurse attracted to the tall, thin Irish–American with the laughing face, black curly hair, and peat-brown eyes. She was, however, the only one in love. He occupied her mind every waking minute of every day.

He had come into the hospital three weeks ago with a badly gashed leg and a dose of double pneumonia. Tomorrow, he was being sent to convalesce in a hospital in Calais. As soon as he was fit, he would return to an American Army unit to fight again. As a reminder of his imminent departure, there was a clanking sound as the ambulance train was shunted into place on the railway sidings behind them, ready for morning.

By comparison, he knew little about her, just that her name was Olivia Jones and she was the same age as himself. She had been born and bred in Wales and had never left its borders until she'd come to France two years ago as a nurse. He also knew, because he could see, that she wasn't even faintly pretty, almost insipid with her pale face and pale blue eyes.

'What will you do when the war is over?' Tom asked casually.

'Finish my training. I hadn't taken my final exams when I left Cardiff.'

'Would it be possible to finish training in the States?'

She caught her breath. 'Why should I do that?'

'Because it's where I'll be.' His voice was very low, intense. 'It's where my job is. And it's where I'd like *you* to be. Will you marry me, Olivia?'

'But we hardly know each other,' she gasped, though it was silly to sound so surprised when it was a question she'd hoped and prayed he'd ask.

He gestured impatiently. 'My darling girl, there's a war on, a hideous war, the worst the world has ever known. There isn't time for people to get to know each other as they would in normal times. I fell in love the first time I set eyes on you.' Pressing her hand to his lips, he said huskily, 'You are the loveliest woman I've ever known.'

He must be in love if he thought that! It was time she answered, said something positive, told him how she felt. He was kissing her now, her neck, her cheeks. He took her face in both hands and kissed her lips.

She was a timid person, withdrawn, and this was the first time she had been properly kissed. She pressed herself against him and felt her body come alive. 'I love you,' she whispered.

He held her so tightly she could hardly breathe. 'The minute this damn war is over we'll get married,' he said hoarsely. 'I'll write you every day and let you know where I'm posted so you can write me. Have you a photograph I can have?'

I've one taken with the other nurses a few months ago,' she said breathlessly. 'I'll let you have it before you go.'

'I'll let you have something of mine.' He held out his hand. A circle of gold glinted dully on the third finger – she had noticed the ring before, and had thought he was married until she realised it was on his right hand. 'It's my grandpop's wedding ring,' he explained as he removed it, dark eyes shining. 'He gave us all something before he died. I got his ring. It'll be too big, but might fit your middle finger. Or you can wear it around your neck on a chain.'

The ring was too big for any of her fingers. She put it in the breast pocket of her long white apron. As soon as she could, she'd buy a chain.

'I feel as if we're already married.' Her voice was thick in her throat. It was almost too much to bear. She wanted Tom to kiss her again, do the things that, until now, she'd thought wrong. She slid her arms around his neck and began to pull him along the side of the hospital building. He put his hands on her waist and they moved as if they were doing some strange sort of dance. In the distance, the troops began to sing, a desolate, haunting sound.

Tom said, 'Where are we going, honey?'

'Round here.'

They reached the corner of the building. About 100 feet away, a tangle of railway lines shone silver in the light of the moon. Beyond the lines stood a small, single-storey building without a door.

'This used to be a station,' she said. 'That building was the waiting room.'

'And is that where we're going?' There was incredulity in his voice.

By now, she felt utterly shameless. Every vestige of the respectability and conformity that she'd been fed over her entire life had fled. In just an instant, the world had turned 180 degrees. 'If you want,' she said.

'If I want! Gee, I can't think of anything I want more. But you, Olivia, is it what you want?'

Her answer was a laugh. She grabbed his hand, and they began to step over the silver lines. The stars continued to shine in their hundreds and thousands, the troops continued to sing, but Olivia and Tom were aware of none of these things as they entered the small, unused building into an intoxicating world of their own.

The war would be over in a few months' time, so everybody said: the experts, the newspapers, the pundits, the tired, hopeful men on the ground. But people had been saying the same thing for the last four years, ever since the fighting had begun.

It was something they wanted to believe, Olivia Jones included. But now she had her own pressing reason for wanting the fighting to end, to be over before Tom returned to battle.

Next morning, she saw him off, slipping him the promised photograph when no one was looking – she would get into serious trouble if Matron discovered the magical thing that had happened the night before. A few nurses in their shoulder-length voile caps, dark-blue gowns, and full-length aprons, came out of the hospital to wave goodbye to the men they had tenderly nursed back to health. Tears were shed on both sides as the train puffed away in the brilliant sunshine towards Calais.

Olivia hadn't thought it possible to feel both unbearably sad and blissfully happy at the same time; sad that Tom had gone, happy thinking about their future together. She fingered the ring in her pocket as she watched the train disappear round a bend. She'd examined it the night before. Inside was engraved, the words worn away until they were barely legible: RUBY TO EAMON 1857.

'If – no, *when* me and Tom have children, we'll call them Ruby and Eamon,' she decided, rubbing her hands together in anticipation.

The vacated beds weren't empty long. Later that morning, a horse-drawn ambulance arrived full of casualties who'd already been cursorily seen to in a dressing station on the front line. The rest of the day was spent re-bandaging wounds, comforting those for whom there seemed no hope because their injuries were too severe. Some were taken to the operating theatre to have limbs removed, returning, dopy from the anaesthetic, waking later, shattered and terrified.

As she walked from bed to bed, smiling at the stricken men, fetching water, making them as comfortable as possible, Olivia cursed the politicians who were responsible for the slaughter, who'd allowed it to continue for so long. A generation of young men had been sacrificed for no real reason, and a generation of women had lost husbands, fathers, sons.

The injured men would never have guessed the little nurse with the sweet smile – Olivia wasn't quite as plain as she thought – was so pre-occupied with thoughts of the previous night, a night when she'd taken a lover, become a woman, and had promised to become a wife.

'Mrs Thomas O'Hagan!'

She practised saying the words underneath her breath.

'What was that, darlin'?' a little Cockney with a broken arm enquired.

'Sorry, I was talking to myself.'

He grinned. 'Well, that way you won't get no arguments.'

She grinned back, tucked the sheet tightly around his waist, and told him to rest.

It was after tea by the time the men had been seen to and those able to eat had been given a meal – the inevitable corned beef accompanied by mashed potatoes. While they ate, a dozen weary nurses collected in a windowless recess outside the ward which they regarded as their staff room, for a hot drink, the first since morning.

The conversation turned, as it often did, to rumours that the fighting would soon end. After all, someone said, the Battle of Amiens had just been won, mainly by Australian and Canadian troops, and there'd been only 7000 casualties on their side.

'Only seven thousand!' someone else remarked sarcastically.

'There's been ten times that number before now.'

Olivia hardly listened. She held her hand against her breast and, through the pocket of her apron, could feel Tom's ring pressing against her palm. For the hundredth time that day, she went over the events of the previous night.

'What's the matter, Olivia?' said a voice. 'You look as if you might cry.'

'Nothing.' *She couldn't see him any more.* His face, so clear all day, had suddenly become a blur. The hairs on her neck prickled and she felt convinced something was dreadfully wrong.

It wasn't until the following day, after a sleepless night, that she learnt that Thomas O'Hagan was dead. The ambulance train had been passing over a bridge that had been heavily mined by saboteurs operating behind Allied lines. Not everyone had died when the bridge exploded and the train and those on board had plunged into the river below.

But Tom had and, for Olivia, it was the end of everything.

She sighed and wriggled uncomfortably on the bed. She was perspiring freely and the clothes felt damp. The contractions were only minutes apart, painful, but bearable.

Suddenly, she felt her stomach heave and she no longer had control of her body. There were a series of violent spasms, followed by a cloud of pain, so savage that she nearly fainted. Then the heaving stopped and she felt empty.

'It's a girl,' Madge cried triumphantly.

'A girl!'

'A lovely girl, very dark. I'm cutting the cord. Do you want to look at her, Olivia?'

'I'm not sure,' Olivia whispered. She half-closed her eyes and saw a creamy-skinned baby being picked up by its feet. Madge gave the plump bottom a sharp slap, and the baby responded with an angry howl. 'She looks fat.'

'No, she's just right. She's a fine, healthy baby. I'll clean you up, then take her downstairs, make a bottle of tepid water and give her a cuddle. She deserves it after all that effort. Is there a name you want to call her?'

'I never gave a thought to names.' She half-saw Madge wrap the baby in a sheet and put her in a basket, then she lay back and allowed herself to be washed and patted gently dry. The bedclothes and her nightdress were changed, her hair quickly combed.

'I'll make us both a cup of tea in a minute,' Madge muttered. 'I need one as much as you.' She picked up the basket and made her way carefully downstairs, leaving an exhausted Olivia warmly tucked in bed with only a feeling of soreness as a reminder of her ordeal.

She lay, watching the sharp line between light and shade creep across the wardrobe with its dusty suitcases on top as the sun gradually disappeared from sight. The singing had stopped. The children had gone indoors. The world seemed to have paused for breath and Olivia paused with it.

She had just had a baby!

Tom's baby. His daughter.

And now she felt oddly incomplete. She had to see Tom's daughter so as always to remember what she looked like. Otherwise, she would wonder until her dying day.

It hurt, getting out of bed, going downstairs, not making a sound in her bare feet. The basket was on the floor in front of the living room fire. Olivia saw a tiny foot appear and kick away the sheet. Another foot appeared, followed by a little flower-like hand. The baby was making faint chirruping noises, like a bird. Madge was humming to herself in the kitchen as she prepared the bottle.

Olivia crept into the room and knelt beside the basket. The baby was naked and, oh, she was so pretty! Dark curly hair, dark creamy skin, rosebud mouth, a perfect nose, not squashed like some babies. Her limbs were smooth and round, unwrinkled. The baby regarded her calmly with big blue eyes, though she'd been told that babies couldn't focus for weeks.

'You're beautiful,' Olivia whispered. She put her finger inside the dimunitive hand and it was gripped with surprising strength. As the flesh of the mother touched that of the child, Olivia shivered, and the parts of her that she had thought had died with Tom, became magically alive. She knew then she would never bring herself to give up her daughter. Never!

She slipped the nightdress off her shoulder, reached down and picked up her baby, cradling her in her arms. 'Are you thirsty, darling? Would you like a drink?' She put the child to her breast and she began to suck noisily. Olivia smiled and began to sway from side to side.

'Olivia! Oh, no, dearie. No!' A shocked Madge had come into the room with the bottle. She sank into a chair. 'That's torn it,' she groaned.

'Oh, Madge!' Olivia cried, eyes shining. 'I remember now what Tom looked like, just like his daughter. And Madge. I'm going to call her Ruby. It was Tom's grandmother's name. Ruby O'Hagan.' She stroked the soft cheek with her thumb. 'Don't you think that's lovely?'

'Lovely,' Madge agreed, sighing.

She was slightly unhinged. The emotions that had been supressed for months bubbled to the surface. She couldn't stop smiling as she nursed her baby hour after hour, cooing, stroking and kissing, marvelling at her fingers, her toes. Entranced, she watched the blue eyes gradually close as Ruby fell asleep.

Eventually, Madge told her sharply to put the child down. 'You're wearing her out. She needs rest. And so do you. You're much too excited.'

'I'm happy, that's all, happier than I've been in ages.' Olivia reluctantly laid the sleeping Ruby in the basket. 'I want to keep her, Madge,' she said quietly.

'I thought as much.' Madge's lips tightened.

'I think that's best, don't you?'

'I've no idea what's best, Olivia.' Madge looked sober, not a bit her cheerful self. 'Whether you keep her or not, either way misery lies. Keep her and you'll have to find somewhere to live, not easy with a baby, even less without a husband. Little Ruby will grow up without a dad. You'll need money, but with a baby you'll find it hard to get a job. You can't go back to nursing. You'll feel trapped. You might come to resent Ruby for ruining your life. You might start thinking, "If only I hadn't kept her, everything would be fine".'

Olivia shuddered. 'Tell me about the other way?'

'With the other way,' Madge continued, 'You can go back to nursing, pass your exams, maybe get promoted. You'll have friends, money, nice clothes, enough to eat. You'll be respected. You might get married, have more children you won't be ashamed to call your own.'

'You make that way sound so much better,' Olivia cried.

'I hadn't finished, dearie. Despite all the good things, you'll never forget your little girl. Every time you see a child of Ruby's age, you'll wonder how she is, what she looks like now she's four, ten, twenty. You'll wonder where she is, how she is, is she being properly looked after? Is she happy? Is she sad? Does she ever think about her mother, her *real* mother? You might try to find her, even if it's only to have a little look to set your mind at rest.'

'Oh, Madge! How do you know all this?'

'I've made the same speech a dozen times before, dearie, that's how. I've another young lady coming at the end of May and I'll probably be making it again.'

'What do you think I should do?' The idea of being free, able to do anything she wanted without the burden of a baby was tempting. But the thought of giving up Ruby was intolerable.

'Don't ask me, Olivia. I don't even know what *I'd* do in the same position. It's a decision for you and no one else to take.'

In the early hours, Ruby, in her basket on the floor beside her mother's bed, woke up and began to howl and still howled after she'd been fed and her nappy changed. Olivia was rubbing her back when Madge appeared in an emerald green dressing gown.

'If you were in rooms, there'd be people hammering on the walls shouting for you to keep the baby quiet.'

'What's wrong with her?' Olivia asked fretfully.

'Nothing's wrong. She's behaving like a perfectly normal baby.'

'But why is she crying, Madge?'

'Maybe you haven't brought up all her wind.'

'She's burped twice.'

'She might want to burp three times.'

Ruby fell asleep and woke up at six for another feed. Olivia fed her. There was something almost sensual about the sound the baby made as she sucked on her breast. A thrill of emotion swept through her, almost as intense as when she'd made love with Tom.

'We're starting on a big adventure soon, you and me,' she whispered. She could look for a job as a housekeeper, say she was a widow.

Madge appeared again, much later, this time wearing a hat and coat. 'I'm going out a minute, dearie. I won't be long.'

Olivia dozed, the baby in her arms. Madge came back and made a cup of tea. She'd hoped she would offer to look after Ruby while she had a proper sleep, but Madge made no such offer. Perhaps she was making a point instead – this was how it would be when she and Ruby were on their own with no one to help.

Midday. She'd bathed her baby, marvelling again at how perfect she was, how beautiful. Ruby made cooing sounds and waved her arms. Olivia dried her, dressed her in the new white clothes Madge had bought, hugging her tightly. 'I love you,' she said. 'I love you so much.'

There was a knock on the front door, followed by Madge's

footsteps in the hall, then whispering that went on for a long time. Then the whispering stopped and someone came upstairs, not Madge, because the tread was too heavy. Her heart did a somersault when her father came into the room. Madge must have sent him the promised telegram.

Olivia wasn't sure if, for the briefest of seconds, she glimpsed a softness in his stony eyes when he looked down on his daughter nursing her tiny, dark-haired baby.

Father and daughter stared at each other across the room, neither speaking. Olivia kept her eyes on his, willing the softness to return. If only she could talk to him, he might offer to support them, come and see them, bring her mother.

Instead, her father strode across the room and tore the baby from her breast. Ruby whimpered and Olivia heard someone give a thin, high-pitched scream that seemed to go on and on and on as if a single note was being played on a violin.

Then Madge seized her shoulders and shook her hard and the screaming stopped. '*RUBY!*' Olivia screamed as her father and her baby vanished from the room.

'Shush, dearie. It's for the best. It's what you asked of me, isn't it?'

But that was then, and this was now. She loved Ruby with all her heart, she wanted to keep her. Even so, Olivia made no attempt to leap out of bed and try to get her baby back. Afterwards, during the dark weeks that followed, she wondered, horrified, if in some secret, horribly selfish, part of her mind, she didn't want Ruby after all, that she was relieved she'd been taken away.

Now, though, she felt only desolation and despair.

It was the second occasion the little Ford Eight had made the long journey from the south to the north of Wales. This time, there was a baby in a basket on the back seat who made not a sound for most of the way. The driver had almost reached his destination when it began to cry. Instead of stopping to give it the bottle Mrs Cookson had prepared, Daffydd Jones pressed his foot harder on the accelerator. Nearly there.

He recognised the white convent when it came into sight, perched on a hill three miles from Abergele. He had been before. The Mother Superior knew him, but not his name. Daffyd Jones wasn't a Catholic, he had no truck with Papist nonsense, but the convent was also an orphanage and had agreed to take the child if it was a girl. Arrangements had been made elsewhere in the event his daughter's bastard turned out to be a boy.

The small car groaned its way up the hill and seemed to breathe a sigh of relief when it stopped outside the convent's thick oak door. He got out, pulled the bell, and returned to collect his tiny passenger whose cries by now had become screams of rage.

An ancient nun, as curved as a question mark, was waiting for him, nodding, like a puppet, when he came back and handed her the basket.

She nodded at him to come inside. He refused, saying gruffly, 'I've to give you this.' He handed her the scrap of paper Mrs Cookson had given him. 'After all, what harm will it do?' she'd said.

Tipping his hat, he bade the nun goodbye. She nodded again and closed the door.

Daffydd Jones watched the door close and wondered why there were tears in his eyes.

Inside the convent, the nun peered at the paper. Her eyes were old, but she could still see, particularly when it was nice, clear print like this.

'Ruby O'Hagan,' she read. Well, at least the child had a name, even if the poor, wee mite had nothing else.

Emily

Chapter 2

1933–1935

The Convent of the Sisters of the Sacred Cross near Abergele was renowned for its orphan girls, all superbly trained by the age of fourteen to enter the world of live-in domestic service. They could sew the neatest of seams, embroider, cook, clean, launder, even garden. They were respectful, healthy, extremely moral, highly religious, and had perfect manners.

The girls made ideal housemaids, nursemaids, cooks, seamstresses. Well-adjusted and apparently content with their lot, they had been brought up, if not with love, then with kindness. Physical punishment was strictly forbidden in the convent.

Their education was confined to subjects that would be of use to girls whose role in life would be to serve others until they eventually married a man from the same class as themselves, usually another servant. Apart from domestic skills, they were taught to read and write and do simple arithmetic. They learnt a smattering of history and geography. It was considered a waste for the girls to study science, literature, art, current affairs, or politics. No one was likely to ask a servant girl what she thought of the situation in Russia or which Shakespeare play was her favourite, though she could, if asked, recite the catechism, reel off the names of the last ten Popes, sing several hymns in Latin, and accurately describe the Twelve Stations of the Cross which she had made every Good Friday for as far back as she could remember.

There were applicants anxious for a convent girl from as far away as London, though the girls mainly went to wealthy Catholic homes across the Welsh/English border: Cheshire, Shropshire, Lancashire. Occasionally, a girl stayed in the convent and took the veil.

Until they left, the girls spent most of their time within the confines of the convent. They were taught there. They went to Mass in the tiny chapel in the well-tended grounds, the service taken by a priest from a seminary twenty miles away. If the girls were ill, unless it was something contagious or requiring surgery, the young patients were cared for by the nuns themselves.

On Sunday afternoons, they went for a walk in the quiet, secluded lanes, proceeding in a crocodile, two by two, seeing only the occasional car or cyclist.

Twice a year, on a nice day in spring or autumn, when there were few holidaymakers about, the older girls were taken to the sands at Abergele, marching through the small town, fascinated by the shops, amazed and slightly scared by the traffic, particularly if a single decker bus drove by, chugging smoke from its rear. They had never seen so many people and tried not to stare at the women with uncovered heads and bare legs, lips painted red for some reason. So far, men had hardly featured in their lives. The priests who took Mass were old. For a long time they had assumed the world to be peopled mainly by women. Yet here were young men, strange creatures, with deep, loud voices. Some even had hair on their faces which the girls took to be an affliction and said a quick prayer. And there were boys, with short trousers and scabby knees, who grinned and shouted at them rudely, even whistled. The girls, in their antiquated brown dresses and long white pinafores, walked demurely past, hands clasped, eyes fixed on the girl in front, as they had been taught.

The convent might have been considered a gloomy place, with its stone walls and stone floors and high, cavernous ceilings. Cool in summer, freezing in winter, the furniture was sparse and as plain as the food. There were no adornments apart from holy pictures, statues, and numerous crucifixes that hung on the white-painted walls. Nor was a clock evident, but someone, somewhere, must have known when to ring the bells, indicating it was time for classes, time for meals, time to pray.

However, the presence of so many children, obviously happy, despite their tragic backgrounds, dispelled any gloom the occasional visitor might have felt when they entered the big, oak door.

'Cannon fodder,' said Emily Dangerfield to her sister, Cecilia, Mother Superior of the convent, one breezy day in March. Trees could be glimpsed through the high window of the always chilly office, the long branches curtseying this way and that against the bright blue sky. 'You're producing cannon fodder.'

'Are you suggesting that one day my girls will be shot out of guns?' Reverend Mother smiled from behind her highly polished desk. She'd had the same argument with Emily before.

'You know what I mean,' Emily said crossly. 'The girls are being raised for one purpose only: to serve others, do their washing, cooking, cleaning, wait on them hand and foot. You're like a factory, except your products happen to be human.'

'What do you suggest I do with them?' Reverend Mother smiled again. She rarely lost her temper, but was secretly annoyed. What did Emily know about running an orphanage? 'Encourage them to become actresses, doctors, playwrights, politicians? How many do you think will succeed after they've been let loose into the world on their own? Our girls have no family. We ensure they have the security of a home where they will be made welcome and be of use to others.'

'Of use!' Emily laughed shortly. 'You make them sound like chairs. I saw a picture a few years ago, *Metropolis*, all about a mechanized society. It reminded me very much of here.'

'Don't talk nonsense, Emily.' Reverend Mother tried hard not to snap. 'I see age hasn't taught you to consider other people's feelings.'

'And age never will.' Emily got up and began to wander round the room. She was a tall woman who had once been beautiful, fifty-seven, smartly dressed in a houndstooth check costume and a little veiled hat on her dyed black hair. A fox fur was thrown casually over the chair she had just vacated. She was proud of her still slim, svelte figure. Her sister was two years older and similarly built, though her shape was little evident beneath the multitudinous layers of her black habit. Her face, unlike Emily's, was remarkably unlined.

'Out of interest, sister dear, why are you here?' Reverend Mother enquired. 'Have you driven all the way from Liverpool just to lecture me? We nuns are only allowed one visit a year for which notice has to be given beforehand. I couldn't bring myself to turn you away, but you've made me break my own rules.'

'It isn't just a visit, sis. I came because I want a girl.'

'I beg your pardon?'

'A girl. I want one of your girls.'

'Excuse me, but aren't you being a trifle hypocritical?'

'No. I shall educate her, broaden her mind, teach her all the things you've managed to avoid.'

'If you want to conduct an experiment, Emily, I suggest you buy a Bunsen burner.'

Emily returned to her chair. She removed a silver cigarette case and lighter from her bag, then replaced them when she saw her sister frown. 'Sorry, I forgot you disapprove. Mind you, you smoked like a chimney when you were young.'

'There are all sorts of things I did when I was young that I haven't done in many years.'

'And smoking was one of the mildest.' Emily winked.

Reverend Mother refused to be riled. 'Those things are long behind me.' She didn't go on about the sinner that repenteth, because it would have only made Emily laugh.

'Seriously, though,' her sister said. 'About a girl. Since Edwin died and the children left home, I've felt terribly lonely in Brambles by myself. It's so big, so isolated. Since I became a widow, my so-called friends have deserted me. I haven't been invited out socially in ages.'

'Why not sell Brambles and move?'

'I can't.' Emily made a face. 'It's not mine to sell. Edwin left it to the boys, but they can only have it if I leave – or die. I think he had visions of me getting married again to some awful cad who'd inherit the place and deprive his children of their inheritance.'

'I always thought Edwin very wise.'

Emily ignored this. 'I'm nervous on my own. I have servants, naturally, but they're part-time. I hear noises during the night and can't sleep.'

Reverend Mother raised her brows sardonically. 'And you think a fourteen-year-old child will protect you?'

'She'll be company, and I'll feel better, knowing there's another human being under the same roof.'

'I'm not sure if I'd trust one of our girls with you, Emily. You'll corrupt her. She'll be smoking and drinking within a week.'

'What shallow principles you must have taught them, Cecilia, that they can be dispensed with so swiftly.'

The sisters laughed.

'Why not employ a companion?' Reverend Mother suggested.

'Gawd, no.' Emily shuddered. 'Not some poor, pathetic woman

without a home of her own. She'd agree with every single word I said, scared I'd sack her.'

'And you think one of our girls will disagree? Doesn't that rather contradict the cannon fodder theory?'

'I'll teach her to disagree as well as smoke and drink.'

Reverend Mother opened a drawer and took out the book in which she kept a list of applicants for her girls. She always vetted them carefully, insisting they come for interview beforehand. She pretended to study the book while considering her sister's request. It would be the worst sort of nepotism if she let Emily go to the top of the list. Yet Emily was the only flesh and blood she had and Cecilia loved her. Their only brother had been killed in the final days of the Boer War and their parents were long dead. Could she indulge her love for Emily by letting her have a girl whose head she would stuff with nonsense?

Looked at another way, it would be an opportunity for one of the more intelligent children to escape what was, let's face it, a life of drudgery, and make something of herself.

'Well?' Emily folded her arms and subjected her sister to a fierce stare. 'I know you, Cecilia. Stop pretending to read and give me an answer. Can I have a girl or not?'

Reverend Mother suddenly had a brainwave, seeing an opportunity to help her sister and herself at the same time. 'We do have someone,' she said carefully. 'She's fourteen next month. But I must warn you, she's impudent, naughty, loud, opinionated, and completely unbiddable. We do, rarely, have girls who are difficult, if not impossible, to place. She's a hard worker, but has too much lip – remember Nanny used to tell you that?'

Emily made a face. 'Has she anything nice about her?'

'She's generous, kindhearted, amusing, curious about everything, and completely fearless.'

'Hmm! What do you know about her background?'

'Very little.' The nun shook her head. 'Fourteen years ago I was visited by a man, middle-aged, Welsh, well-dressed, rather pompous. He refused to give his name and told me one of his wife's parlour maids was expecting a child and would I take it when it arrived in a few weeks' time if it were a girl. I agreed, of course.'

'Did you believe him?' Emily asked curiously.

'Not for a minute. He looked the sort who would have shown the door to any parlour maid he discovered was pregnant. I thought it might be his own child from an illicit liaison, but he didn't look that sort, either. I decided it was almost certainly a relative's, his daughter's, maybe.'

'Has this unbiddable child got a name?'

'Of course, she's got a name. What do you think we've been calling her by all these years?'

'I meant, did she *come* with a name? Or has she got one of your made-up ones?'

'She came with a name. Ruby O'Hagan. Shall I send for her?

'Why not!'

Ten minutes later, there was a knock on the office door. Reverend Mother called, 'Come' and a nun entered accompanied by a girl much taller than Emily had expected for a not-quite-fourteen-year-old. Had she not known the children were more than adequately fed, she would have suspected the child hadn't eaten in weeks. She looked pale and starved, with great dark eyes set in a peaky face, a sharp nose, and wide thin lips with an exaggerated bow. The brown uniform dress was too short, the sleeves and the hem, and her wrists and ankles were almost pathetically slight, the bones protruding as white and glossy as pearls. She had a great mane of black wavy hair tied back with brown ribbon, and she gave a bewildering impression of both fragility and strength.

The nun departed, bowing wordlessly, and the girl came and stood in front of Reverend Mother's desk, hands clasped behind her back. 'Have I been naughty again, Reverend Mother?' she asked in a loud, deep voice with an Irish accent – not surprising as most of the nuns were Irish. She didn't look concerned that the answer might be in the affirmative.

'Well, you should know that more than I, Ruby.'

'I don't *think* I have,' Ruby said earnestly. 'But sometimes I do things that don't seem the least naughty, but I'm told they are.'

Reverend Mother raised her fine eyebrows. 'Such as?'

'Such as on the way here. Sister Aloysius told me off for skipping. She said it wasn't ladylike, but she didn't answer when I asked why.'

'Young ladies are expected to conduct themselves with a certain amount of decorum, Ruby, that's why.'

It was on the tip of Emily's tongue to query this statement, but she thought better of it. 'Decorum' was such a boring word, so inhibiting. If the child wanted to skip, why shouldn't she?

Her sister spoke. 'If you have been naughty, Ruby, unwittingly or otherwise, I haven't been told. You're here because I would like you to meet Mrs Dangerfield.'

The girl transferred her big bold eyes on to the visitor. 'Hello,' she said easily.

'Hello, Ruby.' Emily smiled.

'Am I to work for you?'

'Would you like to work for me?'

'No,' Ruby said baldly, glancing briefly at Reverend Mother, who rolled her eyes heavenwards, as if asking God for patience.

'Why not?' asked Emily, taken aback.

'Because I don't want to go into service.'

'How will you support yourself, dear?'

Ruby tossed her head and her thin nose quivered. 'I'd sooner find a job on my own, like in a clothes shop, or one of those tea shop places I've seen in town. And I'll find somewhere to live on my own too. I don't like being bossed around.'

Reverend Mother's expression was grim. 'You'll be "bossed around" as you put it, in a clothes shop or a cafe, Ruby. Have you not thought of that?'

'Yes, but I won't *belong* to them, will I?' The dark eyes blazed. 'Not like in service. I don't want to belong to anyone except myself.'

Hear, hear, Emily echoed silently. Aloud she said, 'I don't want a servant. I want a live-in friend.'

It was Ruby's turn to look taken aback. She put her narrow head on one side and thought a moment. 'I'd make a good friend,' she said eventually. 'I've got friends already, lots.'

'Would you like *us* to be friends, Ruby?'

There was a choking sound from behind the desk. Reverend Mother rose and said coldly, 'Please leave, Ruby. I would like to talk to Mrs Dangerfield alone.'

The girl looked mutinous. 'But I want to be her friend!'

'I said, leave.'

'There was no need to bite her head off,' Emily said lightly when Ruby had gone.

'What on earth do you think you're doing?' Her sister's voice shivered with anger, anger mainly directed at herself for having allowed the situation to proceed this far. Emily was an entirely unsuitable person to have a child and she should have told her so straight away. 'Ruby's not a toy, or a piece of furniture to decorate your home. She's a child, a human being. How long is she likely to remain your friend? Until you decide to go on another round-the-world cruise? What happens if you get married again?'

'If I go away I'll take Ruby with me. And the idea of remarrying horrifies me. I'll treat her as a daughter, honest. Let's face it, sis,' Emily said reasonably, 'You've got an awkward customer there. Put into service she won't last a week. We'll be doing each other a favour if you let me have her.'

'That's putting it very crudely, Emily.'

'And very wisely, Cecilia. By the way,' Emily twinkled. 'Are you allowed to lose your temper? God *will* be annoyed. I think this calls for an extensive bout of flagellation tonight.'

The other residents of the convent, nuns and girls alike, would have been alarmed had they witnessed the calm, controlled face of Reverend Mother turn such a deep red. 'You're impossible. Please go. As regards Ruby, I'll think about it.'

Ruby prayed extraordinarily hard over the next few weeks that Mrs Dangerfield would come back. It wasn't that she wanted a grown-up friend, but the idea of going into service, being at the beck and call of a houseful of strangers, made her sick. She'd run away before she'd do it. Sister Finbar had once said she was no good at being good, and then got cross when Ruby had agreed. Ruby had no intention of being good unless she felt like it.

Reverend Mother also prayed. She asked God for guidance in her dilemma. Would she be denying a child the chance of a better life by refusing her sister's request? Or would the child be damaged if she acceded to it? And did it make a difference that the child concerned was Ruby O'Hagan who would present an equally troublesome dilemma next month when she reached fourteen and it was time for her to leave the walls of the convent?

She couldn't visualise the girl settling in the kindest, most accommodating of households. She would question the simplest order if she couldn't see a reason for it. The sisters were always complaining. Why couldn't she make her bed her own way? Ruby wanted to know. Why did all beds have to be made the same? Why did everyone's shoes have to be laced identically? Why did her hair have to be tied back when she would have liked it loose? What difference did it make to God how she did her hair? Why couldn't she wear her long winter socks if it was cold in September? It made no sense waiting until October just because it was a rule. Reverend Mother had changed the rule because she couldn't see the sense in it either.

Maybe the world needed people who wanted to change the rules. Ruby O'Hagan would undoubtedly be better off with Emily than a place where unnecessary orders had to be obeyed. She wrote to her sister and suggested she visit again in the middle of April, after Ruby's birthday. 'It will give you plenty of time to get her room ready,' she put at the end.

Emily Dangerfield didn't pray. She didn't believe in it. It would be a bore having to drive Ruby to Mass at St Kentigern's, the pretty little Catholic church in Melling, where she hadn't been since Edwin died, a fact her sister was unaware of. Cecilia assumed her faith was as strong as it had always been and Emily saw no need to disabuse her. They met so rarely and she preferred to reproach Cecilia about the regressive policies of the convent about which she didn't, in fact, give a damn, rather than have Cecilia reproach her for her loss of faith.

What had praying ever done for her? She'd prayed for happiness, but look what she'd ended up with – a dry-as-dust husband who showed no interest in physical contact of the most basic sort once he'd sired two sons, forcing Emily to go elsewhere. And the sons! Adrian was in Australia, sheep-farming of all things, and she was unlikely ever to see him again. Rupert lived in London, but may as well have been in Australia with his brother for all she saw of him and his wife. She'd met her grandchildren, Sara and James, just twice.

If Ruby came, she would treat her as a daughter. Bestow all the love that no one else apparently wanted on a fragile, orphan child. And perhaps it wouldn't hurt to start going to Mass again, either.

Four weeks later, on a cool, sunny, spring day, Ruby emerged from the convent carrying a brown paper parcel tied with string and accompanied by a tearful nun. There was no sign of Reverend Mother, Emily hadn't been invited inside. The girl's eyes were dazzling. She joyfully threw back her narrow shoulders, ready to face the world.

Emily opened the passenger door of her grey Jaguar car and patted the leather seat. Ruby put her hand on the door and looked curiously inside. Then she slid on to the seat with a quiet smile and the ease of someone who had been getting into expensive cars all her life. She threw the parcel on to the back seat and waved to the nun. 'I haven't been in a car before,' she said.

'I'd never have guessed,' Emily said drily. She started up the engine and they drove away. 'Aren't you sad?' she enquired.

'A little bit,' Ruby conceded, taking the brown ribbon off her hair and tossing it loose. 'But it's silly to feel sad over something that can't be helped.'

'Very sensible, but not a concept that can be taken literally throughout one's entire life.'

'What's a concept? And what does literally mean?'

'I'll give you a dictionary when we get home and you can look it up for yourself.'

'What's a dictionary?'

'You'll see when you get one.'

At first, Ruby found going fast exciting, but a bit scary. She tensed whenever another car came towards them, convinced they'd crash, but the cars easily passed and she quickly forgot her fear. She said little, but her eyes sparkled with interest, even if the countryside they drove through was the same as that she'd been used to all her life: vast green fields, undulating hills, untidy hedges full of birds. They came to the occasional village that looked dull compared to Abergele.

'We're in England now, dear, Cheshire,' Emily said – she'd been told to call Mrs Dangerfield 'Emily'. 'We've just crossed the border.'

'You mean we're in another country!' Ruby was impressed.

'Yes. In a few years, people won't have to drive such a long way round to Liverpool. There's a tunnel under the River Mersey, but it isn't ready for cars yet.'

'Reverend Mother said I was going to live in Liverpool. It's where Sister Frances comes from. She said it's bigger than Abergele.'

'Much, much bigger, but it isn't exactly Liverpool where you'll live. My house is on the outskirts, a place called Kirkby. Tomorrow, we'll go to town and buy you some clothes. I'm sure you'll be pleased to get out of that ugly brown frock.'

'Clothes from a shop?'

'Of course, Ruby. Where else?' Emily thought the girl's naivety utterly delightful.

'I've always wanted to go in a shop.' Ruby gave a blissful sigh.

'I must warn you, dear, that Liverpool is terribly noisy. There's loads of traffic and crowds of shoppers. You mustn't be frightened. Cities are very busy places.'

'I'm never frightened,' Ruby said stoutly, having forgotten her recent fear that the car might crash. 'Are we nearly there?'

'We've still got some way to go.'

Ruby snorted and began to twiddle her thumbs, bored. England looked exactly the same as Wales. She visibly perked up when the scenery became more industrialised and squealed with delight when they reached Runcorn and the car drove on to the transporter bridge and they were carried across the shimmering Mersey on a metal sling, a process that Emily always found daunting.

They drove through a forest of tall chimneys spewing black smoke into the blue sky. 'They look ugly,' Ruby opined.

Emily nodded agreement. 'This is Widnes.'

'Ugly, but interesting. Everything's interesting. Are we nearly at Kirkby?' she said impatiently.

'Not far.'

The countryside became flatter, houses more frequent. Ruby bobbed up and down at Emily's side, exclaiming at every single thing, asking so many questions that Emily's head began to spin.

'What's that little boy doing?'

'He's riding a scooter.'

'I've never seen a scooter before. What's that building there?'

'A church, dear.'

'It's *big*. The church in the convent was only little. Can I go there to Mass on Sunday?'

'No, Ruby, it's too far away, and it's not a Catholic church.'

'What was it then?'

'I didn't notice,' Emily said desperately. 'A Protestant church of some sort.'

Ruby screamed. 'Look! What's wrong with that man's face?'

'Nothing. He's got a beard.'

'He looks like an animal. Are we nearly there, Emily?'

'In a minute.'

Emily gave a sigh of relief when she turned the car into the drive of Brambles, the house that wasn't hers any more, but belonged to her sons. If it hadn't been for that she would have sold up the minute Edwin died and moved somewhere more exciting: London, Brighton, or even abroad, Paris, or Berlin which was said to be fascinating, although this Hitler business was worrying. Edwin had left her well provided for, but she was scared to give up the security of her home and rent a place – the sort she aspired to would eat up a goodly portion of her income.

'Is this it?'

'Yes, Ruby, this is it.' Emily opened the car door and got out. Ruby collected her parcel and followed.

'It's not as big as the convent,' she said, a touch disparagingly Emily thought.

'Maybe not,' she said defensively, 'But it's bigger than most houses. It has twelve rooms, six upstairs and six down, that's not counting the kitchen and two bathrooms. Let's go inside so you can see.'

It was a relief to enter the empty house accompanied by another human being – the staff had all had gone home by now. Emily felt grateful for Ruby's loud cries as she ran in and out of the rooms, admiring the furniture, the ornaments, ending up back in the hall, where she examined herself critically, from top to toe, in the full-length mirror, twisting and turning, peering over her shoulder at her back.

'We didn't have mirrors in the convent.' She glanced pertly at Emily. 'We used to look at ourselves in the windows when it went dark. The nuns got cross if they saw us. Vanity is a sin, they said. *I* said, surely God wouldn't mind a person wanting to look nice.'

'And what did they say then?' Emily asked, interested.

'They said it was one thing to look nice, but quite another to dwell on it. I still think that's rubbish, but they got annoyed if I argued too much.' She pointed. 'What's that?'

'A telephone, dear. I'll show you how to use it one day.'

'Can I see where I'll sleep?'

Upstairs, Emily threw open the door of the pretty white and yellow room she'd had prepared next to her own bedroom. 'This is yours.'

Ruby flung herself joyfully on to the bed, oohed and aahed over the yellow flowered curtains that matched the dressing table skirt, and had another hard look at herself in the wardrobe mirror.

'Will you mind sleeping by yourself,' Emily asked. 'You're used to a dormitory, aren't you?'

'I *hate* dormitories,' Ruby said with feeling. 'We were made to go to bed awful early and had to be quiet even if we couldn't sleep. It wasn't so bad in summer, 'cause you could read under the covers, but when it was dark and they took the paraffin lamp away, you couldn't see a thing.' She smiled cajolingly at Emily. 'Will you let me have a lamp to read in bed? After all, I'm your *friend*.'

Emily laughed. 'You can read to your heart's content, Ruby. And you don't need a lamp, you switch the light on here, just inside the door.'

'Jaysus, Mary and Joseph!' Ruby gasped when the already bright room was flooded with more light. 'What's that when it's at home?'

'It's electricity, and please don't ask me to explain it to you, dear. You can look it up in the encyclopaedia. That's a book, and you'll find it with the dictionary in the room that used to be my husband's study,' she added quickly when Ruby opened her mouth to ask what an encyclopaedia was. 'Shall we go down and see what Mrs Arkwright has left for tea?'

On her way to bed that night, Emily paused outside Ruby's door, her hand on the knob, about to go in and make sure the child was all right after the day's upheaval. But say if she *wasn't* all right. She might be upset, even crying. She'd never known how to comfort people, not even her own boys when they were little. A nursemaid had carried out the task on her behalf until her sons went to boarding school at the age of seven. If they required sympathy of any sort during the holidays, they'd never said. Even when Edwin was dying, she hadn't known what to say. Emily removed her hand from the knob and hurried into her own room.

Unusually, that same night Reverend Mother couldn't sleep for the worry that bobbed about in her mind, like a yacht in a stormy sea. A memory surfaced, of when Emily was eight and she was ten. It was Christmas and they each found a doll beside their bed when they woke up, huge dolls, bigger than a real baby and dressed as an adult, in bunchy, silk, lace-trimmed frocks, frilly bonnets, underclothes, and even tiny necklaces. Emily's doll was blonde, its clothes pink, Cecilia's had dark hair and wore blue.

Emily had glanced from one doll to the other and announced in a weepy, whining voice that she wanted the blue one. Cecilia had held out, wanting her own, but gave in eventually, preferring a quiet life to a blue doll on Christmas Day. Anyway, the pink doll was quite nice. They swapped dolls, Emily calmed down, and the girls played happily with their presents throughout the day.

Nanny was putting them to bed, when Emily burst into tears and said she preferred the pink doll after all. This time Cecilia refused, having grown quite fond of the doll which she had christened Victoria after the Queen. Emily screamed, Nanny pleaded, 'After all, it's the one she was given, Cecy, dear.'

'All right, she can have them both. I don't want the blue one back.'

Emily had played with the pink doll all Boxing Day, then abandoned it for something else. The dolls had been put in a cupboard and Cecilia couldn't remember having seen them again.

The same thing had happened on numerous other occasions, but none stuck in her mind quite so clearly as the case of the two dolls. Emily wanted things to the exclusion of everything else, but once she got them, used them, played with them for a while, she lost all interest.

Reverend Mother had no idea what time it was when she eventually fell into a restless sleep. She woke with a start when Sister Angela knocked on the door at five o'clock, interrupting a vivid dream. The dolls, she'd been dreaming about the dolls, the blue one and the pink one. Emily had thrown them away in the little woods not far from where they lived and Cecilia had gone to rescue them. She'd found them face down at the foot of a tree amid a pile of rotting leaves and when she turned them over both dolls had the thin, pale face of Ruby O'Hagan.

The nun got out of bed, knelt on the hard stone floor, and began to pray.

Chapter 3

Ruby always woke up long before Emily. She would sit up straight away, stretch her arms, and look to see if the sun was shining through the yellow curtains. Whether it was or not, she would leap out of bed, get washed – she actually had her own little sink in the corner – and put on one of the frocks Emily had bought for her in Liverpool or Southport.

Of these places, Ruby preferred Liverpool. She liked the big, crowded shops, the bustle and noise. She loved the tramcars – there seemed to be hundreds and hundreds of them trundling along the metal lines making a terrible din and throwing off showers of sparks. She envied the occupants of these wonderful vehicles and longed to ride in one – Emily went everywhere by car. Liverpool buildings were magnificent: the Corn Exchange, the Customs House, the Town Hall, and her favourite, St George's Hall which, according to Emily, was famous throughout the world for its elegant design.

Emily preferred Southport, which Ruby thought all right, quite pretty, but very limited, and a bit too posh. She couldn't take to posh people, which Emily said was due to the way she'd been brought up.

'What do you mean?' Ruby demanded.

'The convent made sure you didn't have ideas above your station,' Emily explained. 'The girls weren't encouraged to have ambitions beyond becoming head cook or marrying the butler. You can't take to posh people, as you call them, because they make you feel inferior.'

'No, they don't,' Ruby argued. 'I just don't like the way they look down their noses at people who aren't as posh as themselves. I had no intention of being a cook, or marrying a butler come to that.'

Emily had merely shrugged, which Ruby took to mean her

argument was inescapable. She considered herself as good as anyone in the world.

One morning, when Ruby had been living in Kirkby for just over three months, she woke to find the August sunshine dancing through the window of her room, turning it into a grotto of golden light. She scrambled out of bed, drew back the curtains, and surveyed the back garden, which consisted of a vast square lawn surrounded by neat flower borders, an orchard, a tennis court, and a vegetable patch tucked away at the bottom. Everywhere was surrounded by birch trees with silver leaves which she'd been told would turn gold in the autumn. There wasn't another house in sight, the nearest was over a mile away.

What would she do today?

A few weeks ago, Emily had suggested she might like to go to school in September. At some schools, girls could stay until they were sixteen or even eighteen. Ruby had made a face and said she'd learnt enough, thanks all the same. Emily said she could do whatever she liked, it was up to her.

Emily didn't mind if she did, or didn't do, all sorts of things. She could stay up as late as she liked, read all night if she wanted, not eat her vegetables, have two helpings of pudding if there was enough, go out to play, or come back, whenever she pleased. Ruby found this a tiny bit unsettling and she quite missed the rules she'd been so fond of breaking at the convent. It was as if Emily didn't *care*, a suspicion that grew as the weeks passed and Emily seemed to lose all interest in taking her out, whether to go shopping or just for a ride. She'd made new friends, the Rowland-Graves, who'd just come back from India to live a few miles away in Knowsley. The Rowland-Graves threw loads of parties: bridge parties, cocktail parties, theatre parties, and parties that could go on all night. Emily was forever getting her hair done and buying new clothes, going out almost daily, draped in furs, even when it was hot. Despite this, she was always very glad Ruby was there to talk to when she came home.

Ruby decided to go to Humble's Farm for the milk and eggs, to save Mr Humble delivering them. She put on what Emily called a housefrock: red cotton patterned with big white flowers and white piping on the collar and sleeves. Emily said her taste was garish and she hoped she'd grow out of it one day. She liked flowery patterns too much. 'Plain clothes are so much more tasteful, Ruby.' Even so, she was allowed to have whatever caught her eye. She pulled on white ankle socks, pushed her feet into sandals, and collected a jug and basin from the kitchen.

It was going to be another scorching day, already hot as Ruby ran along the edge of the fields planted with an assortment of crops. Mr Humble's farm wasn't big, more a smallholding. He had a few cows, a few sheep, a few pigs, quite a lot of hens, a plough horse called Waterloo, a downtrodden wife, five grown-up children who had left home – 'And who could blame them?' said Emily – and a farm hand called Jacob whom Ruby found quite interesting, mainly because he was the only other young person she knew.

Jacob Veering was eighteen, not enormously tall, but broad and solid, with hair a lovely buttery shade and eyes the colour of bluebells. He was very dirty, very handsome, and also, said Emily, a bastard. 'Just like you, I expect,' she added.

Ruby had looked up bastard in the dictionary. It meant illegitimate, so she looked *that* up, and it meant 'out of wedlock'. Wedlock meant, 'in a wedded state'. By this time, Ruby had rather lost track and given up.

Jacob's mother lived in a little cottage opposite Kirkby church. Her name was Ruth, and she was a 'fey creature', according to Emily, supporting herself by making coloured candles that were sold in big shops like George Henry Lee's and Henderson's. She wasn't interested in Jacob, and he'd lived on Humble's Farm over Waterloo's stable since he was twelve.

'Is Jacob a Catholic?' Ruby enquired. 'So I can talk to him?'

'For goodness sake, Ruby, dear. You can talk to Jacob if he's a heathen, which I suspect he is.'

Mrs Humble was collecting eggs when Ruby arrived, out of breath having run all the way. Everywhere in the area of the farmyard was thick with dirt and smelled strongly of manure, particularly when it was hot. Ruby dreaded to think what it would be like in winter when it might smell less, but the caked dirt would turn to mud.

'The usual?' Mrs Humble asked in her sad, beaten voice. She was as bent as an old woman, yet only forty-nine. She wore a frayed shawl, holding the ends together with a gnarled, red hand.

'Yes, please. Six eggs and a jug of milk.'

'Jacob's doing the milking right now.'

'I'll just say good morning.'

Ruby approached the cow shed on tiptoe, though wasn't sure why. Unusually for her, she felt nervous around Jacob. He was polite, but a bit reserved, and she always got the feeling she was in the way. She reached the door and said shyly, 'Hello.'

Jacob wore grubby corduroy trousers tied up with a rope and a frayed collarless shirt with half the sleeves cut off. His arms and face were very brown and his unlaced boots were planted in the straw, as if he'd grown there like a tree. He didn't look up from the task of pulling expertly at the teats of a black and white cow, each teat squirting a thin stream of creamy milk into a metal bucket.

'Hello,' he said, in a voice that wasn't exactly friendly, but wasn't unfriendly, either.

'It's a nice morning.'

'Known few better,' he grunted.

Ruby searched her mind for something to say. Jacob never started a conversation, only speaking when he was spoken to. 'Do you ever listen to the wireless?' she enquired.

'Haven't got one,' Jacob replied.

'We've got one in the house. And a gramophone, too.'

'Have you, now.'

'They play music. Do you like music?'

'Music's all right,' Jacob conceded.

'You can come and listen, if you like. Come on Saturday, after six o'clock. Emily's going to the theatre – that's a place that puts on plays,' she added, in case Jacob didn't know.

Jacob showed no sign of having known or not. 'I'll think about it,' he said.

'Mrs Humble came in with a ladle, scooped milk from the bucket and poured it into Ruby's jug. 'The eggs are ready,' she said dully.

'Ta.' Ruby looked anxiously at Jacob. 'See you Saturday?'

'You might.' He still didn't look up.

Ruby sighed and made her way slowly back to Brambles, where Mrs Arkwright, the cook, was just hoisting her stout, perspiring body off her bike.

'Got the eggs and milk,' Ruby announced.

'Have you, now,' Mrs Arkwright replied, tightlipped, before wheeling the bike round to the back. Ruby followed. The two didn't get on. Months ago, on Ruby's first visit to the kitchen, she had helpfully pointed out the ham currently boiling on the stove would taste better with the addition of a bay leaf – something she had learnt in the convent – and Mrs Arkwright immediately saw her as a threat, intent on taking over her job if she wasn't careful. From thereon, Ruby was discouraged from entering the kitchen.

The cleaner, Mrs Roberts, was just as discouraging. She was old and weary and made it obvious that Ruby's constant chatter got on her nerves.

At least Ernest, the gardener, was friendly, even if he couldn't hear a word she said, being totally deaf. He'd thrown a rope over one of the apple trees to make a swing.

Ruby was badly in need of a friend. She found the countryside very dull. There was plenty to do, but she would have liked someone to do it with – she got no satisfaction from playing in the orchard by herself. Tennis was frustrating when there was no one to hit the ball back. She wondered if it was too late to agree to school, though she'd like to bet it was full of posh girls whom she wouldn't like and she'd regret it straight away. If only Emily would *make* her go. There was a world of difference between being made to do something you didn't want, and taking the decision yourself. If it turned out horrid you had someone else to blame.

She went through the kitchen, deposited the eggs and milk on the table and made a face at Mrs Arkwright's disapproving back.

For the next half hour, she studied the dictionary in Emily's late husband's study. Edwin Dangerfield had been a solicitor specialising in conveyancing which meant transferring things, usually property – Ruby had looked it up. The dictionary was her favourite book and every day she learned six useful words. Last week, she'd reached 'B'. She was wondering if there was any point in remembering 'Bacterium', when she heard Mrs Arkwright make her heavy way upstairs with her employer's morning coffee. She put the book away and, as soon as the cook came down, she flew up the stairs to see Emily.

'Oh, Gawd!' Emily groaned when Ruby put her smiling face around the door. 'You look inordinately cheerful and so bloody *young!* You make me feel at least a hundred. What's it like outside? I told Arky not to open the curtains. My head's splitting from last night.' Last night, the Rowland-Graves had held a dinner party.

'It's nice outside, sunny and warm.'

Emily winced. 'I'd prefer it dull and cold.'

'I thought we could go shopping,' Ruby said hopefully as she sat on the edge of the bed.

'Sorry, dear. I'm going to a garden party this afternoon. I'm urgently in need of a rejuvenating bath and you know how long it takes me to get ready.'

It took hours of massaging the sagging skin, painting the ageing face, teasing the dyed hair into a satisfactory style, trying on at least a dozen outfits, deciding which shoes went best with the frock or costume that had been chosen, searching for appropriate jewellery, the most flattering hat.

'I need new shoes,' Ruby growled. 'All the ones I've got now are too small.'

'Oh, dear!' Emily bit her lip, feeling guilty that she was neglecting the girl. If Mim and Ronnie Rowland-Graves hadn't appeared on the scene, Emily would have leapt at the idea of shopping for shoes. But to her everlasting relief, Mim and Ronnie had. They'd led a fast, slightly *risqué* life in India and were set on doing the same in England. In their early fifties, their main aim in life was to have a good time. They paid no regard to the married status of their guests, nor their ages, as long as they shared their quest for excitement, which involved drinking too much, engaging in spicy conversation, and even spicier party games, all of which would have shocked Edwin to the bones were he still alive.

She stared at Ruby's thin face, no longer cheerful, still looking as if she hadn't eaten a decent meal in ages, and wondered if she was lonely by herself for so much of the time. Emily couldn't possibly have taken her to the Rowland-Graves, which was no place for a young girl. She had an idea. 'If you like, later, I'll drop you off at Kirkby station and you can go to Liverpool and buy shoes yourself.'

Ruby couldn't have been more delighted had she been offered the Crown Jewels. She leapt off the bed and danced around the room. '*Can* I? Oh, *can* I? Oh, Emily, I'd *love* to. I've never been on a train. What time are you leaving? Shall I get changed?'

'But how will you get home from the station?' Emily was already wishing she hadn't been quite so hasty. Was she being irresponsible? No, she decided after a few seconds' thought. Had Ruby gone into service, she would have been given all sorts of onerous tasks to do, shopping among them. It would do the girl good to go out by herself.

'I'll walk home from the station. It's not far, only a few miles,' Ruby said fervently, her big, dark eyes suddenly anxious that the wonderful treat might be denied.

'Are you sure?'

'Absolutely certain.'

The big train came charging into Kirkby station like a monster, snorting clouds of dirty smoke. Ruby, in her best dress – white, patterned with rosebuds – climbed into a carriage, hugging herself with glee. She had two ten-shilling notes folded in her purse, as well as a further five shillings in coins for her fare and any other expenses that might occur.

All the way to Liverpool, much to the irritation of the only other passenger, a woman, she flew from one side of the carriage to the other to look at the view, at the way it changed from soft green fields to rows of cramped brick houses then to a forest of factories before drawing into Exchange station where she got off, marvelling at the vastness of the building and the steaming, panting trains.

Happiness bounced like a ball in Ruby's chest as she made her way through the crowded, vibrant city to Lewis's department store where, feeling terribly important, she bought a pair of Clarks' sandals for four and eleven, and black patent leather shoes with a strap and button for seven and six. It had been *almost* true to claim she'd grown out of the shoes she already had. She'd said it in an attempt to persuade Emily to take her shopping. And it had worked better than she'd hoped. It was nice being on her own, able to go where she pleased, not keep retreating to the Adelphi Hotel for coffee and a cigarette, as Emily felt the need to do.

Emerging from Lewis's, she stood on the busy pavement, buffeted by the crowds, breathing in the choking fumes and the various smells that she liked better than those of the country, wondering where to go next. Not back to Kirkby, it was too early.

She wandered along, starry-eyed, looking in shop windows – window shopping Emily called it. Blacklers had a display of frocks and one in particular caught Ruby's eye: navy-blue with bold red spots, it had a frilly neck with a red bow and flared sleeves like little skirts, and was only one and elevenpence, about a quarter of what

47

Emily usually paid. It was a lady's frock, not a child's, but Ruby was tall enough to wear it. She went inside and tried it on, twirling around in front of the cubicle mirror.

'It looks the gear on you, luv,' the assistant said.

'I'll take it.' The frock was calf-length, whereas all her others came to just below the knees. She thought it made her look very adult. She handed the assistant half a crown which was sent whizzing high across the shop in a little tube attached to a wire towards a woman in a glass case who removed the tube and, a minute later, Ruby's change whizzed back with the bill. She never ceased to be facinated by this process.

Outside again, she decided to wear the frock on Saturday in case Jacob came. She crossed the road, dodging through the traffic, and just missed being mown down by a tramcar with Number 1 and its destination, Dingle, on the front.

'Dingle'. She said the word aloud. It sounded pretty, like something out of a fairy-tale. She noticed that the tram had stopped and people were getting on. It took barely a second for Ruby to decide to get on with them. She'd always wanted to ride on a tram. She climbed to the top and sat on the hard front seat, which gave a perfect view.

The tram set off, clicking noisily along the lines, swerving round bends, breaking suddenly, when a queue appeared, waiting to board. Ruby clutched her parcels with one hand, and held on to the edge of her seat with the other, worried she might be thrown through the window as the tram rocked dangerously from side to side. They passed the soaring tower of the Protestant cathedral which had been started in the last century but still wasn't finished.

The conductor came. Ruby bought a penny ticket which would take her all the way to the Dingle. 'Will you tell me when we get there?' She'd heard him shouting the names of the stops.

'You'll know, luv. We don't go no further than the Dingle.'

The tram was rolling along a long, colourful and very busy road, full of traffic and lined with every conceivable sort of shop, interrupted frequently by little streets of terraced houses. Groups of men lounged outside the pubs that seemed to be on every corner, hands in pockets, idle. Women chatted eagerly over their bags of shopping, children hanging on to their skirts or chasing each other up and down the pavements, in and out of the shops.

Ruby's eyes were everywhere, taking it all in, the way the women were dressed, some almost as smart as Emily, some with shawls over their heads like poor Mrs Humble. There were men in suits and bowler hats, and jackletless men with braces showing, no collars to their shirts, tieless. She saw scrubbed, neatly dressed children, glowing with health, and felt a surge of pity when she saw the scabby-faced mites with bare, dirty feet who were much too thin.

It was like being at the very hub of the universe and Ruby, clutching the seat, knew with utter certainty that this was where she belonged: amid people, noise, and city smells. She felt at home in the clutter of the busy streets in a way she never would in Kirkby where there wasn't another house in sight.

'I'll come back,' she whispered to herself. 'I'll come back tomorrow or the next day, and one of these days, I'll come back for good.'

She got off at the tram sheds and walked up and down the tiny streets. Women sat contentedly on the whitened steps outside their neat houses, enjoying the brilliant sunshine. Children swung from the lampposts, played hopscotch on the pavement, whip and top, or two-balls against the walls.

Ruby sighed enviously and supposed she'd better be getting home.

On Saturday night, Emily went to the theatre wearing a new grey silk costume and a little matching hat with a veil, her fox fur laid casually around her shoulders despite the gloriously hot day.

'You'll be all right won't you, dear?' she said worriedly. 'You can read a book or listen to the wireless. I'll tell you what the play was about when I get home.'

'I'll be fine,' Ruby said stoutly.

As soon as Emily had gone, she went upstairs and changed into the spotted dress from Blacklers. It clung to her thin body and, she was pleased to note, emphasised her small breasts, making her look very grown-up, particularly when she piled her black hair on top of her head, securing it with a slide.

She went into Emily's room, searched through the jewellery box on the dressing table which had been left in a terrible mess, and helped herself to a pearl necklace and earrings – Emily had gone out

49

wearing her 'good' pearls. She tried on a pair of red, high-heeled shoes. They were only a bit too big.

Downstairs, she switched on the wireless and was met by a thunderous blast of classical music which she turned off in disgust, deciding to play one of her favourite records instead: a selection of ballads sung by Rudy Vallee, and so hauntingly lovely, they made her go all funny inside.

Ruby began to sway as she watched the record spin around. 'Goodnight, Sweetheart', was one of her favourites. Unable to resist, she kicked off the shoes, flung her arms in the air, and danced around the room, very slowly, hugging herself. The music was causing a sweet, nagging ache in her tummy, it always did, making her want things she couldn't define. She closed her eyes and tried to imagine someone in the room with her, a man. They were dancing together. She was being kissed by invisible lips in a way she'd never seen people kiss before. Ruby had no idea where the thoughts came from. She must have been born with them.

Rudy Vallee began to sing 'Night and Day', and still Ruby danced, losing herself completely in the glorious, romantic music, unaware that she had an audience.

Outside the window, Jacob Veering, his face shiny after a thorough scrubbing, wearing his one and only suit, didn't think he had ever seen anything so beautiful as the strange young lady fluttering like a butterfly across the room. He had never known anyone like her. His tongue would form a lump in his throat whenever she spoke to him, and it was all he could do to answer.

Jacob already had a girlfriend, Audrey Wainwright, whose father owned a farm much bigger than Humble's. There was an unspoken agreement that they would marry one day and he would transfer his labour from Humble's farm to Wainwright's, where he would live and work for the rest of his life. He wasn't particularly looking forward to the future, but nor did he regard it with dread. As long as he could work on the land, have a place to live, enough to eat, and no one abused him, Jacob would be content, if not happy. Being a man he would need a wife and Audrey Wainwright would fill this role. He assumed she felt the same. The word 'love' had never been uttered during their relationship, but if either had noticed they didn't seem to mind.

But now, as he watched Ruby dance, sensations he'd never felt before were causing tremors in Jacob's normally stolid heart. It was pounding for one thing, so hard and so fast that he felt frightened. He had the urge to smash the window, climb inside, catch Ruby by her tiny waist and twirl her round and round till they both fell dizzily to the floor in each other's arms. Yet he knew he could never bring himself to touch her. She was out of bounds to someone like him. She was a creature from another world to which Jacob, the farmhand, didn't belong.

She looked so strong, and yet so frail, and there was an expression on her face that he envied, a dreamy, lost expression, as if she was somewhere else entirely than the room in which she danced. Jacob had never felt like that and he wondered what it was like. He also wondered if she remembered she had invited him to the house that night. Well, there was only one way of finding out. He knocked on the front door.

When she answered, Jacob gasped. Her eyes were starbright, her cheeks were flushed, and she bestowed upon him a warm look of welcome that caused his heart to pound even more.

'I didn't think you'd turn up!' She reached for his hand. 'Come and listen to the music. I've been dancing. Can you dance?'

'No,' Jacob said thickly. He allowed himself to be pulled inside and immediately felt ill at ease in the richly furnished house with carpets on the floor and ornaments and pictures all over the place. There were velvet chairs in the room into which she led him and the music was louder here. A man was singing about his heart standing still and Jacob wished his own heart would do the same. He couldn't take his eyes away from the little curls that clung damply to Ruby's slender neck and his hand was tingling from her touch.

She smiled at him. 'Would you like something to eat? There's a big apple pie for tomorrow, but Emily won't care if we eat it.'

'Wouldn't mind,' Jacob grunted, wishing he didn't sound so surly.

He was dragged into a big scullery where he gaped at the extraordinary cream stove, the shallow cream sink, the green painted cupboards, the black and white check-tiled floor. She took a golden-crusted pie out of the larder. 'Would you like tea or coffee?' She gestured him to sit at the big table in the centre of the room.

'Tea.' He had never had coffee and had no idea what it was like. She made him feel very ignorant, a bit of an oaf, with her gramophone and coffee and a scullery the likes of which he'd never seen before – he had a feeling people like her called them 'kitchens'.

He watched as she poured water into what was definitely a kettle, but instead of putting it on the peculiar stove to boil, she attached it to the wall with a plug. Overcome with curiousity, he said, 'What's that?'

'It's an electric kettle. Haven't you seen electricity before?'

'They have it in the pub by the station, The Railway Arms.'

'I didn't even know electricity existed until I came to live with Emily. We had paraffin lamps in the convent and the food was cooked in an oven by the kitchen fire. It was called a range.'

'The convent?'

She put milk and sugar on the table and sat opposite him, folding her thin arms. 'The convent where I grew up.'

'But Mr Humble said you were Mrs Dangerfield's niece or something, a relative.'

'Oh, no.' She laughed and her wide mouth almost reached her ears. 'I'm an orphan. The convent was an orphanage, still is. Emily just wanted a friend and she picked me.' She preened herself.

'Don't you mind being an orphan?' Jacob missed not having a father, but at least could boast a mother, even if she hadn't been up to much.

Ruby shrugged carelessly. 'Seems a waste of time, minding. What help would it be?'

Jacob stared at her, blinking. The fact that she was an orphan, that she didn't truly belong in a grand house like this, had brought her, in a way, down to his level. At the same time, it only made her seem more remarkable and untouchable that she had so quickly made herself at home, fitting so easily into rich people's ways, though she didn't talk posh like Mrs Dangerfield.

The kettle boiled. She got up, switched it off, and made the tea. 'Do you take sugar?'

'Two spoons, ta. How did your mam and dad die?'

'I don't know if they're alive or dead. Sister Cecilia said I wasn't even a day old when I arrived at the convent. There was a note to say I was called Ruby O'Hagan, that's all.'

'O'Hagan sounds Irish. Ruby's nice.' Jacob blushed.

'So's Jacob. Would you like some pie?'

Jacob nodded. 'I'll have to be going soon. I'm meeting someone in the pub for a drink.' He didn't say it was his future father-in-law.

'Oh!' Ruby pouted. 'I thought you'd come for longer. You can come again next week. Come whenever you like, 'cept when Emily's here. You can tell if the car's in the drive.'

'OK, ta.'

The pie finished, Jacob left by the rear door. When he got to the front, he heard music. Looking back, he saw Ruby bending over the gramophone. Suddenly, she turned and began to dance. Jacob stood watching for ages and ages, and it was all he could do to tear himself away.

From that week on, life for Ruby was no longer dull. Two, three, sometimes four times a week, whenever Emily was out, she would catch the train to Exchange station and explore Liverpool – the centre of the city and its environs. She discovered the Pier Head where ferries sailed across the Mersey to Birkenhead, Seacombe, and best of all, New Brighton where, if she had enough money, she bought fish and chips, ice cream, and made herself pleasantly sick on the fairground.

'I hope you're not coming down with something,' Emily would say in a concerned voice when she couldn't eat her tea.

'I'll eat it later.' She usually did, better by then. Her appetite was voracious, though she never put on weight. Emily remarked she was growing taller.

She went by tram to every possible destination: Bootle, Walton Vale, Aigburth, Woolton, Penny Lane, getting off along the way, or at the terminus, where she roamed the streets, envious of the way people lived so closely together. A few times, she strolled along the Dock Road, possibly the busiest and most frenziedly noisy place of all, with its foreign smells, hooting, blaring traffic nose to tail, the funnels of enormous ships soaring over the dock walls. The pavements were packed with people jabbering away in languages that were rarely English. She had to push her away through, heart lifting at the exhilerating strangeness of every single thing.

The Dingle remained her favourite place, perhaps because she'd gone there first. A few of the tram conductors got to know her and greeted her as a friend.

The money for fares Ruby found in Emily's large collection of handbags where there were always a few coins that would never be missed. It wasn't stealing. She knew, if asked, Emily would give her money to buy sweets or comics or coloured pencils from the post office, but possibly not to travel the length and breadth of Liverpool by various means. It seemed less troublesome to help herself to money than tell a lie.

Sometimes Emily arrived home before her and when she got in Ruby would say she'd been for a walk.

'In the dark, dear!'

'It was light when I left. I didn't realise I'd walked so far.' Emily didn't notice she always made the same excuse.

Jacob usually turned up in the evenings when Emily was out. Since the night he had seen Ruby dance, Jacob had discovered that sitting in the Wainwright's, as he did most nights, with Audrey, her mam and dad, and two younger sisters, talking or playing cards, drinking tea and eating Mrs Wainwright's rather dry home-made scones, then retiring with Audrey to the stuffy parlour to exchange a few chaste kisses, had lost what little thrall it had. It had never held much, but seemed the thing to do when you were courting.

He still felt uncomfortable in Brambles with its satin cushions, pleated curtains, and electricity. He felt uncomfortable with Ruby who was teaching him to dance, had taught him to drink coffee, and told him things she'd heard on the wireless or read in Emily's newspaper, about people he didn't know who lived in countries he'd never heard of. He'd never opened a newspaper in his life and could read and write only a little.

She dazzled him. He was in awe of her, She knew everything. At night, he went to sleep with her graceful, twirling figure in front his eyes, hearing her voice. He forgot what Audrey looked like. He used some of the money he was saving for the wedding to buy a suit in Ormskirk market.

'We could have bought it in town on Saturday afternoon when you're off,' Ruby said when she admired the cheap suit which was navy-blue with a lighter blue stripe. She squeaked with horror when Jacob said he had never been to Liverpool.

'Never *been*! Lord, Jacob, I've been dozens of times. *Dozens*!'

'I know.' Her frequent expeditions, by train, tram and ferry filled him with admiration. He hated leaving Kirkby. Even in Ormskirk, a small market town, he felt overwhelmed by so many people, panic-stricken in the narrow streets, his chest tight, wanting to run away to where there were open spaces and a clear, unrestricted sky, to where he could breathe. He only felt at home with the soil and the crops and the animals that he tended. There were times when he wished he'd never met Ruby, who'd caused such havoc in his heart that he no longer knew what he wanted.

Christmas was never-ending party time at the Rowland-Graves. Emily ate Christmas dinner with Ruby – the food had mostly been prepared the day before by Mrs Arkwright – nursing the pleasant thought that later she would enjoy herself in a very different way.

She regarded herself as having been doubly blessed. She genuinely loved Ruby, who was a perfect companion; loyal, uncomplaining, intelligent, with a cheerful disposition. It was a pleasure to be met by her sunny, happy face whenever she entered the house. They'd been to Midnight Mass together and it was a delightful experience that she would have missed if the girl hadn't been there. At the same time, the Rowland-Graves were providing all the excitement and fun that Emily had always longed for. Life had never been so good or so fulfilling.

'Will you be all right on your own?' She asked the inevitable question while making preparations for the evening ahead.

Ruby was sitting on the bed, watching the painstaking proceedings. She gave the inevitable answer. 'I'll be fine.'

As soon as Emily had gone she put the light on in her bedroom without drawing the curtains, a signal to Jacob, watching across the fields, that it was safe to come.

Fifteen minutes later, Jacob came, drawn to the light like a moth to a flame.

Ruby had been at Brambles for two years and would shortly be sixteen. 'We should really have a party,' Emily said the week before. 'But you don't know anyone do you?'

'Not a soul,' Ruby said innocently. Only Jacob, scores of bus conductors, a barrow lady called Maggie Mullen from whom she regularly purchased an apple, Mrs First, who had a sweetshop in the Dingle, a girl her own age, Ginnie O'Dare, who worked by Exchange station and whom she often met on the train. There were loads more people she knew by sight. But none of these people could she ask to a party.

'We can't just let your birthday pass without doing something,' Emily said. If she took her out to tea, as she had done last year, it wouldn't interrupt her hectic social life. Perhaps it was guilt that made her decide to splash out on an expensive gold watch for a present.

'Can we go to the pictures?' Ginnie O'Dare was always on about the pictures and Ruby was curious as to what they were like.

'What a lovely idea! We'll go to a matinée. There's a Greta Garbo picture on in town, *Grand Hotel*. I'd love to see it.'

Unknown to Emily, Ruby went to see *Grand Hotel* another half a dozen times. She practised saying, 'I vant to be alone,' Greta Garbo style, in front of the mirror. She gave up tram rides for the cinema, sitting open-mouthed and totally absorbed in the cheapest seats during matinées in half-empty cinemas where she learned more about human nature in the space of a few weeks, than she'd done during her entire life. She discovered what treachery meant, jealousy and betrayal, and that she'd never realised people could so easily be provoked to murder. She learnt about love, how pure it could be, how good, yet sometimes very evil, driving people to do all sorts of terrible things in its name. Ruby knew the film stars were only acting out stories that had been written for them, yet they must be reflecting real life, the sort of life she hadn't known existed.

After a while, she felt as if Bette Davies, Joan Crawford, Claudette Colbert, were her friends. She fell in love with Van Heflin and would have liked Herbert Marshall for a dad.

It was about this time, a few months after Ruby's sixteenth birthday, that Emily Dangerfield fell in love herself.

Bill Pickering was forty-three, the first American she had ever met, which only added to his warm, relaxed charm. Tall, slender, deeply tanned, with luxuriant blond, wavy hair and a full moustache, he had lived the last ten years in Monte Carlo where he owned a chain of hotels. His clothes were well cut and expensive, extremely dashing, and he wore them with elegant grace. He had come to stay with his old friends, the Rowland-Graves, for the summer, feeling ever-so-slightly tired of Monte Carlo's ritzy glamour, leaving the hotels to the care of experienced staff.

Emily was thrilled when he began to flirt with her, flattered that a man sixteen years her junior should find her attractive. And she wasn't just imagining it. Mim Rowland-Graves had commented enviously that Bill was obviously smitten. Emily was already in love by the time he asked her out. 'I think it's time we got to know each other properly,' he said in his light transatlantic drawl.

She invited him to Brambles for drinks and to sample Mrs Arkwright's delicious miniature pork pies.

'I didn't know you had a daughter!' he exclaimed in surprise when introduced to Ruby.

'Ruby is my ward,' Emily explained, flattered again that he thought her young enough to have a sixteen-year-old child – mind you, she had vaguely admitted to being forty-nine.

'How do you do,' Ruby said nicely, liking Bill Pickering on the spot. He had a lovely smile that crinkled the skin around his light brown eyes.

'And how do *you* do. Ruby. Gee whizz, Em, this little lady will break a few hearts when she grows up,' he said, thus pleasing Ruby with the compliment and Emily with the dimunitive 'Em', which made her feel as if they were more than just friends.

Emily showed him around the house, which he found very impressive. 'Great place, Em,' he enthused. 'Love the garden. Best house I've seen round these parts, in fact. Furnished with exquisite taste, as my old ma back in the States would say.'

'Thank you.' Emily blushed. 'I chose everything myself.'

From then on, Bill Pickering appeared frequently at Brambles. He played tennis with Ruby and sometimes let her win. Emily, watching wistfully from a deckchair, tried hard not to feel old.

'They're potty about each other,' Ruby told Jacob one night. 'They kiss all the time. Sometimes they go into Emily's bedroom and make the most peculiar noises.' She looked at him coyly. 'Have you ever wanted to kiss me?'

'Yes,' Jacob said daringly.

'Shall we try it? See what it's like?'

Before he could answer, she'd thrown herself on to his knee and pressed her mouth against his. For a few seconds he didn't respond, but the light pressure of her lips was creating turmoil in his stomach. He pulled her down so that they were squashed together in the velvet armchair and his arms were wrapped around her as tightly as a fist. Her ribs were like a little delicate ladder under his splayed hand, her shoulder blades as sharp as knives. He was kissing her fiercely now, rubbing his thumb against her soft breasts. And to his joy and astonishment she was responding, curling her arms around his neck, caressing the nape, touching his ears.

It went on and on the kiss, on and on, until it felt as if they'd been kissing for hours, until Jacob, unable to help himself, slid his hand under her skirt. Ruby groaned and opened her legs and he moved her gently to the floor and crouched on top of her. He looked into her eyes which were huge and black and slightly scared, framed like a picture with long, smoky lashes.

He wanted to ask if it was all right to do what he was about to do, but then she might say no, and he couldn't have borne it. Somewhere deep within the ferment in his brain he felt a tiny prick of conscience. He wondered how much she knew? What had she been told in the convent? Had Mrs Dangerfield informed her of the facts of life?

Then Ruby said, 'Don't stop,' and Jacob couldn't have stopped to save his life, though he retained enough sense to withdraw at the proper time. It wouldn't do for her to get pregnant.

Afterwards, she was unusually quiet and subdued. She looked puzzled, as if she wasn't quite sure what had happened. They went into the kitchen and it was Jacob who made the tea. Ruby sat in a chair, kicking her heels against it absently, like a child.

'Does this mean we'll get married?' she asked after a while.

Jacob's heart did a somersault. 'If you want,' he replied.

'I think I do. When?'

'When you're older,' he said gruffly.

'Where will we live?'

'I don't know.' Nor did he care. To be with Ruby, he'd live on one of them tram cars she was always on about. He'd go anywhere, do anything, if they could be together.

She was sipping the tea, watching him over the cup with her dazzling black eyes. 'Shall we go upstairs and do it again?' she whispered.

'I hope you're not coming down with something,' Emily said a few days later when it dawned on her that Ruby had been very quiet for several days.

'I feel all right, thank you.'

'Are you sure?' Even the reply wasn't quite like Ruby. Perhaps she was concerned what would happen to her when Emily and Bill got married – he had only hinted so far, but she was expecting a proposal any minute. 'I think the confirmed bachelor will shortly be confirmed no more,' Ronnie Rowland-Graves had said with a wink the other day. Ruby was smart and could no doubt sense the way the wind was blowing.

Bill was thinking of selling his hotels and living permanently in England. Emily was already making plans. They would live in Brambles at first, the house he so much admired, then look for a place in London. A flat in Mayfair or Belgravia would be ideal and perhaps a little hidey-hole in Paris, or even New York – they could travel to and fro on one of those great cruise liners which would be a holiday in itself. Whatever happened, once she became Mrs Pickering, there would be no more need for Ruby in her life.

Yet she couldn't just abandon the girl. She had been wondering if Adrian in Australia would be willing to take her until she was eighteen? Or perhaps the Rowland-Graves could be persuaded, though they wouldn't provide a particularly healthy atmosphere for someone so young.

She forgot about Ruby and concentrated on Bill, a less taxing way of occupying her mind. For the first time in her life she was properly in love. When she looked in the mirror she saw the lovely woman she'd once been. Her blissful happiness showed in her eyes and she could feel it in her heart. This coming weekend, Bill was taking her to the Lake District. She couldn't wait. She began to plan what to wear. It was when she was deciding which nightdress to take that she remembered Bill would see her first thing in the morning when she looked a miserable wreck. She prayed she'd wake early so there'd be time for the massive preparations required to make herself present-able for when Bill woke up himself.

It was fine when they left Kirkby after tea on Saturday, a clear August day, warm but not muggy. But they'd gone only twenty miles when the sky began to cloud over, getting ominously dark. Spots of rain splattered on to the windscreen and in the blinking of an eye became a deluge. They were in Emily's Jaguar as Bill couldn't drive. 'There just doesn't seem the need in Monte Carlo. I can easily walk to my hotels. Otherwise I use taxis.'

Emily hated driving in the rain. She reduced her speed and bent over the steering wheel clutching it tightly in both hands. A headache arrived as quickly as the rain and she could hardly see. The windscreen wipers didn't seem to be working properly and were making her dizzy. The headlights were useless, the beam absorbed by the pelting rain. Beside her, Bill made encouraging noises, but after a while, Emily drew into a lay-by and announced she couldn't go on. They'd travelled less than a quarter of the way, and at this rate they wouldn't get there till midnight.

'But, honey, the hotel's booked,' Bill cried.

'I'm sorry, but we'll just have to wait until the rain goes off. I'm no good at driving in this sort of weather.'

An hour later, the weather showed no sign of clearing.

'Where are we?' Bill asked.

'I've no idea. In the middle of nowhere, I suspect. I wonder, darling, would you mind very much if we went home? This is bound to have cleared up by morning and we can start off early. If we turn round at least I'll know where I'm going.'

'I don't mind a jot, hon.' He kissed her cheek. 'As long as I'm with you, that's all I care.'

The journey back was hazardous, but it wasn't long before she began to recognise the way and felt able to relax.

'Well,' Bill laughed when the Jaguar squelched to a halt outside Brambles. 'That was quite an adventure, unexpected though it was.'

'What time is it?'

'Not quite ten.'

'The house is in darkness. Ruby sometimes goes to bed early, but she always leaves a light on. I hope she's all right.'

'We'll soon see, hon.'

Ruby appeared on the landing in response to Emily's shout. She must have been about to get undressed as the buttons down the front of her frock were undone. There was something odd about her face. She looked uncomfortable. When she saw Bill, she drew the edges of her frock together – perhaps that was the reason.

'You didn't leave a light on, dear.'

'I wasn't expecting you back till Sunday.'

'You'd forgotten that, hadn't you, honey?'

Bill's intervention made Emily feel doddery and vague. To her surprise he went over to the foot of the stairs, looked up. 'Why don't you come down, Rube? Join me and Emily for a drink?'

'She's only sixteen,' Emily snapped. She had been thinking that now was a perfect time for him to propose, over drinks, rain lashing against the windows, lamps switched on instead of the central light, a romantic record on the gramophone . . . She would have lit a fire had she known how.

'A little drop of sherry wouldn't hurt,' Bill smiled.

'I don't want any, thanks all the same,' said Ruby, tossing her head.

Bill continued to stand by the stairs. An irritated Emily followed his upward gaze – and caught her breath! Ruby had grown up without her noticing. There was something about her stance, feet slightly apart – bare feet – the way her hands clutched the frock so that the material was pulled taut over the breasts that seemed to have happened overnight. She looked like a woman, a woman very much aware of her sexuality as she stared haughtily back at a transfixed Bill.

Emily broke the spell. 'Would you like a bite to eat, darling?' Mrs Arkwright had roasted a large joint of beef that morning, enough for several days. She'd slice some on a plate with tomato, pickles, and bread and butter, open some wine.

'A bite to eat would be most welcome.' Bill jumped, as if he'd forgotten she was there.

'Would you mind putting on some music? I won't be long.'

Upstairs, a door slammed. Ruby had gone into her room. Emily's face was grim as she went into the kitchen. Pretty soon, Ruby would be gone for ever. No matter how much she loved the girl, there was no alternative. It was dangerous for her to stay.

She threw a lace cloth over a little occasional table and put it in front of the fireplace, lighting a candle for the centre. The dancing orange flame was reflected in the rose red wine so the bottle looked as if it was on fire. In the background, Paul Whiteman and his Orchestra were playing. 'Rhapsody in Blue'.

'This is very nice.' Bill seemed to have forgotten about Ruby and was eating the snack with boyish enjoyment. He winked. 'You'll make someone a wonderful wife one day, Emily.'

Emily fluttered her lashes. She had changed out of her tweed costume into a pair of Chinese silk lounging pyjamas in a stunning shade of yellow and felt rather daring. She was more than a little dismayed to hear him say, 'someone'. There was only one person whose wife she wanted to be and she had thought he felt the same.

But apparently he did. He reached across and took her hand. 'And honey, I'd like that someone to be me.'

'Oh, darling!' She almost burst into tears, but remembered her mascara just in time. 'I'd like it too.'

He kissed her hand. 'Let's drink to us.' He picked up his glass.

'To us!' She had never been so deliriously happy.

'When I finish this delicious food, I'll kiss you like you've never been kissed before.'

Emily couldn't eat another thing. She lit a cigarette and poured the remainder of the wine. 'Shall I fetch another bottle?' There were still several cases left from Edwin's once considerable wine cellar.

'Why not!' He waved his fork. 'Let's celebrate. It's not every day a couple decide to get married.'

The second bottle quickly went and Emily felt quite gloriously tipsy. By now, they were sitting on the settee and Bill was kissing her thoroughly as he'd promised. Her heart thumped wildly in her chest as she responded with an almost fierce passion. She would never know another night like this.

Bill opened more wine and they began to discuss wedding arrangements. 'I think we should get hitched pretty soon, hon. We love each other, so what point is there in waiting?' His voice, like hers, had become slurred.

Emily couldn't have agreed more. 'I wouldn't want a grand affair. A register office would suit me.'

'Me, too.' he stroked her breast. Emily shivered with delight. 'And where shall we go for our honeymoon? How about Rome, my favourite city? I'll do this to you all day long.'

She sighed pleasurably. 'Rome's perfect. Where shall we live? Please say London. You know how much I love it. I've told you so many times.'

'Then London it shall be, my lovely Em.' He stretched his arms and glanced around the room. 'Though I love this house. It will be a shame to sell it, but if you're intent on London, we have no choice. I can't get rid of the hotels at the drop of a hat. It will take at least a year, possibly longer.'

Emily laughed. 'Then I'm afraid we're stuck in Brambles until then. I can't sell it. It isn't mine to sell.'

Bill reached for his glass, a strange expression on his face. Emily, trying to discern it, decided it was expression*less*, very still, telling nothing. 'I beg your pardon?' he said politely.

'Edwin left the property to the boys.' She wrinkled her nose. 'I can – we can – live here as long as we want, but I'm afraid that's all. If it hadn't been for Edwin's ridiculous will, I would have sold up the minute he died.'

'But I thought . . .' he paused. He was very pale.

'Thought what, darling?'

'Nothing. Will you excuse me for a moment?'

He walked unsteadily out of the room. She heard him trip on his way up to the bathroom which she badly needed herself after so much wine. She slipped off her shoes, lifted her feet on to the settee, and hugged her knees, a demure, girlish pose in which to welcome him back. Her mind felt blurred and, afterwards, Emily wondered how, while she was in such a blissfully confused state, the truth should arrive so clearly and so cruelly.

She was wondering idly why his face had changed so suddenly, then gone so pale? What was it he'd thought but wouldn't say?

The answer came unexpectedly, like a physical blow. *He'd assumed she owned Brambles.* It was the reason he'd wanted to marry her. He was after the money he'd thought she'd get from the sale of the house.

Edwin had been right about the will.

Bill was coming downstairs, entering the room. Their eyes met. Emily's were sick with horror. She felt as if her bones were corroding inside her body, that any minute she would collapse into a flabby, boneless lump of flesh. Everything he'd said had been a lie – and she'd fallen for it, she thought bitterly, silly old woman that she was.

'How many hotels do you have in Monte Carlo, Bill?'

He shrugged, her face, the tone of her voice, made it obvious she had guessed the truth. Her blood boiled when his handsome face twisted in a grin. 'None, though I've worked in quite a few.'

'What as, a waiter, or a kitchen hand, collecting the swill for the pigs? Or did you pimp for the rich guests, procure – I think that's the word – procure old tarts and young boys for a fat tip? That would be just up your street.'

He flushed an ugly red, every scrap of charm gone. He took a step towards her and she felt frightened for having spoken so venomously. But she was speaking from the heart which he had broken only a few minutes ago.

'The only old tart I know is you, Emily,' he sneered and she wondered how she could possibly have thought him likeable, let alone fallen in love. It was as if he'd shed an outer skin and revealed the real man underneath. 'You were very easy to seduce. And I'm not the only one who's a liar. Forty-nine! You're sixty if a day.'

'You bastard!' She picked up her glass and threw it at him. It merely glanced off his arm, but a few dregs of wine stained the sleeve of his grey tweed suit. It looked like blood.

'You're a bad loser, Emily.'

It dawned on her that he no longer spoke with an accent. Instead, he had a trace of Cockney whine. He wasn't even an American! She'd been set up!

All the love that had recently flowed so sweetly through her veins turned to acid. She launched herself at him, knocking over the little round table that still held the debris of their meal and catching Bill by surprise, so that he stumbled and almost fell. He blinked, raised his hand, and hit her hard across the face.

Emily screamed, just as Ruby rushed into the room wearing a dressing gown that was much too short.

'What do you think you're doing?' She leaped on Bill's back, wrapping her arms like a vice around his neck. Bill seized the arms, easily pulling them apart, and pinned the slight, valiantly struggling figure against the wall.

'You pig!' Ruby yelled, doing her best to bite his hands, kicking at him with her bare feet which only made Bill laugh.

He turned his laughing face to Emily. 'You know how I managed to kiss you without puking, Emily, dearest? I thought about Ruby. I pretended I was kissing her instead. Like this!' He bent his head and kissed the still wriggling Ruby full on the lips. Emily watched, horrified, as his hand reached for the belt of her dressing gown, undid it.

Suddenly, someone was pulling him away and Emily nearly fainted when she saw who it was – Jacob Veering! He was barefoot, like Ruby, naked to the waist, and the savagery of his anger was awesome. Emily was trying to digest the awful fact that the two young people must have been upstairs together, when Jacob pulled Bill round to face him as effortlessly as if he'd been a rag doll. He drew back his fist and aimed a blow that sent the man hurtling across the room, slamming him against the wall with a thud that shook the house. Bill's body bounced forward like a ball and he fell to the floor, where he lay face down, absolutely still.

Nobody spoke for several minutes. Then Emily said in a dull voice, 'You could have killed him!'

Ruby ran across the room, knelt beside the prone figure, and felt the limp wrists for a pulse, then turned the body over and laid her head against the chest. She straightened up, eyes huge and fearful, and shook her head.

'Oh, my God!' Emily screamed.

It was the girl, not the woman, who took charge of the situation. 'Jacob, you've got to get away,' Ruby said crisply, shaking the young man's arm. He looked at her dazedly, as if he was being shaken from a deep sleep. 'Jacob! Bill's dead. You've killed him.'

'He shouldn't have touched you.' Jacob's eyes blazed briefly, then his broad shoulders slumped, all anger gone.

'They'll hang you.' Ruby shook him again. 'You've got to get away.'

Jacob sighed. His arms hung hopelessly at his side. He looked lost. 'I don't know where to go, Ruby.'

Ruby flung her arms around his neck. 'I'll come with you. I know where we can go. But we must leave straight away. Emily will have to call the police soon. Come on, Jacob.' She dragged him towards the door. 'Let's get dressed.'

They left without a backward glance. Emily heard them go upstairs, heard their voices in the bedroom – Ruby's full of reckless urgency, Jacob's slow and muffled. They came down again. Ruby was wearing the ghastly spotted dress she'd bought in Blacklers, much too grown-up. It looked silly with her childish red shoes. There was a handbag and a white cardigan over her arm. She'd never seen Jacob in a suit before. It looked the cheapest you could buy. There was something terribly brave and vulnerable about the pair. They looked too young to be throwing themselves at the mercy of a capricious fate.

'You'll be all right, won't you, Emily?' Ruby said anxiously.

Emily nodded.

'You'll give us a chance to get away before you call the police?'

Emily nodded again. She would have spoken, offered money, suggested Ruby take a coat, asked if it was still raining, but her lips were too stiff to move.

'We're going now, Emily. Look after yourself.'

All Emily seemed able to do was nod.

'We might see each other again, you never know.'

Another nod.

Jacob grunted something. Shortly afterwards the front door opened and closed and a sense of emptiness descended over Brambles, along with an oppressive silence that was so palpable that Emily felt she could have reached out and touched it with her shaking hands. She hid her face in the velvet arm of the settee and wondered what would happen to her now? She was friendless. There was a feeling in her bones that the Rowland-Graves had been behind Bill's scheming. They had encouraged her pathetic belief he might be interested in a woman old enough to be his mother. She vowed never to see them again.

She thought of Ruby, making her way through the dark countryside with Jacob and wondered if the girl loved him as much as he obviously loved her. She was far too good for him in every way. Jacob might be physically strong, but Ruby would have to carry him through whatever life they might have together.

After a long while, Emily got wearily to her feet, averting her eyes from the body on the floor. It was time she got washed, made herself look respectable. She painted her old face, changed into a sensible frock, and wondered as she returned downstairs what to tell the police. What explanation could she give for her lover having been punched so hard by a local farm hand that it had killed him? Not the truth. It was too shameful and was bound to be pounced on by the press. She'd be a laughing stock.

Then Emily had an idea she desperately wished she'd had before. She gritted her teeth and dragged the still warm Bill by his heels to the bottom of the stairs. He'd been drinking, she'd say, and had fallen the whole way down. It would still cause a bit of a scandal, but more bearable than the truth. She put a cushion under his head so it would look as if she'd tried to care for him and checked there was no blood on the carpet where he'd lain. The carpet was clean. The injury that had killed him must have been internal.

She picked up the telephone, dialled the operator, asked for the police, and was waiting to be connected when she heard a noise, a groan, that sent shivers of ice down her spine. From the corner of her eye she saw a movement at the bottom of the stairs. Emily could scarcely bear to look, not sure if she could stand any more shocks that night. When she did, she saw Bill was trying to sit up, groaning, and holding the back of his head. He looked at her fearfully. 'Where's that bloody maniac who hit me?'

'Gone.' Emily replaced the receiver, weak with relief, and regretting she hadn't the sense to feel for a pulse herself. 'And I'd like you to be gone by the time I get back if you don't mind. If you're still here, I'll call the police and have you thrown out.'

He was struggling to his feet, holding on to the banisters. She felt no inclination to help. 'Where are you going?' he asked in an old man's voice.

'Never you mind.'

She was going to look for Ruby, fetch her back. There was no need, now, for her and Jacob to have gone. In the dark, lonely days that lay ahead she would need Ruby as she had never done before.

Outside, the rain had stopped. A brilliant moon, almost whole, shone out of a dense, black, cloudless sky, making long, glistening ribbons of the still wet roads. The tyres of the Jaguar sizzled in the wet as Emily drove for miles and miles in every direction, until she felt giddy, and realised she was passing places she'd already passed before.

Still Emily drove, hopeless now, looking for Ruby, until the moon disappeared and a glimmer of yellow light on the horizon signalled the night was over and a new day was about to dawn.

Jacob

Chapter 4

1935–1938

She made an impressive sight, the pawnshop runner. Tall for a woman, taper thin, she proudly walked the streets of the Dingle in her polka dot frock and shabby red shoes, her sleeping baby tucked in a black shawl. Her long hair was thick and wavy and as black as night and it billowed like a cloud behind her, reminding her many admirers of a ship in full sail. The baby was a girl and her name was Greta – no one was surprised that the remarkable pawnshop runner hadn't given her child a conventional name like Mary or Anne.

It was said she was only seventeen, though she looked older. Her long face with its sharp nose and wide mouth could appear pinched when she wasn't smiling, but as she seemed to be smiling all the time, not many people noticed, just as they didn't notice when her dark eyes grew sombre as they sometimes did when she looked at her child who wasn't thriving as well as she should. She lived in Foster Court, an appalling slum, where twenty or thirty people dwelt in a single house, whole families in just one room. And, yes, she had a husband – she wasn't *that* sort of girl. It was rumoured that he, the husband, drank his wages. The pawnshop runner supported him, just as she did her baby and herself.

Those who had spoken to her said she was clever. She used long words and knew all sorts of funny things, though she didn't talk posh. Her accent was more Irish than Scouse and she'd obviously fallen on hard times. Oh, and her name was Ruby – Ruby O'Hagan.

When Ruby and Jacob left Brambles, they'd headed straight for Kirkby station. 'It's too late for a train,' Ruby said, 'but we'll be safer inside the waiting room, out of sight.'

They walked quickly. The rain had stopped, the moon was out, though the midnight air was chilly. Ruby regretted not bringing a coat.

Jacob followed like an obedient animal. He hadn't said a word since they left the house. Ruby spoke to him gently. He'd killed Bill Pickering while protecting her. Who knows what Bill might have done if Jacob hadn't been there. She doubted if Emily had been in a fit state to help.

During the hours spent in the waiting room, she held his hand and murmured comforting words of support. 'We'll be all right,' she told him. 'We'll bury ourselves where no one knows us, the Dingle, I've been there loads of times. We'll find a nice place to live and get jobs. I've always wanted to work in a shop.' The more she thought about it, the more she tried to convince herself it was an adventure, the sort of thing they might have done, anyway, at some time in the future.

A train came puffing in just after six o'clock by which time a watery sun had risen in a pallid sky. Jacob had only seen trains in the distance and found the noise terrifying. He put his hands over his ears to shut it out, wishing he could shut out the world as easily.

When they reached Exchange station, Ruby remembered they hadn't bought tickets. She paid the fares at the barrier and looked worriedly in her purse. 'I've only got tenpence left. Have you got money, Jacob?'

He shook his head. He had more than five pounds saved, but it was in his loft on Humble's farm.

'We'd better walk to the Dingle,' Ruby was saying. 'We'll need to buy food later.'

For Jacob, the walk was a nightmare. So many tall buildings rearing skywards, threatening to collapse on top of him, tramcars almost as noisy as the trains, buses, cars, lorries, the occasional horse-drawn cart that made him think longingly of Waterloo, the horse that kept him company on the farm. Ruby said, 'It's only early, so it's not so busy as usual,' as if he'd like it better when it was, when he already hated it with all his heart.

It started to drizzle, and he felt as if they'd been walking for ever by the time they reached the Dingle, a rabbit warren of little streets. It was only then that Ruby paused, looking lost.

'How do we find somewhere to live?'

Jacob hoped she wasn't asking him because he had no idea. He had no idea about anything any more.

'I know, I'll ask in a shop,' she said cheerfully. She went into a sweet and tobacconists and emerged with a piece of paper clutched in her hand.

'There's a room to let in Dombey Street. The landlady's called Mrs Howlett. It's along this way, second on the right. I think we should take it, whatever it's like. If necessary, we can look around for somewhere better when we've got more time.'

He trudged behind her in a daze, wanting to die, yet knowing he would have followed her to the ends of the earth. She knocked on a house with steps up to the front door and it was opened by a nervous looking girl of about eighteen.

'I've come about the room,' Ruby said importantly.

'Me mam's gone out a minute.' The girl had a nice, kind smile. 'Come and have a decko. She won't be long. It's upstairs at the back.'

The room was small and cramped and had too much dark furniture including a great double bed. Jacob felt his insides shrink. It was like being inside a coffin.

'It's nice,' Ruby said. She sat on the bed and bounced up and down a few times. 'We'll take it. How much is the rent?'

'Half a crown a week in advance, but you'll have to wait for me mam.'

'What does "in advance" mean?'

'It means me mam wants paying now. People have been known to do a moonlight flit and she ends up out of pocket.'

Ruby had never heard of a moonlight flit, but got the meaning. She didn't have half a crown, but she was wearing the gold watch Emily had bought for her birthday which had cost five guineas. She'd offer Mrs Howlett the watch as a deposit until she earned enough to pay the rent.

'I hope she lets you have it,' the girl said wistfully. 'It'd be nice to have young people for a change.'

The front door opened and a voice shouted, 'Dolly!'

'I'm upstairs, Mam,' the girl shouted back. 'There's people here about the room.'

'Coming.' Mrs Howlett puffed up the stairs like a train. She appeared in the doorway, a big, stout woman, redfaced from her exertions. Her small eyes took in the young couple, Ruby sitting on the bed, Jacob hunched and awkward, wishing he were anywhere else in the world.

'Where's your luggage?' she snapped.

'We haven't got—' Ruby began.

'And where's your wedding ring?'

'I haven't—'

Mrs Howlett gestured angrily towards the stairs. 'Get out me house immediately. I'm not having the likes of you under me roof.'

'But—'

'Out!' the landlady said imperiously.

It was the first time Jacob had ever seen Ruby stuck for words. She drew herself to her full height, tossed her head, and stalked downstairs. By the time she reached the bottom she must have recovered her composure, because she said in her loudest, most penetrating voice, 'Come on, Jacob. This place is a pigsty. I wouldn't live here if they paid me.'

They were outside, on the pavement, it was raining properly now, and Ruby was shaking, her face the colour of a ripe plum. Jacob longed to comfort her, as she had comforted him during the night, but nothing in his body seemed to be working, only his legs, which stumbled after Ruby wherever she chose to take him.

She took his hand. 'What shall we do now?' she whispered. It didn't feel like an adventure any more.

Jacob's head drooped. He didn't know.

The door of the house from which they'd just been evicted opened and Dolly crept stealthily out. 'Me mam's gone to the lavvy.' She touched Ruby's hand. 'I'm sorry, luv. I would have liked you to have the room, but mam's a stickler for convention.'

'She's got awful manners,' Ruby said spiritedly.

'I know.' Dolly sniffed. 'And I've got to live with 'em, an' all. Would you like a piece of advice, luv?' She ignored Jacob. Perhaps she thought him deaf and dumb as well as useless.

'What sort of advice?' Ruby enquired.

'If I were you, I'd buy meself a wedding ring from Woollies. They only cost a tanner.'

'I will, thanks. We only got married yesterday,' she lied shamelessly. 'It was very sudden and we couldn't afford to buy a proper ring. I didn't realise you could get them for sixpence.'

'Good luck – what's your name, luv?'

'Ruby.'

'Good luck, Ruby.'

Dolly smiled and was about to leave when Ruby said, 'Do you know if there's a room going anywhere else?'

'No, luv. There's bed and breakfast places around, though they might get a bit sniffy if you haven't got luggage and a ring. Anyroad, have you got the money?'

Ruby made a face. 'Only tenpence.'

'That's not nearly enough. Mind you, if you're stuck for cash, you could always pawn that lovely watch. In the meantime, you could try Charlie Murphy in Foster Court, number 2. He charges by the night, only thruppence, and he won't care if you're wearing a ring or not. But I warn you, it's a terrible flea pit. Scarcely fit for human beings to live in.'

'Your mam's just made me feel less than human, so that won't matter all that much.'

In all the times she had happily roamed the streets of the Dingle, Ruby had never come across anywhere like Foster Court. It was hidden, out of sight, between a billiard hall and a butchers, a narrow alley, barely six feet wide, with a handful of four storey dwellings on either side, the filthy bricks bitten and crumbling, as if they'd caught a repellent disease. Despite the rain, barefoot children were playing in the water that ran along the cracked flags separating the houses, paddling, splashing their hands. One little boy, wearing only ragged short trousers, was trying to sail a paper boat. There was a sickening lavatory smell and the place was very dark, buried within its own shadows, as if the sun, when it was out, had been forbidden to shine in the hideous man-made chasm that was Foster Court.

She was tempted to go no further, turn back, but it wouldn't hurt to know they had a place to sleep that night, even if it was horrible. It was only early. They could spend the rest of the day looking for work. If things went well, they might not have to come back. Mr Murphy could keep his threepence.

Ruby knocked on the unpainted door with the number 2 scratched on crudely with a knife. There was no letter box, as if letters were unknown in a place like this.

'Mr Murphy?' she said faintly when a ghostly figure appeared, an old man with a grey face and skin the texture of wet putty. His white hair was long and dirty, the ends the colour of tobacco, as if he was turning rusty with age.

'That's me, queen,' he said chirpily.

'I . . . we, we're looking for a room.'

'Are you now! Well, I've got a room. Second floor back, thruppence a night, payment up front.' He grinned, showing the occcasional yellow tooth. 'No parties, no drinking, no dancing.'

'We'd like to take it, please. Just for tonight.'

'Give us the ackers, queen, and it's yours. You can find your own way up. The lavvy's in the yard, the scullery's below stairs. I'll fetch you the keys.' He threw open the door, and Ruby winced when she saw the damp-stained walls, the uncarpeted stairs worn to a curve in the middle from the tread of a thousand feet. She wondered if the owners of the feet had felt as miserable as she did as she went up one flight of stairs, then another, Jacob behind, as he had been all day, not speaking, his face a mask of despair. The sound of a woman screaming came from one of the rooms, using language Ruby had never heard before. A baby wailed plaintively in another.

The first thing she noticed when she went in the room was the threadbare curtain on the window. One of the panes was missing and there was a piece of cardboard in its place.

'There's no bedding.' There was no sink either, no carpet or linoleum on the floor, no ornaments, hardly any furniture, no light, only a stub of metal tubing where a gas mantel should have been. The bed didn't have a headboard, the palliase looked disgusting, and the bolster had turned an unhealthy shade of yellow. A small fireplace was heaped with ash. Ruby crept over to the window and saw a communal yard with just two lavatories for the use of the residents of all the properties on that side. Her heart sank and she turned away. Jacob was sitting on one of the wooden chairs beside a little square table with oilcloth nailed on top.

He spoke at last. 'Go home, Ruby,' he said in a voice as wretched as his face. 'Go back to Emily. I'll manage on me own.'

'Don't be daft!' Ruby said spiritedly. 'We're in this together.'

'I was thinking of turning meself in.'

'And letting them hang you!' she gasped.

'I didn't mean to kill him,' Jacob groaned.

'I know you didn't.' Ruby considered this fact. 'I suppose,' she said thoughtfully, 'you mightn't be tried for murder, but manslaughter instead. You'd be sent to prison for years.'

Jacob would rather hang than be shut for years in a cell with bars on the window, possibly never feel the sun again, smell the flowers, see the trees blossom in the spring and watch the leaves fall in autumn.

'Let's go and buy a cup of tea,' Ruby said encouragingly. 'Then look for a job.'

He shook his head and tucked his arms protectively across his chest. 'I'd sooner stay.' He needed to rest, come to terms with what he'd done, get used to the fact he was a murderer. The day had already been confused enough without having to look for work that he didn't want. He would never be happy working anywhere other than on the land. As far as today was concerned, he'd had enough. He'd look for a job tomorrow.

Ruby must have lost patience with him at last. She stamped her foot. 'If that's how you feel, Jacob Veering, I'll find a job on my own.'

Finding a job was just as difficult as finding a room when you didn't know where to look. Did you just walk into a shop and ask if there was a vacancy? Although not one to refrain from pushing herself forward, Ruby couldn't quite raise the nerve. And the shops she peered in appeared to be fully staffed. No one looked over-worked. She passed a pub with a notice in the window, 'Cleaner Required', and sniffed in derision. She hated cleaning. She wanted to work in a shop. But how?

Some jobs were advertised in newspapers, but it meant writing a letter, waiting for a reply, going for interview with half a dozen other people, then waiting again for the interviewer to make up their mind – it had happened to Priscilla Lane in a picture she'd seen.

If only she'd brought a coat. Better still, her new mackintosh with check lining and a hood. Or an umbrella. It might be August, but it wasn't exactly warm, particularly if you were soaked to the skin. Her shoes had begun to squelch and the rain showed no sign of stopping. She thought balefully that it was the rain's fault she and Jacob were in such a mess. If it hadn't rained yesterday, Emily and Bill Pickering would be in the Lake District. For the first time, she wondered what had caused last night's fight? Alerted by the shouting, she'd arrived just in time to see Bill, whom she'd thought so nice, giving poor Emily a whack about the face. And now Bill was dead! Ruby tried not to think about it.

It was two o'clock by the time she came to Park Road, the route the tramcar took when it carried her to the Dingle. Briskly busy, lined with shops, there were even more people around on a Saturday afternoon. Ruby remembered it was where she'd decided, months ago, that this was the place she wanted to be, though she hadn't thought it would be under such horrible circumstances.

The first dress shop she came to, she plucked up courage and went in. A smart lady in black approached and wished her, 'Good afternoon, luv. What can I do for you? You look like a drowned rat, if you don't mind my saying.'

'Good afternoon,' Ruby gushed. 'I'm looking for a job – and I feel like a drowned rat at the moment.'

'Sorry, luv,' the woman said smilingly, 'but I only employ mature staff. I hope you have better luck somewhere else.'

Encouraged by the polite reception, Ruby made the same request several more times including a chemist and a haberdashers when she ran out of dress shops. The chemist offered her a form to fill in and said she could bring it back any time, so obviously weren't anxious for another member of staff. 'We'll be taking an extra person on for Christmas,' the woman in the haberashers said helpfully. 'Try again in November.'

It was quarter past four, she was passing a cafe, and longed for a cup of tea – she'd had nothing to eat or drink since last night, though the thought of food made her nauseous. She went in, ordered a pot of tea for one, bringing the contents of her purse down to fourpence which was worrying. Tomorrow was Sunday and it would be a waste of time searching for work. If they had to stay in Foster Court a second night, it would cost another threepence and she'd be left with a penny. She'd intended buying Jacob something to eat and they'd need food tomorrow. She wished she hadn't bought the tea, though it was nice, sitting in the warmth, making the tea last out, giving her time to think, not that thinking had helped much so far.

Being short of money was a new experience. She recalled the abundant amount of coppers and silver that Emily left in her various bags that she'd helped herself to whenever she needed, for the pictures and her journeys around Liverpool.

It crossed her mind that the pennies she had left might be best spent calling Emily from a telephone box and asking for money – they could meet somewhere in town, because Ruby couldn't afford to go to Brambles. She gave the matter serious thought before deciding, reluctantly, that she couldn't rely on Emily not to tell the police. She might be followed when she returned to Foster Court and Jacob, who was wanted for murder.

A girl came to remove the tea things. 'Have you finished, luv? You look like a drowned rat.'

'Someone's already told me that. I'll be finished in a minute.' Ruby poured the last of the hot water into the pot and managed to squeeze out half a cup. 'By the way, I don't suppose you need any more staff?' It was worth a try.

'No. We're not much busy during the week. I only work Sat'days meself.'

'Thanks, anyway.'

Nothing had happened in Ruby's short life to make her feel as disheartened as she did now. She'd faced few problems – she couldn't remember what they were, but was sure she'd always come out on top. But now she felt beaten, not knowing which way to turn. If she kept on trying, she would get a job one day, next week perhaps, but she needed one *now*.

She looked at her watch. Five o'clock. Only a few people were left in the cafe and the sign on the door had been turned to Closed. She looked at her watch again. What was it Dolly Howlett had said? Something about pawning her lovely watch. Ruby had no idea what that meant.

The girl returned to clear the table. 'Excuse me,' Ruby said, 'but what does "pawn" mean?'

'Y'what?' The girl looked at her vacantly.

'Someone said today I could pawn my watch. I've never heard of it before.'

'Oh, *pawn*. It means taking it to a pawnshop and they'll lend money on it. You get a ticket in case you want to redeem your pledge, buy it back, as it were. Of course,' the girl smiled grimly. 'You have to pay more than they gave you. They're nothing but a racket, pawnshops. I'd steer clear of them if I were you.'

Ruby didn't have much choice. A ray of sunshine had appeared, making the immediate future look considerably brighter. 'Is there one near here, a pawnshop?'

'There's Overton's. Turn right outside the door and it's a few blocks away, on the corner. You'll know it by the three brass balls outside. You'd better hurry. They close at half five.'

'Thank you.

The window of Overton's was heavily barred and full of jewellery which an elderly man with rimless glass and hardly any hair was in the process of removing. She opened the door and a bell jangled loudly. The man removed his head from the window.

'Yes?'

'I'd like to pawn—' Ruby began.

'Door's round the side,' the man snapped.

The side door was small and unobtrusive. Another bell rang when Ruby entered a small, dimly-lit lobby, coming face to face with a metal grille over a wooden counter that was as curved in the middle as the stairs in Foster Court.

A man appeared, very like the one in the window, but younger and with slightly more hair that was combed over his bare scalp in an unsuccessful attempt to hide the fact he was bald. His eyes were the palest she had ever seen.

'We're closing in a minute,' he said abruptly. 'What do you want?'

'I want to pawn my watch, please.'

'Hand it over.'

There was a slit between the counter and the bottom of the grille. Ruby removed the watch which had an expanding strap and of which she was very fond and pushed it through. 'It cost five guineas,' she said. 'It's pure gold.'

'I can see that for meself, thanks.' He was examining the watch carefully, turning it over, running his fingers along the strap. He lifted his head and regarded her sharply with his pale eyes. 'Where did you get it?'

'It was a birthday present.'

'It ses on the back "Ruby O'Hagan".'

Emily had had the back engraved. 'I know, that's me.'

'Can you prove it?'

'How am I supposed to do that?' Ruby demanded sharply.

'Show me something with your name on; an official document of some sort – your birth certificate, or the receipt for the watch, a letter addressed to yourself would do.'

'I haven't got anything like that with me.' She didn't know if she'd ever had a birth certificate, Emily had the receipt for the watch, and no one had ever sent her a letter.

'Where do you live?'

Ruby paused, knowing instinctively not to say Foster Court where no one was likely to own a watch, let alone one worth five guineas. The man was watching her suspiciously and had noticed the pause. It dawned on her that she probably looked a sight, soaking wet, her hair plastered to her head, her cardigan all shrivelled. She should have tidied herself up before she came in. 'I live in Kirkby,' she replied.

'And you've come all this way to pawn a watch?' he said in mock disbelief.

'I'm staying in the Dingle for a few days with a friend.' Ruby was beginning to feel a touch desperate.

'What's the name of this friend?'

'Dolly Howlett. She lives in Dombey Street.' She rarely told lies because she was quite happy for people to know the truth, but today she seemed to be tying herself up in knots.

'I tell you what, bring Dolly Howlett along on Monday to vouch for you, and I'll let you have a guinea for your watch.'

'All right. Until then, I'd like it back if you don't mind.' She had no intention of entering a pawn shop again as long as she lived. The watch would have to be got rid of another way.

The man smiled, though it was more like a sneer. 'I don't think so. I'd like to check it against our list of stolen property. The police might be interested in this watch.'

Ruby lost her temper. 'Are you suggesting it's stolen?'

'Are you suggesting it's not?'

'Of course it's not. It's mine, I got it for my birthday.'

'Who off, the King?'

'No, off Emily. You can't just keep it. I need it.'

'If you need it, why are you trying to pawn it?'

'Because I want the money, stupid.'

The man scribbed something on a piece of paper and shoved it beneath the grille. 'Here's a receipt. You can have the money on Monday under the conditions already described. Now, if you don't mind, we're closed.' He pulled down a shutter behind the grille with a bang. An enraged Ruby hammered on the grille with her fist, to no avail. She marched round to the front, found the front door locked, and no sign of the other man inside. Despite more hammering, no one came.

It was the second time that day she'd been made to feel about two inches tall; first Mrs Howlett, now in a pawnshop. Angry tears stung Ruby's eyes mingling with the rain, still falling steadily. She couldn't go back for the watch even if she knew someone who could vouch for her. If the man contacted the police they might recognise the name on the back: Ruby O'Hagan, who'd left Brambles last night in the company of Jacob Veering. She'd lost her watch for ever.

What could she do now other than go back to Foster Court? At least she could get dry, have a rest. She thought about lying on the grubby palliase, resting her head on the discoloured bolster, and her stomach turned. For the briefest of moments, she considered returning to Brambles, even if it meant walking there, spending the night to come and all the nights to follow, in her yellow and white bedroom wearing one of her pretty nighties – she remembered she hadn't brought a nightie with her. If asked, she would swear she had no idea where Jacob was. Emily would need her company after what had happened with Bill, with whom she'd seemed so much in love and he with her.

But she couldn't desert Jacob. She would never sleep easily that night, or any night, if she did. The memory of her treachery would haunt her the rest of her days. Jacob needed her far more than Emily ever would. What's more, he loved her and she loved him. She felt guilty for being so impatient when she'd left Foster Court and began to hurry. He was probably wondering why she'd been gone such a long time.

The shops were all closed now, hardly anyone was about. Trams rolled by, crowded, taking lucky people back to their homes or out for the night. Still smarting from the way she'd been treated in Overton's, Ruby eyed them enviously as she splashed through puddles, uncaring, her feet couldn't get more wet than they already were. She walked past the pub with the notice, 'Cleaner Required' in the window, then stopped and retraced her steps. She'd been good at cleaning in the convent. She'd been good at everything. It was her attitude that was at fault according to the nuns. She made no secret of the fact she didn't like carrying out a single one of the tasks she was given to do and would like them even less if she was put into service and had to do them for a living.

'I wouldn't mind doing them for myself,' she would say with a superior expression on her face that drove the nuns wild, 'but not for anyone else.' She resented the notion she'd been put on earth solely to make other people's lives more comfortable.

But now Ruby was willing to throw her principles to the wind and apply for the job as cleaner in the Malt House as the pub was called according to the sign outside. The landlord's name was painted over the door: Frederick Ernest Quinlan.

She threw back her shoulders, confident again, and went through the swing doors into a large, brightly-lit room, with a polished floor and round, polished tables. The bar occupied most of one wall and was backed by a decorative mirror with a gold painted border, reflecting the whole room. The mirror also reflected the back of the middle-aged barmaid, a tiny whisper of a woman, a whole head shorter than Ruby, wearing a mauve crocheted jumper and diamanté earrings, her hair as gold as the border on the mirror, except for the roots which were black. Expertly made-up, she looked worn out, despite the night having scarcely begun – there were only four customers present at such an early hour, all men.

'I'd like to see Mr Quinlan about the cleaning job,' Ruby said, coming straight to the point.

'Then you're out of luck,' the woman said tiredly. 'But I'm Mrs Quinlan and you can see me if you like. I need someone straight away.'

'I can start straight away, now if you want.'

A man entered and came over to the bar. 'A pint of best bitter, Martha, luv. Where's your Fred?'

Showing slightly more animation than before, the woman replied acidly, 'Where d'you think? In bed, bloody asleep.'

'So, Fred's in bed with a sore head,' the man chortled as he took the drink.

'Only a man would find it funny, the landlord drinking the profits and leaving his wife to tend the bar,' Mrs Quinlan remarked when the man went to take a seat.

'Is that what he does? That's disgraceful,' Ruby said sympathetically.

'Isn't it?' The sympathy was clearly appreciated. 'He manages to stagger down at midday, but by three o'clock, closing time, he's as drunk as a fiddle and ready for his bed. He might condescend to join us about nine in the evening to get tanked up again, which means he can't be raised next morning, leaving yours bloody truly to clear this place up. I'm working fourteen hours a bloody day, flat out, and I can't stand it any more. That's why I need a cleaner, mornings, eight till ten, half a crown a week. Fred thinks it an extravagence which is a bloody cheek when you consider the amount of ale he consumes a day.'

'It certainly is,' Ruby agreed. 'About the job . . .'

'Oh, yes.' Mrs Quinlan looked properly at Ruby for the first time, clearly liking what she saw, and no doubt influenced by the fact she was on her side against Fred. 'How old are you?'

'Sixteen.'

'I'll pretend I didn't hear that. Under eighteen, you're not allowed on licensed premises. You shouldn't be here, in fact.'

'In that case, I'm eighteen. My name's Ruby O'Hagan, by the way.'

'In that case, Ruby, you've got the job,' Mrs Quinlan said promptly, looking slightly happier than when Ruby had come in. 'I wouldn't expect you Sundays. I'll just have to clean the bloody place meself, but you can start Monday.'

'Make it three shillings a week and I'll work Sundays. And I'd appreciate being paid by the day, Mrs Quinlan, if you don't mind,' Ruby said daringly, having gauged Martha Quinlan was a good-natured person and open to such suggestions.

'I don't mind, luv. I don't mind so much, I'll pay you beforehand.' She opened the till. 'Here's a tanner for tomorrer. You've got an honest face. I trust you not to let me down. Oh, and call me Martha, everyone does.'

She'd done it! She'd got a job. Added to that the rain had stopped, she had tenpence in her purse again, and there was the most delicious smell that made her taste buds water.

A fish and chip shop! She was about to buy two-pennyworth of chips and take them back to Foster Court, but decided to fetch Jacob first. They could buy the chips together and go for a walk. It would do him good to get some fresh air.

But Jacob was fast asleep in their decrepit little room, fully dressed and snoring softly, his face buried in the yellow bolster, his nice new suit all creased as he lay, curled up like a baby, one arm shielding his face.

Ruby no longer felt hungry. She removed her damp cardigan, folded it into a pillow, and lay beside him, putting her arm around his waist. In no time at all, she was asleep herself.

Martha Quinlan was a hard taskmaster. Due to the fact she no longer had a watch to know the time, Ruby arrived more than half an hour early and got her out of bed. Without her make-up, in a shabby dressing gown, she looked wretchedly weary. It was midnight by the time she'd gone to bed, she complained. 'Fred came down and a couple of his cronies stayed long after closing time. I had to hang about and lock the bloody place up. I don't trust Fred to do it proper.'

The bar, so spruce and shining the night before, looked as if a hurricane had swept through it. The tables were laden with dirty glasses, empty cigarette packets, and overflowing ashtrays. There were more glasses on the floor, cigarette butts, spent matches, two dirty hankies, and a copy of yesterday's *Daily Herald*, which Ruby put aside to read later.

She set to, taking the glasses into the kitchen, emptying the ashtrays in a bucket, wiping the tables, sweeping the floor. She washed the glasses in hot, soapy water, dried them, and took them into the bar, hanging the tankards on the hooks provided, putting the others on a shelf underneath.

'I've finished,' she announced to Martha who was perched on a stool, smoking, and watching her with a hawk's eye.

'In a pig's ear, you've finished. Them tables need polishing and the glass marks removed, floor has to be buffed. You'll find everything you need in the kitchen. After that, I'd like the place dusted; window sills, doors, chairs, and them bottles behind could do with a wipe. Then you can take a look in the men's lavvies in the yard, mop 'em out. We only had a few women in last night and none of 'em used the lavvy, so the Ladies won't want touching.' She grinned. 'Oh, this is nice. I feel like a lady of leisure, I do. If you weren't here, I'd be doing all this meself. When you've finished, I'll make us a nice cup of tea and some toast.'

'How long have I been here?' Ruby felt as if she'd been slaving away for hours.

'Not long enough to earn even half the tanner you got last night,' Martha said with another grin. 'I suppose you think I'm finicky, Fred does, but I like to keep the place nice. There's some pubs just sprinkle a handful of sawdust on the floor each morning, but not me. Come on, luv,' she urged, 'get a move on. The sooner you finish, the sooner we can have that tea.'

'Do you want the bread cut thick or thin?' Martha asked an hour later, though to Ruby it felt more like ten. They were in the kitchen, the kettle was about to boil, and the grill was on waiting to toast the bread.

'Thick, please.'

'I'll put the jam on the table and you can help yourself. I suppose you're fair worn out.'

'Yes, but I'll get used to it,' Ruby said stoutly.

'I'm sure you will. You're a hard worker, I can tell. Thorough, like meself. We'll get along, you and me.' Martha turned the toast over. 'Do you live nearabouts?'

'Foster Court – but it's only temporary.'

Martha wrinkled her nose. 'By yourself?'

'No, with Jacob. He's my husband.'

'Jaysus, Mary and Joseph, girl,' Martha gasped. 'You're never married at your age!'

'We did it secretly, then we ran away from home. It only happened on Friday. I haven't even got a wedding ring yet.'

'Your poor mam and dad, I bet they're dead upset, wondering where you are.'

'I haven't got a mam and dad. I'm an orphan. Oh, look, the toast's burning.'

'She always burns the toast,' said a caustic voice and a woman came in, a much younger version of Martha. Her blonde hair was pinned in curls against her scalp and covered with a flesh pink net. She wore a flowered crêpe dressing gown and fluffy slippers. 'Is that piece mine, Mam?' she demanded.

'It's Ruby's. If you want toast, our Agnes, make your own.'

'I'm not Agnes, I'm Fay,' the young woman said crossly. 'I don't know how many times I've got to tell you.'

'As far as I'm concerned, miss, you were christened Agnes

Quinlan, and Agnes Quinlan you'll stay. Fay!' Martha hooted. 'I've never heard such nonsense.'

The newcomer pouted. 'Agnes is a horrible name. What do you think, Ruby? Isn't Fay much nicer?'

'I like them both,' Ruby said tactfully, more interested in the toast.

'Just because she works in the Town Hall she wants her name changed,' Martha sneered. 'Agnes isn't good enough for her any more. She's ashamed of living in a pub in the Dingle, an' all.'

'So would you be,' Agnes/Fay said hotly, 'if you worked with people from places like Aigburth or Woolton. Some even live in houses with names, not numbers.'

'Where you live's got a name, it's called the Malt House.'

'Oh, shurrup, Mam. I'm going back to bed. You can wake me up in time for midday Mass.'

'Ta, very much, *Agnes.*'

'She's me daughter,' Martha announced, as if Ruby hadn't already guessed, after Agnes/Fay had gone in a huff. 'She's too big for her boots these days. You'd think she was lady-in-waiting to the queen herself, not just a bloody receptionist in the Town Hall. Mind you,' her face grew fond, 'I'm proud of her. What mother wouldn't be? Though I'd appreciate some help with this place, but our Agnes wouldn't be seen dead behind the bar. As to cleaning, she wouldn't know where to start.' She sighed. 'Our Jim now, he's a different kettle of fish altogether. Always willing to lend a hand, but he's in the Merchant Navy and we only see him once in a blue moon. Would you like more toast, luv? That piece went quick. And, oh, I'll give you tomorrer's money now, if you like, seeing as how you're obviously short. It works out to fivepence a day.'

Jacob had been asleep when she left that morning. When she returned to Foster Court, having been to nine o'clock Mass in a church called St Finbar's on the way, he was still in bed, wide awake, staring glumly at the ceiling. His eyes flickered in her direction when she went in.

'I've got a job, cleaning,' she announced breezily, 'and I've got money, too. We can have fish and chips for our dinner. With your wages on top of mine, we can be out of here by the end of the week.'

He didn't answer, but rolled over, away from her, facing the wall.

'Your suit's in a terrible state,' Ruby continued in the same breezy voice. 'And my dress is even worse, it was damp when I lay down to sleep. We need an iron. We need all sorts of things: soap and towel, dishes, knives and forks. If we had a saucepan, I could make us something to eat in the kitchen downstairs. Perhaps tomorrow. Oh, and we definitely need bedding, except I'm not sure if we'll need our own once we're living somewhere else. Another thing, Jacob . . .'

'I want to die, Ruby.'

'Jacob!' She leapt on to the bed and folded him in her arms. 'Don't talk like that. Everything's going to be all right, you'll see. We'll soon be out of here.'

'I don't want to be out of here,' he said despairingly. 'I don't want to be anywhere except back on the farm.'

'But that's not possible, Jacob. You can't go back to Humble's, not ever. But in a while, once we're on our feet, maybe we can move out to the countryside, find another farm.' She'd hate it, perhaps not as much as he hated the town, but she was hardier than him, she realised that now. She could stand up to things, make the best of them.

'I'm a murderer, Ruby.' He turned over and she shivered when she saw the dead empty eyes in a face that had lost all its colour, like the face of a corpse. 'I killed a man. I don't think I can live with it. That's why I want to die.'

'It was an accident, love. Oh, please don't be like this. I can't stand it.' She put her head on his chest and began to weep.

Jacob would have wept with her, but he was beyond tears, beyond everything, except sleeping and staring at the wall. And loving Ruby, yet wishing she would go away, back to Emily, leaving him to rot on the stinking bed. It made everything worse, seeing her so dishevelled when she'd always looked so smart, knowing the girl who could dance like a butterfly had got a job cleaning. It was enough that his own life was ruined. It wasn't possible to imagine feeling better, but he wouldn't feel so bad if Ruby hadn't been there, sharing the agony with him.

'Take your suit off, Jacob. It's getting ruined.' She began to help him off with his clothes, tugging at them.

Something stirred within him, a longing to forget, to lose himself within her. But even that didn't help. They made half-hearted love and the furore in Jacob's brain continued unabated and he forgot nothing.

Later, he couldn't bring himself to go with her to look for food although, despite everything, he was hungry. Ruby went alone, returning with a bottle of lemonade and two bars of chocolate – the fish and chip shop wasn't open on Sundays.

'We'll have something nice and tasty tomorrow,' she said comfortably, resting her hands on her rumbling stomach.

Next day, Jacob felt exactly the same, as if he was secured to the bed with invisible chains, capable only of using one of the unspeakable lavatories when it was dark and no-one could see him.

'But we'll never get out of this place if you don't go to work!' Ruby cried. She had been to the Malt House and bought a comb, soap and towel on the way back. Her frock was off and she was in her silky petticoat, trying to remove the frock's creases with her hands, shaking it. Having fetched water from the kitchen in the lemonade bottle, she was pouring it into her hands, splashing it on her face and under her arms, drying herself with an energy that made Jacob wilt, knowing he couldn't match it to save his life. Then she combed her hair, tugging at the knots, looking almost her own self again, and suggested he went out and found a job.

'No,' said Jacob, wishing there were bedclothes he could hide under.

A few weeks later, there were. Ruby got them secondhand: thick, flanelette sheets, frayed at the hem, a bolster cover. There were other things: dishes, cutlery, a shaving brush and razor that Jacob hardly used, though Ruby had insisted he wear the moleskin pants and thick shirt she'd got for when he started work. It saved his suit, now hanging behind the door, waiting for when she could afford to have it dry-cleaned.

The saucepan she'd bought had disappeared off the kitchen stove, along with a quarter of a pound of stewing steak and potatoes for their tea, poor Ruby unaware she should have stayed and kept watch. Anyone could have taken it: the woman who lived on the first floor with her eleven children, the mad man in the basement who wore nothing but a dirty blanket and shouted obscenities at everyone, the two women on the ground floor who entertained a suspiciously large number of male visitors.

By this time, Ruby had another cleaning job because she wasn't earning enough at the Malt House. There were still things needed to make life bearable. She was desperate for an iron, a rope to hang the washing on, and doubted if there would ever be sixpence to spare for a wedding ring.

It was Agnes/Fay who got her the job in the Town Hall, evenings, six till eight, five days and half a crown a week, mopping floors, cleaning stairs, polishing the chairs and tables in the stately council chamber.

'Why do you do it?' Agnes/Fay, with whom she'd become quite friendly, wanted to know. 'You could get a proper job. You talk nice, you're presentable, at least you would be if you ever ironed your frock.'

'I'd sooner clean,' Ruby replied. She was so busy, she didn't have time to think about Jacob, mouldering away in Foster Court which she would do if she worked in a shop, as she would have preferred. Jacob was asleep when she left for the Malt House and ready for sleep again by the time she went to the Town Hall. It meant she could keep him company during the day. All he did was sleep, or lie on the bed staring at the ceiling while she talked to him, tried to cheer him up. He would leave the bed only to eat the food prepared in the cockroach-ridden kitchen, which Ruby did her best to use when it was empty of the sullen, angry women who lived elsewhere in the house.

Jacob had fallen apart. His hair was dirty, he smelt. His beard was a tangle of stiff, matted hairs. But it was Jacob's weakness that gave Ruby the strength to carry on. She told herself that one day he would get better, find a job, and they would live somewhere nice. Anywhere would be an improvement on Foster Court.

'Would you do us a favour, Ruby, luv?' Martha Quinlan said. 'I'm expecting a delivery from the brewery today, and I'm a bit short o'cash. Would you mind taking something to uncle's for me?'

'Uncle who?'

'Uncle no one, luv. I'll just have to pawn me engagement ring, not for the first time, I might add,' she said darkly.

'You want me to take your engagement ring to the pawnshop?'

'Otherwise known as uncle's, that's right, luv. I'll give you something, two and a half per cent's the going rate.'

'Two and a half per cent of what?' asked Ruby, mystified.

'Of whatever you get, girl. Are you thick or something this morning? Old Nellie, the pawnshop runner, popped her clogs last month. I've been stuck ever since.'

'Stuck for what?'

'Someone to take me valuables to the pawnshop, that's what,' Martha said impatiently. 'I've got me reputation to consider. I couldn't be seen going anywhere near the place meself.'

'All right.' Ruby forgot her vow never to enter a pawnshop again. 'Where shall I go?'

'Reilly's on Park Road pays the best rates. I'll give you a note. Mrs Reilly knows me by name, if not by sight.'

Mrs Reilly had a hard, businesslike manner, but was a great improvement on the man who'd stolen her watch. Like Overton's, the window at the front displayed jewellery and various items of silver. Ruby found an entrance round the back leading to a small room with the now familiar grille. She had to wait while a child, much to her amazement, pawned a man's suit.

'Have you taken over from Old Nelly?' the woman asked when Ruby eventually gave her the envelope containing Martha's ring and a note to say who it was from.

'No. I'm just doing a favour for Mrs Quinlan.'

'That's a pity. There's quite a few people who've missed Old Nelly since she passed on. Hang on a minute while I show me husband the ring.'

Ruby waited, the woman returned, 'Twenty-five shillings,' she said.

'What's two and a half per cent of that?' They hadn't taught percentages in the convent.

'Sevenpence a'penny.'

A few days later, Ruby was sent to redeem the ring with the promise of the same sum. It seemed an extraordinarily easy way of earning one and threepence.

'These people you mentioned,' she said to the woman behind the grille, 'What would I have to do?'

'Can you be trusted?'

'Mrs Quinlan trusted me with her ring.'

'So she did. This needs a bit of sorting. Come back tomorrow and I'll let you know.'

A few days later, Ruby crossed Dingle Lane into Aigburth Road, where the properties suddenly became larger, the streets wider. Brocade curtains hung in neat folds on the bay windows, every step had been ruthlessly scrubbed, door brasses glittered in the late October sunshine. She found the road she was looking for, went down the back entry, as she'd been instructed, and entered the house, number 14, through the yard where she was met by a dazzling display of net curtains. She knocked on the door and it was opened by an anxious woman of about forty who looked frantically around, as if expecting heads to appear over the adjacent walls to see who the visitor was.

Ruby was dragged inside a kitchen very like the one in Brambles, only smaller. The woman whispered hoarsely, 'Are you from Reillys?'

'I am so' Ruby announced grandly.

'I've got the stuff ready, some jewellery.' The woman's name was Mrs Somerfield. Her hands trembled as she reached inside a drawer and drew out a paper bag. 'How long will it take? I need the cash urgent like.'

'About an hour. I've someone else to see.'

Mrs Somerfield's eyes narrowed. 'Who?'

'That's confidential,' Ruby said officiously. 'You wouldn't want me telling the other person where I've been, would you?'

'God, no!'

'I'll be back as soon as I can.'

The next house was detached, backing on to Princes Park. It was a large, friendly, russet brick house, with an untidy tangle of roses around the door, and gardens front and back full of trees and overgrown shrubs. The bay windows were badly in need of a good clean and the grass urgently required mowing. Even so, it would be a perfect place to live, Ruby thought longingly, so close to the shops, yet affording a certain amount of privacy. She'd become quite keen on privacy after so long in Foster Court. A fluffy, striped kitten was sitting unhygienically on the table in the cosy, old-fashioned kitchen, giving itself a thorough wash.

Mrs Hart, the owner of this enviable house, was a friendly

woman, tall and carelessly dressed, and remarkably open about her need for money. She gave Ruby a small parcel wrapped in tissue paper. 'It's Dresden, so be careful with it, won't you, dear. That son of mine will have me in the poor house before long. He's at university, living the life of Riley, and draining my pitiful finances – my husband only left me a small pension. I'm forever having moneylenders banging on the door or sending threatening letters. Would you like a cup of tea, dear? You look cold.'

'I'd love one, thanks.' Mrs Somerfield would just have to wait for the cash she urgently needed. Ruby sat down and stroked the kitten who obligingly washed her fingers.

'Have you taken over from Old Nelly?' asked Mrs Hart.

'I think I might have.'

Chapter 5

By the time Christmas came, Ruby was earning almost as much from her role as a pawnshop runner as she did from cleaning. But she could never manage to get enough together to escape from Foster Court. Now that winter had descended, there was fuel to buy as well as food. She wore a shawl instead of a more expensive coat and could have done with a pair of stouter shoes.

Christmas was also the time when Ruby finally had to admit to herself the alarming fact that she was expecting a baby. She'd been deliberately ignoring the non-appearance of periods, the slight sickness in the mornings. She knew little about babies, but recognised the rudimentary signs. It must have happened the first Sunday in Foster Court when Jacob hadn't pulled out as he usually did. They hadn't made love since, which meant she was four months gone and the baby would arrive in May.

It was Martha Quinlan who pointed out what was becoming increasingly obvious. 'Are you in the club, luv?' she asked on Christmas Eve.

Ruby sat down with a thump on the chair she was polishing. 'Yes.' It was scary, saying the word, 'yes', agreeing that in five months' time she would have a baby and it was no use ignoring it any longer, hoping it would go away.

'Congratulations, luv. I expect you're dead pleased,' Martha said warmly. 'Though I can't say I'll be glad about losing you. I'll never get another cleaner as good.'

'Oh, I won't be leaving.' Ruby tried not to sound as worried as she felt. She couldn't afford to lose one of her jobs. 'I feel fine, and I can bring the baby with me once it's born. Can't I?'

Martha looked doubtful. 'I dunno, luv. We'll have to see.'

★

The news that he was about to become a father jolted Jacob out of his all-consuming lethargy. It was Christmas Day and Ruby, usually a source of never-ending chatter, was unnaturally quiet. Her peaked face bore a sober expression he'd never seen before and her dark eyes were inscrutable. She'd done her best to make the room look festive with a few pathetic strands of tinsel around the window and draped over the tiny fireplace, in which an equally pathetic fire smouldered, giving off more smoke than flames. There was a lamb chop for dinner followed by a piece of home-made cake, a present from the woman in the pub.

'What's wrong?' Jacob asked when they had finished eating, unable to stand the silence any longer. He had always found the chatter irritating, but found the silence worse.

'I'm having a baby,' she said matter-of-factly.

Jacob turned to look out of the window, at the brilliant afternoon sun sinking in the cloudless sky, at the ice-skimmed walls and roofs. There was a sprinkling of snow in the yard. The crazy man from downstairs was peeing against a lavatory wall, his feet bare, wearing only his blanket. Somewhere, a carol was being sung, 'Christmas is coming, the goose is getting fat . . .'

He sighed. 'I think you should go back to Emily.'

Ruby unexpectedly exploded, furiously waving her arms. 'I phoned Emily last night to wish her Merry Christmas, to see how she was, and she doesn't live in Brambles any more. She's gone abroad. So I can't go back even if I wanted.' She glared at him. 'Not that I do.'

Jacob wilted under the glare. 'What are we going to do, Ruby?' he asked in his hopeless, tired way.

She jumped up, stamped her foot, and began to pace up and down the room, her shoes clattering on the floorboards. 'We?' she screamed. 'What are *we* going to do? I know this much, Jacob Veering, *you're* not going to do anything other than lie rotting on the bed, never getting washed, so that you smell disgusting and look like a tramp. But I'll tell you this for nothing, it won't be on *this* bed, not any longer. You can rot somewhere else. I wish I'd never stuck by you. Better still, I wish we'd never met. I wish they'd hung you by the neck until you were dead.'

Jacob's shoulders hunched lower and lower under the onslaught. 'I wish I *were* dead, Ruby,' he whispered.

'In that case, why haven't you killed yourself? What's to stop you.' She flung her arm in the direction of the line slung across the room. 'There's a rope. I'm out long enough, working, so you've had plenty of opportunity.'

He felt a slight rumble of anger. 'That's a coward's way out.'

She laughed sarcastically. 'You're a coward already, letting yourself be kept by a woman.'

'Hold on a minute, Ruby—'

'I'll do no such thing. I'm not holding on another minute. You can get out, Jacob. I'll be better off without you. You're a dead weight. With you gone, there'll be more money for my baby.'

'But it's *our* baby,' he spluttered.

'No, Jacob.' She shook her head furiously. 'It's *mine*. If you're not willing to support it, you've no right to lay claim it's yours.' She threw her shawl around her. The fringed ends flicked against Jacob's cheek, stinging.

'Where are you going?'

'For a walk.'

'But it's Christmas Day!'

'I don't care if it's Judgement Day, I'm going for a walk.'

Ruby's anger was too hot to let her feel the cold as she walked swiftly along the empty streets of the Dingle. It was dusk now, and the lamplighter was doing his rounds

'Merry Christmas, miss,' he said as she walked through the pool of light that appeared like magic on the icy pavement.

'And the same to you.'

Curtains were being drawn against the dark and the coldness of the night, leaving only the occasional chink of light. Families had gathered together for the anniversary of the birth of Christ. For the first time in her life, Ruby felt very alone, but it didn't make her sad. Instead, she felt more angry with Jacob for letting her down, not pulling his weight. He'd become a burden she wasn't prepared to shoulder any more, not now that she was expecting a child. Resting her hands on her swelling stomach, she made a vow that her child would come first, always.

As she walked, Ruby wondered curiously if her mother was celebrating Christmas behind curtains somewhere in the land. In the past, occasionally, she'd thought about her mother, but never for long. What point was there? She could think about it till the cows came home, but it was a waste of time. Mrs, or Miss, O'Hagan might be dead. And if she was alive then she hadn't wanted her baby for some reason which, as far as Ruby was concerned, was more her mother's loss than hers. Until the last few months, she'd always been very happy, mother or no mother. Even now, most of the time, she wasn't *un*happy, not even about the baby once she'd got used to the idea. There were occasions, admittedly, when she had bouts of despair, but she managed to cope, somehow. If Jacob had done his share, she would have coped even better.

He'd better be gone when she got back, she thought grimly. If not, there'd be hell to pay.

When Ruby returned to Foster Court, Jacob had washed, shaved, combed his hair, put on his suit, and looked a new man. If it hadn't been for the hollow cheeks and flabby neck, he would have been the Jacob of old. He glanced at her shyly. 'I'll look for a job straight after Christmas, Ruby. I'm sorry about . . .'

She didn't let him finish, but danced across the room and threw herself into his arms. 'Oh, Jacob, I love you. Everything's going to be perfect from now on.' She cupped his face in her hands. 'It is, isn't it, Jacob?'

'Yes, Ruby. I promise.'

Unemployment had been rising for years. When Jacob Veering set out in search of work, there were almost a million men in competition. Jacob, unskilled in everything except farm work, found there was a limit to the jobs he could do. The docks, the mainstay of male employment in the area, was out – even experienced dockers were being laid off. The wages he'd been hoping to earn, two pounds a week at least, possibly three, according to Ruby, seemed more like pie in the sky as he was turned down for job after job, each paying less than the one he'd last applied for and, despite the paltry wages, all with a dozen men after them who'd done the work before.

Jacob was almost tempted to take to his bed again, give up altogether, but Ruby was having their child, growing bigger and bigger, waiting for him, bright-eyed and expectant, when he returned to Foster Court after another dismal, unsuccessful day.

'Never mind. Your luck might change tomorrow,' she would say encouragingly when she saw his dejected face.

One night, she came home from the Town Hall in a rage. 'They're making me leave,' she said hotly. 'All because of the baby. I said I felt fine, but they wouldn't listen. They said I might fall and weren't prepared to answer for the consequences.' She grimaced. 'And Martha Quinlan keeps threatening to let me go. I make her feel uncomfortable, she says, working my legs off while all she has to do is watch. In fact, she's started giving me a hand. "It's not right," I keep telling her, "paying me to clean and doing it yourself." You'd think I was an invalid or something,' she finished indignantly.

He wondered if Ruby had been a weaker person, not so independent, he might have risen to the occasion months ago, not given in. But she sapped any confidence he might have had, made him feel less than a man. Nothing got her down. Her initiative knew no bounds. Undeterred by the loss of her job, next morning she neatly wrote out half a dozen postcards and took them to pawnbrokers in the vicinity:

RUBY O'HAGAN
PAWNSHOP RUNNER
Available to collect and redeem pledges
Far and wide

She was delighted with the response. Names and addresses were promptly supplied of people urgently in need of cash, but too ashamed to show their faces in the place where it could be had. From then on, she visited the shops every morning in case there'd been a telephone call or a note delivered when it was dark requesting the pawnshop runner to call.

Without exception, the customers were women, not solely from better off places like Aigburth or Princes Park. There were poverty-stricken families in the Dingle, too proud to let their neighbours know they had to pawn the man's best suit on Monday to make ends meet, redeeming it for weekend use on Friday when the wages arrived. Ruby had to call at some ungodly hour, early morning or late at night, in case she was recognised, earning only a penny or twopence for her pains.

Not all the pathetic bundles of bedding, children's boots, canteens of cutlery, chiming clocks, or wedding rings, were redeemed. At the end of the week, Ruby might be told, 'Sorry, luv. I can't afford it. I'll get in touch once I've got the cash together.' Until then, beds would remain bare and childish feet unshod, or they might stay that way for ever.

Mrs Hart, the nicest of her customers, had so far never redeemed a pledge. Her big house was gradually being stripped of the pretty things that had been wedding presents or had belonged to her or her late husband's family since before she was born, to pay the ever-increasing debts of her son, the awful Max.

'I'd get much more for the damn things if I sold them,' she groaned, 'But I pawn them in the hope that one day I'll get them back, though where the money will come from, I've no idea.'

'They only keep them six months, then they're put up for sale,' Ruby said as she nursed the growing kitten, appropriately called Tiger.

At first she had been intrigued as to why so many apparently well-off women should so frequently require an urgent injection of cash. After a while she was able to tell the signs. There were women who drank, women who gambled, who overspent the housekeeping, who juggled a load of debts, borrowing from one source to pay off another. One sad lady she regularly called on was secretly supporting her dying father, unable to tell her husband because he wouldn't approve.

Some of the posh houses Ruby went in were anything but posh inside, with bare floors and mean furniture little better than Foster Court. The only decent things were the curtains on show to the outside world.

She was becoming a familiar figure on the streets of the Dingle. 'There's the pawnshop runner,' people would say as she walked by. 'Which tuppenny-a' penny toff are you off to see today, Ruby?' they would call, but Ruby would smile enigmatically and put her finger to her lips.

Martha Quinlan was no longer prepared to let an increasingly pregnant Ruby clean her bar and insisted she leave. 'You make me feel terrible, luv. But promise you'll still come for a cuppa regularly. I'll miss you something awful and so will our Agnes.'

'I'll miss you too.' Martha and Agnes/Fay had become her friends. She was sorry to lose her job, but was earning enough to manage without it, particularly now that Jacob was working, earning twenty-one and sixpence a week.

At long last, Jacob had found a job where his past experience was relevant – he knew about horses. For the past month he had driven a horse and cart around Edge Hill delivering coal. He hated it with all his heart. The black, pungent dust got up his nose and on his chest, making him cough and wheeze. At six o'clock, he came home covered in the stuff, his clothes stiff with it, his face and neck filthy. Ruby had to boil pans of water for him to wash in, though he never seemed able to get the dirt out of his hair. But she couldn't wash the clothes and the room stank of coal. Jacob could smell it even when he was asleep. One of the worst times of the day – and there were many – was getting out of bed and putting on the moleskin pants and the shirt that felt like a suit of armour they were so hard. And, finally, the leather waistcoat to protect his back and shoulders when he humped the heavy sacks down narrow entries into someone's back yard or emptied them down a manhole into the cellar.

Even the horse had no personality, not like Waterloo, the horse who'd been his companion on Humble's Farm. It was a dull, tired creature, as miserable as himself, showing no interest when he tried to talk to it.

Unlike Ruby, Jacob could see no end to this wretched existence. While she talked about leaving Foster Court and how their life would improve, he couldn't envisage a brighter future.

Winter was coming to an end, the nights were getting lighter, the days warmer. It was March and the baby was due in six weeks' time. A woman was coming to deliver it at Jacob's command, no matter what the hour. She charged ten shillings, but was very reliable and experienced.

Jacob came home one Friday, his spirits at their lowest. Charlie Murphy, their landlord, was sitting on the step, sunning himself in the evening sunshine. 'Nice day,' he remarked.

'Is it?' Jacob grunted. He hadn't noticed anything nice about it.

Charlie regarded him thoughtfully. 'Pay-days are always a bit special, lad.'

'I suppose.' He always gave his entire wages to Ruby who handled the family's finances.

'While you're flush, d'you fancy putting a tanner on a horse running tomorrer? Twenty to one, a sure-fire winner.'

'How much would I get if it won?'

'It's bound to win, mate, and you'd get ten bob plus your place money which isn't a bad return in my book.'

'And if I put on a shilling I'd get twice as much?'

'You would so.' Charlie nodded emphatically.

'Then I'll risk a shilling,' Jacob said recklessly.

Ruby called him the biggest fool under the sun when he told her. He had to tell her because she counted the wages carefully, pointing out he was a shilling short. She still claimed he was a fool when the horse won and he gave her a pound, keeping the place money for himself. On Sunday night, he celebrated his win with a couple of pints of ale, the first he'd had since coming to Foster Court. In the pub he got chatting to a group of young men who called him 'Jake', and made him feel one of the crowd, a proper man, unlike at home where he felt worthless.

All the following week he felt better about himself. On Friday, Charlie Murphy was waiting on the step when he came home and Jacob put another shilling on a sure-fire winner running next day. The horse lost and Ruby flatly refused to give him a few coppers so he could drown his sorrows in drink.

'I still want things for the baby, a shawl, and where's the little mite to sleep I'd like to know?' she said crossly. 'We need a cot. You're being very irresponsible, Jacob.'

The next time he was paid, Jacob, feeling daring, deducted half a crown before giving Ruby his wages, a shilling for a bet, the rest for ale. He'd go to the pub, the Shaftesbury, tonight. She could rant and rave all she liked, but he'd put in a hard week's work and was entitled to a bit of relaxation over a pint. Other men did it. Why not him?

Ruby didn't rant and rave. 'I've worked hard, too, Jacob,' she said quietly. 'But if that's how you feel . . .' She shrugged.

It *was* how he felt. In the pub he could forget about Foster Court, Ruby, and the coming baby. She made him boil his own water to wash in and silently perused the little notebook in which she kept a record of her pawnshop dealings while he changed into his newly cleaned suit. She didn't look up when he said 'tara'.

In the Shaftesbury he was made welcome with shouts of, 'Hello, there, Jake, ould mate. We didn't think we'd be seeing you again. What are you drinking?'

There were eight of them altogether, including Jacob. He felt obliged to buy a round and by closing time he'd consumed eight pints of ale, more than he'd ever had before. He was pickled to the gills when he got home, to find Ruby sitting up in bed with a sleeping baby in her arms. A strange woman was folding blood-stained sheets. She looked at him with contempt.

'You've got a daughter, Mr O'Hagan,' she said in a voice full of loathing. 'Fortunately, your poor wife was fit enough to send one of the downstairs' kids to fetch me. Christ knows what she'd have done if I hadn't been here.'

'She'd have managed.' Sober, Jacob would have felt ashamed, but brimming with ale, he didn't care. Left alone, Ruby could have delivered the child on her own, cut the cord, done whatever else was necessary, saved herself ten bob. And he resented being called 'O'Hagan'. There was good reason for not admitting to Veering which would be on the police files, but having to use Ruby's name instead of his own, only added to his feeling of inferiority.

'I'm off now, Mrs O'Hagan. Are you comfortable, luv?' Ruby nodded. She looked flushed and happy. 'I'll pop in tomorrow, see how you are like. You can pay me then.'

'Thank you.'

The woman left. Overcome with curiosity, Jacob swayed drunkenly towards the bed. 'It's a girl?'

'Yes, she's only little,' Ruby said distantly. 'Mrs Mickelwhite reckons about four pounds. It's because she came early. She wasn't due till next month. She needs fattening up.'

'What are you going to call her?' He took for granted he would have no say in the naming of his daughter and he was right.

'Greta, after Greta Garbo.'

He nodded, though he thought it a daft name. 'Look, Ruby, I'm sorry I wasn't around.' He felt it necessary to make amends. 'I wouldn't have dreamt of going out if I'd known the baby would come tonight.'

'It would have been nice if you'd been here to hold my hand,' she said reproachfully.

'Say if she had come when I was at work,' he reasoned.

'That's different. Work's necessary, not like ale.'

Jacob felt tempted to disagree, but held his tongue. 'Did it hurt bad, Ruby?' He suppressed a hiccup.

'No, it was very quick and hardly hurt at all. Mrs Mickelwhite said it was one of the easiest births she'd ever known. Would you like to hold her?' She must have decided to forgive him and carefully laid the tiny baby in his arms. It was muffled in clothes: a long, flannelette gown, knitted cardigan, bonnet, booties, all well worn. Ruby had got them from a secondhand market stall. Only the shawl was new, a present from the woman in the Malt House.

The child felt as light as a feather in his arms, but to Jacob she weighed heavier than the sacks of coal he humped around Edge Hill. He stared at the perfect little face, the long lashes trembling on white, waxen cheeks, the prim, pale mouth, and wanted to run away and never come back. Some men might regard their first child as a blessing, but he saw it as a cross he would have to bear for the rest of his life. There would be no end to the years of dirty, back-breaking work, earning a measly few bob. He put his daughter back in Ruby's arms. 'She's lovely,' he said briefly.

'Isn't she?' She stared at the child adoringly. 'I love her more than life itself, Jacob.'

'Do you, now!' He felt jealous.

Within a week, Ruby had returned to work, the baby wrapped up warmly and tucked inside her shawl, acknowledging the congratulations from various passers-by with a queenly gesture of her hand, and moving the shawl a fraction to expose Greta's pretty, pale face to be admired.

Mrs Hart gave the baby a tiny silver bangle. 'My godmother bought that when I was born,' she said to Ruby. 'I'd like Greta to have it, otherwise it will end up in Reilly's along with everything else of value from this house.'

The christening took place the following Sunday, the day after Ruby's seventeenth birthday. It was a quiet affair: just Ruby, Jacob, and their daughter, who was turning out to be an ideal baby, sleeping all night, sucking contentedly at her mother's breast, burping on cue. Though she wasn't gaining weight, Ruby reckoned, balancing Greta in her arms. 'She's hardly any different from the day she was born,' she said worriedly.

'How can you tell?' Jacob wanted to know. He was fed up with Greta commanding her entire attention.

'I just can.'

The night of the christening he went to the pub, saying he wanted to wet the baby's head. The horse he'd backed the day before, which Ruby knew nothing about, had come in third and the odds had been good. He wasn't sure which was more important, the drink or the horses. It certainly wasn't Ruby, or their baby.

By the time Greta was three months old, Jacob was handing over barely half his pay. Every Friday he put a couple of bob on the horses. The occasional wins made his heart sing so sweetly they were worth the more frequent losses. The weeks passed more quickly, each day bringing Friday closer. There would be a feeling in his gut that this week he'd make a killing.

The hours flew by too, knowing the evening ahead would be spent in the Shaftesbury with his mates. Ruby could scowl all she liked; he was a man and he'd do as he pleased. The men in the pub boasted of how they gave their wives a clout if they stepped out of line. If Ruby didn't buck up her ideas, show him some respect, one of these days he'd box her bloody ears.

Charlie Murphy had been badgered into repairing the window in their room and Ruby had made curtains, bright red. There was a patchwork cover on the bed, a rag rug on the floor, and a lace cloth hid the scratches on the chest of drawers. Everywhere was spotless, the room a little, bright oasis in the otherwise cheerless house.

When Jacob came home one hot evening in August, covered with coal dust as usual, the evening sun was pouring through the open window giving the place an extra sparkle. Greta was lying on the bed wearing only a ragged nappy, cooing and lazily examining her toes. She wasn't an active child. She caught colds easily and was still underweight according to Ruby, who worried about her constantly.

The table was set. A large dish in the middle emitted a thin spiral of smoke through a hole in the lid indicating there was the inevitable stew for tea. Ruby acknowledged Jacob's presence with a brief nod. 'Tea's ready when you've had a wash.'

'Is there water boiled?'

'I'm not boiling water so you can get tarted up and go drinking in the pub. I've told you that before. You can boil your own water.' She sat down and opened a newspaper she must have found, an action that always particularly irked Jacob. He could hardly read and felt she was showing him up. 'I'll have a cup of tea while I wait,' she said.

'I'd sooner you boiled the water.' There was a threat in his voice and she looked at him in surprise.

'You'd sooner what?'

'I'd sooner you got off your backside and boiled some bloody water.' He took a step towards her.

Ruby laughed. 'This is the first time all day I've sat down and I've no intention of moving.'

It was the laugh that did it. He wanted her cowed. He was fed up with her being so superior, always on top, him in the wrong, making him feel like a naughty lad. Jacob raised his hand and slapped her across the face, hard enough to make her cry, beg his forgiveness.

Except it did no such thing. Ruby screamed, jumped to her feet, grabbed the saucepan that had held the stew, and swung it against his head. There was a cracking sound as metal hit bone and Jacob collapsed back on to the bed.

Ruby screamed again and grabbed Greta out of the way. She stood over him, saucepan in one hand and the baby in the other, her cheek as red as a flame. 'If you ever hit me again, Jacob Veering,' she said in a grating voice, 'So help me, I'll kill you stone dead.'

Jacob didn't doubt it.

'I tripped,' he explained later in the pub. 'Banged me head against the wall.'

'Sure it wasn't your missus that did it,' joked one of his mates. 'If so, I hope you gave her what for.'

'Me missus wouldn't dare!' He seethed all night at the unfairness of it all. The feeling grew the drunker he got. Other men got away with knocking their wives about, why not him? But then you couldn't compare Ruby with normal women. There was something unnatural about her. The harder things got, the greater she thrived, as if life was a battle she was determined to win. Something inside Jacob melted. This extraordinary woman belonged to *him*! A memory surfaced in his sozzled brain, of Ruby, the way she used to poke her head around the cowshed. 'Hello, Jacob,' she would say shyly.

She'd loved him then, but not now. He'd spoiled things. Jacob began to feel sorry for himself. As soon as he got home, he'd show Ruby how much he loved her, make everything better.

She was fast asleep, the window open, the curtains drifting to and fro in little puffy waves. His working clothes were hanging over the sill, though the room still smelled of coal dust. Greta was in her cot at the foot of the bed.

Jacob quickly undressed, trembling with desire not felt since he'd left Brambles. He wanted Ruby as he'd never wanted her before. She'd been little more than a child when they last made love, but now she was a woman, a desirable woman, famous throughout the neighbourhood.

He slid naked into bed, put his arm around her waist, and pulled her towards him.

She woke immediately. 'What are you doing?' she said warily, pushing him away.

'I love you, Ruby,' he whispered hoarsely. By now, there was a fire in his gut that had to be extinguished or he would go mad. The slippy, struggling, protesting body only added to his passion, egging him on, making the fire get hotter and hotter, until it was scarcely bearable.

'Jacob!' she spat. 'You're drunk, I can smell it. Let go of me. You'll wake Greta.'

He didn't care if he woke the world. The petticoat she slept in tore as he pulled it waist high, dragging her underneath him, positioning himself between the thin legs. He plunged inside her and shuddered with relief. She felt looser than he remembered, but then she'd had a baby since. It did nothing to dampen his enjoyment or inhibit his tumultuous, tumbling climax. He rolled off her, sated, satisfied, ready for sleep.

He never went to the Shaftesbury again, but to a pub where he was a stranger. He felt ashamed of what he'd done and all the things he hadn't done. They never spoke of the night when he'd taken Ruby against her will. Next morning, there were angry marks on her arms and a bruise on her face where he'd hit her earlier on.

By now, he needed the drink, not just to escape from the frigid atmosphere of Foster Court. In the pub he kept to himself, not wanting to make friends.

His shame increased when, a few months later, Ruby announced she was pregnant, her face accusing. It was his fault. Everything was his fault.

Their second daughter was born the following year, 1937, April again. Ruby called her Heather, after some actress, Heather Angel, who'd been in one of her favourite films of all time, *Berkeley Square*.

Unlike Greta, Heather was an active, boisterous baby, hardly sleeping, always crying, demanding her mother's breast, scarlet with incomprehensible anger. Ruby, the pawnshop runner, acquired a giant pram, pushing it along the streets of the Dingle, a baby at each end: quiet Greta, sitting up, and Heather, bawling her bad-tempered little head off.

The girl approached him first. Jacob wouldn't have dreamt of talking to a woman on his own initiative. It was Saturday night, the pub was crowded, a pianist was thumping out tunes he vaguely remembered from the time he'd spent in Brambles listening to the gramophone with Ruby.

'When they begin, the beguine,' the clientele roared lustily.

'You look lonely, luv,' the girl said, slipping on to the bench beside him. She was neither white nor black, but an attractive pale brown, with dark gingery hair a mass of curls and ringlets.

'I'm all right, thanks,' Jacob said stiffly, assuming she was on the game and looking for a customer. If so, she was out of luck. He had ninepence in his pocket, not enough to pay for the cheapest prostitute in all of Liverpool. Which was a shame, because she was very pretty. Her small, pointed breasts showed prominently through her red jumper, and she had smooth, satiny skin. He was a normal, virile man, with a normal man's desires – desires that went unfulfilled. He and Ruby slept in the same bed, but he was too scared to touch her.

'What's your name, luv?' the girl enquired.

'Jake Veering.'

'I'm Elizabeth Georgeson, but everyone calls me Beth. D'you come from round here?'

'No, Kirkby.'

'What are you doing in these parts, Jake?'

Jacob wasn't sure what he was doing there. Ruby had brought him and he'd meekly followed, but he couldn't tell the girl that.

'Lost me job,' he said, 'came looking for another.'

'Did you find one?'

'I'm a coalman, Edge Hill way.'

'Me Gran lives in Edge Hill,' she cried, smiling delightedly. 'I'll tell her to look out for you in future. I live in Toxteth meself.' She worked on the tool counter in Woollies in Lord Street. 'But I'm hoping to be transferred to cosmetics any minute.' Her brown, velvety eyes glowed. 'I can't wait.'

Her father was Jamaican, her mother Irish, and she had two brothers and three sisters, all living at home. She was eighteen, the same age as Ruby, which Jacob found incredible. Ruby seemed more like twenty-five, thirty, compared to this pretty, carefree girl, whose main ambition in life was to sell lipsticks and scent.

'You didn't mind me talking to you, did you, Jake?' she said later. 'You *did* look lonely, and I thought it was a shame, someone as nice as you sitting on their own.' She looked at him shyly. 'Have you got a girlfriend?'

Jacob swallowed. 'No,' he said boldly. He didn't want to drive her away. It made a change to be flattered. She wasn't on the game, but in the pub only because it was someone's birthday from work. She made him feel big, whereas Ruby made him feel small. She was soft, Ruby was hard. When closing time came, he daringly suggested they meet again next Saturday in the same pub.

She looked disappointed. 'But that's a whole week away! Couldn't we see each other sooner?'

'I'd like to but . . .' Jacob paused, but having told one lie, it was easy to tell another, '. . . I'm a bit short of cash. I send money to me mam in Kirkby every week, see. She's a widder and I've got three brothers, all younger than me. She has a job making ends meet since I left home.'

Beth looked at him emotionally. 'You're even nicer than I first thought. Tell you what, we'll go to the pictures Wednesday, it'll be my treat.'

From then on, they saw each other twice a week, which quickly became three. His wages rose by one and six a week and he didn't tell Ruby, but kept the money for himself. When Beth introduced him to her big, strapping father and red-haired mother, they regarded him with a critical eye and apparently liked what they saw. He said he was a Catholic and was welcomed with open arms into their home, regarded as Beth's suitor, just as he had been Audrey's what seemed like a million years ago. It was a position that Jacob liked, uncomplicated, with few demands, apart from the necessity to have a good time. He rather enjoyed his double life, though knew it couldn't last. One of these days Ruby would find out about Beth, or Beth about Ruby.

The double life came to an end in an unexpected way.

It was New Year's Eve, snowing, the grey sky was heavy with sludgy black clouds. In the coalyard, a mountain of glossy coal had been turned into a thing of beauty by a spangle of snowflakes. Jacob wore gloves as he threw the bulging sacks on to the cart, whistling cheerfully as he worked. His employer, Arthur Cummings, too old and frail to carry on the business by himself, was rubbing his gnarled hands in the doorway of the small house overlooking the yard where he lived alone. His wife had died two years before, they'd had no children.

'Watch'a doing tonight, lad?' he enquired.

He knew about Ruby and the girls. Christmas had proved complicated with two women having demands on his time. Beth had been told he was spending the holiday in Kirkby. He was seeing her tomorrow. 'Just staying in,' Jacob replied, 'having a drink with the wife.'

'Good lad,' Arthur said approvingly. 'You're welcome to share a bottle of Guinness with us when you're finished here. We can toast the New Year a bit early, like.'

Jacob nodded, though he'd no intention of accepting. Arthur was a nice man, obviously lonely, always offering cups of tea and trying to engage him in conversation. But Jacob couldn't be bothered. He finished loading the cart, patted the unresponsive horse whose name was Clifford, between the ears, and was about to leap on board, when Beth walked through the wooden gates, startling Clifford, who tossed his head and gave a nervous snort.

'What are you doing here?' he demanded a trifle shortly. The yard was neutral territory. Ruby had never thought to come near.

'I've got something to tell you, Jake.' She looked very pale and her eyes were swollen. 'I'm in the club.'

'In the what?'

'The club, Jake. I'm expecting a baby. I haven't told me mam and dad, but we'll have to get wed straight away. They'll guess, eventually, but it won't matter once we're married. We'll go to St Vincent de Paul's tonight and see Father Vincent, arrange to have the banns called.'

Jacob froze with shock. 'I can't, tonight,' he stuttered. 'It's New Year's Eve. I promised to spend it with me mam.'

Beth looked disappointed. 'The next night, then.'

That night and the next, to Ruby's surprise, Jacob stayed in, terrified out of his wits. It occurred to him he wasn't married to Ruby and was therefore free to marry Beth. But he didn't want a wife, particularly not one who was pregnant. It would be a case of exchanging one miserable life for another, possibly worse. At least Ruby earned a goodly sum and had worked right through both pregnancies. Beth might want to leave Woollies and the responsibility for supporting her and the child would rest entirely on him. He began to see all sorts of qualities in Ruby that he hadn't appreciated before.

Beth knew he lived in Foster Court, but not the number. 'It's a hovel,' he told her. 'Only temporary. I'd sooner you didn't come.' Any minute she'd come looking for him or she'd turn up again at the coal yard. Even worse, she might send her father. Jacob didn't know which way to turn.

Another day passed. He told Arthur Cummings he needed a day off. 'I've a bit of business to see to. I'll work all day Sat'day instead.' He'd been a good worker and had never taken time off before. Arthur willingly agreed.

Next morning, he put on in his working clothes and hid in a doorway at the end of the court until he saw Ruby leave with the children in the pram, then went back and changed into his suit.

He had no idea how to escape the tangle his life had become, other than to run away, get a job on a farm, never look at a woman again for as long as he lived. There were railway stations in town where he could catch a train as far away from Liverpool as he could afford.

The city throbbed with the noise of traffic, he was jostled on the pavements, his head began to ache as he made his muddled way towards Lime Street station. He paused, trying to get his bearings. He was outside a shop that wasn't really a shop. 'Army Recruiting Office' said the sign over the window.

Jacob stared at the sign for several minutes before going in.

He hadn't expected to return to Foster Court, but he did. It would take at least two weeks for his application to join the Army to be processed. He'd given the address of the coalyard, Mr Cummings wouldn't mind, and he'd think of a reason for the different surname, Veering, if it was noticed. His first posting would be with the Army Educational Corps to have his reading and writing skills brought up to standard. Accommodation would be provided, food, his pay would be his own. Most importantly of all, he would be taken care of. From now on, his only obligation would be to King and country.

Tonight he'd go round Beth's before she sought him out, arrange to have the banns called, pick a date for the wedding. By the time it arrived, he would be gone.

Ruby didn't worry when Jacob didn't come home for his tea. She'd got used to the way he seemed to lead his own life these days. Sometimes, she wondered if she still loved him, or if she never had, that it had just been a childish crush. He was the first young man she'd ever met, undoubtedly handsome, but under different circumstances, she doubted if she would have given him a second glance. Without the incident with Bill Pickering, their romance would probably have petered out years ago.

But then she wouldn't have had her girls. They were on the bed, both asleep. She went over and touched Greta's white cheek. 'What would I have done without you?' she whispered. The pale lips were curved in a wistful smile and she was clutching the rag doll she had christened 'Babs'. She resembled her father, with the same butter coloured hair, the same blue eyes and long, fair lashes. She had Jacob's placid temperament.

Poor Jacob! Ruby sighed. He was a nice man who'd been expected to act in a way that was quite beyond him. Jacob needed peace, quiet, to be left alone. Jacob, the farmhand, would have worked as hard as any man, harder than some.

Ruby made no attempt to touch her other daughter for fear of waking her. At nine months, Heather was a minx, crawling now, into everything. Twice she'd burnt her hand on the iron that had been hidden under the bed to cool. Mother and daughter were very alike. Heather had black hair and almost black eyes. Thin and wiry, very strong, she was almost as tall as Greta who was a year older, often sickly, and still underweight.

She supposed she may as well eat the stew going cold on the table. Stew was easiest to make on the gas ring in the kitchen – she wouldn't have dreamt of putting anything in the filthy oven. Cooking was difficult since Heather had started crawling. She didn't know whether to leave the child in the room with everything dangerous out the way, or take her downstairs where there were different hazards, including cockroaches which Heather couldn't be trusted not to catch and eat.

When, oh, when, would they get away from Foster Court!

It was only in the dead of night that the house was still and silence descended. For this reason, Ruby never minded the occasional times when she woke, able for once to hear the girls' gentle breathing and Jacob's soft snores. No babies were crying, no women screaming, doors slamming. No one was fighting. Sometimes, she would lie, quite content, until the wheels of the milk cart rattled along the main road, followed by the clink of bottles. As if this was a signal for the area to come to life, doors would open, voices could be heard, whistling, and the steady beat of booted feet as men marched towards the docks to start their day's work. At this point, Ruby would wake Jacob and get up herself and hope to reach the kitchen before anyone else to boil water for tea.

When she woke up that night, she realised something was wrong, something was missing. She remembered Jacob wasn't home by the time she'd gone to bed. And he still wasn't there.

She had no idea what time it was. Apart from the children's breath, the world was soundless. She sat up and lit the candle and for the first time noticed Jacob's suit wasn't behind the door on its cardboard hanger. She stayed sitting up, sick with worry and freezing cold, until the milk cart arrived, the dockers had gone to work, when she got dressed, fed the girls, put them in the pram, and pushed it round to the coal yard.

The sky was leaden and the January morning bitterly cold. When she arrived at the yard, a strange young man was loading the cart with sacks. A grey horse, already harnessed, stared moodily at the ground, tossing its head fearfully when it saw her.

'Where's Jacob?' Ruby demanded loudly. Had he lost his job and was too scared to tell her?

'You'd better give Arthur Cummings a knock. He'll tell you.' The young man grinned and nodded towards the small house standing on its own in the corner of the yard. 'Sounds as if he was a bit of'a lad, our Jacob.'

'How would you know?' Ruby snapped.

An old man, very bent, with rheumy eyes, answered the door. For some reason, he looked extremely moidered. Ruby didn't waste time with polite niceties. 'Where's Jacob?'

'Who are you?'

'His wife.'

'But I thought . . .' He pulled at his snow-white hair and looked even more moidered.

'Thought what?'

'Well, his wife's already here.'

'I never said I was his wife. I'm his fiancée.' A girl had come into the hall from the back of the house. She wore a brown fitted coat and a Fair Isle tam-o'-shanter with matching mittens, and would have been exceptionally pretty had her eyes not been so red with weeping. 'Jake hasn't got a wife.'

'Oh, yes he has,' Ruby said fiercely. 'Me!' She pointed to the pram. 'And these are his children. But where the hell's their father, that's what I'd like to know. His name's Jacob, by the way, and you can't possibly be his fiancée.'

The girl screamed and burst into tears. 'Jaysus! It's even worse than I thought. He's double-crossed me on top of everything else.'

'Yes, but where is he?' Ruby insisted.

'He's joined the Army, girl,' Arthur Cummings said nervously. 'The Royal Tank Regiment. He said his wife knew.'

Arthur was a gentle old man, genuinely upset by his ex-employee's disgraceful behaviour as if, somehow, it reflected on him. He made a pot of tea, which, he said, he was as much in need of as his visitors. The pram was parked in the hall and the two women sat at a chenille-covered table in a comfortable back room which looked as if nothing had changed since the last century. A cheerful fire spat and crackled in the black grate.

There seemed little point in blaming each other. Jacob had duped them both. Perhaps it was perverse, but Ruby couldn't help liking the girl who was clearly heartbroken. She loved him, she sobbed, they were getting married next month. Last night they'd arranged to go window shopping to look at wedding rings and intended to buy one on Saturday. When he didn't turn up, she'd been worried.

Ruby glanced at the sixpenny brass ring she'd bought from Woolworth's. She'd paid for it herself and her finger turned green if she didn't take it off when she went to bed. She wasn't sure how she felt other than totally betrayed. Jacob! Having an affair! She hadn't thought he had it in him. But adversity had never sat well on Jacob's shoulders and at that moment her own shoulders felt a fraction lighter, knowing that he had gone out of her life. She might cry, tonight and the next night and a few nights to come, if only because the thing that had started so sweetly had ended on such a sour note. But then it had turned sour a long while ago.

By now, Beth was weeping inconsolably. Ruby reached over and touched her arm. 'You'll have to try and forget him,' she said in the tone of a mother addressing a child. 'You're only young. You'll find someone else.'

'I'll never forget him and I don't want anyone else,' the girl wept. 'Me life's ruined. I can't go back to work. I've told everyone I'm getting married. Some of 'em have already got me a present. They were coming to St Vincent de Paul's to watch.'

'Tell them you've called it off,' Arthur suggested. He was sitting between them like a referee, having taken their predicament to his heart.

'That's a good idea,' Ruby said encouragingly. 'Say you've changed your mind.'

Beth looked at them, her face tragic. 'I would, I could, except . . . except, I'm having Jake's baby. When me dad finds out, he'll kill me.'

There was a knock on the door. 'Not another young lady looking for Jacob, I hope,' Arthur said plaintively when he went to answer it, but it was only his new employee announcing he was on his way.

The knock must have reminded Heather she was being neglected and she set up a plaintive wail.

'I'll have to be going,' Ruby announced. 'I've got things to do, important things, people to see.'

'But what about me?' Beth cried.

Ruby frowned. 'What about you?'

'You've got to help me.'

'No, I haven't. I've been left in a bigger pickle than you. I've got two children to support, rent to pay, a job to do.'

'But you haven't got a broken heart, not like me,' Beth said passionately. 'You're not the least upset, I can tell. No wonder he turned to me. You must have been neglecting him something awful. It's your fault he went away. You drove him to it.'

'Hold on a minute, girl,' Mr Cummings interjected. 'I don't think you're being entirely fair.'

'Nothing *is* fair.'

'Jacob only left home after he met you,' Ruby pointed out. 'It was probably learning about the baby that did it. He wasn't capable of supporting one family, let alone two.'

'He supported his mam and little brothers, didn't he?'

'Did he thump! He hasn't seen his mam in years and he was an only child. He could hardly bring himself to support his children. It was the bookie and the beer that took most of Jacob's money.'

'Oh!' Beth started to cry again.

Perhaps that last remark had been unnecessarily brutal. Ruby felt sorry for the girl. She looked too soft-hearted by a mile and was right to claim Jacob had been neglected, but it was his own fault. He'd been treated with the utmost sympathy when they'd first arrived at Foster Court. Another woman wouldn't have let him lie on that damned bed for more than a couple of days, let alone six months, supporting him, fussing over him. He'd probably still be there, she thought darkly, if Greta hadn't arrived. He'd treated his daughters with indifference, as if they were nothing to do with him, that somehow Ruby had managed to conceive them on her own.

'You're better off without him,' she said abruptly.

'How can you possibly say that!' the girl cried.

'She's been married to him for two years,' Mr Cummings put in. 'She should know. Meself, I considered him a nice lad, but he's gone down in me estimation as from this morning.'

Beth shivered. 'I'm nearly three months gone. I'll have to leave home before I start to show. I'd prefer to go sooner rather than later, under me own steam, as it were, because I'll be chucked out, anyroad, once me dad finds out. At least I'd avoid a good hiding.'

'That makes sense to me,' the old man opined, nodding his white head.

'Yes, but where would I go?' She spread her hands and shrugged helplessly. 'Could I stay with you?' She looked hopefully at Ruby. 'I'm sorry about what I said before. I didn't mean it.'

Ruby snorted. 'Believe me, you wouldn't want to stay with me. No one in their right mind would want to live in Foster Court. The room was cramped enough with Jacob and he was out most of the time. You and me'd be falling over each other and there isn't the space for another baby. And what happens when you stop work? Am I supposed to keep you?'

'I don't care how squashed it is. I tell you what,' Beth said eagerly, 'I'll do the cleaning in return for me keep. You won't have to lift a finger.'

'I can't exactly afford a housekeeper,' Ruby said tartly.

'You can pretend I'm the wife and you're the husband. I'll look after the children and make the meals while you go out to work. What sort of work d'you do?'

'She's the pawnshop runner,' Arthur said proudly.

'I don't want to be anyone's husband, thanks all the same,' Ruby snapped. 'Not only that, my main aim in life is to get out of Foster Court, not take in a lodger.' She folded her arms, a sign her mind was made up. In the hall, her younger daughter was screaming the fact she had completely lost patience with being ignored. 'I'll have to go before Heather takes the roof off.'

'I know what you can do,' Arthur said. 'Both of you. You can move in with me. There's two rooms empty upstairs and a parlour that's never used. I wouldn't want paying, like, just the cleaning and cooking done in return.' He sniffed pathetically. 'I haven't had a decent meal since me ould missus passed on. It'd be nice to have company for a change.' He looked from one to the other with his rheumy eyes. 'Oh, and I like kiddies,' he added as if another inducement was needed before they would agree. 'What do you say?'

'Yes!' Beth cried without hesitation.

Ruby contemplated the idea for several seconds. She liked Beth. They had something in common, both having been betrayed by the same man. And she liked Arthur and his comfortable little house. 'All right,' she said after a while, 'Beth can do the cleaning and cooking and look after the children. I'll pay for the food. It wouldn't be fair otherwise. But I am *not*,' she said warningly, 'under any circumstances, to be regarded as a husband.'

Arthur sighed happily. 'Then it's agreed?'

'Agreed,' the two women said together, and Ruby thought that Jacob would probably die of shock if he could have seen the way they smiled at each other and shook hands.

Beth

Chapter 6

1938–1945

Beth's little boy fought his way into the world six months later on a sultry August night, causing his mother considerable agony and a certain amount of agitation to Arthur Cummings who paced the living room like an expectant father. 'Is she going to die?' he asked in a trembling voice when a scream more piercing than the others rent the air.

'Of course not,' Ruby snapped. Her own children having arrived without inconveniencing a soul, apart from herself, she had little patience with Beth's hysterical carryings on. Mrs Mickelwhite, who'd delivered Greta and Heather, was in the bedroom with her now. Ruby ran upstairs to make sure the latest exhibition hadn't woken the girls, but they were fast asleep, one at each end of a single bed. She sat there while the screams in the next room rose to a crescendo, then suddenly stopped. A baby yelled lustily. Ruby waited until the gory bits were over and went into the bedroom, where Mrs Mickelwhite was putting a vast, chubby baby in Beth's arms. The new mother looked exhausted. Bathed in sweat, her gingery hair stood on end.

'He's at least ten pounds,' the midwife said with a satisfied cluck. 'His poor mother went through hell. What are you going to call him, luv?'

'Jake.' Beth stuck out her tongue at Ruby.

'Bitch!' Ruby said amiably. The two girls shared a love-hate relationship. Ruby accused Beth of being indolent and too extravagent, though secretly conceded these trifling faults were more than made up for by her sweet nature and kind heart. In turn, Beth told Ruby she was bossy and mean enough to skin a flint, though was forced to admit she was an incredibly hard worker and extremely caring. They'd argued over calling the baby Jake if it were a boy. Ruby didn't want to be reminded of Jacob, particularly in human form. Beth wanted reminding all the time. She called herself Beth Veering and had kept his shaving brush – Ruby had been about to throw it out – and it stood, like an ornament, on the dressing table in her room.

'Isn't he handsome?' Beth smiled proudly at her new son who was wide awake and waving his chubby fists like a boxer. A fluff of light brown hair covered his scalp and his skin was lighter than Beth's, a pale tan shade.

'He's beautiful,' Ruby said truthfully. She kissed Beth and shook hands with Jake.

'Where's his father?' Mrs Mickelwhite enquired.

'In the Army.'

'And where's your fella nowadays, Mrs O'Hagan? I met him a few times if you recall.'

'He's in the Army too.'

'They joined together.' Beth grinned.

'They're best friends.' Ruby grinned back.

'That's nice,' Mrs Mickelwhite remarked.

It was pleasant living with Arthur Cummings. The house was cosy, though very small. Beth complained it was cramped but, after Foster Court, Ruby appreciated not eating and sleeping in the same room and having a proper kitchen for their sole use. The washing got covered in coal dust and the lavatory was at the bottom of the yard, but at least it wasn't used by all and sundry and Beth managed to keep it more or less clean if she was nagged hard enough.

There was no need nowadays to take the girls as she sped to and fro between her customers and the various pawnshops. They were happy to be left with Beth and Arthur giving Ruby the opportunity to drop in on Martha Quinlan for a cup of tea and a chat, feeling quite the lady of leisure. Mrs Hart had also become a good friend and Ruby often called to see her and Tiger, even if nothing had to be pawned that day to pay off her incorrigible son's debts.

On Sundays, Beth's day off, Ruby reluctantly took over the cooking. Saturday, the old man babysat while the two women went to the pictures: the Dingle Picturedrome or the Beresford. At first, there'd been terrible arguments over what to see until they decided to take turns in choosing. Ruby preferred romances, Beth liked comedy best and anything starring Franchot Tone.

Everyone was happy with the arrangement. Arthur paid the bills and was provided with company in his old age, Beth had a roof over her own and her baby's head in return for doing the housework, although not very well, according to Ruby who bought the food. The money left over she shared with Beth, leaving enough to buy things she'd never been able to afford since leaving Brambles.

Even Jacob's replacement, the young man whose name was Herbie, proved his usefulness by seeing to Clifford the horse every night after they'd finished their day's work.

Arthur was the only one concerned about the war clouds that were gathering on the horizon. He read the *Daily Herald* every day and had his ear glued to the wireless. 'That Hitler chap's throwing his weight about far too much for my liking,' he said frequently. 'I've lived through enough wars in my lifetime. It's not meself I'm concerned about, I've had a good innings. It's you young 'uns.'

'There's nothing to worry about.' Ruby flatly refused to believe anyone, including Adolf Hitler, would be so stupid as to start the war some columnists claimed was imminent. She ignored the ominous signs: the booklet called, 'The Protection of Your Home Against Air Raids,' which had been delivered to every household in the land, followed by others describing how to mask the windows with tape to prevent them from shattering, or explaining what a gas mask was. Martha Quinlan had joined the Women's Voluntary Service, the WVS, and was learning first aid and hoping Fred would feel patriotic enough to run the Malt House in her absence.

Germany annexed Austria, threatened Czechoslovakia, mobilised its Armed Forces. Benito Mussolini installed a Fascist government in Italy. Still Ruby felt convinced that war would somehow be avoided.

In September, the British Prime Minister, Neville Chamberlain, met with Adolf Hitler in Munich, returning home waving a piece of paper guaranteeing, 'Peace in our Time'.

'See, I told you there wouldn't be a war,' Ruby crowed when she heard it on the wireless.

But the paper proved worthless and Germany blithely continued with its objective of conquering the entire continent of Europe.

★

Christmas, which they'd been so much looking forward to, was thoroughly spoiled by the arrival a few days days beforehand of three adult gas masks – junior ones would be issued at a later date and there would be a special one for Jake, now five months old. Arthur was the most badly affected and seemed to sink into a depression from that day on from which he never recovered. The 1914–18 conflict had been termed, 'the war to end all wars', yet now there was about to be another. He had lost faith in humanity, he moaned, there was no goodness left in the world, otherwise how could a man like Adolf Hitler prosper? 'Look what he's doing to the Jews!' He stopped going to Mass because he no longer believed in God and made a desperate fuss of the three small children he had so kindly taken into his home. 'What's going to happen to the poor little mites?' he would say despairingly.

They wondered what the New Year, 1939, would bring, and as the weeks and months passed, it seemed that war was becoming more and more inevitable. The signs were everywhere. Brick shelters were built on the corners of the streets, walls of sandbags appeared outside important buildings. First Aid Centres were established. Agnes/Fay Quinlan reported the staff had practised evacuating the Town Hall in case of an air raid. Martha said that when the war started, the children of Liverpool would be evacuated to places like Southport or Wales.

'Over my dead body,' Ruby swore. 'There's no one going to separate me from my kids.'

'It's not compulsory,' Martha assured her. 'Anyroad, mothers can go with their children if they want.'

'I wish they were grown-up like yours,' Ruby said with a heartfelt sigh. 'They wouldn't be such a worry.'

Martha gave her arm a little shake. 'Don't you believe it, luv. Kids are always a worry, no matter what their age. Our Jim's in the Merchant Navy. The seas will be the most dangerous place of all. By the way, he's home this weekend, the first time in months. We're having a bit of a do on Sat'day. You're welcome to come. I've never asked before because you couldn't get away due to the kids.'

'Can I bring Beth?' They could wear the new frocks they'd got for Christmas from C & A.

'Bring whoever you like, luv. How's your Jacob? Have you heard from him lately?'

'Not for a while.'

'Is he still in Aldershot?'

'As far as I know. That's where I last wrote to him, but he still hasn't answered. He was never much good at writing.' She'd heard that the Royal Tank Regiment was based in Aldershot. It wasn't a lie that Jacob had joined up. She just hadn't mentioned that it was his way of leaving his family for good.

'I bet his heart's in his mouth, wondering where he'll be posted when the fighting begins.'

'I bet it is.' She wondered if Jacob would be braver in the Army than he'd been in civilian life.

Ruby had never met Jim Quinlan before. He was, she supposed, unremarkable, though at times there was something almost beautiful about his still, tranquil face. She loved the way he always managed to give everyone his undivided attention, making them feel special, no matter how unimportant other people might think they were.

The Merchant Navy was his life. He'd signed on as a cadet with the Elder Dempster line sixteen years ago. Recently, he'd passed his First Master's Certificate and was now a First Officer, the equivalent of a captain, though so far he'd never had a ship of his own. There was scarcely a country on earth he hadn't visited on the ships, big and small, that carried goods and sometimes passengers, across the oceans of the world.

'So, this is the famous pawnshop runner,' he said when Martha introduced them in the Malt House on Saturday night. 'Mam often mentions you in her letters. It's nice to meet you in the flesh at last. You're every bit as pretty as she said.'

'Am I?' Ruby stammered, strangely tongue-tied, glad she was wearing her new emerald green frock. Emily would have approved of the plain style, but not the colour.

'You've got a husband in the Army, so I understand. And two children as well. How old are they?'

'Greta's three, Heather's two. Their birthdays were last month.'

'You don't look much more than a child yourself.' He smiled into her eyes.

'I had my birthday last month too. I'm twenty.'

'Twenty! You make me feel very old. I'm thirty-one.'

'That's not old,' she protested.

'Old enough to put pretty girls like you out of my reach – unmarried ones, I hasten to add.'

Jacob would have to be killed as soon as the fighting started, Ruby decided. She would become a widow and put herself within the reach of Jim Quinlan.

Beth, sitting on her other side, joined in the conversation. 'I suppose you've got a girl in every port,' she said, fluttering her lashes and glancing at him coyly. She looked very pretty tonight in pale blue.

'Only every other port. Will you excuse me? Me mam wants me a minute.' Martha was beckoning to him from behind the bar.

'Is that how you caught Jacob?' Ruby said furiously when Jim had gone. 'Looking at him like a dying cow?'

'He'd be well used to cows, Jacob, after being married to you for so long.'

'Women who flirt make me sick.'

'You're only saying that because you can't flirt yourself.'

'I wouldn't want to. It's degrading. Men either take me for what I am, or they don't take me at all.'

'They don't take you at all as far as I can see. There's only been Jacob and he did a runner.'

'That was your fault, not mine.' Ruby put an end to the argument by going to the Ladies. When she came out, she leant against the wall and watched Jim Quinlan who was sitting with an elderly couple, nodding now and then, oblivious to the noise in the crowded bar. His face was brown from the sun, the skin smooth, not weatherbeaten as she would have expected from someone who spent so much time in the open air. Tiny lines were etched around his hazel eyes and the lashes were short and stubby, very thick. She imagined him standing on deck, shielding his eyes against the sun with a hand that was surprisingly long and slender and also very brown.

Ruby shivered, imagining going to bed with Jim Quinlan, waking up in his arms. The delicious thought was interrupted by Martha shoving a plate of sausage rolls in her ribs.

'Do us a favour, girl. Take these around. I'm up to me eyeballs behind the bar.'

'OK.' It would give her another chance to talk to Jim.

★

In June, Mrs Hart decided to leave the country for America. 'I've a sister there, Nora. She lives in Colorado, I think I told you before. Once this damn war starts, it won't be safe to cross the Atlantic.'

Ruby thought about Jim Quinlan who would have no choice but to cross the Atlantic no matter how unsafe. 'What about Max?' she asked.

'He's already been called up. He's joined the Royal Air Force – he learnt to fly at university.' She smiled. 'I'm pleased to say he appears to have turned over a new leaf.'

'Are you taking Tiger?' Tiger had grown to an enormous size, though still considered himself a kitten. She scratched his chin and he purred appreciatively.

'Unfortunately, I can't. Nora already has two cats, both female. Tiger would be in his element, but I doubt if the resultant kittens would be welcome. No, he's going to my friend in Childwall. I'm sure he'll be happy there, won't you, Tiger?' The cat didn't look particularly pleased about this arrangement and stared impassively at his owner. 'I wonder, Ruby, dear,' Mrs Hart went on, 'If you'd do me a big favour?' She took a small, brown envelope from out of the dresser drawer.

'You know I will,' Ruby assured her. Mrs Hart had become a dear friend and she was sorry she was leaving.

'If I give you the keys, will you keep an eye on the house for me? It seems silly to sell it. They say the war will only last a couple of months and I'll be back. Just look in every few weeks and make sure everything's all right. I'm having the mains cut off, so there shouldn't be any floods or gas leaks, but I've put Nora's address in there, so you can write and let me know if there's a problem. And help yourself to anything from the garden, dear. You've had apples off the tree, so you know how lovely and crisp they are, and there's rhubarb too. It tastes like wine.'

'I'll miss you,' Ruby said, taking the envelope.

'And I'll miss you, Ruby dear, and your two lovely little girls.' Mrs Hart looked close to tears. 'But it won't be for long, will it? In no time at all, I'll be back and we'll have tea together again; just you, me, and Tiger.'

It was a wonderful day, not hot, but comfortably warm, the golden sun dazzling in the cloudless blue sky, entirely appropriate for a

*Sun*day. It was the sort of day that, under different circumstances, would have been regarded as a blessing from God, an example of how perfect the world could be when He felt in the mood.

In reality, the day was anything but perfect.

Ruby and Beth strolled through Princes Park. Jake was fast asleep in the pram that had once held Greta and Heather. The girls were scampering over the thick, dry grass, running in and out of the trees, calling to each other, their childish voices echoing sharply in the late afternoon air.

The faces of the young women were sombre. At eleven o'clock that morning, Great Britain had declared war on Germany after Hitler had invaded Poland, a country they had been bound by treaty to protect.

'What are we going to do, about being evacuated, that is?' Beth spoke in a low voice, as if half to herself.

'I think we should go, though I don't like leaving Arthur.'

'Me, neither. But I suppose the children should come first.'

'Arthur would be the first to agree. He'd hate it if he thought we were staying in Liverpool because of him.' Ruby watched Heather pull her older, more fragile sister, up a slight incline. Heather watched over Greta like a mother hen with a chick. Tears sprang to her eyes at the thought of either of her daughters being harmed. Or Beth and Jake, come to that. She loved Beth like a sister and Jake as a son.

Arthur had made a fuss when they said they were going for a walk. He was expecting an air raid any minute. 'Don't go far,' he'd warned. So they hadn't.

Ruby looked anxiously at the sky, half-expecting to see an enemy plane loaded with deadly bombs, but the blue sky was clear from horizon to horizon except for the brilliant sun. 'Martha Quinlan's helping to organise the evacuation. Shall we call in the Malt House on the way home and arrange to go tomorrow?' she said. 'They're running special coaches and trains for evacuees.'

Beth sighed. 'OK, but let's go on a train no matter where it takes us. It'll be murder stuck on a coach with the children.'

'A train it is.'

Coaches went to Wales, trains to Southport, Martha told them. They should turn up at Exchange station at ten o'clock next morning.

'Who will we stay with?' enquired Beth.

'No one knows, luv. I understand it's a bit like a meat market at the other end. You just have to stand around until you're picked.'

As they walked back, Beth said wistfully, 'I'd love to go and see my brothers. Ronnie's eighteen and Dick's twenty-one. They're bound to have been called up.'

'I'll come with you,' Ruby offered.

'No, ta, Rube. Thanks all the same, but me dad won't consider it too late to give me a walloping. I don't want to arrive in Southport with me arm in a sling.'

'I'll stay and keep the home fires burning,' Arthur promised manfully when they left next morning with Jake in his pushchair, a few hastily packed carrier bags, and gasmasks slung over their shoulders. The old man was obviously on the verge of tears. His hands were visibly shaking and he looked particularly frail today. 'Never forget this is your home,' he said emotionally. 'You're free to come and go whenever you please.'

'Thanks, Arthur,' Ruby said, flinging her arms around his neck. 'It's the first *proper* home I've ever had.'

The train was packed with excited children, weeping children, and some pale with fear. A few mothers accompanied the smaller ones. A uniformed WVS lady distributed sandwiches *en route* and tied name labels around wrists. Ruby pinned her label to the collar of her green frock.

In Southport, they were herded into an open space beside the station where several cars were parked. The occupants immediately got out and began to walk among the new arrivals, assessing them openly. The nicely dressed children were pounced upon and quickly whisked away.

'Martha was right,' Ruby said hotly. 'I feel like a piece of meat. Any minute now someone's going to ask how much I cost a pound.' Nevertheless, she was glad they were all wearing their best clothes. The girls looked like the royal princesses in their frilly cotton frocks, and Jake was adorable in a blue and white sailor suit, a present from Arthur for his first birthday.

'Would you like to come with me, dear?' A tall, grey-haired woman with a mild good-natured face put her hand on Ruby's arm. She wore an expensive navy-blue serge coat and matching hat.

'Come on, Beth!' Ruby called. 'Greta, love, hold Heather's hand. I've got these bags to carry.'

The woman shook her head. 'I'm sorry, dear. I meant you and your little girls. I haven't room for any more.'

'In that case, I'll wait for someone who has,' Ruby said.

A WVS lady bustled up. 'Then you'll wait forever, Mrs . . .' she peered at the label on Ruby's frock, '. . . O'Hagan. I doubt if anyone can accommodate two adults and three children.'

'You go, Ruby.' Beth gave her a little push. 'I'll meet you here, by the station, tomorrow. About two o'clock.'

'But I wanted us to be together!'

'That's out of the question, Mrs O'Hagan. Miss Scanlon has kindly offered to take you. I'd appreciate it if you left immediately. You're holding up the proceedings.'

Miss Scanlon led them towards a small Morris saloon. She chatted amiably throughout the journey. Ruby sat in the back, hardly answering, hugging the silent children and blinking back the tears. It was bad enough leaving Arthur; she hadn't expected to be parted from Beth as well.

'Here we are!' They stopped outside a smart semi-detached house on the outskirts of the town. 'I'll take the bags, you look after your little girls,' Miss Scanlon said helpfully. 'You must all feel very strange.'

The house was pleasant inside. The furniture was light oak. Patterned rugs were scattered over the polished floors and there were numerous bowls of roses: red roses, yellow, and a lovely peachy colour. Their heady perfume filled the house. Yet Ruby experienced the same sinking sensation she'd had on first entering Foster Court, when she went into the place where they were now to live.

Greta started to cry.

'Don't like here, Mammy,' Heather whispered.

'Shush, both of you.'

They were shown upstairs. 'I decided to let the evacuees have the big room, it accommodates more beds. I've moved into the back.' Miss Scanlon waved her arm at the double bed with its flowered eiderdown. Two campbeds were made up with blankets.

'It's kind of you to put us up,' Ruby muttered.

'I'm only too pleased to do my bit, Mrs O'Hagan.'

★

The bed was comfortable, they all slept well on their first night, the food was well-cooked and plentiful. Miss Scanlon was doing her best to be friendly and make them feel at home.

But it *wasn't* home. Greta and Heather didn't know where to play and Ruby didn't know where to put herself. The parlour seemed out of bounds, the living room had Miss Scanlon in it most of the time and they felt in the way. The garden contained only rose bushes and a vegetable patch. It was impossible to run around – Heather tried and badly scratched her arm. The bedroom was the only place where they could be alone, yet it felt rude to shut themselves away for long periods.

It was a relief, after dinner, to catch a bus to the town centre to meet Beth.

The bus dropped them off in Lord Street, a lovely wide boulevard with trees down the centre, where Ruby used to go shopping with Emily. The weather was as lovely as the day before. 'We'll go to the sands later,' Ruby promised. 'After we've met Beth and Jake and had a cup of tea.'

'When we see Arfur?' Greta asked in a quivery voice.

'I'm not sure, love, soon.'

The small face crumpled. 'Wanna go home to Arfur.'

'We will, eventually.'

Beth was late. Ruby's nerves were already on edge, Greta made no secret of how miserable she felt, and Heather quickly got bored while they sat on a bench outside the station, complaining about her scratched arm.

Two hours later, when Beth and Jake still hadn't arrived Ruby, deeply concerned, gave up. By now, Greta was sobbing helplessly, demanding they go home to Arthur, and Heather was in a filthy temper. She took them for the promised cup of tea and a brief play on the sands, then caught the bus back to Miss Scanlon's.

'Have you got the telephone number of anyone in the WVS?' she asked the woman anxiously.

'I'm afraid not, dear. Is something wrong?'

'I've lost my friend. She didn't turn up and I've no idea where she is.'

'She can't have gone far, Mrs O'Hagan. I shouldn't let it worry you.'

It worried Ruby all night long. When Beth didn't turn up at the station the following day, it worried her even more. She called the Malt House from a telephone box and asked Martha Quinlan if she knew where Beth and Jake might be. Martha had no idea, but promised to try and find out.

'If you speak to her, tell her I'll be at the station at two o'clock every day until she comes.'

Two more days were to pass before a perspiring Beth bearing a carrier bag and a grizzling Jake turned up at Southport station. 'I think he's cutting a tooth.' Beth's pretty face collapsed and she burst into tears. 'Oh, Rube! We're living in this horrible place, miles from anywhere. This woman, Mrs Dobbs, she's got five children, and considers me a maid-of-all-work. I couldn't get away, there's no buses, and one of the kids broke the pushchair. I share a camp bed with Jake and we've hardly slept at all.'

'Sit down, love,' Ruby said angrily. 'Here, give me Jake.'

'I'm not going back, Rube,' Beth sobbed. 'I've brought our things. I don't care about the pushchair. I walked for ages until I came to a bus stop. I've never prayed so much that you'd be here.'

'Of course you're not going back. Somehow or other, we'll find a WVS woman and she can get you somewhere else to stay.'

'No, she won't, Ruby. The other night, the day we came, we waited till it was dark, but no one wanted Jake and me. There was just us left and the woman in charge had to take us back to her house. Next day, she drove us into the depths of the countryside and dumped us on Mrs Dobbs.'

'But you and Jake looked dead respectable compared to most of the others. I thought you'd be taken straight after us.'

'You don't understand, do you, Ruby?' Beth stopped crying and managed to smile ruefully at her friend.

'What's there to understand?'

'We're coloured, me and Jake,' she said in a matter-of-fact voice.

'I know you're coloured,' Ruby said impatiently, 'a very nice colour as it happens. What's wrong with that?'

'Not everyone's as tolerant as you. It's all right round Toxteth and Dingle where there's lots of black people, but there's parts of Liverpool where we wouldn't exactly be welcome.'

Ruby wiped Jake's tearful face with her hanky. He was a lovely baby with a lovely nature. It was beyond her comprehension how anyone could be prejudiced towards an innocent one-year-old child because he wasn't white. 'What's going to happen now?' she asked Beth.

'I'm going home, that's what, back to Arthur.'

'Come back with us,' Ruby said tersely. 'Miss Scanlon won't mind if I explain what's happened. There's plenty of room. I can sleep in the big bed with the girls and you and Jake can have a camp bed each.'

Miss Scanlon listened, her mild face expressionless, while Ruby explained the reason for Beth and Jake's presence, finishing with, 'You don't mind if they stay, do you?'

'Show your friend where's she's to sleep, then I'd like a word with you in private, Mrs O'Hagan.' Her voice was as expressionless as her face.

Ruby returned downstairs alone when the sleeping arrangements had been sorted out. She found Miss Scanlan in the kitchen. 'You wanted to speak to me?' she said with a smile, grateful that the woman had been so willing to help.

Miss Scanlan turned and Ruby felt her blood turn to ice when she saw the look of hatred in her eyes, her ugly twisted lips. 'I don't appreciate having niggers brought into my home,' she spat. 'I'd have turned her and her nigger baby out on the spot if it hadn't been for the fact I've got a weak heart and I couldn't have stood a scene. But I want them out tomorrow, first thing. After they've gone, *you* can wash the things they've used; the dishes, the cutlery, the bedding. I'm not touching them.'

It took several seconds for the odious words to sink in, and when they did Ruby could hardly speak for the ball of anger in her throat. 'Don't worry,' she said in a voice she hardly recognised as her own, 'they won't use any of your precious things, because they're going home, Beth and Jake. And me and my children are going with them.'

The woman must have realised she had gone too far. She immediately changed her tune. 'But there's no need for you to go, Mrs O'Hagan,' she cried. 'You and me, we'll get along fine. You talk nice, your children have lovely manners. Lord knows who I'll get landed with if you leave.'

'*You* don't talk nice, Miss Scanlan. Oh, your accent's posh enough, but what you say is filthy. I don't want someone like you anywhere near my girls. You're worse than Hitler with your views.

133

Oh, and I hope tomorrow you get landed with a family of gorillas. At least they'll have better manners than you.'

'I don't know why we had to up and leave so suddenly,' Beth said on the train back to Liverpool. 'That woman seemed OK to me. I was looking forward a nice long kip.'

'Has there been the faintest sign of an air raid since we left?'

'No, but . . .'

'Well, that's why we went away in the first place, isn't it?' Ruby raised her eyebrows, daring Beth to argue. 'To escape the raids. It seemed daft to stay. None of us were happy there. Were we girls?' Greta and Heather emphatically shook their heads. 'Even Jake has bucked up since we got on the train.' Jake was gurgling happily at everyone. Ruby sighed blissfully. 'Another few stops and we'll be home.'

To their surprise, when the small company entered the coal yard, the door to Arthur's house was open and there was a strange young man standing in the hall.

'Who are you?' Ruby demanded.

'I'm Doctor Brooker,' the man said crisply. 'Who are you?'

'Ruby O'Hagan and I live here. All of us do.'

'You're acquainted with Mr Arthur Cummings?'

'I must be, mustn't I, if I live here? What does Arthur want with a doctor?'

'Would you mind coming inside, please?'

'Where's Arthur?'

'I'll tell you inside.'

'What's the matter, Rube?' Beth asked shakily.

'I don't know. Let's go in and find out.'

'I'm afraid there's bad news,' Dr Brooker said gravely when the women were seated. By now they had realised that must be the case, but weren't prepared for how bad the news actually was. 'I'm sorry to say that last night Arthur Cummings died peacefully in his sleep. He suffered no pain. Indeed, there was a smile on his face when he passed away. He was eighty-one years old. I pray I live so long myself and die so happily.' He spoke gently. 'Are you relatives?'

'No, friends,' Ruby whispered. Beth began to cry. The little girls caught her mood and cried with her, little hacking sobs, as it dawned on them that their dear Arthur was dead.

'I'm so sorry,' Dr Brooker murmured.

'Is he still here? I'd like to say goodbye – we all would.'

'He was taken to the morgue only minutes before you arrived. It's not long since his body was found. The young man, Herbie, was worried there was no sign of life when he returned this evening with the cart. Apparently, Mr Cummings always came out to greet him.'

'He'd still be alive if we hadn't gone away,' Ruby said, her voice suddenly harsh. 'It was us going that finished him off. Five days, the war's only started five days ago, and already we've lost someone we love.'

It was the saddest night they'd ever known. The children were worn out and went to bed willingly. Greta and Heather were upset about Arthur, but not old enough to mourn. Ruby and Beth stayed up until the early hours, talking about their old friend, reminiscing, crying sporadically, taking turns to comfort each other. They blamed themselves for deserting him.

When Beth began to fall asleep in front of her eyes, Ruby made her go upstairs, then stayed in the chair, staring at the empty fireplace, while other thoughts flitted in and out of her mind. The scene with Miss Scanlon had brought home to her an aspect of life she hadn't known existed; colour prejudice. She would never repeat to Beth the terrible things that Miss Scanlon had said, but the words would forever stay seared on her soul.

Her thoughts turned to Jim Quinlan, as they often did when she was alone. They'd only met a few times since the party in the Malt House. Looking into his warm eyes, she'd hoped to see something more than the friendly interest he took in everybody's affairs, but had looked in vain. Ruby sighed. Even if he considered her the most desirable woman in the world, she couldn't imagine Jim Quinlan allowing himself to show a scrap of interest when he thought she was married.

Next morning, there were practical issues to consider. Would the landlord let them have the house? Beth wondered aloud.

'Not unless we take over the yard as well. They both go together. I don't know about you, but I don't fancy running a coal business.'

'I didn't think of that. Which reminds me, I'll just have a word with Clifford. Just because he's a horse, it doesn't mean he won't be as upset as anyone that Arthur's gone.'

Herbie arrived soon afterwards, wanting to know if he should deliver the coal as usual and who would pay him if he did. 'And there's more needs ordering. We're running low.'

'I think you should nip round the landlord's first, tell him about Arthur,' Ruby advised. 'Things need sorting out.'

'Would he let our dad take over the place, d'you think?' Herbie asked, his young face bright with hope. 'He lost his leg on the docks a few years back, our dad, then our mam did a bunk and we lost the house an' all. Me and him and our Mary have been living in rooms ever since. We could run the place together. Mary could do the paperwork, she's good at sums. We talked about it last night.'

'All you can do is ask, Herbie. If you move in, I won't have to worry about Clifford being looked after.'

Beth came up and overheard the last remark. 'No, but you can start worrying about something else, Ruby – where are *we* going to live?'

'I know exactly where we're going to live,' Ruby sang. 'In a nice, detached, five-bedroomed house overlooking Princes Park.'

'What if she comes back, this Mrs Hart?' Beth asked next day as they toured the house, upstairs and down. The girls ran ahead, gleefully exploring, Arthur forgotten. Jake tottered along on his chubby legs, clutching his mother's hand.

'She went to America to escape the war. She's not likely to come back now it's started, is she?'

'I'll be worried all the same.'

'So will I, a bit, but I'd sooner be worried than live somewhere like Foster Court. I'd write and ask Mrs Hart if it'd be all right if we stayed, but her sister's address turned out to be a laundry list when I opened the envelope with the keys. She was always a bit of a scatterbrain. Isn't everywhere lovely and big!'

The hall and the landing were enormous and four of the spacious bedrooms had bay windows with padded seats – one was still full of Max Hart's childish toys. The furniture was old and shabby and the carpets as faded as the curtains and the upholstered suites in the two big reception rooms at the front. Here and there, a young Max had scribbled with a crayon on the pale, knobbly wallpaper, though was unlikely to have been chastised by his indulgent mother. Mrs Hart hadn't thought to cover the furniture or put things away before she set sail for America. The beds hadn't been made, there was half-finished knitting in the kitchen where dishes had been left to drain. Ruby hadn't felt inclined to tidy up the times she'd come to make sure everything was all right.

'It looks as if she's just popped out to do a bit of shopping,' Beth remarked. 'It's creepy. She's even left a record on the gramophone with the lid up. It's full of dust.'

Ruby thought the place had a run-down, appealing charm that hadn't been evident in the more sumptuously furnished Brambles. 'Stop moaning and count your blessings,' she said sternly.

'Oh, I'm counting them, don't worry.' Beth smiled. 'I never dreamt I'd ever live in a house like this. Bagsy me a bedroom overlooking the park.'

'Bagsy me the other. Anyway,' Ruby frowned and looked thoughtful, 'I think it best if we kept to the back, downstairs too, we'll use the living room next to the kitchen, so as few people will notice us as possible, but we'll have to think of a story for the neighbours to explain why we're here – say we're housesitting, for instance, that we've got permission to stay. We'll have to get some blackout curtains. It's lucky Mrs Hart put sticky tape on the windows before she went away.'

'There's a sewing machine in the little bedroom, a treadle. Me mam had one the same at home. It'll do to sew the blackout curtains – and I can make us some clothes.'

They returned downstairs, leaving Greta and Heather trying out the inside lavatory. 'I'll arrange to have the mains turned on,' Ruby said, thinking aloud. 'I'll say I'm Mrs Hart's daughter if anyone asks. It means we'll have bills to pay, electricity, gas. Tomorrow, I'll start work again. Probably no one's noticed I've been gone – there wasn't time to tell them.'

'Oh, this is the gear!' Beth picked Jake up and gave him a little excited twirl. 'You're a miracle worker, Ruby O'Hagan, you really are. I'm ever so glad I met you.'

'You can thank Jake's dad for that. Don't forget, it was him you met first.'

Chapter 7

It wasn't long, a matter of weeks, before Ruby was forced to declare the pawnshop runner another casualty of war. Most of her former customers no longer needed to pawn their valuables. Unemployment had vanished at a stroke and wages had risen. Women were taking over men's jobs, earning fabulous amounts in factories. They delivered post, read meters, joined the Forces, became tram and bus conductors, did all sorts of jobs that had once been the preserve of males.

The world had changed. There was a different spirit in the air. Germany had laid down a challenge and the British people had taken it up with enthusiasm. The pawnshop runner was out of date. She belonged to a world that no longer existed. Ruby would have to find another, quite different job.

Ironically, the new poor were women with families whose husbands had been called up. They were allowed a pitiful sum to make up for the breadwinner being away risking his life for his country.

'Why aren't you getting an allowance?' Beth enquired when Ruby, rather foolishly, conveyed this piece of information and expressed her disgust. 'You've got a husband in the Army.'

'I told you, it's pitiful.'

'How much is pitiful?'

'About twenty-five shillings,' Ruby replied, uncomfortably aware the conversation had taken a dangerous turn.

'Twenty-five bob!' Beth gaped. 'Don't be daft, we could do a lot with that.'

Ruby yawned. 'I can't be bothered applying.'

'I'm surprised you didn't get it automatically as soon as Jake joined up.'

'Are you?' She couldn't think of anything else to say.

Beth went into the kitchen and Ruby to the garden to watch the children play. She gave a sigh of relief, thinking the subject of allowances had been dropped, but her interrogator appeared a few minutes later.

'Why are you known as Ruby O'Hagan, not Veering?'

'Why not?' Ruby countered weakly.

'Because it's what happens when people get married, soft girl. The woman takes the man's name. Me, I was looking forward to becoming Mrs Veering.' Her eyes narrowed. 'You and Jake weren't married, were you? Don't argue,' she snapped, when Ruby opened her mouth to insist they were. 'I know for sure because there's no way in the world you'd turn down twenty-five bob without good reason.'

'Oh, all right, we weren't.' Ruby shrugged.

Beth went pale. 'So, he *could* have married me.' She burst into tears. 'I've always told meself he went away with a broken heart because we couldn't get wed.'

'Well you were wrong.' Ruby was inclined to give the occasional emotional outbursts concerning Jacob short shrift. 'I bet he went away happier than he'd been in a long time. He was escaping from us both, not to mention his children – including Jake.'

'You're as hard as nails, Ruby O'Hagan.'

'No, I'm not. I'm a realist. I've never seen the point of crying over spilt milk. We've got more important things than Jacob to think about at the moment – ourselves. I'm not making enough for us to live on. I need to find another job. Just try thinking about that!'

'I've already thought about it.' Beth sniffed and wiped her eyes with her sleeve. 'Why don't *I* get a job instead of you?'

Ruby stifled a laugh. Beth was upset enough, it wouldn't do to upset her further, but what on earth could she *do*? She thought the world of her, but to put it bluntly, Beth was useless. She wasn't very strong nor particularly clever. She glided dreamily through life and nothing could hurry her. Looking after children, doing housework, was the most she could be trusted with. 'What sort of job?' Ruby asked, feigning interest.

'In one of them munition factories. You said yourself the wages were good. I can be the husband for a change. You can stay at home and be the wife.'

'You think you can manage that, do you?'

'Well, I can try.'

'All right then, try.' Ruby hid a smile, knowing it would all end in the inevitable tears and she'd be looking for a job herself in a few weeks' time. She could take over Beth's! 'Let's see how you get on.'

Ten days later, Beth started work as a fly presser at A. E. Wadsworth Engineering, a small factory on the Dock Road that had recently converted to war work.

'I'm going to stamp out parts for aeroplanes,' she said importantly when she returned from the interview. 'The wages are three pounds, five and six a week. I get a five bob rise after six months. It's ever such hard work.' She grimaced. 'You should see the size of the press I have to operate. It's *huge*.'

The first day she came home, her hands wouldn't stop shaking and she went to bed straight away. During the night, Ruby heard her sobbing quietly, but decided to leave her to it, doubting that she'd last the week.

On the second day, her right arm was paralysed from using the heavy machine and she could hardly walk from the tram stop on her swollen feet. She refused anything to eat and cried again in bed.

Wednesday, she cried before she went to bed. The women she worked with were horrible and the men made fun. 'One of 'em said I had the strength of a gnat.'

'Cheek!' Ruby expostulated.

Thursday, she arrived with a bandage on her thumb. 'I caught it in the machine.'

'Is it still all there?'

'The machine or me thumb?'

'I don't care about the machine. What about your thumb?'

'It's just bruised, Rube. Don't worry.'

Ruby worried again on Friday when there was no sign of Beth by half-past five. She arrived two hours later, slightly unsteady on her feet, and looking twenty years older than at the beginning of the week. 'I went for a drink with me mates,' she announced. 'I'm a little bit tiddley.'

'Mates!' Ruby shrilled. 'What mates? I thought everyone was

horrible or made fun. You've got a cheek! I took ages making your tea and now it's ruined. I'm not making another.'

'S'all right, Rube. I'm not hungry.' Minutes later, she was fast asleep in the chair.

Ruby wouldn't have felt quite as irritated at the way things had turned out if she hadn't found it so hard to look after three small children as well as clean a very large house and keep the garden tidy. Now that Jake was walking, he couldn't be let out of sight.

'We need a playpen,' she informed his mother.

'I'll buy one as soon as I can afford it,' Beth promised in the same airy tone Ruby used to adopt in Arthur's house when told something was urgently required.

Greta and Heather demanded constant attention. 'How am I supposed to play with you, keep an eye on Jake, clean this place, and prepare the food?' Ruby shrieked.

'Beth didn't shout at us,' growled Heather.

Six months later, in March, Beth got the promised five shilling raise. She loved her job and claimed it made her feel very much part of the war effort.

Ruby sulked. She didn't feel she was contributing anything towards the war. By now, a playpen had been acquired, the girls were encouraged to help with the housework, a rota had been drawn up so only a certain number of tasks were carried out each day. There was time for a walk to the shops each morning, a visit to the park in the afternoon, an occasional ride into town on the tram. She responded to the call to 'Dig for Victory', and planted vegetables in the garden.

But it wasn't enough. She was bored out of her skull. Martha Quinlan suggested she join the WVS and Ruby said she'd love to, 'But what would I do with the children?'

'We can have meetings in your nice big house,' Martha said. 'You don't have to be an active member like me. We meet regularly to roll bandages, knit blankets, make toys, do all sorts of useful things. Before Christmas, we made gift parcels for the troops. Last week, we stuffed mattresses for evacuees – some of the poor little mites still wet their beds.'

Ruby agreed. It was better than nothing.

There was a meeting the following week. The children were lectured beforehand on the necessity of behaving themselves, and about a dozen women of various ages turned up armed with refreshments and a pile of old sheets to be turned. This involved tearing the sheets in two, cutting away the frayed centre, and sewing the good ends together to make another, almost new. The women were delighted to discover the sewing machine and took turns using it, apart from Ruby who wanted nothing to do with the damn thing.

It turned out to be an unexpectedly enjoyable afternoon. They told jokes, some quite near the knuckle, gossiped, and sorted out the war between them. When they were leaving, one of the younger women approached Ruby. 'Would you mind if I brought my kids next week? I have to leave them with me mam and she moans like hell. They could play in the garden. One of us could be designated to look after them.'

'I'll do it,' Ruby offered, groaning inwardly. She didn't like children much apart from her own and Jake, but she disliked sewing even more. Still, she wanted to do something towards the war effort and it didn't mean she had to like it.

'I'll tell Freda. She can bring her kids too.'

'If you're looking after eight children, two more wouldn't make much difference, would it, Rube?' Beth remarked a few weeks later.

'What do you mean?' Ruby asked suspiciously.

'It's just that Olive Deacon, one of the women in the factory, is having to leave because her mam's gone in hospital and there's no one who'll have her two little boys. They're lovely, Rube, honest. Olive showed us their photey once.'

'Most kids look nice in photographs. And I'd be having them every day, not once a week like now.'

'Ah, come on, Rube,' Beth said in her most cajoling voice. 'If Olive leaves, they'll get someone else who won't be nearly as good. She's one of our best workers. In a way, it's your patriotic duty to look after her kids. She'll pay, naturally.'

'You bitch!' Ruby hissed. 'OK, I'll have them.'

Roy and Reggie Deacon were little horrors. They told lies, fought with the girls, and taught Jake to wee against the trees. One day, when Ruby thought they were innocently occupied upstairs, she discovered them playing with Max Hart's well-preserved toys and had beheaded several wooden soldiers and unstuffed a bear. She comforted herself with the thought that Roy was starting school in September and without him Reggie might behave when he was outnumbered two to one by the girls.

But when September came, Roy's place was taken by a girl called Mollie whose mother also worked with Beth. Mollie was more badly behaved than Roy and Reggie put together and broke a pretty vase on her first day, one of the few valuable objects in the house that hadn't been pawned. Ruby gritted her teeth and told herself she was doing her patriotic duty though wasn't sure if she believed it. Nevertheless, she threw herself whole-heartedly into the task of looking after the children, just as she had done with the cleaning jobs which she'd loathed almost as much.

For almost a year, the bulk of the population had remained unaffected by the war. France had fallen, thousands of French and British troops had been rescued in the great evacuation of Dunkirk, the slaughter on the seas at the hands of German U-boats was horrific. Martha Quinlan was in a constant state of fear for Jim – so was Ruby, though she told no one. These events occurred outside the lives of ordinary people. Although food rationing was in place, the main inconvenience was the tiny amount of tea allowed. But when, in June, 1940, the air-raid siren sounded for the first time, the fact of war became a brutal reality.

Ruby had prepared a shelter in the vast cellar which was as big as the ground floor area of the house and separated into four sections by thick, brick walls. It was full of mysterious lengths of timber, boxes of books and old clothes, furniture even older than that upstairs, rolls of tattered linoleum and carpet. She cleaned one of the sections, laid a carpet, and furnished it with two discarded easychairs, a sofa with a curled end which she covered with a blanket to hide the holes, and a folding bed. Jake's cot, which he didn't use any more but could still squeeze into, was brought down. She fixed a splint on a table which had a broken leg, and filled a box with matches, candles, an assortment of books and board games, and a pack of cards. Then she prayed the shelter would never be used. But her prayers were in vain.

Beth was a light sleeper and heard the siren first. She woke Ruby and they ushered the children into the cellar. Jake stayed asleep and the others played Snap and drank lemonade, while gunfire rumbled in the distance. After about an hour, the all clear sounded and they returned upstairs.

'Well, that wasn't so bad, was it?' Ruby commented.

'It was scarcely worth breaking our sleep for,' grumbled Beth.

The next time the siren went, the gunfire sounded closer and they thought they could hear a plane and hoped it wasn't German. The following day, they heard that six bombs had landed harmlessly in a field.

The siren continued to sound throughout July and bombs continued to drop on fields on the outskirts of the city. Ruby and Beth decided these incidents weren't worth getting out of bed for, but two weeks later, in August, four people were killed and several injured when a stick of bombs fell on Wallasey.

'Jaysus!' Beth gasped when she heard. '*Killed*!' They looked at each other with scared eyes.

Ruby nodded bleakly. 'It's the cellar from now on. No more staying in bed when the siren goes.'

It seemed to happen all of a sudden, as if the Luftwaffe had been playing with them and had now decided that it was no longer a game. The raids continued, getting heavier, lasting longer, until one night saw three separate raids on Liverpool causing serious damage throughout the city and killing more people.

The unthinkable had finally happened. In the cellar, Ruby and Beth listened to the planes droning overhead, the bombs screaming to earth, the inevitable explosions, and wondered how such madness could have been allowed to happen. Their worst nightmare had become a reality.

'I'm almost glad Arthur died when he did,' Ruby said softly. 'At least he missed all this.'

There was one good thing to be thankful for; Greta and Heather regarded the raids as a great adventure. They enjoyed playing games and being read to in the middle of the night and Jake usually slept through everything.

No matter how little sleep she'd had, Beth always left promptly for work. One morning, after Beth had gone and Mollie and Roy Deacon had arrived and the five children were in the living room with drawing pads, crayons, and Max Hart's wooden blocks, Ruby went into the kitchen and was washing the dishes when she heard scratching on the back door. She opened it to find a skeletal cat outside. It miaowed weakly when it saw her, walked shakily inside, then flopped in a heap of scraggy, tortoiseshell fur on to the floor.

'Tiger!' Ruby fell to her knees and stroked the strangely thin, furry body. 'Oh, Tiger, what's happened to you? You're no more than skin and bone.' Tiger regarded her pathetically with his amber eyes. 'Let's get you some milk.'

She poured milk into a saucer and the cat managed to raise his head and lap most of it up. He ate half a slice of bread and Marmite, then Ruby wrapped him in a piece of old blanket and cuddled him, sniffing tearfully, the dishes forgotten. Greta came in and was instructed to look under the stairs for his basket.

'I can remember seeing it there,' said her mother.

Tiger was put in front of the fire with stern instructions he wasn't to be touched. 'He's not well,' Ruby said. 'I'm nursing him better.'

'I can't stand cats,' Beth said when she came home and was informed of Tiger's presence.

'You'd better learn to stand this one because he's staying.'

'What if the woman he was left with comes looking for him?'

'It's taken weeks, possibly months, for him to get in such a state. If anyone was going to look for him, they'd have done it long before.'

'Ruby?' Martha Quinlan said in the tone of voice of someone about to ask a favour.

'Yes, Martha?' Ruby rolled her eyes and wondered what the favour was.

'You know Mrs Wallace who has a wart on her nose and who sometimes comes to meetings? Well, her granddaughter, Connie, lives in Essex, but she's coming to work in Rootes' Securities in Speke and needs somewhere to live. Her gran can't take her, the poor dear only lives in lodgings.'

'What d'you want me to do, build her a house?'

Martha grinned. 'No, luv, put her up. You've plenty of room. The extra few bob a week will come in handy, won't it? Connie's giving up a wonderful job in order to serve her country. She's a beautician in a posh London hotel, the Ritz, or something. She wanted to join the forces but they wouldn't take her because her sight's not too good, so she decided on munitions instead.'

'Don't they have munition factories down south?'

'Of course, luv, but her mam's dead, her dad's been transferred to Scotland for some reason, and her brother's in the Army. She thought it would be nice to be near her gran.'

'OK,' Ruby said with a sigh. It was a waste of time trying to refuse. Her patriotic duty would be called into question and she'd be made to feel guilty. 'Will she expect to be fed?'

'Only breakfast and an evening meal, luv.'

'Is that all?'

Mrs Hart's linen cupboard was raided and a bed prepared for Connie Wallace whose bespectacled, perfectly made-up face had to be seen to be believed. She was a plain woman made striking by the skilful use of cosmetics. Her eye shadow was two different shades of blue and the lashes were so long that Ruby and Beth were green with envy until told that they were false. Rouge was applied with a brush and lipstick with a pencil. 'They're from America,' she said. There was a beauty spot on her chin when she remembered.

Her spectacles were shaped like bird's wings, the frames black flecked with gold, also from America. 'I'm terrified of breaking them, because they can't be replaced till this ruddy war's over.'

In the cellar during the raids, she taught Ruby and Beth how to apply make-up so it showed off their best features, though the exercise usually ended in shrieks of laughter.

By now, the evidence of the damage caused by the raids was all around them. Houses had been replaced by mounds of rubble or just the roofless skeleton left, like a grotesque statue, the sky visible though the gaps that had once been windows. Churches had been damaged, hospitals, schools, cinemas, numerous factories. Hundreds of people had been killed and hundreds more injured.

Ruby wondered how she, how everyone, managed to carry on. Yet somehow they did, and mainly, they managed to do it with a smile and a cheerfulness that was catching, including Ruby herself. She had no choice. It was either that or be miserable and admit defeat, and there was no way Ruby O'Hagan would do either.

In November, two things happened, both totally unexpected.

Beth always arrived home with the *Liverpool Echo*, which Ruby would read if she had time. The paper wasn't only concerned with war news. Other things, mundane in comparison, were happening on the domestic front. People were getting married for one, and having their wedding photographs published. Ruby never read the weddings page, but one night a man's vaguely familiar face caught her eye as she was about to turn over. Interested, she scanned the text beneath.

'The marriage took place last Saturday at the Holy Name church, Fazakerley, between Mr William Simon Pickering and Miss Rosemary Louise McNamara . . .'

Her insides did a somersault and she read no more.

Bill Pickering! He wasn't dead. Jacob hadn't killed him after all. He'd been alive all this time.

'What's the matter, Rube?' Beth asked in a concerned voice. 'You've gone as white as a sheet.'

'Nothing.' It had all been in vain – the running away, the years spent in Foster Court. She could have stayed in Brambles and Jacob could have continued to work on the farm. By now, she would have long grown out of him, she felt sure of that. She bunched the paper in a ball and threw it across the room.

'I thought we were supposed to save waste paper?' said Beth.

'We are.' The gesture had got rid of some of her anger. Things that had happened couldn't be undone. Anyway, had things gone differently, she wouldn't have had her girls.

It was Beth who discovered Jacob Veering was dead. A woman at work had shown her a photograph of her brother who was in the Royal Tank Regiment and shortly due home on leave. 'He was with this other chap in the photey. They had their arms around each other. I couldn't believe me eyes when I saw the other chap was Jake. "Who's that?" I asked, pointing to him. Me heart was in me mouth. I wasn't sure what I wanted her to say, perhaps that Jake might be coming home with her brother. Instead, she said, "Oh, that's Jacob, one of Albie's friends. Poor chap got killed at Dunkirk." "Are you sure?" I asked. "Sure I'm sure," she said. "They were sitting next to each other waiting for a boat to fetch them home when the Jerries strafed the beach. Jacob was hit in the head. He died in Albie's arms. Albie was dead upset."

There was silence for a while, then Ruby sighed. 'Well, I'm glad he died in someone's arms.'

'Is that all you've got to say?'

'What d'you expect me to say, Beth?'

Beth was stronger now. She didn't cry. 'Oh, I dunno. I don't know what to say meself. I'm surprised I'm not more upset.'

'It means we're both widows, in a way. We're only twenty-two, we can have new relationships.' She thought of Jim Quinlan.

'I don't want a new relationship,' Beth said flatly. 'One was enough.'

Ruby wondered how she would tell people that the man who was supposed to be her husband was dead? She wasn't prepared to cry and mope around, pretend to be sad. Though, thinking about it, she *was* sad. Jacob was the father of her children, the first man she had ever loved. She hadn't even a photograph to show the girls when they grew up. 'This woman at work,' she said, 'would she loan you the photo to have a copy made?'

'What excuse would I give?'

'Use your imagination for a change and think of one.' Ruby went upstairs for a little cry.

By Christmas, they had another lodger, a fussy, mild-mannered young man called Charles Winner from Dunstable who took very seriously his position as the only man in the household. As an engineering draughtsman, he was in a reserved occupation and wouldn't be called up. He had moved to Liverpool to be near his girlfriend, Wendy, who was a WREN and had been posted to the Admiralty Operations Room in Water Street. Sometimes, Wendy slept overnight in the small bedroom, the only one now empty – at least Ruby presumed she slept in the small bedroom, but felt in no position to lay down the law if she didn't.

It seemed to have got around that Mrs Hart's house was somewhere people could stay if they were in Liverpool overnight, a few days, a week – Ruby suspected it was all Martha Quinlan's doing. If Wendy wasn't occupying the spare room, then more often than not someone else was: a serviceman on leave who couldn't stay with his family because they'd lost their house in a raid, or their girlfriends lived in places where men weren't allowed. Wives came to see their sailor husbands when their ships docked briefly in

Liverpool. When all the bedrooms were in use, people kipped down on a settee in one of the living rooms. They brought their ration books so the coupons could be used to buy the extra food.

Ruby was up at six every morning preparing half a dozen breakfasts. The children ate at a later sitting. She was never sure how many people would turn up for tea. During the day she looked after hordes of children, somehow managed to shop, and washed endless sheets and pillowcases so that the rack in the kitchen was always full of washing that took ages to dry and there was never time to iron – by now, Mrs Hart's linen cupboard had been stripped bare.

'You'd never guess. Tiger,' Ruby commented more than once, 'but I swore I'd never enter domestic service.'

Tiger was his old self again, possibly bigger than before. He was a very understanding cat and purred sympathetically whenever she complained.

'Another thing, I wanted to keep our presence in the house as unobtrusive as possible, but people come and go by the minute and the noise is horrendous. The neighbours must wonder if it's been turned into a hotel or a school.'

'Don't worry about it,' Tiger purred.

Christmas was less than a week away. A box of decorations had been discovered in the cellar, a paper tree. The living room at the back, supposedly private, but which everyone considered they were at liberty to use whenever they pleased, was festooned with chains, the tree decorated with gold and silver stars. Ruby made a Christmas cake that contained no eggs, very little fruit, and had only a thin suggestion of icing. Beth won a pudding in a raffle at work, and Connie had come by a turkey by mysterious means she wasn't prepared to divulge. Charles Winner was staying in Liverpool because Wendy hadn't been allowed leave. 'But she's coming to dinner on Christmas Day,' he told Ruby when he presented her with two bottles of sherry.

'That's nice of her !' Ruby remarked, seeing herself stuck in the kitchen just like any other day.

But Beth and Connie, who'd made herself very much at home, offered to do the cooking on the day. 'You won't have to lift a finger, Rube,' Beth promised.

Ruby began to look forward to the festivies. Suddenly, she didn't mind the house being full. For the first time, there was money to buy presents for the children, though finding them in the shops wasn't easy. She'd managed to get Greta and Heather a doll each, little shopping baskets, hairslides. There was a wheelbarrow for Jake, a toy bus, and a lovely enamelled compact for his mother. She rubbed her hands together excitedly. This year, Christmas was going to be the gear.

Apart from a few light raids that had caused little damage, December had been remarkably free from the attentions of the Luftwaffe. Liverpool breathed a sigh of relief and everyone anticipated a peaceful holiday.

But they were wrong.

Five days before Christmas, the siren went at half past six. Tiger, terrified, immediately made for the cellar. The children had eaten, but Ruby, Beth and Connie were in the middle of a meal. Charles wasn't yet home. They followed the big cat down the narrow wooden stairs with their food. When Ruby finished, she went back for the tea she wasn't prepared to waste, raid or no raid. She was about to return, when the front door opened and Charles came in accompanied by Wendy and another WREN, a pretty blonde. 'This is Rhona. She's on her way to see a friend, but I thought she could shelter with us until the raid's over. It's probably just a light one, but it's not worth taking the risk.'

'I hope you don't mind,' Rhona said.

'Of course, I don't mind.' Ruby gave her a warm, welcoming smile. 'You'd best get down the cellar quick. Take the pot and I'll fetch more cups.'

There'd never been a raid like it before. The world became one large, never-ending explosion. The house shook, dust drifted from the ceiling. Shut away as they were in the bowels of the earth, the sound of breaking glass could still be heard, the urgent clamour of fire engines, the occasional scream.

Even the children were frightened, not interested in games or stories tonight. The grown-ups hardly spoke, but looked at each other, biting their lips, when a bomb shrieked to earth, wondering if they were to be its target.

During a lull, Ruby went upstairs to make more tea, not caring if she used the entire week's ration. She drew back the curtains and looked at the crimson sky shot with streaks of black smoke. A fire crackled nearby. It was like a scene from hell.

'It looks as if it's been soaked with blood, the sky,' said a voice. It was Charles. 'I've come for the sherry,' he explained. 'I thought it might cheer us up a little. I know where I can get more tomorrow.'

'If there is a tomorrow.'

'Tomorrow always comes. Ruby.'

'It might not come for us,' Ruby said harshly. 'It's no good pretending everything's going to be all right, being positive, because we've lost control of our lives. In the past, no matter how bad things got, I'd grit me teeth and make them better. But now I can't. No one can.'

'In that case, you've just got to grit your teeth and hope for the best. Forget about the tea for now, let's have sherry instead. And I got you a box of chocolates for Christmas. I'll fetch them too.'

It cheered her that he'd thought to buy her a present. She'd got nothing for him or Wendy. She'd buy something — tomorrow!

Charles said, 'I don't know if it's just my imagination, but I can hear singing.'

'I'll just get some glasses.' Mrs Hart had some in her china cabinet. The children could have lemonade.

They returned to the cellar, where Rhona had removed her tunic, loosened her tie, and was leading a sing-song in a fine soprano voice. 'Good King Wenceslas looked down, on the feast of Stephen . . .'

Greta and Heather had livened up miraculously. They were singing along, bright-eyed and full of smiles. Jake didn't know the words, but stared intently at Rhona's pretty face and tried to mouth them. Beth glanced at Ruby and winked. 'Isn't this the gear!' she whispered. 'I can't hear the bombs any more.'

The sherry and lemonade were poured, the chocolates opened, spirits were lifted. Connie and Wendy danced an Irish jig and Ruby sang, 'Yours till the stars lose their glory', astonished to find she knew all the words. Greta and Heather recited a poem they'd learnt from Roy Deacon, unaware it was full of innuendo and *double entendres*. The audience laughed until their sides ached and drank more sherry.

'Do your impersonation of Paul Robeson,' Wendy urged Charles, so he sang 'Old Man River' in a deep, mournful voice that made them want to cry. Rhona cheered them up again with a chorus of carols.

Outside, bombs fell, the earth was being shaken to pieces, but they didn't hear, or pretended not to hear. They were too loud, too boisterous, needing to shut out reality in favour of make-believe.

It meant they didn't notice the candle flicker when the cellar door opened, or see the young man wearing an air force blue greatcoat limp down the stairs. 'Evening folks,' the young man said, bringing the entertainment to an abrupt halt. 'Hope I'm not interrupting, but do you mind if I join in?'

'Who are you?' demanded Ruby, but she knew before the words were out of her mouth. She hadn't met him before, but a photograph of the curly-haired young man with the same mischievous, smiling features was on the sideboard upstairs.

It was Max Hart.

'This is Max,' she said quickly to the assembled company, praying he wouldn't demand to know what they were doing in his mother's house. But he didn't look as if he was about to make a scene. Instead, despite his smile, he appeared bone weary, his young face creased with exhaustion. 'Max, meet Beth, Connie, Charles . . .' She reeled off the introductions.

'Take your coat off, luv, and sit down,' said Connie.

Removing the coat was easier said than done. Max could hardly raise his arms. Charles sprang forward to help.

'My God!' Charles gasped when the coat was off, revealing the blue-grey uniform underneath. 'You're a Flight Lieutenant and you've got the Distinguished Flying Cross.' He shook Max's hand vigorously, close to tears. 'This country owes everything to young men like you. You're the bravest of the brave. What was it Churchill said about the battle in the skies? "Never have so many owed so much to so few."'

Max Hart blushed uncomfortably. 'Would you mind if I had a drink?'

'It's only sherry,' said Ruby.

He managed a tired grin. 'That'll do fine.' He went on to explain it had taken two days to get from his base in Kent using public transport or hitching lifts. 'An ambulance at one point. In Bedford, a chap lent me his bike to get as far as Northampton where I left it with his cousin. The cousin used his entire petrol ration to take me to Birmingham.' He'd slept on a train and had arrived in Liverpool only an hour ago and, ignoring the danger, began to walk. 'Then this Civil Defence chap stopped and gave me a lecture and a lift. I've got ten days leave on account of the fact I sprained my damn ankle. I was determined to spend Christmas in my own home, don't ask why.' He grinned again. 'I think I wanted to be assured there were a few remnants of normality left in the world, but instead I found Liverpool being blown to pieces and the house apparently haunted. It gave me a shock, I can tell you, when I heard singing from the cellar.'

'Didn't your mum tell you she said Ruby could have the house while she went to America?' Connie enquired.

'It must have slipped her mind,' Max replied with a straight face. 'Look, you were having a good time before I showed up. Please go on. It sounded fun, better any day than listening to the noise outside.' The bombardment was continuing unabated.

Rhona said, 'This is especially for you,' and began to sing, 'There's a boy coming home on leave . . .'

By midnight, they had begun to wilt, having run out of songs and energy, though the Luftwaffe showed no sign of wilting and the bombs continued to rain down. Thankfully, the children had gone to sleep. They talked instead.

'I know who you are,' Max said quietly to Ruby. 'The pawnshop runner. Mum said you were like an exotic stick insect.'

'I don't know if that's a compliment or not!'

'I'd take it as a compliment if I were you.' He winked. 'Out of interest, what are you doing here?'

She'd known this was coming. 'Your mam asked if I'd keep an eye on the house,' she explained, 'but when me and Beth were desperate for somewhere to live, I thought it wouldn't hurt to move in, just us two and the children. But I kept being told it was my patriotic duty to take in more people or look after other women's children. I suppose,' she added ruefully, 'it's all got out of hand. Lord knows what your mam'll say when she finds out.'

'Well, she won't find out from me. You're doing a great job while mum is having a grand time in the States according to her letters. Let's regard it as *her* contribution towards the war.'

'You're being very kind and understanding.'

'Don't mention it,' he said dismissively. 'I was halfway to Liverpool when I began to wonder if I was mad, wanting to spend

Christmas alone in a cold house where there wouldn't be any food. I've rarely been so pleased about anything as finding you here. Bloody hell, Tiger!' he exclaimed when the big cat appeared and launched itself on to his knee. 'I didn't know you were still around.'

'There's an old wardrobe he regards as his own special shelter.'

'Me and Tiger used to be best friends when I was home from university.' Tiger purred ecstatically as he feverishly licked the familiar face.

'It looks as if you still are.'

It was almost four when the all clear sounded. They looked at each other thankfully, knowing they'd shared an experience they would never forget. Charles insisted Max use his bedroom. 'I'll just get some clothes first . . .'

Ruby was the first to emerge from the cellar, half-expecting the house to have blown away and be met by open air. But Mrs Hart's house had survived. A strange, sour smell turned out to be soot which had fallen down all the chimneys. They went straight to bed. Heather shared Wendy's room and Charles slept on a settee.

Four hours later, everyone had gone to work as usual. Ruby peeped in to look at Max; he was dead to the world. Roy Deacon was delivered by his mother, but there was no sign of Mollie. The family had been sheltering in the understairs cupboard, Ruby learnt later, and the house had received a direct hit. Mollie, four years old, was dead.

The heavy raids continued in the run-up to Christmas. Ruby wondered if Hitler's aim was to wipe Liverpool and its people off the face of the earth as the terror continued, night after night. Max Hart didn't leave the house and spent much of his time in bed. He was having a lovely rest, he said, enjoying being made a desperate fuss of. People kept bringing him little treats; cream cakes, chocolate, a quarter bottle of whisky. The children had spent hours making a Christmas card especially for him – he had vowed to keep it for ever. The creases in his face had smoothed away, he looked more relaxed.

On Christmas Eve, Beth finished work at midday and announced she was taking Greta and Heather out to buy their mam a present.

'They haven't got any money,' said Ruby.

'I'll soon remedy that. I'll take Jake an' all, let him get some fresh air.'

It was the first time Ruby could recall being in the house alone since they'd moved in – she didn't count Max who was asleep upstairs. She sprawled in an armchair, luxuriating in the unaccustomed silence. When Beth returned, she might go out herself and buy a few last-minute presents. Although it was distressing to witness the devastation caused by the last day's raids, there was also the feeling of being lucky to be alive. So many people had died: people who had worked with Beth or Connie, or she knew slightly, such as Charlie Murphy who'd been their landlord in Foster Court. Arthur's little house in the coal yard had been damaged, though the occupants, Herbie and his family, were thankfully unhurt.

Ruby sighed and supposed she'd better get on with some work. She was heaving herself reluctantly out of the chair when she heard a shout, quickly followed by another and knew it could only be Max.

She raced upstairs and found him thrashing wildly about in the bed, covered in perspiration.

'Max!' She shook him. 'Max! Calm down. Everything's all right. You're quite safe.'

He opened his eyes and looked at her fearfully, like a small boy. 'I'm sorry. I was having this ghastly dream.'

'The dream's over now, love. You're safely at home with us.'

'God!' He shoved himself to a sitting position. 'It seemed so real.'

'What was it about?'

'I can only remember bits. I was in my plane, over Germany, and I'd lost my way. I didn't know how to get home. The world was drowned in blackness, not a light anywhere. I was worried for my crew, that I was letting them down. I began to panic . . .'

Ruby stroked his brow. 'It was only a dream. Here, have a drop of your whisky. It'll calm you down.'

'You're very kind,' he said when she put the glass in his hand.

'Why shouldn't I be?' she asked, surprised.

'You can't have a very high opinion of me. I presume you know why Mum had to pawn so many of her things.'

'To settle your debts at university. Yes, but it doesn't alter what you are now: a pilot in the Royal Air Force who won a medal for bravery.'

'I got in with this crowd of chaps who had money to burn,' he said ruefully. 'I wanted the things they had; clothes, a car. I spent a fortune on booze. We played cards, the minimum stake was a quid.'

'That's all in the past,' Ruby soothed.

'As for my medal, I don't deserve it. I'd only been in the air a matter of seconds when I came face to face with a bloody Heinkel. I knew my plane had been hit, but just carried on with what I was there for, to bring down every Jerry plane in sight. I got the Heinkel and half a dozen others. When I got back to base, there was a bullet in my shoulder.' He gave an ironic shrug. 'I hadn't felt a thing, but they gave me a medal all the same. The thing is,' he went on, suddenly angry, 'every man in every damn aircrew deserves a medal for bravery.' He frowned irritably. 'Why is this house so damn quiet? It feels eerie. And where's that bloody cat?'

'Everyone's out except you and me. Tiger was up a tree when I last saw him.'

His face crumpled. 'I was as mad as hell when mum said in a letter that she'd given him away.'

'He'll be here when you come back,' Ruby said consolingly.

'Will you be? Here when I come back, that is?'

'Only if you come back soon. As soon as the war ends, your mother will come home and we'll have to find somewhere else to live. Could I have your mother's address before you leave?'

'It's in my locker at the base. I'll have to send it to you.' He gave a satisfied sigh. 'It's nice, knowing you're here, keeping the place warm.'

He looked so young and vulnerable, had suffered so much, that Ruby felt an impulse to plant an affectionate, sisterly kiss on his cheek, though was unprepared for his response. Max immediately grabbed her and kissed her back in a way that was anything but brotherly.

'Max!' She was about to push him away, but hesitated. For months, he'd been risking his life for people like her. He could have died a hundred times. It wasn't much to ask, she thought impulsively, to give herself in return for the sacrifices he had made. She slid her arms around his neck.

'You're so lovely,' he was saying gruffly. 'I've been wanting to do this ever since we met.' There was desperation in the way his lean hands caressed her body, as if he was trying to shed the nightmare that was now his life and lose himself in the curves and secrets of a woman's body. She wondered if any female body would have done as she let him remove her clothes, at the same time she felt concerned that Beth might come home.

Max said no more, just gave a rapturous groan when he plunged inside her.

Ruby tenderly stroked his face, pretending to respond, appear as passionate as he was, listening with one ear for Beth and the children. All that mattered was that Max momentarily forgot the violent times in which they lived.

'That was wonderful,' he whispered when it was over and she lay in his arms. 'I'll come back for you one day.' His face was soft with emotion and he was about to kiss her again when a shout from down below made them both jump.

'I'd better go.' Ruby struggled into her clothes. At the door, she paused, 'It was wonderful for me too, Max.'

The siren went that night at seven and the onslaught didn't stop until the early hours of Christmas morning.

Dinner would have been a sober affair if they hadn't done their best to appear in good spirits for the sake of the children who had never received so many presents. Their happiness was infectious and by the end of the meal the good spirits were quite genuine.

'After all,' Charles pointed out, 'if the good Lord has seen fit to spare us, we should celebrate that fact, not mope.'

Max Hart left on Boxing Day. It could take days to return to the base in Kent. A friend of Charles had offered to take the young airman as far as Manchester from where he might catch a train – or he might not. Nothing was certain any more.

The car arrived at eight o'clock that morning. Everyone gathered outside the door to say goodbye. Max hugged the children, kissed the women, shook hands with Charles. 'It's been the best Christmas of my life,' he told them with a happy sigh.

'See you next Christmas, if not before,' Connie called as he backed towards the gate, waving all the time.

'Try and make it before,' shouted Beth.

Ruby held her hands to her face, not knowing what to say. Max was about to get in the car when she ran down the path.

'Take care Max,' she cried. 'I'll never forget you.'

She watched the car, waving frantically, until it turned a corner and Max was gone.

She never saw him again and he never sent his mother's address.

Chapter 8

In April, Greta started school. 'Why can't *I* go too?' demanded an outraged Heather.

'Because you're not old enough. You'll have to wait until next year.' Ruby badly missed her eldest daughter, though not Roy Deacon who'd started at the same time. It hurt, handing over the care of her precious child to strangers. Would they understand her nervous little ways, her shyness? Would she be bullied? If so, Ruby would descend upon the school and raise Cain. Heather sulked and worried Greta wouldn't cope without her.

Beth was informed that Ruby had exhausted her patriotic duty when it came to looking after other women's kids and not to bring any more home.

'Anything you say, Rube,' Beth replied easily. 'By the way, what's wrong with Charles?'

'I've no idea. I'll ask him.'

Charles was moping around like a sick puppy. Wendy had met someone else, he confessed when Ruby questioned the reason for his miserable face. The someone else was a sub-lieutenant in the Navy. 'It's the uniform,' he said gloomily. 'Men in civvies are at a distinct disadvantage these days.'

'I'll take him out of himself,' Connie Wallace vowed. 'I've always liked Charles and I don't give a damn about uniforms. After all, you can't wear 'em for the rest of your life. They've got to come off sometime, even if it's only for bed.'

Charles was taken out of himself so thoroughly that three months later the couple announced they were getting married.

'Straight away,' Connie said with a grin. 'Charles thinks it's silly to hang around while there's a war on, one of us could get killed any day,' which Ruby thought a touch morbid. She was pleased they wanted to continue living upstairs, sleeping in Connie's room which had a double bed and, if Ruby didn't mind, using the small bedroom for storage.

The wedding would take place two weeks on Saturday. Clothes rationing had just been introduced and Connie was given the choice of using all her precious coupons on a bridal gown or getting married in ordinary clothes.

'I always wanted a white wedding,' she said wistfully. 'But never mind, eh!'

But Beth had other ideas. She enjoyed showing off her skill on the sewing machine. A pair of Mrs Hart's lace curtains would make a fine wedding gown, she claimed. 'And there's enough for a veil, though you can't have it over your face, it's too thick.'

Roses from the garden would do for a bouquet and Martha Quinlan offered a supply of beer as her and Fred's present. The church wasn't far away so everyone could walk. The reception would be held in the house. There were some very old records under the gramophone for those who wanted to dance. Thirty guests had been invited.

'What am I supposed to give them to eat?' Ruby wanted to know. 'It takes me all my time to feed you lot.'

'Spam?' suggested Charles.

'Spam with what?'

'Just sliced on a plate with bread and pickles.'

'And when did you last see pickles in the shops?' Ruby replied tartly. 'I can't remember what a pickle looks like.'

'I'll show you what a pickle looks like.' Charles disappeared, returning minutes later with three large dust-covered jars which he put on the table with a thump. 'Pickled onions, pickled cabbage, pickled plums,' he announced, clearly enjoying the look of astonishment on Ruby's face.

'You don't pickle plums, you preserve them. Where did these come from?'

'The cellar. Max's mother must have done them.'

'Good gracious me! I never noticed before. Will they be all right after all this time? I don't want to spoil the wedding by poisoning the guests.'

'We'll try them out beforehand.'

'*You* can try them out beforehand, Charles. If you don't die, I'll serve them to your guests. It's a pity the apples aren't ripe yet, else I could have done something with them. And that rhubarb would make lovely wine, but one of the things they never taught us at the convent was how to make wine.'

Fortunately, the guests saw fit to contribute items of food towards the wedding do. The bridal pair began to bring home tins of Spam, fruit cocktail, peaches and cream that they'd been given. Charles's mother was fetching a cake from Dunstable, though as she said in her letter, it would be sadly lacking most of the essential ingredients.

Connie arrived one night with a basket containing a live rabbit. 'I got it off this chap at work. He can't feed it any more. Apparently, rabbit tastes just like chicken.'

Ruby screamed. 'Only when it's dead, and there's no way I'm going to kill the poor thing. It's beautiful.' The rabbit was sleekly black with two white paws. It was nibbling a piece of carrot, innocently unaware what fate might have in store.

'Chicken would be a real treat compared with Spam. Maybe Charles is willing to kill it,' Connie said thoughtfully.

'He can bone it and cook it too. I'd feel as if I was cooking Tiger.'

By the time Charles arrived, the children were playing with the rabbit and it had a name – Floppy. Tiger regarded it warily, unsure whether it was friend or foe.

Charles professed his unwillingness to lay a hand on the creature and Beth burst into tears at the very idea. 'I couldn't possibly eat it,' she cried. 'Anyroad, you can't take it off the children now. They love it.'

'You're nothing but a shower of yellow bellies,' Connie said scathingly.

'Why don't *you* kill it?' demanded Charles.

His bride-to-be shuddered delicately. 'Oh, I couldn't. It's much too cuddly.'

Mrs Hart had several glorious hats stored in boxes in her wardrobe. Ruby borrowed a navy-blue straw boater that went perfectly with her new blue and white flowered frock which had puffed sleeves and a sweetheart neck.

'You'll not come across a frock like this again until this ruddy war's over,' the shop assistant said sadly. 'From now on, they'll be made from the minimum amount of material. Puffed sleeves are definitely out.'

Beth's suit was strawberry red moygashel with a pleated skirt – pleats were something else that would take a long time to come back. With it, she wore Mrs Hart's cream organdie picture hat trimmed with silky cabbage roses.

'Don't we look wonderful!' Ruby sang on the morning of the wedding when they were dressed in their finery. 'I feel very elegant in this hat and you look like a Southern belle in yours – Vivien Leigh had better look out.' She turned to the bride. 'But neither of us can hold a candle to you, Connie. You're a sight for sore eyes. Mrs Hart would be thrilled to bits if she could see you in her curtains.'

Connie's perfectly painted face, surrounded by a frill of lace, glowed with happiness, and her eyes behind her smart glasses were misty with love for Charles, whose wife she would shortly become. She looked at herself in the full-length mirror. The dress had a high neck, long, tight sleeves and a gathered skirt with the curtains' original scalloped hem. 'This is the loveliest wedding dress in the world,' she said huskily. 'I couldn't have got anything half as nice from the poshest shop in London.' She flung her arms around Beth. 'Thank you! You've made my wedding day extra-special. I'll be grateful for as long as I live. And thank you, Ruby. You've worked wonders with the food. I bet Queen Elizabeth herself didn't sit down to such a grand do when she married the King.'

Ruby rescued her hat which had fallen off during Connie's emotional embrace. 'I bet she didn't sit down to rabbit either. I'm glad we didn't kill Floppy. It would have ruined the day – and such a glorious day too. The sun's hot enough to crack the flags and there's not a cloud in sight.'

Greta and Heather were bridesmaids, their frocks peach-coloured slipper satin made from the skirt of a genuine bridesmaid frock that had belonged to Agnes/Fay Quinlan. Jake was adorable in a borrowed page boy suit of blue velvet, only a mite too big.

People came to their doors on that lovely July day, to watch and wave, to clap and smile, to shout their good wishes, as the wedding procession made its way on foot to the church. Hearts were warmed and tears were shed as the bright little pageant passed, reminding them that great joy and happiness was still possible even if their country was embroiled in a vicious war.

They arrived at a scene of devastation, where two houses had recently stood. Connie removed a rose from her bouquet and threw it on to the tumble of bricks. She gave another rose to a very old woman who was smiling through her tears as they approached.

'God bless you, luv,' the woman gasped.

A third rose went to a young soldier, a fourth to a woman with two babies in a pram. By the time they reached the church, Connie had only one rose left. But it was enough.

Ruby doubted if Mrs Hart's house had ever rung to so much laughter. People laughed at the slightest thing or sometimes at nothing at all. It was as if on this one, special day, they had forgotten their troubles and were determined to enjoy themselves to the full. They danced and laughed, laughed and sang, and split their sides when the best man, a friend of Charles's, made a speech that wasn't remotely funny. 'Ladies and Gentlemen,' he began, and everyone collapsed into giggles.

The children couldn't contain their excitement. Their shrill, urgent cries could be heard above the music, their abundant energy evident by the way they flashed, like lightning, from room to room, where they were petted and made a desperate fuss of, to such an extent, Ruby began to doubt if she'd ever be able to control them again.

The Spam, bread and pickles rapidly disappeared, and the dry-as-dust cake went down a treat, much to the relief of Charles's grey-haired mother, elegantly clad in peacock blue brocade, who'd been worried it would be spat out in disgust.

'These plums are delicious,' she said to Ruby. 'Did you bottle them yourself?'

'No. They were a sort of gift, like most of the food.'

'You've done my son proud, Mrs O'Hagan. I only wish his brother and sister could be here, but Graham is in Egypt and Susie expecting a baby any minute. This is quite the nicest wedding I've ever been to. I can't wait to tell everyone what a wonderful send-off Charles had. I'm very grateful, and not just for the wedding. Charles tells me the household buzzes around you, that you're always here, always cheerful, keeping everyone going and looking after them so well.' She gave Ruby's shoulder an affectionate squeeze. 'That's quite an achievement for someone so young.'

'Why thank you.' Ruby had never looked at it that way before. It came as a pleasant surprise to know she was so highly appreciated.

'I suppose your husband's in the forces?'

'He was. He was killed in the evacuation of Dunkirk.'

Mrs Winner's face went pale with shock. 'Oh, my dear girl! I'm so terribly sorry. Charles never mentioned that.'

The strangest thing happened – it had happened before when she'd told people – Ruby felt her eyes fill with tears. 'I'm getting over it,' she said gruffly.

Later, when someone put an old Rudy Vallee record on the gramophone and he began to sing 'Night and Day', she thought of Jacob again, remembering the first night he'd come to Brambles and she'd danced for him. *That* Jacob had been so sweetly innocent, so very nice. The same Jacob had punched Bill Pickering across the room in order to defend her, because he loved her so much. In her eyes, it was *that* Jacob who'd died on the sands of Dunkirk, not the scared, pathetic man she'd lived with for two years. Ruby mourned the real Jacob, before he'd become twisted with fear, forced to live in a world he found totally alien.

At six o'clock, the newly-married couple left for their two day honeymoon in New Brighton, a mere ferry ride across the Mersey, but a place easy to get to, and just as easy to get back from, better than going further afield and spending their precious time waiting on stations for trains that might never come.

The mood became quieter. The air was already cooler and they lounged in the garden, watching the shadows creep across the untidy grass with its clusters of tiny daisies and brilliant yellow dandelions, praying the siren wouldn't go to signal a raid. But since May, after an horrific week, when every night the city had been subjected to a relentless barrage of bombs and mines, when it seemed that Liverpool would completely disappear off the face of the earth, when thousands of people had been killed or injured, Hitler seemed to have given up. There'd been few raids since.

Ruby was sitting on the back step with Martha Quinlan, when suddenly the woman leapt to her feet. 'Jim! It's our Jim!' she cried.

'Hello, Mam. Dad said you were here.'

His voice was unusually dull, as were his eyes. He had lost his suntan and looked thin. Martha began to pat him all over, as if to make sure he was real, exclaiming in distress at his thinness.

'I wasn't expecting you, son. Oh, but I'm so pleased to see you I could cry.'

Jim raised a wry smile. 'That's a bit of a contradiction, Mam. I'm changing ships, that's why I'm here. I'm off again on Monday. I just thought I'd come and sample what ordinary life feels like for a change. It's easy to forget on a ship. Hello, Ruby. You look very smart.'

'How are you, Jim?' She felt concern that he looked so low. At the same time, her heart was racing. It was months since she'd seen him, almost a year, though he was rarely far from her mind. Did he think of her as often as she did him? she wondered. Did he think of her *ever*?

'I'm OK,' Jim shrugged. 'I was sorry to hear about your husband.'

Martha broke in before Ruby could reply. 'She's bearing up remarkably well, son. Beth too. Oh, so many widows,' she cried, 'so many fatherless children. What has the world come to!'

Mrs Wallace, Connie's gran, the only one of her relatives who could be there, came to announce she was going and to thank Ruby for the lovely day, followed shortly afterwards by several of Charles's friends. After seeing them out, she returned to the garden where Jim Quinlan was deep in conversation with Beth. She was about to join them, but there was something about the way their heads were bent together, an air of intimacy, that stopped her in her tracks. She felt a flush of jealousy. What were they talking about? Did they have to be so close?

Until then, she hadn't wanted the day to end. Now she wanted it to be over, for everyone to go. She had difficulty keeping her temper with the girls. The excitement had made them silly. They were showing off, rolling over on the grass in their bridesmaid's frocks. Tiger was discovered on the draining board licking a tin of conny-onny that had been almost full. The best man was drunk, having had far more than his fair share of the beer. Ruby resisted the urge to point this out.

And still Beth and Jim talked. It wasn't fair, Ruby raged inwardly. Beth was leaving everything to her. She was beginning to feel like the mother of the bride as the guests began to depart in greater numbers, shaking *her* hand, thanking *her* for the wonderful time they'd had.

'You put so much effort into everything.'

'Thank you so much. It's been a marvellous day.'

At last, there were only three people left: Mrs Winner, Martha, and Jim, all inside listening to the wireless. Beth had taken Ruby's not very subtle hint and was putting the children to bed, no easy task if the shrieks and yells coming from upstairs were anything to go by. Mrs Winner was sleeping in Charles's room and returning to Dunstable next day. She was dead on her feet, she said contentedly, but insisted on washing the dishes before retiring. 'I'll help tidy up in the morning.'

Martha yawned. 'We'd best get going, son. I've got to be up at the crack of dawn to clean that bloody pub. Thanks, Ruby. You did a cracking job today. I really enjoyed meself.'

Jim nodded briefly. 'Me too, for the short time I was here.'

'Come again tomorrow,' Ruby said eagerly. 'Sample a bit more ordinary life. Come to tea! There's some tinned fruit left.'

'Thanks all the same, but I've made arrangements for tomorrow.'

'Then I'll see you next time you're home.' How many months would pass before that happened? And then they might exchange no more than a few words, like today. For some reason she wanted to cry and was horribly pleased when mother and son left and Jim made no attempt to shout goodbye to Beth upstairs.

Beth came down not long after the front door closed. 'What's up with you?' she demanded. 'You've got a cob on, I can tell. I can't think why. I thought today was the gear.'

'I'm tired, that's all,' Ruby answered shortly.

'You don't usually have a face on when you're tired.'

'Well, I have this time. I'm going to bed. The house is in a state and there'll be loads to do tomorrow.'

She was halfway up the stairs, when Beth said. 'I hope you don't mind, but I'm going out tomorrow.'

'Going out!' An awful suspicion entered her mind. 'Where to?'

'To a matinée at the pictures with Jim Quinlan, then for a meal afterwards.'

'That's not fair!' Ruby said furiously, knowing she was being unreasonable. It was the first time Beth had done such a thing, but she wouldn't have cared had it been with someone else. 'Connie was your friend as well as mine. I organised the wedding. At least you could help with clearing up.'

Beth looked so penitent that Ruby felt ashamed. Had the positions been reversed, she would have told Beth where to go. 'I'm sorry, Rube. But I couldn't possibly have turned him down.'

'Why not?'

'He's in a bit of a state – well, more than a bit.' Her eyes filled with tears. 'He's expecting to die any minute.'

At midday on Sunday, after an emotional goodbye and a fervently expressed hope they would meet again, Mrs Winner left for Dunstable. Beth accompanied her on the tram and would take her to the station before meeting Jim Quinlan.

Ruby was glad he wasn't calling for her. She couldn't have stood watching them go off together. What was it about Beth that had made him confide in her? Had he thought she, Ruby, would laugh, make fun, dismiss his fears? Though it wasn't fear, according to Beth, more the total conviction he was going to die. 'And it's not the dying itself he's worried about, but the way it might happen. He doesn't mind if it's quick, but he has nightmares about freezing to death in the seas around Russia, or dying in a fire.'

'Why on earth should he think like that?' asked Ruby.

'When he left school, ten lads from his class joined the Merchant Navy. Now they're all dead except Jim. He doesn't see why God should spare him and not his mates. He said it doesn't seem right.' Beth shivered. 'Oh, Ruby! It's only natural he'd feel like that. There's death everywhere. I feel a bit the same when we're sheltering in the cellar, like we could die any minute. Why should we be allowed to live, when there's people dying all around us? At least raids stop eventually, but the danger never stops for the men at sea.'

When the two women had gone, Ruby walked through the empty house to where the children were playing in a desultory fashion in the garden, having expended a week's energy at the wedding the day before. It seemed strange, not having to think about preparing a meal for tonight. Charles and Connie were away, Beth was eating out. She'd just make something light for her own and the children's tea – beans on toast. It was Jake's favourite. There was plenty of tinned fruit for afters.

She paused in the kitchen to make a cup of Camp coffee – a bottle of the disgusting stuff had been provided for the wedding. She drank it on the back step, grimacing with each sip.

The children were playing school, Heather the teacher, Greta and Jake the class. Tiger and Floppy lay on the grass pretending to be interested observers. A lump came to her throat at this picture of sweet, childish innocence, and she thanked God that Mrs Hart had gone to America, leaving her house for them to commandeer.

But what would they do when the war was over? Where would they live then? She and Beth couldn't stay together for always. Ruby would have to get a job, which she didn't mind a bit. But what sort of job? She didn't think there would ever again be a need for the pawnshop runner. Anyway, she'd moved on from that. As for cleaning, she'd no intention ever again of wielding a duster or mopping a floor on behalf of anyone except herself. Her thoughts went back to the convent when the height of her ambition had been to work in a shop or a restaurant. She hadn't realised then that women could become teachers, doctors, actresses, that women went to university, flew planes, discovered radium like Marie Curie, had all sorts of fascinating jobs.

Much as Ruby wanted to, she couldn't imagine doing any of these things, not because she considered herself incapable – she would have had a shot at any one of them – but circumstances in the shape of two young children were against her.

Of course, the future could lead in a different direction. She might get married . . .

A scream jolted her out of her musings. The picture of sweet, childish innocence had been spoilt by a classroom revolt. Three-year-old Jake had got tired of being taught how to spell, particularly by such a hard task master, and was making for the swing – a piece of rope suspended from a tree. Heather was trying to drag him back. 'It isn't playtime yet,' she yelled.

Ruby clapped her hands and the children froze. Heather glared at the little boy who had a mutinous look on his handsome face.

'Let him go, Heather,' Ruby ordered.

'He's being naughty, Mam.'

'No, he isn't. He wants to play on the swing, that's all. Let him go.'

Heather reluctantly released a joyous Jake. He seized the rope and began to swing with the liberated air of a child who'd spent the day in a real school.

It was a good job Beth wasn't there. She got annoyed when Heather bossed her son around.

'I'll have to put a stop to it,' Ruby thought. 'Not just with Jake, but with Greta too.' It had seemed touching once, the concern Heather felt for her sister, but since Greta started school, it was as if the younger girl resented the older being out of her control, dominating her totally when she was home. Ruby wasn't sure if it was fortunate or *un*fortunate that Greta didn't seem to mind, allowing herself to be ordered about without a murmur of complaint. She seemed content never to make a decision for herself, to play what Heather wanted, go where Heather went, unlike Jake, who preferred to run his young life on his own with only occasional interference from a grown-up. He was a lovely child with a lovely nature. Ruby felt sure he would become a fine young man, whereas Heather, she thought wryly, seemed destined to grow up a shrew and Greta a doormat.

She looked at her daughters. Greta was sitting patiently on the grass. Her tiny heart-shaped face, framed by a mop of babyish blonde hair, was fixed on that of her sister, waiting for her to return to her role as teacher. She was still small for her age, as if her body had never recovered from those first lean years in Foster Court when she always seemed to have a cold and there wasn't enough to eat – yesterday, quite a few people had assumed she was the four-year old and Heather, an inch taller, was five.

Looking at Heather was like looking at herself: the same strong features, dark eyes, boney frame. 'But was I ever quite so sour?' Ruby wondered. The nuns had said she was wilful, always wanting her own way, but she hadn't stamped her feet in rage if she didn't get it, which Heather was apt to do.

'She'll grow out of it,' Ruby consoled herself. 'Or at least, I hope so.'

Not long after the wedding, a downstairs room became a bedroom for Marie Ferguson, a gruff, good-natured widow in her fifties who worked as a cook in Sefton hospital. She found it easier to live close by, rather than travel daily to her house in a small village near Wigan.

Marie quickly became a member of what was, by now, almost a family. Weekends, she was happy to babysit while Ruby and Beth went to the pictures or, occasionally, a dance.

Beth loved dancing, but Ruby was no good at small talk. She got bored when asked the same questions over and over again. 'What's your name? What do you do? Where do you live? Can I take you home?', the last being met with a firm, '*No!*'

'They all seem so *young*,' she grumbled.

'You're not exactly old,' argued Beth.

'I *feel* old compared to them.'

'Anyroad, they're not all young. There's plenty in their thirties, even older. What's wrong with them?'

'They're married, that's what. Their poor wives would have a fit if they saw them dancing with other women, taking them home, where they'd get up to even worse mischief if they were allowed.'

Ruby had the feeling that she'd gone from young to old in the space of the few days it had taken to leave Kirkby with Jacob and move into Foster Court. Once, she'd loved to dance, but the urge had gone and dancing now seemed a frivolous way of occupying her time. She had lost her sense of fun, she realised sadly. She had grown up too quickly, become an adult too soon, a rather serious, very sober adult.

The following Easter, Heather started school. Ruby didn't like to admit, not even to herself, that she was relieved to see the back of her troublesome daughter. Jake was happy on his own, and equally happy to start school himself a year later, giving Ruby the long-cherished opportunity to do her bit, even if only part-time.

Martha Quinlan, always an opportunist on behalf of the WVS, immediately found her something to do. Liverpool Corporation were gradually repairing the thousands of houses damaged in the blitz, but this didn't include decorating the insides; the walls and ceilings stained when water tanks had broken, discoloured when a chimney-full of soot had fallen, or scorched by fire.

'It's the elderly that need help,' Martha explained. 'Young 'uns can distemper the walls in a jiffy. The old people get distressed when their homes look a mess, and painters and decorators are as hard to find as ciggies, not that they could afford 'em if they weren't.'

So Ruby spent four hours every morning painting houses. She

learnt how to plaster holes and mix cement, arriving home stinking of Turpentine, her black hair streaked with paint.

It was 1943 and the war showed no sign of ending, though the people were continually promised victory was 'just around the corner'. The invasion of France was expected any day, but in the meantime, another invasion had taken place, much to the delight of young women throughout Britain – and the dismay of the men.

The Yanks had arrived. Hordes of cheerful, outgoing, engaging young men in well fitting uniforms, generous to a fault, had taken over the country. They were everywhere, pockets stuffed with chewing gum and cash, convinced that every British woman, young or old, could be had in exchange for a pair of nylons.

Nowadays, Ruby looked forward to the weekend dances. It was like entering a fresh, new world, talking to young men from places like Texas or California who had done things she'd only seen in films; worked on ranches, driven Cadillacs, played baseball, been to Radio City, Hollywood, Fifth Avenue, Niagara Falls . . .

Or so they said. She only believed half she was told, but the Americans' good-natured high spirits came as a relief after the horror of the air raids and the continuing shortage of virtually every single thing that made life bearable, particularly food.

She went out with quite a few, never more than twice, otherwise she would have found herself engaged, a crafty way the Yanks had of getting women into bed who couldn't be got there by easier means. There was a measure of cynicism in Ruby's fraternation with the 'enemy', as Charles called them, and she often returned home laden with oranges, candy, tins of ham, and other delicacies rarely seen in war-torn Britain and which Charles happily consumed, despite their dubious source.

Ruby had known Beth was in love before Beth knew herself. They were at a dance at the Locarno, a foxtrot had just ended, and Ruby returned to their spot under the balcony. Beth was already there, holding hands with a tall, black American sergeant.

'Rube, this is Daniel,' Beth said shyly, and there was a look on her face, and on Daniel's, that said everything.

It came as no surprise when they got married six months later in the same church where Connie had married Charles, though it was a very different sort of wedding. Beth wore a simple white frock she'd made herself and there were no bridesmaids. The only guests were Beth's immediate friends whom she now regarded as her family. There was hardly time for a sandwich and a glass of wine before Daniel and the best man had to return to the base in Burtonwood, where he would continue to live, while Beth and Jake remained in Mrs Hart's house.

Daniel Lefarge was a lawyer. Back in Little Rock, Arkansas, he fought for equal rights for negroes. He was one of the few educated black men in the state.

'It's terrible there,' a wide-eyed Beth said to Ruby on the night of her wedding. Everyone else had gone to bed and they were finishing off the last of the wine. 'We're not allowed in restaurants or bars. We can't sit by whites on the buses. We have to use separate lavatories.'

Ruby raised her eyebrows. 'We?'

'Black people,' Beth said firmly. 'I'm black, like Daniel.'

'I always thought of us, of you and me, as the same.'

'If I was the same as you,' Beth explained, 'Daniel would have been refused permission to get married. Black servicemen aren't allowed to marry British girls if they're white. It was decided in the Senate because it would cause trouble when they returned home with a white bride.'

'That's daft!' Ruby expostulated.

'It may seem daft to you, but not to Americans, particularly in the South where Daniel comes from. White people there consider negroes less than human.'

'Will you be happy in that sort of atmosphere?' Ruby felt fearful for her gentle, sensitive friend, who didn't seem to realise the awfulness of what she was saying. 'Remember the time when we were evacuated to Southport? You were terribly upset.'

'I'd be happy anywhere with Daniel.' Beth's face shone. 'And so will Jake. They adore each other.'

In June, 1944, on D-Day, Daniel Lefarge was among the first American troops to storm the French beaches. From that day on, Beth lived in a state of terror. Daniel's letters were few and usually arrived weeks late. Beth rarely ate breakfast, but lingered behind the front door with a cup of tea, praying that the postwoman would come. If she did, and there was nothing from Daniel, her disappointment was evident in her tragic face. On more than one occasion, Ruby travelled all the way to A. E. Wadsworth Engineering to deliver a letter with a French postmark that had arrived after her friend had gone to work.

Another Christmas, the sixth of the war, and hopefully the last. Allied troops were slowly advancing across Europe and, at last, victory was in sight.

In the New Year, Charles and Connie found a place of their own, a little cottage in Kirkby, not far from Brambles where Ruby used to live. Beth was advised that shortly she would no longer have a job. Marie Ferguson was making plans to go home.

As soon as the conflict was over, Beth and Jake were going to live in America with Daniel's mother – he would join them as soon as he was demobbed. There would only be Ruby and her girls left in the house, to which its owner could return any day.

She took down the blackout curtains and began to put the house, as far as she could, back to its original order. There were marks, scars, wear and tear, things broken, missing, changed, that couldn't be hidden. Mrs Hart was unlikely to think Ruby, who'd only been asked to keep an eye on the place, had tamed the wild garden out of the kindess of her heart – even established a vegetable patch – or varnished the front door when the original varnish had worn away altogether and she'd felt ashamed of the bleached, bare wood.

She had every intention of facing Mrs Hart, confessing what she'd done, but preferred not to be living on the premises when the woman walked through her newly varnished door. But finding somewhere to live was proving difficult, if not impossible. She roamed the streets, anxiously perused the cards in newsagents' windows, scoured the *Echo*, but nearly half the properties in Liverpool had been destroyed or damaged. It wasn't just Ruby desperate for somewhere to live.

The months passed. February gave way to March, March was suddenly April, the Allies were approaching Berlin and victory was imminent, but still Ruby hadn't found a job or somewhere to live. She and Beth had built a little nest egg between them, but her half would quickly disappear if there wasn't a wage coming in. She had nightmares about returning to somewhere like Foster Court, and the bad dreams occurred almost nightly as time went by and still nothing had turned up.

At the beginning of May, it was reported that Hitler had killed himself. The following day, Berlin fell. A victory announcement was expected by the hour. Ruby, working in the home of Mrs Effie Gittings, was listening to the wireless in the next room while she distempered the parlour walls an insipid pale blue, the only colour available apart from white. Mrs Gittings kept abandoning the wireless to discuss the latest news and fetch cups of tea as insipid as the distemper.

'You work ever so neat,' the old lady said admiringly. 'It's nice having a woman do the decorating. Men make splashes on the furniture and look daggers if you dare complain. At least one good thing's come out of this terrible war; women have shown they can work as good as men in most jobs.'

Later, as Ruby trudged home, she had an idea that made her want to dance along the pavement. *She would become a painter and decorator!* She liked the idea of being her own boss, working her own hours, being home when the children finished school. As soon as she was settled elsewhere, she'd have leaflets printed and deliver one to every house in the Dingle. She would become well-known again, like the pawnshop runner, not that fame was her objective, but making a living was. The future suddenly looked challenging and exciting, full of hope, and by the time she reached the house, her decorating company had expanded to the extent it had a staff of ten, all women. She would think of a clever name to call herself, something catchy.

At the gate, she paused. The 'settled elsewhere' bit had still to be resolved. Some of her excitement faded. Before she could lift a paintbrush, she had to find a place to live.

Sighing, she opened the front door, ready to make for the wireless in case there'd been any news, but froze when she heard footsteps upstairs, heavy, male footsteps.

'Who's there?' she called shakily. For a brief second she wondered if it might be Max Hart.

A young man appeared at the top of the stairs, nothing like Max. 'Who the hell are you?' he demanded angrily. 'There's people living here, but there bloody well shouldn't be. This house is supposed to be empty.'

It had always been Ruby's belief, ever since she was a little girl and couldn't have put it into words, that the best form on defence was attack. Besides which, she disliked the young man on sight. He looked about twenty-one, five years younger than herself, was very tall, very thin, with brilliantined black hair and a pencil moustache. The trousers of his cheap, chalk-striped suit were several inches too short, exposing shabby brown boots. Not that she presented a pretty picture herself in her paint-stained slacks and jumper.

'Who the hell are *you?*' she replied spiritedly. 'How dare you break into my house!'

'Break in!' The man clumped downstairs brandishing a key. '*Your* house!' he snorted. 'This house belongs to Mrs Beatrice Hart, but not for long, 'cause I'm going to buy it.'

Ruby tossed her head haughtily and hoped she didn't look as shaken as she felt. 'She hadn't told us it was to be sold.'

The visitor frowned. 'Why should she?'

'Because she writes to me from Colorado,' Ruby lied. 'She's been living with her sister. Mind you, I haven't heard from her in a while. She said we could live here for the duration. Her son, Max, stayed with us for a time. Do you know where Max is?'

'Never heard of him.' The man's frown faded, though he still looked suspicious. 'Why didn't she say the house was occupied when she wrote and told the estate agent to sell?'

'I've known her for years, she was always very forgetful. Did you say she was *selling* the house?'

'Yes. She's got married again and she's staying in America. 'I'm surprised she didn't write and tell you *that!*'

'I expect she will.' They glared at each other. His eyes were brown, his cheeks hollow, lips thin and stern. There was something hungry about him, and she suspected he'd been raised in poverty worse than she'd ever known. To her horror, a little excited shiver coursed down her spine, shocking her to the core, because he wasn't a bit attractive.

'Anyroad,' he said bluntly, 'as soon as the final contracts are exchanged, you can scram sharpish. How many live here?'

'Me and my two children. There's also my friend and her little boy, but they'll be leaving soon. How long will it be before the contracts are exchanged?'

'A few weeks.'

Ruby nodded. Suddenly, the idea of leaving the house in which everyone had been so happy, despite the war, made her feel inordinately sad. She touched the wooden banister and sighed. 'It's a lovely house,' she murmured. 'You'll like living in it.'

'I'm not going to live in it. I've already got a house. I'm a property developer. Here's my card.'

His name was Matthew Doyle according to the badly handwritten card. 'You've spelt property wrong,' Ruby pointed out. 'It only has one "p" in the middle.'

'Thanks for telling me,' he sneered, but looked embarrassed.

'I hope you're not going to pull the place down.' She sighed again. 'It would be such a shame.'

'I will, one day, when the time is ripe. Until then, it'll be rented out.'

'What's happening to everything in it?'

'You mean the furniture and fittings?' He made an attempt to look knowledgable and superior. 'It's being sold as it is. I'll keep some stuff and sell the rest.'

'I see.' She wondered where he'd got the money from to buy the house. And why wasn't he in the Forces like most men of his age? There was something despicable about speculating, buying up property, while there was a war on and other men were risking their lives. Her lips curled in disgust.

'Why are you covered all over in paint?' Matthew Doyle enquired.

'I've been decorating an old lady's house.'

He chuckled. 'I've just bought a whole row of bomb-damaged houses. When they need painting, I'll get in touch.'

Ruby looked at him directly, hating him. 'Don't bother. I do it for nothing, something I doubt you'd understand.'

He flushed angrily. 'You know nothing about me.'

'I know enough. How much rent will you want for the house?'

'More than you can afford,' he replied, blinking at the sudden change of tack, 'seeing as you work for nothing, like. Unless you've got a husband who can pay what it's worth.'

'My husband died at Dunkirk. I'm a widow.' She knew he would never let her have the house which she couldn't possibly afford, but was hoping to get under his skin, make him ashamed, though doubted if he was capable of shame.

To her surprise, he didn't answer straight away, but seemed lost in thought. She watched him, hands stuffed in the pockets of his ill-fitting suit. There was something almost pathetic about such a badly-dressed individual who couldn't spell passing himself off as a property developer. She'd like to bet the estate agents he dealt with laughed like drains behind his back, yet he could probably buy and sell the lot of them. She neither respected or admired him, but there was something to be said – she couldn't think what it was just now – for someone who'd so clearly pulled himself up by his boot straps to get on.

'You could turn it into a boarding house,' he said.

Ruby's jaw dropped. 'I beg your pardon!'

'Live downstairs and let the upstairs rooms. Take lodgers. Make their meals, do their washing, and they'll pay more.' He smiled sarcastically. 'Or is being a landlady too good for you?'

'Oh, Rube! That's wonderful news,' Beth cried when she came home.

'Is it?' Ruby loathed every aspect of housework and regarded with horror the idea of looking after a houseful of lodgers. But it seemed she had no choice. Matthew Doyle wanted eight pounds a week rent. If she let the upstairs rooms for four pounds each, she'd be left with eight pounds for herself. It sounded a lot, but there'd be mountains of food to buy and tons of washing powder. It seemed she was destined to wallow in domesticity for the rest of her life.

No! No, she wouldn't. Ruby tightened her fists and gritted her teeth. She'd hang on to her little nest egg, add to it week by week, *buy* a house if she couldn't find one to rent. Somehow, in some way, she'd *do* something with her life, no matter how long it took.

At twenty to eight that night, it was announced on the BBC that the following day was to be a national holiday.

The war in Europe was over.

They took the excited children to a street party by the Malt House, where bunting was strung from the upstairs windows, where the tables were laden with a feast that made young eyes glisten and mouths water. Ruby had been saving food for this momentous day and arrived with two dozen home-made fairy cakes, a jelly sprinkled with hundreds and thousands, a tin of cream, two bottles of ginger beer, and mounds of sandwiches filled with cress she'd grown herself.

It was a mad day, crazy. Total strangers flung their arms around each other and hugged and kissed as if they were the greatest friends. When the children finished eating, the grown-ups sat down to what was left over, by which time half the men were as drunk as lords. They sat on the pavement outside the pub, hugging their ale, reliving the war, fighting the battles all over again, savouring the victory, which they claimed they'd expected all along, having forgotten the dark times when everything seemed to be lost and Hitler was winning.

After tea, they danced; the hokey-cokey, knees up Mother Brown, the conga. Ruby and Beth waltzed together, and Beth said longingly, 'Don't be hurt, Rube, but I don't half wish I was dancing with Daniel. There'll never be another day like today. It would have been nice to have spent it together.'

Ruby felt a little knot of envy. What would it be like to fall in love, she wondered? *Properly* in love, not the childish love she'd felt for Jacob, or the hopeless way she loved Jim Quinlan. Would she ever know what real love was?

Jim was around somewhere. He looked withdrawn, a bit lost, not joyful that everything was over but he *was* still alive. Perhaps he felt that death had cheated him, that he had no right to be there, celebrating, when his friends were dead. Ruby had already decided to give up on Jim Quinlan, though he would always retain a special place in her heart.

Still, she had her girls. She looked up to see where they were. They were whizzing round in a circle with Jake, laughing helplessly, as if they, too, were drunk. The girls would miss Jake. He was their brother, although neither she nor Beth had ever felt able to tell them. It was hard to imagine the future without Beth. They'd lived through the war together, shared every single thing. Even Jacob, she thought with a smile.

Connie and Charles arrived. 'We decided you were the only people in the world we wanted to spend tonight with,' Connie cried. 'We've been to the house and guessed you might be here.' She embraced Ruby affectionately, then Beth.

Charles kissed them both. 'You'll always be part of our memories,' he said huskily. 'You took strangers into your house and made them feel at home. I'll always be grateful.'

He took them into the packed Malt House for a drink, where

Martha was working frantically behind the bar. Above the din, Ruby managed to convey the news that she'd found somewhere to live. 'In other words, I'm staying put. Some chap's buying the house, a Matthew Doyle.'

'Matt Doyle!' Martha screeched. 'You'll have to be careful there, Ruby. He's nothing but a dirty, rotten spiv. He could get you anything on the black market – at a price.'

Dusk was falling when they went outside. The exhausted crowd started to sing, sitting on their doorsteps, lounging against the walls, happier than most had ever known. The moon came out, and then the stars. And still they sang, until a few began to drift away, and then more.

Ruby and Beth walked back through the lamp lit streets, the weary children behind, dragging their feet. Mrs Hart's house came into view. Ruby had switched on the lights before they left, feeling extravagent and very daring. But it was worth it to see every window in every room brightly lit, welcoming them home, a sight never seen before in all the years they'd lived there.

Beth took Ruby's hand and squeezed it, as if in farewell. In another few weeks, she and Jake would be gone.

An era was over and a new one about to begin.

Ruby's girls

Chapter 9

1957–1958

Heather O'Hagan sat on the bed and watched her sister in her frothy pink party dress get made up in front of the dressing table mirror. 'That lippy doesn't suit you,' she said critically. 'It's too dark.'

'D'you think so?' Greta put her head on one side and studied her reflection. 'I thought it made me look glamorous.'

'It makes you look like a tart. Fair-haired women should wear pale lippy.'

Greta pouted. 'You're always saying that, sis, but Marilyn Monroe doesn't, and *she* looks glamorous.'

'No, she doesn't. She looks like a tart.'

'Oh, all right.' Greta rubbed the offending lipstick off with her hankie and applied a lighter shade. 'What's that like?'

'Much better.' Heather smiled, having got her way. For as long as she could remember, she'd felt responsible for Greta, who could very easily make a complete mess of things without her help. She never seemed able to do things right. Say she'd worn that horrible maroon lippy at her party! It was all right Mam saying, 'people learn from their mistakes,' but they could learn better and less painfully with good advice.

Ruby opened the bedroom door. 'Greta, it's eight o'clock and your first guest has arrived.'

Greta quickly dabbed scent behind her ears, then tipped the bottle against a piece of cotton wool which she tucked inside her bra. She jumped to her feet. 'Who is it?'

'I don't know, love. It's a he, and he's very handsome. I told him to put some records on the gramophone.'

'It might be Peter King.' She rushed out of the room.

'Don't let him see you're interested,' Heather called.

'I think that's up to Greta, don't you?' Ruby said pointedly.

'But he's a drip, Mam. He's already got a girlfriend.'

'It can't be all that serious if he's come to Greta's party on his own.'

'I don't want her to get hurt, Mam.' She'd sooner be hurt herself, any day, than let Greta suffer a broken heart.

Ruby's face softened. 'I know. But you can't protect her for ever. Oh, there's the doorbell. Answer it, there's a love. I've sausage rolls in the oven that need seeing to and sandwiches still to make.'

'All right.' Heather stood and smoothed the hips of her plain black skirt, glancing briefly at her tall reflection in the mirror. With the skirt, she wore a white, tailored blouse, and her long, black hair was pinned back with a slide. The whole effect was deliberately severe because she didn't want to overshadow her sister on her twenty-first.

Frankie Laine was singing 'Jezebel' and everywhere smelled of a strange mixture of baking and scent – *June*, the girls' favourite. There was a lovely atmosphere, heady, excited, as if the walls of Mrs Hart's house knew there was going to be a party. Ruby still thought of it as Mrs Hart's house, even though it had belonged to Matthew Doyle for twelve years – twelve long, very tedious years, she thought, making a face as she took the sausage rolls out of the oven. The lodgers lived upstairs and the two downstairs reception rooms had been turned into bedrooms, one for Ruby, the other for the girls. The rather dark room at the back, where the party would be held, was their living room. Fortunately, the kitchen was big enough for the lodgers to eat in. *Un*fortunately, it meant she had to keep it scrupulously clean, or at least she tried.

Every time she thought she had enough saved for a deposit on a house of her own, houses had gone up another few hundred. It was like being in a race she stood no chance of winning. She'd probably end up the oldest landlady in the world.

The doorbell rang again. 'Will someone get that,' she yelled.

'I'll do it.' Mr Keppel appeared at the kitchen door. 'I'm just on my way out.'

'Thanks. Have a nice time.'

'It's the dress rehearsal tonight. I'm a bag of nerves.'

'I hope it goes well.' Mr Keppel had only been living upstairs a few months. He worked in a bank and his spare time was taken up with amateur dramatics. Ruby was going to the play's first night at the Crane theatre on Monday. She was glad Mr Oliver and Mr Hamilton were away for the weekend, leaving only Mr Keppel, who was no trouble, and Mrs Mulligan, who was a pain.

A few seconds later, Martha Quinlan came into the kitchen, a shopping bag in each hand. 'This is the cake,' she puffed, putting one bag on the table. 'And the other's a couple of bottles of wine, for us, not the kids. D'you fancy a glass now?'

'I wouldn't say no. I'm a bit nervous, Martha. I've never thrown a party before.'

'It's not like you to be nervous. Remember that wedding during the war? I've never had such a nice time since.'

'That was different. People were more easily pleased. Let's see the cake.' Ruby had made the cake herself and Martha had iced it. 'Oh, it's lovely!' she exclaimed when the elaborate pink and white creation was removed from its tissue wrapping. 'Very artistic. Did you actually make the roses yourself?'

''Course, I did. That's what I went to night school for, cake decoration. I've got the candles separate.'

Martha was nearing seventy, grey-haired, slightly stooped, deeply wrinkled, but as hard-working as ever. It was almost a decade since Fred had retired as licensee of the Malt House, and the licence had passed to Jim and his wife, Barbara. The older couple still lived on the premises and Martha was often called upon to lend a hand behind the bar. According to her, Barbara was a lazy bitch. 'You'd never dream she'd been a nurse,' she frequently remarked. 'I used to think our Agnes was idle, but at least she bucked up her ideas when she got married and had kids. That Barbara won't have a baby, she's too scared.'

'Do you want white wine or red, luv?' she asked now.

'White, please.'

A bottle was expertly uncorked, the wine poured. Martha began to put twenty-one pink candles on the cake. 'How many's coming to the party?'

'Twenty, half girls, half boys – that sounds like more now,' she said when the doorbell rang. 'They're mostly Greta's friends from work, a few of Heather's. Charles and Connie might pop in later, but only if they can get a babysitter for the boys.'

'They can stay in the kitchen with us,' Martha said comfortably.

'We can have a nice natter. It will be quite like old times, except Beth won't be here.'

'She rang earlier to wish Greta a happy birthday.'

'How's she getting on?'

'Just fine,' Ruby lied, because Beth wouldn't have wanted Martha to know anything else. 'Jake's at university in Boston and her other three kids sound incredibly clever – much cleverer than mine. Daniel's got his own law firm and they've just bought a lovely new house. It's got central heating, a double garage, and its own swimming pool.'

Martha looked impressed. 'She certainly fell on her feet, didn't she, our Beth, when she married Daniel.'

Ruby gave a non-committal smile. Only she knew how unhappy Beth was. She recalled the very first letter she had written from Little Rock; how pretty the place was, how the sun always seemed to be shining, the clothes in the shops so smart, Daniel's brother, Nathan, was teaching Jake to play baseball. Everything sounded wonderful until Ruby reached the end and there was a PS which she could remember almost word for word.

'Oh, Rube,' Beth had written. 'I'm so miserable I could die. Daniel's mam doesn't like me, you'll never guess why; because I'm too pale.' The 'pale' was underlined. 'She says I'm "high yeller", whatever that is. And my poor Jake is almost white. We don't fit in anywhere, Jake and me. The whites hate us because we're black, and the blacks don't like us for not being black enough. Nathan's OK, but he's the only one. I can't wait for Daniel to be demobbed and come home.'

Daniel came home, but things only got a little better. With her husband deeply involved in his work, and his spare time taken up with advancing the cause of black people, Beth felt increasingly lonely and friendless. Everywhere was segregated; shops, restaurants, buses, even schools. She yearned to return to Liverpool. Yet she loved Daniel and couldn't bear to leave.

'Oh, listen!' Martha suddenly yelped. 'It's Bill Haley and The Comets singing "Rock around the Clock".'

'Someone must have bought Greta the record as a present.'

'Fred ses I'm turning childlike in me old age, but I love rock and roll.'

'I'm not averse to it myself. I wonder what time I should serve the food?'

'Nine-ish?' suggested Martha.

Ruby began to arrange the sausage rolls on a plate. 'I should have done this earlier, but I've been run off my feet all day. I hope fifty sarnies are enough; salmon paste and cheese – not together,' she added hastily. 'I made the little vol-au-vent things and the cheese straws last night.' She laughed. 'Lord! If the nuns could see me now, they'd be so proud. I used to hate cookery lessons – well, I hated everything they taught us, but some of it must have sunk in.'

At nine o'clock, she sailed into the noisy, crowded, smoke-filled living room with the refreshments and put them on the sideboard for the guests to help themselves. Most were dancing, a few attempting to talk above the din, and one couple were squashed in an armchair in a passionate embrace, though the young man quickly disengaged himself when he saw the food.

'I'll fetch the cake later,' she called, but no one heard.

Charles and Connie had arrived earlier, but could only stay a little while. They'd asked a neighbour to watch over their two little boys, but she wanted to be home for ten o'clock to see a play on television.

'I'd love a television,' Martha sighed. 'But our Fred claims they're nothing but a time waster. Mind you, he should know. If anyone knows how to waste time, it's bloody Fred.'

'A chap upstairs, Mr Hamilton, has one,' said Ruby. 'I switched it on once when I cleaned his room, but nothing happened. I was worried I'd broken it.'

It was Charles's opinion that televisions would never catch on. 'People are too intelligent to sit and watch a little screen all night long.'

Connie grinned. 'Then I must be very unintelligent, because I wouldn't mind having one a bit. I'd love to see *What's My Line*, and the lads would enjoy *Watch With Mother*.'

'I think this calls for an instant divorce,' Charles said sternly, grinning back.

They waited for Ruby to carry the cake with its twenty-one flickering candles into the other room, following behind with Martha, singing 'Happy Birthday to you . . .'

'You've done them kids dead proud, d'you know that, Ruby,'

Martha said when Connie and Charles had gone and they were alone again in the kitchen.

'It's only a party, Martha.'

'I don't just mean the party, girl. I mean over their whole lives. And you've done it on your own, without a husband most of the time, and not a single relative around to give a hand. Yet they've turned out such lovely girls.' She gave Ruby a look of real affection. 'I'll not forget the day you came into the pub about the cleaning job. You looked as if you'd just got out the bath with your clothes on. Fred said I was a fool, advancing you sixpence. He didn't think I'd ever see you or the tanner again. But I knew I would.' She patted Ruby's hand. 'I wonder if your mam's around somewhere? If so, it's her that's the fool, giving up such a lovely daughter.'

'Oh, Martha, stop it.' Ruby blushed. 'You've had too much wine and it's made you maudlin. You'll be crying any minute.'

Martha seemed about to continue with her eulogy, but was interrupted by a knock on the kitchen door and Iris Mulligan came in, her stout, fiftyish body wrapped in a tweed dressing gown, a thick brown net covering her mousey hair, and her face greasy with Pond's cold cream. Mrs Mulligan had occupied a front upstairs room for nearly five years and was a champion complainer, almost certainly the reason she was there now.

'Is that noise going to go on for much longer, Mrs O'Hagan?' she whined. 'It's ten o'clock and some of us have to sleep.'

'I told you the other day we were having a party, Mrs Mulligan,' Ruby said plainly. 'I apologised in advance for the noise, remember? It's Friday, you don't have to work tomorrow. It's also my daughter's twenty-first. I'm afraid the noise will continue until midnight and then everyone will go home.'

'That seems most unreasonable, Mrs O'Hagan.'

'I'm afraid it can't be helped, Mrs Mulligan.'

'You'll just have to read a book,' Martha growled. 'Jaysus! How do you stand it?' she exlaimed when Iris Mulligan had departed in a huff.

Ruby shrugged. 'I've stopped taking any notice. She complains about every single thing. If it's not the noise, it's the food, or the other lodgers – Mr Oliver snores and Mr Hamilton has his television on too loud. At least she does her own washing and ironing, not like the men.'

'Fancy ending up at her age living in a room in someone's house! Has she got any kids?'

'No. Actually, Martha,' Ruby dropped her voice, concerned she might be overheard, 'someone told me her husband brought a woman home only half his age, and she was given the choice of putting up with it or getting out.'

'He couldn't do that!' Martha gasped.

'He did. She ended up with nowhere to live and without a stick of furniture. That's why she's here.'

'Bloody hell! My Fred doesn't seem so bad after that. No wonder the poor woman's miserable. I'd be the same if I was her.'

Next morning, the party was declared a great success. It had gone suspiciously quiet over the final half hour, but Ruby hadn't bothered to investigate. She could hardly complain if they were indulging in a bit of snogging when she'd got up to far worse with Jacob when she was only sixteen.

'Are you staying in town this afternoon?' she enquired over breakfast. The girls had appeared at half-past seven in their dressing gowns, as fresh as daisies, despite going to bed so late. Both worked in the city centre; Greta as a switchboard operator for a firm of accountants and Heather as filing clerk in the Royal Liver insurance company. Saturday, they finished at midday and usually spent the afternoon roaming the clothes departments of the big shops, always arriving home with something new. Ruby would have done the same at their age, but lack of money, followed by clothes rationing, had proved rather inhibiting.

'I might spend my birthday money on a new frock,' Greta announced, munching on a piece of toast.

'And I need new shoes.' Heather regarded her long, narrow feet. 'Wedge heels would be nice for a change.'

'I wouldn't mind new shoes myself.'

'You can have my red ones if you like, Mam. I don't like them anymore. The heels are too squat.'

'Squat!' Ruby hooted. She and Heather took the same size. 'I've heard of high heels and flat heels and cuban heels, but never squat. I'll try them on later. It's come to something, a mother inheriting her daughter's cast-offs. You've got more money than sense, the pair of you.'

An hour later, she waved them off into the soft April sunshine, arms linked, heads bent towards each other, already deep in conversation. In her spindly-heeled sandals, Greta was almost as tall as her sister. She wore a stiff, taffeta petticoat under a flowered dirndl skirt, and her wide belt was pulled so tight it was a wonder she could breathe. On top, she wore a gathered peasant blouse with smocking on the yoke. Her hair was held back with wide pink ribbon. Ruby smiled. She would have looked perfect stuck on top of a Christmas tree.

Heather favoured a more tailored look. Her suit was classically styled grey flannel, worn with a white blouse, black shoes, and a black felt beret.

They made a striking pair; Greta small and pretty, a pale, natural blonde, Heather elegantly tall and very dark. Her sombre face could look quite beautiful when she smiled.

A van passed, and the driver had to brake sharply as he almost ran into a lamppost, his attention distracted by the sight of Ruby's girls. He caught her eye, looked her up and down, and winked appreciatively. She would be thirty-eight in a few weeks' time, but could turn male heads as easily as her daughters.

Ruby closed the door and began to sort through the post which had just arrived. There were two belated birthday cards for Greta, letters for the lodgers, and an electricity bill for herself – she winced when she opened it and saw the amount. She left Greta's cards on the hall table and took the rest upstairs, shoving the letters under the appropriate doors.

Downstairs again, she met Tiger, ancient now, emerging from a marathon sleep in the cellar where he spent most of his time in his wardrobe. Floppy had disappeared years ago and hopefully hadn't ended his days as someone's dinner. She gave the big cat a cuddle and a saucer of milk, then went into the girls' room and tried on Heather's red shoes. The heels *were* a bit thick, but otherwise very smart. They fitted perfectly, but she had nothing to wear with them. She searched through Heather's clothes, found a nice navy-blue frock she hadn't seen her wear in ages, and wondered if she dropped a hint she'd be given the frock as well. It would have been nice to wander round the shops with the girls, buy herself new clothes, she thought ruefully, but every spare penny went in the bank towards a house.

★

In Owen Owen's, Greta was agonising over whether or not to buy a short-sleeved angora jumper. 'It's a lovely blue and ever so soft.' She rubbed the stuff between her fingers.

'It's daft buying a jumper in April,' Heather said. 'It'll itch like mad in the heat.'

'I could keep it till winter, sis.'

'But it's only got short sleeves!'

'Oh, all right.' Greta abandoned the jumper and made for a rack of blouses. 'These are pretty. Oh, see! They've got lace panels down the front. They'd go nice with your suit.'

'Mmm!' Heather frowned and began to pull out the various colours. Buying a blouse, buying clothes of any sort, was a serious matter, demanding total concentration. 'I wouldn't mind the black. I tell you what, let's keep these in mind and perhaps come back later. We haven't been to Lewis's yet, nor T. J. Hughes, and you still haven't seen a frock you like.'

'Shall we go for a coffee? We can think about the blouses and that white handbag I saw earlier.'

'That's a good idea! There's a new coffee bar at the top of Bold Street.'

On the way, they earnestly discussed the things they'd seen. If Greta bought the white bag, she would need white sandals to match. Heather wondered if diamanté earrings would be too dressy for work.

'You wear a diamanté brooch,' Greta pointed out.

'Yes, but earrings are different.'

They ordered coffees and took them to a table in the window, too embroiled in their own concerns to show interest in the people passing by. They'd led a cosseted, sheltered life, the O'Hagan girls. Foster Court had made no impression on their young minds. Their memories stretched back only as far as living cosily with Arthur in the coal yard. Lack of a father had never bothered them. A man had always been around; first Arthur, then Charles, then mam's lodgers, to make a fuss of them. Other children, not just Jake, had been there to play with, in a house that was always full of people. They'd never felt lonely or unloved. So far, neither had been called upon to take a decision about anything remotely important apart from what clothes to buy or whether to go out with a particular young man.

Last night, Peter King had asked Greta for a date but, on Heather's advice, she had turned him down. Whenever possible, they went out in a foursome, because they enjoyed each other's company as much as they did that of the various young men. Greta, more so than Heather, knew that one day this would change, that a man would appear she would want to spend the rest of her life with to the exclusion of everyone else, including her sister. Heather couldn't imagine Greta coping with marriage, and certainly not motherhood, without her unwavering support. Sometimes, she wondered if she should remain unmarried, become a spinster, so that she would always be available for Greta.

'I think I'll buy something for Mam,' Greta said. 'A sort of "thank you" for the party.'

'I'll go halves,' offered Heather. 'What shall we get?'

'I was thinking about a scarf, a nice georgette one.'

'How about a scarf and a scarf ring?'

'Perfect.' They smiled at each other, imagining the way mam's eyes would light up when she was given the presents. They loved Mam with all their hearts.

At first, neither saw the two young men outside the coffee bar window, waving their arms, pressing their faces against the glass, in an attempt to make themselves noticed. Greta gave a tiny scream when she became aware of a squashed nose and staring eyes only inches away. She burst out laughing, and the young man leapt back, did a thumbs up sign, said something to his equally contorted friend, and they made for the door.

'They're coming in!' Heather cried, aghast. 'Do you know them?'

'Not from Adam.'

'Then you shouldn't have laughed. 'Oh, look, they're coming to sit by us!'

The young men joined them at the table. 'Good afternoon, ladies,' said one. 'I'm Larry, and this is Rob. We've been looking everywhere for you two.'

Heather scowled. 'Don't talk soft.'

'It's true,' said Rob, looking hurt. 'I said to Larry earlier, "This avvy, we'll find the two best-looking girls in Liverpool and take them to the pics." We've been searching for ages and had almost given up when we saw you.'

'Gary Cooper and Grace Kelly are on the Futurist in *High Noon*.' Larry sniffed pathetically. 'We couldn't possibly go on our own.

We need someone to hold our hands.'

'I can't think why,' Heather snapped. 'Anyroad, we've already seen it and it's not the least bit frightening.'

'How about *Bride of the Gorilla*?' suggested Rob. 'It's on the Scala. You can hide your head on me shoulder during the scary bits. I won't mind.'

'It sounds a load of rubbish.'

'Oh, Heather, it sounds fun.' To Heather's annoyance, Greta was smiling broadly at the intruders, whom she had to concede seemed quite harmless, even faintly funny, not to mention very good-looking. They were remarkably similar in appearance; fresh-faced, wholesome, well-built, almost six feet tall, with the same coloured hair, a sort of mid-brown, though Rob's was curly and Larry's straight. Both were nicely dressed in flannels, open-necked shirts, and tweed jackets.

'Are you brothers?' she enquired.

'Almost,' replied Rob. 'Our mams had us on the same night in the same hospital. They were in the next bed to each other. We've been best friends ever since and so have our mams.'

'Oh, that's nice, isn't it, sis?'

'I suppose so,' Heather grudgingly agreed.

'You're sisters!' Larry gaped. 'I'd never have guessed. You're not a bit like each other.'

'I take after me dad, and Heather's the image of our mam.'

'If that's Heather, who are you?'

'Greta.'

Larry inched his chair closer. 'Greta's always been me favourite name for a woman.'

'Liar!' Greta laughed.

'Me, I've always preferred Heather.' Rob grinned at Heather, and she could have kicked herself, because although she didn't mean to, she couldn't help but grin back.

'Now, about the pics . . .' Larry began.

'We've got shopping to do first,' Greta said. 'And we'll have to ring Mam, tell her we'll be late.'

'We'll come shopping with you. Would you like another coffee before we go?'

'Yes, please,' the girls said together.

★

Ruby was sitting with her feet up, listening to the wireless, and wondering if she could afford a television, when her daughters turned up with two extremely pleasant, polite young men who looked like identical twins, yet weren't even related. One was called Larry Donovan, the other Rob White. They owned a car between them, a Volkswagen Beetle, and had given the girls a lift home. She understood they'd been to the pictures that afternoon to see *Bride of the Gorilla*, which had given them a good laugh.

Heather, usually so sober, had gone all girlish and coy, having paired off with an obviously smitten Rob. Greta and Larry couldn't take their starry eyes off each other.

After making something to eat, Ruby stayed in the kitchen, where she drank a glass of the wine left over from the night before and listened to the giggles and whisperings from the next room. It was one of the rare occasions she wished she had a husband so that when the time came he could sternly demand what Larry and Rob's intentions were towards his daughters. She had a feeling they were already serious. She'd noticed how Larry had managed to slip in the reassuring fact that they were Catholics.

Something miraculous had happened; two inseparable couples had met and fallen in love.

She felt herself go cold. She'd known it was inevitable that one day her girls would get married. Indeed, she had prayed they would settle down, have children, be happy. But now, when it seemed that this might happen, Ruby found it impossible to visualise life without them. She had fashioned her life around her daughters. They were always at the forefront of her mind whenever she made a decision, no matter how trivial. Virtually everything she had done had been done for her girls.

Imagine the house without music, without the wireless on too loud, no bright young voices, arguing, laughing, sometimes crying, shouting 'Tara, Mam,' or 'Mam, we're home'? There'd only be the lodgers who made hardly any noise at all except where Iris Mulligan was concerned.

Rubbish! Ruby drained the glass and returned it to the table with a thump. Without the girls, she could do all sorts of things. Give up being a landlady, for one. There would be no need for a house big enough for three, and she could afford to buy something smaller. Matthew Doyle could have his house back, though she'd be sad to leave. She'd get a job, doing something, she wasn't sure what, but she'd go to nightschool like Martha, learn a trade; book-keeping or typing. Or she could start her own business – she remembered she'd once thought of becoming a painter and decorator.

For the first time since she was child she would have no ties. She could do anything she pleased.

Oh, but she would always miss her girls!

Sunday, the girls went to Southport for the day in Larry and Rob's car. They returned late, with the rest of the week already mapped out; Monday, the pictures to see *Carousel* with Gordon MacCrea and Shirley Jones, Tuesday the Locarno, Wednesday a club called the Cavern that hadn't long opened and played New Orleans jazz, Thursday somewhere else . . .

Ruby lost track of the arrangements. The boys didn't seem short of money, both were toolmakers at the English Electric. When they'd gone, she wondered if she should offer some motherly advice, but couldn't think of any. 'Don't rush things,' perhaps, but doubted if the girls would take any notice – *she* wouldn't have. Years ago, she'd told them the facts of life and felt sure they were still virgins – at least they had been until that morning. It was best not to interfere. They'd go their own way whatever she said. Young people were very perverse and inclined to regard opposition as encouragement.

She got things off her chest in a letter to Beth. On re-reading it, she thought the weekend's developments sounded rather nice, a bit touching, and felt very pleased for her girls.

On Friday, just after she'd changed the beds upstairs and had four sets of sheets and pillowslips to wash, Matthew Doyle paid his monthly visit to collect the rent. It had crept up over the years to fifteen pounds a week. Ruby had raised her lodgers' terms accordingly.

He always breezed in, without an invitation, made himself at home in the kitchen and expected a cup of tea and a long chat as if, Ruby thought nastily, he found it necessary to emphasise the property was his. She found it incredible that a man in his position should still collect his own rents, and detested him as much now as when they'd first met. It riled her that she had to be nice to him, and worried her that one of these days he'd remember that the house had been bought as an investment with a view to having it knocked down and something else put in its place.

Nowadays, he was unrecognisable as the young man she'd met twelve years ago. Gone were the shabby clothes, the boots, the moustache. Today he wore a slick, grey suit over a sparkling white shirt, a silk tie. His expensive black shoes were highly polished and he carried a leather briefcase. It wasn't just his appearance that had changed, but his bearing – he exuded an airy, good-humoured confidence that she found highly irritating, and his accent had lost its rough edge.

Matthew Doyle had become a very rich man with a finger in all sorts of pies. It was Doyle Construction who were responsible for the block of flats being built in Crosby which had been the subject of much controversy – residents in the houses behind had thought they'd have a view of the River Mersey from their front windows for the rest of their lives. He had been elected to Liverpool City Council and his photo was frequently in the *Echo*, attending a charity function or a civic event with his pretty wife who was the daughter of another business tycoon. They lived in an old manor house in Aughton.

'I've brought Greta a present,' he announced, settling himself in the kitchen. He took a box out of the briefcase.

'What for?'

'Her birthday, of course. It's a bit late, but I'm afraid I couldn't get here before.'

'How did you know it was her birthday?'

'She told me last month.'

Greta actually *liked* him, as did Tiger, who had exerted himself sufficiently to rub against his legs. Matthew reached down and tickled his chin.

'Thanks for the present. I'm sure Greta will love whatever it is.'

'It's scent, good stuff. Made in France. Chanel something.' He was sprawled on a wooden chair, long legs stretched in front of him, very elegant.

Ruby turned away to put the kettle on when an excited little shiver made her spine tingle. It happened every time they met, as if her body wasn't listening to her brain. Damn the man!

'You don't think much of me, do you?' He was looking at her, laughter in his brown eyes, making fun of her. Lately, she could have sworn he'd started to flirt. Today she thought he seemed a bit edgy, unusual for him.

'You're all right,' she said grudgingly.

'You've never liked me from the moment we first met.'

'I wouldn't say that.'

'*I* would. You were thinking what a creep I was, making a few bob when most men of my age were in the Forces.'

'It happened to be true,' Ruby pointed out. 'And it wasn't exactly "a few bob", either.'

He nodded. 'You're right, 'cept when we met I was up to me ears in debt to the bank. I was desperate for ready cash. When I first looked over this place, I intended letting out the rooms meself, making a bomb.'

'Why didn't you?' She wondered where this was leading.

'You turned up, didn't you? Your need seemed greater than mine. I let you have the place for eight quid a week when I could have got twice as much.'

'I'm very grateful,' Ruby said stiffly. She hadn't asked for special treatment and wondered why he was telling her twelve years after the event.

He grinned. 'You might be grateful, but you still don't think much of me.'

Sometimes, she found it very difficult to be nice. She slammed a cup of tea in front of him. 'I think you're wonderful, will that do? Anyway, what's brought this on? Why is it suddenly so important that I like you after all this time?'

'Because *I* like *you*,' he said simply.

'And you've only just realised?'

'No, I've liked you since the day you walked through the front door covered in paint.' He shrugged. 'Being rich has its drawbacks.'

'I wouldn't know.' Now what was he on about?

'You lose contact with your roots,' he said forlornly. 'You never meet people who've been as poor as you were yourself. Everyone thinks you've always lived in a mansion and driven a Rolls-Royce.'

'Aah!' Ruby said with mock sympathy.

'It's got to me lately,' he went on, ignoring the interruption. 'I feel lonely, suffocated. I want to talk to someone from the same background as meself, remind meself of who I am, as it were.'

'There's plenty around.'

'Including you.'

'What makes you think we're from the same background?'

'We both lived in Foster Court.'

She gasped. 'I don't remember you.'

'I lived in number five with me gran.' He smiled, as if the memory wasn't totally unpleasant. 'I never went out, that's why you don't remember me. I used to sit in the window and watch the world go by. I'd see you every day, leaving number two in your shawl with your kids in a pram. Gran said you were the pawnshop runner.'

'Why didn't you go out?' She suspected he was like Jacob, set on avoiding a proper job of work.

'Because I had TB,' he said simply.

'Tuberculosis!' No wonder he hadn't joined the Forces. 'Are you better now?'

'Well, I'm not likely to cough up blood on your nice kitchen table, if that's what you're worried about.'

'I wasn't worried about any such thing,' Ruby said sharply.

'Sorry!' He raised his hands and backed away.

'Why are you telling me this?' she demanded irritably. 'You've never mentioned Foster Court before.'

'I'm playing on your sympathies,' he said with a grin. 'I told you, I need someone to talk to. Someone who won't slag off the working classes and argue over the quality of various wines. I'm sick of discussing contracts and arranging deals.'

Ruby folded her arms on the table. 'OK, so talk.'

'I'd prefer to do it over dinner,' he said slyly.

'You've got a cheek!' she cried indignantly. 'You've also got a wife.'

'Caroline's in the South of France, holidaying on daddy's yacht.'

'I don't care if she's holidaying on the moon. I'm not going out with a married man.'

'It would be entirely above-board. We'd sit in a restaurant with about fifty other people and talk, that's all.'

'No!' Ruby said flatly.

He got up and went over to the window. 'I'd forgotten how big this garden is. It must be at least a hundred and fifty feet deep and half as wide. I reckon I could get two pairs of semis on this plot, no problem.' He turned to face her. 'D'you know how much a semi goes for these days, Ruby?' He shook his head incredulously. 'Over two thousand quid.'

At this, Ruby felt so angry that she half-expected a cloud steam to emerge from her mouth. 'Are you trying to blackmail me?' she hissed.

'Yes.'

'Well, it hasn't worked. The answer's still "No".'

Ruby had been invited to tea to meet Larry and Rob's parents and sundry other relatives. She had her hair set and bought a new frock; red cotton to match Heather's cast-off shoes. It had a plain round neck, cap sleeves, and a swirling circular skirt. The boys took her in the car, squashed on the back seat between Greta and Heather, both reeking of Matthew Doyle's Chanel No 5.

She felt unusually nervous, expecting to feel out of things without a husband, a relative, even a friend to take with her in support, but found herself warmly welcomed into the bosoms of both families; the mams and dads, aunts and uncles, brothers and sisters, various grandparents, all crammed into the large Victorian terraced house in Orrell Park. Without exception, they made her feel very special, as if no one in the entire history of the world had given birth to two such outstandingly pretty daughters, such charming, old-fashioned girls, real bobby dazzlers. Though it wasn't surprising, she was something of an eye-catcher herself, and could easily have been taken for their elder sister. What a pity their dad hadn't been around to see them grow up. He would have been dead proud. And what a struggle she must have had, bringing them up all on her own. Well, all they could say was, no one could possibly have done it better.

'Me and Moira often worried that one of the lads would meet a girl and leave the other bereft,' said Ellie, who was Rob's mother, or might have been Larry's – Ruby didn't think she would ever remember who was who. 'But, as it is, it's worked out perfectly, both falling in love at the same time. Mind you, they've always done things together.' Moira was Larry's mother, or possibly Rob's.

'I'm very pleased,' Ruby murmured.

'Of course, we wouldn't dream of letting you pay for the double wedding. That'd be too much to expect. Perhaps we could get together sometime and discuss the expense.'

'I didn't know they were planning on getting married,' Ruby said faintly, deeply hurt that no one had told her.

'Oh, they're having too good a time at the moment to make plans, but Moira and me assume it's on the cards. Don't you?'

Ruby smiled, relieved she hadn't been left out. 'I think I always have, right from the minute they first met.'

Ellie linked her arm. 'Come and have more sherry. You look as if you need it. I bet you feel shattered, meeting so many people in one go. I know I would. Oh, look, our Chris has arrived. I must introduce you to me disgraceful little brother.'

'What did he do that was so disgraceful?'

'He entered a seminary, became a priest, then gave it up. That was fourteen years ago, but our mam still hasn't got over the shock.'

She half-expected an ex-priest to look romantic, slightly decadent, possibly debauched, but Ellie's brother, Chris Ryan, was none of these things. Instead, he was a distracted, untidy man about her own age, with a pleasant face and a lovely smile. She noticed he was wearing odd socks.

'Oh, look at your tie,' Ellie said fussily. 'Have you got it on upside down or something?'

'I don't seem able to get the knot right,' Chris said mildly, smiling at Ruby. 'So, you're shortly to become a member of our family, or I should say families. You must find it all very confusing. I'm never quite sure which of these people I'm related to, yet I've known at least half of them all my life.'

'Don't worry about it, luv.' Ellie patted his hand. 'If you need reminding, just ask me.' She winked at Ruby. 'Don't take any notice of him. He's putting it on. There's a brain as sharp as a razor in that ugly head. Excuse me a minute, while I fetch some sherry.'

'And a beer for me, please, sis.'

'Go on, ask,' said Chris when Ellie had gone.

'Ask what?'

'Ask why I stopped being a priest. I know Ellie will have told you. For some strange reason, she tells everyone. I think she revels a bit in having a disreputable brother.'

'I wanted to ask, but didn't like to,' Ruby confessed.

'That makes a change. Most people ask straight out.'

'OK, so why did you stop being a priest?'

'I'm afraid there was nothing scandalous about it. I didn't have an affair with a nun, as most people seem to think. I lost my faith, which coincided, quite fortunately, with the start of the war. It meant I had no crisis of conscience when I left and joined the Army.'

'Did you enjoy the Army?'

He made a rueful face. 'My only problem was, although I was anxious to fight for my country, I wasn't too keen on killing Germans. I was glad when it was all over and me and a German had never come face to face.' He took her elbow. 'I spy two empty seats. Let's sit down.'

'How do you use this razor sharp brain of yours?' Ruby asked when they were seated.

He looked at her enigmatically. 'You'll never guess.'

'I'm not even going to try and guess what an ex-priest does.'

'I'm a policeman, a detective sergeant. Plain clothes, I'm pleased to say. I could never get used to wearing a helmet.'

Ruby shook her head. 'I can't see you in a policeman's uniform.'

'Thank the Lord you never will. I was hopeless on traffic duty. I used to bless everything and it went in the wrong direction.'

She laughed. 'Is that why you were promoted?'

'I suspect so. The powers-that-be probably wanted me out of harm's way.' He waved his hand dismissively. 'Enough about me, Ruby. Let's talk about *you*. What do you do?'

She told him she was a landlady and how it had come about, going back to the day she and Beth had returned from Southport and found Arthur Cummings had died and they'd moved into Mrs Hart's house overlooking Princes Park. She told him a surprising amount, about Connie and Charles and all the other people who'd stayed, and how they'd sheltered in the cellar and enjoyed a sing-song during the raids, about Beth going to work, the children she'd looked after, Matthew Doyle, her lodgers, Greta's party the other week, how pleased she was the four young people had got together, that she liked Larry and Rob very much.

'Gosh! I've been talking for ages,' she said, flustered, when she'd finished. 'You're a very good listener. I'm surprised you didn't die of boredom.'

'I've been anything but bored.' He was watching her with a strange expression on his face, a face that seemed rather more than pleasant now that she looked at it properly. It was sensitive, intelligent, immensely attractive. Why hadn't she noticed before?

His eyes were dark grey, his nose and mouth a bit too wide. All of a sudden, Ruby's heart began to beat excessively loud and painfully hard.

'Our Ellie never brought the sherry or the beer, did she?' Chris said lightly. 'Don't dare move from that chair while I fetch them.' He threw her a glance that sent her heart into overdrive. 'If I come back and find you gone, you'll become a wanted woman, and the entire constabulary of Liverpool will be dispatched to bring you in.'

Chapter 10

The November sky was the colour of slate. It scowled through the windows of Mrs Hart's house where Ruby was in the kitchen making a list of O'Hagan guests for the forthcoming wedding. Beth was flying over from America, Martha and Fred Quinlan were coming, so were Connie and Charles. Greta and Heather had invited loads of friends from work, otherwise there'd only be six people on the brides' side of the church, including herself. Not that she cared. It wasn't her fault that she didn't have hordes of relatives.

The double wedding would take place on the Saturday before Christmas. Ruby was making a cake for Martha to ice. The Whites were paying for the flowers, the Donovans the cars, and the three families were sharing the cost of the reception. The wedding gowns were already in the hands of a dressmaker – Heather's regal white velvet, and Greta's determination to look like a fairy required dozens of yards of organdie and tulle.

Ruby was buying her own outfit, but couldn't decide on the colour. She changed her mind by the day. Pink was too light, brown too dark, red too bright, blue babyish, white or black out of the question. Purple had been her favourite for two whole days until Chris said it was the colour mourners wore to royal funerals.

'What about peach or apricot?' he suggested.

'Too fruity.'

'Green?'

'Unlucky.'

'There's no colours left. You've rejected the entire rainbow.'

'I'm considering burgundy or maroon.'

'Too miserable.'

'Grey?'

203

'Depressing.'

'You're a lot of help. I know, navy-blue!'

'I'd feel as if I was with a woman copper.'

'I might not go,' Ruby said gloomily.

'That seems the only solution. I suggest that before our own wedding we join a nudist colony so we can get married with nothing on. All you'd have to worry about is the colour of your lipstick.'

Ruby stretched lazily and remembered she'd thrown a cushion at him. This last year, a kind fate had showered the O'Hagan women with the most generous of blessings, first the girls, then their mother.

She and Chris Ryan were in love. They had recognised this remarkable fact the first time they met. 'I love you,' Ruby whispered, as if he was in the room with her, able to hear, able to answer, say, 'I love you too.' Or maybe the precious message had carried across the miles and he *had* heard, sitting at his desk, or out on a case, or in that horrible bar where he went with his colleagues for a drink. She looked at her watch; almost noon. He could be anywhere.

The future stretched ahead, a glorious vision of endless days filled with happiness. As yet, they'd made no firm plans, apart from a wish to get married next summer. They hadn't decided where to buy a house, where to go on their honeymoon, should they have a big wedding or a small one?

'Small,' said Chris.

'Big,' said Ruby.

Once she was married and no longer a landlady, for the first time in her life she would be a lady of leisure, though knew she would quickly get bored. There'd be time to learn things, study, think about a career. Chris had suggested she become a teacher. One of his mates on the force had left and was now in a teachers' training college.

Ruby, who was inclined to think she could do anything on earth, thought it a marvellous idea, until she remembered aloud that she hadn't been very keen on looking after other people's children during the war.

'You'd be teaching them, not looking after them,' Chris pointed out. 'You might need qualifications before they'd let you in, but you can study for them at home.'

She promised to think about it. She also thought, though she didn't tell him, about the possibility of having more children of her own. For the umpteenth time she thought about it again, sitting at the kitchen table, making the guest list for her daughters' wedding. It would be different this time, having babies with a proper husband at her side, enough money to feed and clothe them, loads of Chris's relatives to provide support if she needed it. Ellie White and her family were delighted that Ruby and Chris were together.

The doorbell rang and the sound barely made an impression on Ruby's consciousness. She jumped when it rang again, and prayed it was Chris, who occasionally called if he was in the vicinity.

It wasn't Chris, but a strange woman in an expensive fur coat who was about to ring the bell again. 'I thought you weren't in,' she said in a quiet, cultured voice.

'Can I help you?' Ruby enquired. She looked too posh to be selling something.

'You're Ruby O'Hagan, aren't you? Oh, there's no need to ask, I recognised you months ago, the first time I saw you.'

Ruby searched her memory, but couldn't recall having seen the woman before and certainly not within the last few months. She looked in her sixties, with a small, tight, very ordinary face, greying hair. 'I'm sorry, have we met?'

'I suppose you could say we met briefly. My name's Olivia Appleby.' She swallowed nervously. 'I'm your mother.'

What did you say to a mother who'd dumped you in a convent when you were less than twenty-four hours old? Ruby had no idea. She showed Olivia Appleby into the living room, then went to make tea. In the kitchen, she tried to collect her thoughts, make sense of things while waiting for the kettle to boil. She took out the best china, set the tray with a lace cloth, put sugar in the little painted bowl and milk in the matching jug, polished the teaspoons on her skirt. When everything was ready, she took a deep breath, picked up the tray, and carried it into the next room.

'I suppose you don't know what to say,' remarked Olivia Appleby when she went in. She was sitting uncomfortably on the very edge of the settee, clutching her knees, as if she too found the situation difficult. The fur coat had been thrown on a chair and she wore a smart black suit underneath.

'How did you find me? How long have you known where I live?'

Ruby asked. She was curiously empty inside, as if all emotion and feeling had drained from her body. She felt nothing for this well-spoken, well-dressed woman, neither love nor anger, but there was a vague sense of resentment that she'd turned up to disrupt her life after all this time.

'I've known about you for two months. Since then, I've been trying to pluck up the courage to come.' There was a slight tremor in her voice. 'I found you through, well it's a long story, but I'll tell you in as few words as possible.' She took a deep breath. 'When I was expecting you, I lived in Bristol with a woman called Madge Cookson. She was a midwife of sorts. You'd only been born a matter of hours when someone took you away.' A look of pain passed over her face. 'Madge swore she'd no idea where you'd gone.' She shrugged tiredly. 'We stayed in touch with the occasional letter, Christmas cards, that sort of thing. Earlier this year, in August, Madge died. When her son wrote to tell me, he enclosed a letter. On the envelope, Madge had written it was to be sent to me on her death. It said, the letter, that she'd promised never to tell where my baby had been taken, but didn't want to carry the secret to her grave and you'd gone to the Convent of the Sisters of the Sacred Cross in Abergele. She also said you'd kept your real name, Ruby O'Hagan.' She smiled wanly at Ruby. 'My first thought was truly horrible – I wished Madge hadn't lived until almost ninety, that she'd died years and years before, when you were still a child.'

'Who was the someone who took me away?'

'My father. He dragged you from my arms.' She cradled her arms and shivered violently. 'Do you mind if I smoke?'

'There's an ashtray around somewhere.' Ruby found one on the sideboard and put it beside the untouched tea. 'Have you been to the convent?'

'I went as soon as I read Madge's letter. It's no longer an orphanage, hasn't been for years.' She paused to light a cigarette, breathing in the smoke with an expression of relief, as if she'd been aching for a cigarette for ages. 'At first, I thought they'd refuse to give me the information I wanted, but the Mother Superior was young and very understanding. She couldn't see the harm after so many years. There was a mad search in the basement for files, and the long and short of it is I learnt you'd gone to live in Liverpool with an Emily Dangerfield.'

'Emily left, years ago.' Ruby felt as if she was listening to the story of some other child's life, not her own.

'I found that out straight away. I then resorted to the telephone directory, though thought it unlikely you'd be in. You'd have married, I reasoned. But say you'd had a son? He'd be an O'Hagan. All I had to do was ask his mother's name. I found an R. O'Hagan at this address and drove here straight away, stopped the car outside.' She stubbed the cigarette out and immediately lit another. 'I saw you at an upstairs window. You're so like your father, I wanted to cry. I went away and cried somewhere else, then I drove home. That was September. Since then, I've been trying to pluck up the nerve to come back.'

Ruby knew there were dozens of questions she should ask, but couldn't think of a single one.

'I'm surprised you never married,' commented the woman who claimed to be her mother.

'I did. His name was Jacob and he was killed in the war. I kept my own name. It would take too long to explain why.' She didn't want to. All she wanted was for the woman to go away and never come back because it was disquieting to discover she had a mother when she'd managed quite well without one for thirty-eight years.

'I'm so sorry about your husband. Have you any children?'

'Two girls; Greta and Heather. They're getting married in December. It's a double wedding.'

'I suppose you're up to your eyes. I remember when my own daughter . . .' She broke off, embarrassed. 'I meant, my *other* daughter. Oh!' she cried. 'I don't suppose there's any chance of us becoming friends? It's been too long.'

'I reckon so,' Ruby said slowly and felt ashamed when she saw the look of anguish on Olivia Appleby's pale, unhappy face.

'Perhaps I should go. I'm sure you're very busy and I'm probably holding you up.' She reached for her coat.

'Please, don't.' If she left, Ruby would kick herself later for not asking things she'd always been curious to know. It would also be very cruel. This woman had clearly grieved for her lost child far more than the child had grieved for its mother. She tried to imagine how she would have felt if one of her daughters had been torn from her arms when only a few hours old and she'd never seen her again, but it was impossible. 'Tell me about my father?' she said trying to make her voice sound warm and friendly.

The woman smiled properly for the first time, a sweet, almost childish smile. Her eyes lit up. 'His name was Thomas Gerald O'Hagan. We met in France towards the end of the First World War. I was a nurse, he was my patient.'

'Did he know about me?'

'No, he died before I knew I was pregnant. He was an American, born in Boston.'

'An American!'

'His father had a bookshop where Tom worked. We were going to get married after the war.' Her head drooped. 'He was my one and only love. I never fell in love again. I married Henry Appleby for companionship. He was a widower, much older than me. I never told him about you. I was only forty when he died.' She twisted the wedding ring on her finger. 'It was a good marriage. We were content with each other. We had three children – a daughter and two sons, all married now, leading their own lives, and providing me with grandchildren. I have eight,' she said with a touch of pride.

'Ten.'

She flushed. 'Ten, counting yours.' She leaned forward and looked at Ruby anxiously. 'Tell me, have you been happy? I've thought of you constantly over the years; on your birthday, or whenever I saw a girl your age. Madge told me this would happen. I'd wonder what you were doing, where you were living, but most of all I longed to know if you were happy.'

'I've been happy most of the time.'

'I'm glad. Now, I really must be going. I've intruded long enough. All this must have come as a terrible shock.' She was putting on her coat, lighting another cigarette. 'You need time to think, get used to the idea of your mother appearing out of the blue. Perhaps we could meet again sometime. I'm sure we have loads of things to say to each other.'

'Perhaps we could,' Ruby said politely.

Olivia Appleby winced. 'I'll leave you my card. I'd love to have a photo of your daughters' wedding.' Her lips twisted wryly. 'My *grand*daughters' wedding. Oh, and I brought you something. I nearly forgot.' She fished in her bag and brought out a little velvet box. 'This is the ring that Tom, your father, gave me. It belonged to his "grandpop" – that's how he put it. It's engraved, "Ruby to Eamon, 1857". It's exactly one hundred years since Ruby and Eamon got married. Now you know where your name came from.'

'Thank you,' said Ruby.

They went towards the door, shook hands. Olivia Appleby was walking down the path towards a large, gleaming car Ruby hadn't noticed before. She opened the gate, turned and waved. There was something terribly sad about her bent shoulders, her wan face.

This woman was her *mother*! Yet she'd treated her like a stranger. She wouldn't have expected Ruby to fall into her arms, shower her with kisses, but she must have hoped for something more than the cold welcome she'd been given, some enthusiasm towards the idea of them meeting again.

She must be bitterly disappointed. How far did she have to drive, feeling as as she did? Ruby glanced at the card – Bath. She hadn't asked all sorts of things, important things, about her father, Olivia herself.

Ruby wanted to run down the path, persuade her mother to come back, ask the questions now. But she couldn't. There was still a feeling of faint resentment that she'd come at all.

Olivia had reached the car, opened the door, was about to get in.

'Just a minute,' Ruby shouted.

The wan face brightened hopefully. 'Yes, dear?'

'Why don't you come to the wedding? It's The third of December, a Saturday.'

'I'd love to.'

'I'll send an invitation to the address on the card.'

Her mother got in the car, smiling and nodding. 'Thank you very much.' She closed the door and drove away.

'You're very quiet,' Chris said that night. Larry and Rob had taken the girls out in the Volkswagen and they had the house to themselves, not counting the lodgers upstairs.

'I'm thinking.'

'Could you think aloud? It's more sociable.'

'Sorry.' She wrinkled her nose apologetically. For some reason, she couldn't bring herself to tell him about her mother's visit. Later, after he'd gone, she'd write to Beth, with whom she'd always shared the closest of her secrets.

'I hope you're not still cogitating on what colour frock to wear for the wedding?'

'No.' She laughed. 'I've decided I don't care. Any colour will do apart from khaki. Fuchsia would be nice.' She'd always been drawn to bright colours.

'You'd look lovely in khaki, but even lovelier in fuchsia.' They were on the settee in each others' arms. He traced the outline of her face with his finger. 'You've got a very determined chin.'

'You've got holy eyes. You'd have made a good priest. The women parishioners would have fallen madly in love with you.'

'I doubt if having holy eyes will advance my career in the police force,' he said drily.

'I've never got anywhere with my determined chin.'

He kissed her. 'There's plenty of time. Until then, could you point your chin in the direction of the bedroom and we can continue this conversation there? Better still, *dis*continue it and concentrate on other things.'

Two hours later, a blissfully exhausted Ruby and Chris were in the kitchen innocently drinking tea when the young people arrived home – it probably never crossed their minds they did anything else.

The day was bitterly cold. Tiny flakes of ice were being whipped to and fro in the bone-chilling wind, confetti for a winter wedding.

Heather's short veil was flung into a halo around her regal head, while Greta had to cling on to her longer one for fear she'd take off, be blown away, as it spread around her like two great, lacy wings.

There'd been a gasp from the watching crowd when Ruby's girls came out of the church. They had never looked so beautiful, and probably never would again. Ruby thought with tears in her eyes. Memories chased each other through her brain; Greta's first words, Heather's first determined, stumbling steps, playing with Jake in the garden of Mrs Hart's house, starting school.

But now her girls were married women. They belonged to someone else, two very nice young men whom Ruby felt convinced would make them happy. Their mother was no longer the most important person in their lives.

'Sad?' whispered Chris who was standing behind her while the photographer took pictures.

Ruby nodded and he slipped his arm around her waist and

squeezed. 'It's only natural to feel sad, but I'll cheer you up tonight, I promise.'

'Not tonight. Beth's staying.'

'And you'd prefer me out the way!'

'If you don't mind. Only tonight. She's staying a week, but you can come tomorrow. Get to know her.'

'I mind so much, I'm busting a gut, but I'll just have to put up with it.' He grinned. He was the most understanding man she'd ever known and she was the luckiest woman in the world. There wasn't a single reason to be sad.

'Who's the lady in the mink?' Chris asked.

'Olivia Appleby, a friend from long ago.' She hadn't known the coat was mink until Martha Quinlan had remarked on the fact.

Her mother had asked for their relationship to be kept to themselves. 'I hope you don't mind,' she'd said over the phone, 'but I'm not up to the questions, the explanations, the accusing looks. Perhaps later . . .'

'I'll introduce you as Olivia Appleby and say you're a friend.' It was the way Ruby preferred. She wasn't up to facing people's reactions, either. Even the girls didn't know their grandmother was at the wedding. Only Beth knew the truth.

Beth! She looked across at her friend who was standing with Connie and Charles. She'd lost weight and her lovely hair had been brutally shorn to tight little curls close to her scalp, reminding Ruby of a convict. Above the exaggerated cheekbones in the once plump face, her eyes held an expression that a convict might; desperate, lonely. She was wearing a lovely mohair coat with fur trimming and suede boots. Beth clearly wasn't short of money, but she was short of other, more important things. It was obvious from her eyes.

The photographer had almost finished and some of the shivering guests had begun to pile into cars to drive to the hall where the reception was being held. Ruby and Chris were being taken in an official car. Charles had offered to take the Quinlans, her mother was bringing Beth.

Ruby made sure everyone was being looked after before getting in the car herself.

'Gee, Rube! I had a great time.' It was almost midnight when Beth threw herself into an armchair with an exhausted sigh. She already had a touch of an American accent.

Ruby collapsed wearily on to the settee. She'd danced herself silly and had kissed more people than she'd done in her entire life. It had been an enjoyable day, but highly emotional.

'I can't remember when I last enjoyed meself so much,' Beth said, 'though for all the expense, it wasn't as good as Connie and Charles's wedding all those years ago.'

'Martha said the same – and Connie and Charles.'

'That day will stand out in me mind for ever.' She looked curiously at her friend. 'I've often wondered why you got so ratty with me when it was over.'

Ruby made a face. 'Because Jim Quinlan asked you out.'

'You were keen on him?'

'Excessively keen. I can't think why. It was never reciprocated.'

'You've never mentioned that before.' Beth looked surprised. 'We usually told each other everything.' She unzipped her boots, threw them off, and tucked her legs beneath her. 'Have you got any wine? I feel pleasantly drunk and I don't want it to wear off.'

'I got some specially for my American guest. Red or white?'

'Either.'

When Ruby returned with the wine, she said, 'I didn't tell you about Jim because I was too embarrassed. I loved him, at least I had a crush on him, but he was only vaguely aware of my existence. Then he damn well went and asked you for a date. I was livid, I can tell you.'

'There's no need to tell me. I remember very well.'

'I'm sorry,' Ruby said penitently.

'How is Jim these days? I thought he might have come to the wedding.'

'He has the Malt House to look after, doesn't he? He's never been the same since the war. According to Martha, it knocked the stuffing out of him. His wife doesn't help. Martha claims she has affairs.'

'Poor Jim!' Beth sighed. 'Why is it some people lead incredibly happy lives and others are dead miserable?'

'If I knew that, Beth, I'd write a book about it and make a fortune. I suppose for most people it's a bit of both.'

Beth gave a short laugh. 'That more or less describes me, but leaning heavily towards the dead miserable.'

'Oh, Beth! What's wrong?' It didn't seem fair. Beth was so nice – and so was Jim. Yet she, Ruby, was deliriously happy and wasn't nice at all.

'Can I have more wine?'

'Help yourself – here, take the bottle. But promise not to get plastered.'

'I'm not making promises I might not keep.' She sighed again. 'It's Daniel, it's my kids, it's everything, Rube.'

'Is Jake all right?'

'Sort of. He's at university in New York, I think I told you. I insisted he went there. Daniel was annoyed, but black people can lead relatively normal lives in New York, not like in Little Rock. I shall try to persuade Jake to stay when he finishes the course, though I'll miss him dreadfully. He's the one person who keeps me sane.'

'I never think of Jake – or you – as black.'

'Well, we are,' Beth said flatly. 'Daniel and his friends fight against prejudice all the time. They sit in the white section of buses and wait to get thrown off or barge into hotels or restaurants, knowing they'll be chucked out, often brutally. No one cares that Daniel's a top class lawyer, only that he's black. He's forever coming home with his head split open, covered in blood.'

'I suppose you could say that was admirable, Beth,' Ruby said cautiously. It was the sort of thing she hoped she would do herself.

'It is, it's just that he wants me to go with him, other women do. He considers I'm letting him down, which I suppose I am.' She looked appealingly at Ruby, her lovely velvet eyes moist. 'But I hate violence. I can't stand seeing the hate in people's eyes, their faces all contorted. I'd sooner hide in the house, send Rebecca – she's our housekeeper – to do the shopping. Daniel and his friends are contemptuous of me. They think I'm a coward – I freely admit that I am.'

'What about the other children?' She'd had two girls and another boy.

'I hardly feel they're mine.' Her voice was desolate. 'Daniel's mother sets them against me – she's never liked me much. I'm the wrong colour, the wrong wife for her son, the wrong mother for her grandchildren. She brought her children up to fight and she considers me weak and spineless. My way of dealing with prejudice would be to move to a place where people are more tolerant, where there's no need to fight. Poor Jake is thoroughly confused. He doesn't know whose side to be on.'

'I don't know what to say, Beth.' It was far worse than she'd thought.

'What *is* there to say, Rube?' She shrugged helplessly. 'Sometimes, I wish it was just me and Jake again.' She smiled. 'Except it never was just us, was it? It was you and your girls as well – and dear old Arthur for a while.'

Beth was sleeping in the girls' room. Next morning, just after nine, Ruby went in with two cups of tea. Beth was already awake. She sat up and stretched her arms.

'I slept like a log. This bed's lovely and soft.'

'That's Greta's. Heather prefers a hard mattress.'

'She would!' Beth laughed. 'What a little madam she was! Always bossing Jake around.'

'Not to mention Greta, but she's improved since she met Rob.'

'Good old Rob. Give us that tea, Rube. I'm desperate. Me mouth feels like a sewer.'

'You drank too much wine.' Ruby sat on the bed. 'Though you look better this morning.'

Beth rolled her eyes. 'Are you suggesting I looked awful yesterday?'

'No, but your face is less drawn. Actually, Beth,' Ruby said gratefully, 'I'm glad you're here. The house would have felt peculiar without the girls, knowing they'll never live here again.' There hadn't been time to tidy the room since her daughters had got ready for their wedding. Nighties had been flung over a chair, the dressing table was littered with make-up, face powder had been spilt, the top left off a bottle of June. Ruby put her tea on the floor and went to screw it back on. Heather must have been too excited to be her usual neat and tidy self.

'If I wasn't here, I'm sure you'd have had other company,' Beth glanced at her slyly. 'Chris Ryan, for instance.'

'He's never stayed the night.'

'I'm sure he'd jump at the chance if it was offered. Unless you're worried about your reputation?'

Ruby laughed. 'Since when have I cared about my reputation?'

'What if your lodgers found out and were so shocked they left?' It was a relief to see Beth's eyes dance.

'The men wouldn't. Mrs Mulligan might complain, but if she left I'd be glad to see the back of her. Mind you, she gave the girls a lovely tablecloth each for a wedding present, white damask.' She loathed white tablecloths herself, finding it impossible to get the stains out. Dark, check patterned cloths were best – the stains could hardly be seen.

'Where's Tiger? I haven't seen him since I came.'

'He spends most of his time in the cellar. Remember that wardrobe he hid in during the raids? He just comes up for food now and then, has a weary stroll around the garden, then it's back to the cellar.'

'I'll go down and say "hello" later. I've never liked cats, apart from Tiger. What are we going to do today?' she enquired.

'After Mass – do you still go to Mass?'

'Of course!'

'If we get well wrapped up, after Mass, we could go for a walk in the park, then come back for something to eat. I don't feed the lodgers on Sundays, it's my day off, so we'll have the place to ourselves. We're going to the Quinlans for tea, and tonight Chris is coming.'

'I'll feel like a gooseberry.'

'As long as you don't *look* like a gooseberry, it doesn't matter.'

The week flew by. They went to the pictures, to the theatre, to dinner, wandered around the shops that were decorated for Christmas. Beth bought presents to take back home. Sometimes Chris came with them, but Ruby didn't let on that it was better when he didn't. Beth looked upon the years they'd spent in the house by Princes Park as a golden time when everything was perfect. She talked about little else; 'Remember this, Rube. Remember that.' Ruby had never been inclined to look back, particularly not now that the future seemed so sweet, but she willingly indulged her friend, laughed with her, remembered this and that, held her hand when she cried. She felt more comfortable if Chris wasn't there during these nostalgic reminders of a period long before they'd met.

One afternoon, they walked to the house in Toxteth where Beth used to live. The woman who answered the door was young and had a baby in her arms. She had no idea who'd lived there before, and when Beth asked at the shop on the corner they knew nothing about a red-haired Irishwoman who'd been married to a tall man from Jamaica.

'Well, I suppose that's that,' Beth sighed. 'It would have been nice to see them. Now I'll never know where they are.'

On Friday, Beth's last night, Ruby fed her lodgers early, and Connie, Charles, and Martha Quinlan came to dinner. Chris was on duty, or so he claimed. Ruby wondered if he was just being tactful. He would say goodbye to Beth next morning at Lime Street station where she would catch the London train.

'It's a pity you've come all this way and can only stay a week,' Martha said to Beth. 'And the girls are coming home tomorrow. You've seen hardly anything of them.'

'I'd have preferred to stay longer, but it's Christmas soon and I've loads of things to do.' Beth looked wistful.

'Perhaps next time you could come and stay a whole month.'

'But don't leave it another twelve years until you do,' Connie put in.

'Hear, hear,' echoed Charles. 'And bring Jake with you. We'd love to see him.'

'He'd love to see you.' There were tears in Beth's eyes. She'd cried too much that week.

She cried again when everyone had gone, sobbed uncontrollably because she didn't want to go back to Little Rock. 'I'd forgotten what it was like to feel happy. I almost wish I hadn't come and been reminded.'

Next morning, she managed to remain dry-eyed when Ruby and Chris saw her on to the London train. She was flying home from Heathrow.

Ruby hugged her fiercely. 'Come to *our* wedding,' she urged. 'We haven't fixed a date yet, but it'll be some time next summer.'

'I'll try.'

The train chugged out of the station and they waved to each other until it turned a bend and Beth disappeared.

'I've had an idea where we should go for our honeymoon,' Chris said, putting his arm around a dejected Ruby's shoulders.

'Where?' she sniffed.

'If Beth doesn't come to us, then we could go to her. How about spending our honeymoon in the States, New York? We could fly down to Little Rock for the weekend.'

'Oh!' Ruby flung her arms around his neck. 'You are truly the most wonderful man in the world. Whatever did I do to deserve you?'

Everyone had been surprised when the two young couples had decided to honeymoon separately; Greta and Larry had gone to London, Heather and Rob to Devon. Though perhaps it wasn't all that surprising considering they intended to live together while they saved up a deposit for a house.

'One house or two?' Ruby had wanted to know.

'Don't be silly, mam,' Greta laughed. 'Two, of course.'

'Though we'll live close by so we can see each other every day and take our babies for walks,' Heather announced.

'Babies!' Ruby shrieked. 'Oh, my God! I might soon be a grandmother.'

To her chagrin, Greta had asked Matthew Doyle if he had a place to let. Ruby couldn't understand why he was always so obliging with her family – the girls had been given a beautiful dinner service each as a wedding present. He'd let them have a self-contained, furnished flat comprising the top half of a narrow, four-storied house in the Dingle not far from where Foster Court, now demolished, used to be.

Greta and Heather had had a wonderful time getting the flat ready to live in. They were like children with a doll's house. The rickety furniture was polished, the windows cleaned till they sparkled, pictures and new curtains put up. They would come home from work and excitedly show their mother the flowered teatowels they'd bought in their dinner hour, the various kitchen utensils. Even the purchase of half a dozen pink toilet rolls seemed to give them an inordinate amount of pleasure.

Now Beth had gone and Ruby's girls were expected home any minute to start their lives as married women.

Another era had ended. Another was about to begin.

Chapter 11

Greta Donovan couldn't remember a time when she hadn't been happy, but she'd never thought it possible to be as happy as she was now. Life couldn't possibly be more perfect. Although Heather hadn't said anything, every now and then they would look at each other and smile, and Greta would just *know* she felt the same. There was something about Heather's face – and no doubt her own – a sort of glow, as if she was bubbling over inside, wanting to say things that couldn't be said because words hadn't been invented to describe how they felt.

Since she had become a married woman, Greta was convinced she'd grown taller, looked older, become a more responsible person. During the dinner break, she went with her sister to St John's Market and bought food for their tea. Back at work, she would earnestly discuss what they were having that night with the other married women, who would in turn tell her what they had planned. It was far more interesting than talking about clothes, not that she'd lost *all* interest in clothes.

Larry and Rob always went to a football match on Saturday. If it was an away game, they went in the Volkswagen or on the train if it was very far. The girls took the opportunity to clean the flat from top to bottom, polishing everywhere, changing the beds, and doing the washing. Mam said it was daft, they were doing work for work's sake, the bedding only needed to be changed every fortnight, and the furniture merely needed dusting, and then only if the dust could actually be seen. What mam didn't realise, was her daughters *enjoyed* doing these things. Nowadays, Greta preferred the smell of polish to June.

What they liked most of all was cooking. There wasn't time to make anything lavish on weekdays, but the menu was varied so they didn't have the same meal twice in a week. Greta had discovered she was good at making omelettes which she usually served with sauteed potatoes and salad. Heather could make wonderful puddings, especially trifle, though they only had trifle on Sundays after an ambitious main course of something like Chicken Marengo or Pork and Apple Casserole from Mam's cookery book which she'd never used, preferring to stick to meals she'd learnt to make at the convent. The book had been given her by one of the lodgers, probably as a hint.

Often, Larry or Rob's parents would join them, or Mam and Chris. There wasn't room at the table for more then six people and even then it was a squeeze. Anyroad, they only had five chairs and a stool.

Sundays, Larry and Rob helped prepare the meal in the diminutive kitchen and washed up afterwards – they were the best husbands the world had ever known. Once a month, they all went out to dinner, but not anywhere expensive because they were saving up for a house.

With four wages coming in and such a tiny amount needed in rent – Matthew Doyle had let them have the flat surprisingly cheap – both couples had almost enough for deposits. The boys had already had money saved, not for any particular reason other than there didn't seem much to spend it on. The girls found this amazing, having saved nothing at all, and knowing they still wouldn't have saved a penny if their wages had been two or three times as much. There'd always seemed far too many essential things, like clothes, to spend money on.

Marriage, however, had brought them down to earth. Since the wedding, neither Greta nor Heather had bought a single item of clothing and hardly any make-up. They were very careful with the food, though Larry had asked with an amused grin if they really needed three different sorts of pepper.

Matthew Doyle had informed them when he came to collect the rent that there was a new estate of semi-detached houses planned in Childwall that would cost two thousand pounds which meant they'd only have to put down two hundred.

'What!' Mam had screamed when she was told.

'Two hundred pounds, Mam. That's all.'

'I'm not on about the deposit. Are you saying he collects *your* rent as well? What's the matter with the man? He's got hundreds of people working for him, yet he still goes round marking rent books.'

Matthew had arranged for them to be sent a brochure which showed a plan of the estate which was shaped like a letter U with a smaller U inside.

The following Sunday, after breakfast, they went in the car to look at the site, which was ideal; an old playing field, not far from a row of useful shops.

'Those houses would be best,' opined Mrs White, Rob's mother, when she and her husband came that afternoon. She pointed on the plan to the larger U. 'They're less overlooked, well away from the main road, and they've got bigger gardens. The ones on the curve have the biggest.'

'You and Larry can live on one curve, and me and Rob on the other,' Heather said excitedly. 'We can wave to each other in the morning and before we go to bed.'

'I suggest you put down a deposit immediately before they're snapped up,' Mr White put in. 'We'll let you have a loan if you haven't enough.'

Larry's mam and dad had also offered to lend them money and so had Mam. People were being incredibly nice. Greta took the plans into work to show everybody and they were very nice as well. She was given the name of a good conveyancing solicitor and that of a man who fitted carpets on the cheap.

Greta lay in bed one Sunday morning studying the back of Larry's head. It was almost three months since they were married and Sunday was the best day of all. She felt even more exquisitely happy than usual. They would be in each other's company until it was time for Larry to leave for work tomorrow.

She always found the back of his head particularly endearing and longed to reach out and touch the short hairs on the nape of his boyish neck, kiss his right ear, the only one visible, which was a lovely, rosy pink. But the alarm clock showed only five past seven and she didn't want to wake him yet. He worked hard and needed his sleep. At eight o'clock, she'd sneak out and make a cup of tea. After they'd drunk it, they'd make love which was quite seriously the very, very best part of being married.

Until then, Greta was quite satisfied to lie in bed, look at Larry's head, think about the new house and what colours to choose for the walls and, most importantly of all, the tiny baby that was resting securely in her tummy. Only Larry knew about the baby – it felt awfully odd, almost daring, discussing your periods with a *man*. She was waiting to see the doctor until three had been missed which she would know by next Wednesday. It was just possible that their house might be finished before the baby arrived and things would work out ideally which, in Greta's short experience of life, things usually did.

Her thoughts were so enjoyable that by the time she looked at the clock again it was almost eight. She got up as quietly as she could and tip-toed downstairs to the kitchen. Heather was already there, about to put the kettle on. She looked flushed and starry-eyed and Greta suspected she and Rob had already made love, though didn't say anything. Sex with their husbands was the only subject the girls never discussed.

'Shall we go to ten o'clock Mass?' Heather enquired, a silly question in a way because they always did.

'I think so.' It would give all of them another hour and a half in bed. They didn't have breakfast until they came home from church, a *real* breakfast for a change; bacon, eggs, sausages and fried bread.

Heather said in a small voice, 'We haven't been to Holy Communion since we got married.'

'I know.' It was embarrassing to swallow the body of Christ after an hour or more of enthusiastic love-making. Perhaps Heather, like Greta, had a feeling God wouldn't have approved. 'Perhaps next week,' Greta said vaguely.

'Yes, perhaps,' Heather answered, just as vaguely.

It was Mam and Chris's turn to come to dinner; curried beef and rice followed by a meringue gâteau. Chris had brought a bottle of red wine. Greta was thrilled to bits that Mam had clicked with Rob's uncle and they would stay one big happy family.

The food went down extremely well, though Greta had a touch of indigestion afterwards which was probably due to the baby and she didn't mind a bit. The men, Chris included, went into the kitchen to wash up.

'I have a feeling,' Ruby said to Greta, almost slyly, 'that you've got news for us.'

'No, I haven't.' She'd noticed Mam had been staring at her intently throughout the meal.

'Are you sure?'

Greta felt her cheeks grow extremely hot and knew she was blushing. 'How did you guess?' she stammered.

'From your face, love. You look like the cat that ate the cream. Am I right?'

'I haven't the faintest idea what you're both talking about,' Heather complained.

'I'm expecting a baby,' Greta whispered.

'There! I knew it,' Ruby said triumphantly. 'When?'

'About the end of September, I reckon, but I haven't seen the doctor yet.'

'How long have you known?' her sister demanded angrily.

'Two months.'

'And you didn't tell me! Does Larry know?'

'Of course.'

'That's not fair!'

'Don't be silly, Heather.' Ruby looked annoyed. 'Larry's her husband.'

'*I'm* her sister. I wanted us to have our babies at the same time. Now I'm way behind.'

'It's not a race, luv. Oh!' Ruby groaned. 'I've got a horrible feeling I've put my foot in it.'

'It had sorted itself out by the time we left,' Ruby said in the car on the way home. 'Rob and Larry knew nothing about their little tiff. I think Heather regards them as a foursome, not two separate couples. She expects Greta to be as close to her as she is to Larry. Greta, strangely enough, has always been more independent. But me and my big mouth! I really set the cat amongst the pigeons.'

'I happen to love your big mouth,' Chris replied. 'Anyway, there'd have been an upset whenever Heather found out.'

'I suppose.' Ruby sighed. 'You know, I always feel uneasy when I've been to see them.'

Chris looked at her in surprise. 'Why? I've rarely known such a happy atmosphere. They obviously adore each other. It seems to me the two nicest young women in the world have found the two nicest young men. Honestly, darling, most parents worry if their children are miserable, not the other way round.'

'It's unreal,' Ruby said slowly. 'It's *too* happy, like a fairy-tale, or that film, *The Enchanted Cottage*. I keep feeling that somethings's going to spoil it, that it can't last.'

'Of course, it can't last. Eventually, they'll calm down, get used to being married, get on one another's nerves, lose their tempers, go running to their mam for a moan. But it doesn't mean they'll love each other any less.'

'You wouldn't think you were a bachelor. You sound as if you've had half a dozen wives. Does it mean we'll go like that?'

'No, not us.' He grinned. 'We'll prove the exception to the rule.'

It was April and about time she told Matthew Doyle and the lodgers that she would be abandoning the house by Prince Park at the end of July – she and Chris were getting married on 3 August, his fortieth birthday. 'I'll be getting the best present a man could ever have,' he said jubilantly. 'You!'

Ruby knew she was being unfair. The lodgers needed plenty of notice to find somewhere else to live and, for all his faults, Matthew Doyle had been a good landlord.

Yet she couldn't bring herself to say a word and was glad when Matthew broached the subject himself next time he came. He knew she was getting married, Greta had told him.

'Will your new husband mind sharing you with the lodgers?' he enquired. He was lounging in a kitchen chair, long legs stretched out, finishing in a pair of gleaming handmade shoes. As always, he wore an expensive suit, white shirt, silk tie.

'He won't be sharing me with anybody. We're buying a house.'

'Where?'

Ruby shrugged. 'I don't know yet. We've looked at a few places.'

'When did you intend telling me you were leaving?'

'I meant to,' she said uncomfortably, 'but kept putting it off.'

He looked at her sideways. 'Why?'

'I don't know.' She did, though. It was because she had the strangest feeling she was burning her bridges behind her, which she knew was ridiculous because nothing could possibly go wrong. 'I'm sorry,' she said. 'I'll be leaving at the end of July. I'll tell them upstairs tonight.'

'In that case, I'll apply for planning permission and have this place torn down.'

Everton were playing Arsenal in London. It was the last away match of the season. When Greta and Heather arrived home from work early on Saturday afternoon, the Volkswagen had gone from the place where it was usually parked outside the flat.

'I thought they were catching the train?' Heather remarked.

'They must have changed their minds, probably because the weather's cleared up.' It had poured with rain all night, but the sun had come out on their way to work. 'Shall we have a little snack before we start on the cleaning? Beans on toast, or something. I'm starving.'

'That's because you're eating for two,' Heather said stiffly. It was still a sore point that Greta hadn't confided in her the minute she'd found herself pregnant. It was for this reason, because she'd been so deeply hurt, that she hadn't told her sister she might possibly be pregnant too. She was only a week late, but was normally as regular as clockwork.

'I'll need maternity clothes soon.' Greta gave a little shudder of delight as they went upstairs. 'Shall we look for some next week in the dinner hour?'

'If you like.' Heather's voice was still stiff, but the idea of wandering around the maternity departments of the big shops was so appealing, that she added warmly, 'I'd *love* to!'

They smiled at each other.

As soon as they entered the flat, Heather put the kettle on and Greta switched on the wireless. She turned the knob, hoping to find something nice to listen to and stopped when she came to a woman singing, 'You'll Never Walk Alone', from *Carousel*, the best picture she'd ever seen.

'Listen!' she shouted.

'I can hear.' They sang along with the wireless while they prepared the beans on toast.

Ruby was humming along to the same music while she ironed the lodgers' sheets. She never ironed her own sheets and resented doing it for other people. But the beautiful words of the song were so uplifting, they made her feel quite cheerful. 'Only another couple of months,' she thought, 'and I'll never have to iron another sheet again.'

In a house in Orrell Park, Moira Donovan was searching through her friend's knitting patterns for a matinée jacket. The wireless was on in the background and the sun shone cheerily through the window.

'This looks nice,' she said, pulling a pattern out. 'I think I could manage that. It's a relatively simple stitch.'

'I'll do the lacy borders for you.' Ellie White offered. She was an expert knitter.

'Ta. I wonder if Greta will have a boy or a girl?' Moira mused.

'What does your Larry have to say?'

Moira laughed. 'Whatever Greta has will suit Larry. As long as it's healthy, he doesn't care, same as me.'

'I hope our Rob puts Heather in the club soon. We've always done things together. I'd like us to become grandmothers at the same time.'

'We're ever so lucky with our sons and their wives, Ellie,' Moira said soberly.

'I know. We're lucky all round. Oh, there's that song! What's the name of the picture it's from?'

'*Carousel*. The lads took the girls to see it not long after they met. Ever since, Larry's always sung it in the bath – if you could call it singing. It's more like a bellow.'

'You'll never walk alone,' Ellie began to sing.

Moira joined in.

The phone call came just after six o'clock. Ruby had several things on her mind. What to wear that night when she went out with Chris? Was she prepared to live in the north side of Liverpool when all she knew was the south? Had she made enough food for the evening meal now that Mr Oliver had turned up when he'd said he'd be away?

She went into the hall. The telephone was on a table with a wooden box beside it for anybody who wasn't an O'Hagan to put in the money if they made a call. They usually did. She picked up the receiver and briskly reeled off the number.

'Ruby. It's Albert White.' Albert was Rob's father.

'Oh, hello, Albert. How are you?'

'I've some terrible news, girl. Are you sitting down?'

There was nowhere to sit. A chair only encouraged longer calls. 'What's wrong, Albert?' Perhaps the house purchase had fallen through, which would be a shame. She hadn't the faintest intimation how earthshattering the news would be.

'It's the lads, Ruby. I don't quite know how to say this, but there's been an accident . . .'

It had been raining in London by the time the match finished. The lads were on their way home when a lorry skidded on the wet surface and rammed straight into the Volkswagen. Larry and Rob had been killed instantly. The police had telephoned their colleagues in Liverpool who'd gone to tell the Whites because Rob, who'd been driving, still had his parents' address on his licence.

'Do my girls know?' Ruby screamed. There wasn't a phone in the flat.

'Not yet. Moira and Joan have just set off in a taxi to tell them.' His gruff voice broke. 'Ruby, girl, I don't know how we're going to live with this.'

'I'm going to see my girls straight away.'

'Chris is on his way to collect you. Don't go by yourself, Ruby. Wait for Chris.'

She slammed down the phone. She had no intention of waiting for Chris or anyone. If she ran, she could be with her girls in ten minutes, maybe less.

'Mrs O'Hagan!' Iris Mulligan appeared on the stairs. 'Do you have to leave the kitchen door open when you've got the wireless on so loud? I was trying to take forty winks.'

'Oh, shut up,' Ruby said brutally.

'I beg your pardon?'

'Shut up your moaning.' She snatched a coat off the rail in the hall. It was an old one of Heather's, but she didn't notice.

'Is something wrong, Mrs O'Hagan?'

Ruby didn't answer. She opened the door and ran.

She actually lost her way in the streets that were as familiar to her as the back of her hand. By the time she reached the flat she had a stitch in her side and could hardly breathe. Moira Donovan and Ellie White were getting out of a taxi. Both were weeping and supported each other towards the door. They'd lost their sons and Rob had been an only child, but right then Ruby cared only for her girls.

The door was opened by Heather who was wiping her floury hands on a frilly apron. The sweet smell of baking wafted out.

'Hello!' She smiled, but the smile faded when she saw the expressions on the faces of the three women. 'What's wrong?'

'Oh, love!' Ruby fell upon her daughter, pressed her to her breast. Greta appeared. 'What's the matter, Mam?'

'*Greta!* Come here.' Ruby reached with one arm for her other daughter and for the briefest of moments, they clung together until Greta broke away.

'Oh, Mam!' she wailed hysterically. 'It's Larry, isn't it? And Rob? They're not coming back. Oh, Mam!'

Her girls were beyond help. Nothing could console them. They cried in their mother's arms, in each other's. Rob and Larry's fathers arrived, but for the mother and her daughers, the other people in the room didn't exist.

Someone, a man, tried to embrace Ruby, comfort her, but she pushed him away.

Someone else made tea, sympathetic words were murmured, a doctor came and left sleeping tablets, it was the only thing he could do.

Then everybody went, leaving Ruby with her girls. There seemed no point in staying and they had their own grieving to do.

A week later, early one May morning, the two young men, the best of friends throughout their short lives, were buried together. It was the prettiest of days, sunny and warm. A slight, white mist drifted over the cemetery, but had cleared by the time the nightmare proceedings were over. Greta and Heather could hardly stand and there were no refreshments afterwards because it would only have prolonged the agony.

'Would you like me to come back with you?' Chris asked Ruby.

'No, thanks,' she answered politely. 'I'm not in the mood.'

He looked at her sadly. 'I see.'

Days passed, weeks, a month. Ruby stayed most of the time in the flat with the girls, tending to them, making sure they ate. Both were expectant mothers and needed their food. She had no idea what was happening with the lodgers and didn't care.

'You know what I'd like?' Heather said one day.

'What, love?'

'To go back and live in our old room.' Heather glanced around the dark, drab, little living room that had never seemed dark or drab before. 'I don't want to stay here anymore. Everything about it reminds me of Rob. It's not that I don't want to be reminded,' she went on, 'but this was our special place, where me and Rob belonged. It doesn't seem right to live here now that he's gone.'

'What about you, Greta?'

'I feel the same.'

'Then let's pack your things and go.'

Ruby felt in a muddle. In six weeks' time she was supposed to be marrying Chris. They'd intended buying a house. But she couldn't possibly leave her girls and this wasn't the time to be planning a wedding. Perhaps in the New Year, February or March, by which time the girls would have had their babies and everyone's grief mightn't feel so raw.

It was then she remembered Matthew Doyle had been informed she was leaving at the end of July and the lodgers told to find somewhere else.

The muddle needed to be sorted out. The first person to contact was Chris. Now she thought about it, she was surprised he hadn't been in touch before.

She rang the station and was told it was his day off, so called him at home. His voice was courteous, but lacked its usual warmth. She knew she'd been neglecting him, but surely he hadn't taken offence considering the tragic circumstances? They arranged for him to come and see her that night.

It was ages since she'd looked at herself in a mirror and when she did she was horrified. She'd aged. Her hair, usually so glossy, had become wire wool, her skin was pasty, her eyes were dead. It was important she make herself look presentable because there'd been something worrying about Chris's voice. She used conditioner when she washed her hair, splashed her face with cold water, put drops in her eyes, and decided to wear the red dress she'd had on when she and Chris had first met. Finally, she got made-up, taking particular care. Although she looked much better when she'd finished, she was still pale. She went into the girls' room and asked to borrow some rouge.

Greta and Heather were talking quietly, half-lying, half-sitting on their beds. The endless, wretched weeping had more or less stopped, but the life had gone out of them. They would never be the same again. Yet looking at them, in their old room, on their old beds, Ruby found it hard to believe that Larry and Rob hadn't been part of a dream, that they'd ever actually existed. Her girls were home and it was as if they'd never been away.

She flung her arms around Chris's neck and kissed him. She'd almost forgotten what he looked like. She smoothed his slightly tousled hair, straightened his tie. 'Oh, I've missed you,' she gasped.

'I don't think so, Ruby. I reckon you've only just remembered I exist.'

'Don't be silly.' She shook his arm. 'Come inside.'

They went into the living room where Chris sat in an armchair when she'd expected him to sit on the settee and take her in his arms.

'Would you like tea or coffee?' she asked, slightly scared. This wasn't a bit like him.

'No, thank you.'

'Chris, what's the matter?' She felt a curl of fear in her stomach. Something was terribly wrong.

'How are the girls?'

'Broken-hearted. I doubt if their hearts will ever mend.'

He nodded. 'They'll bear the scars for the rest of their days.'

'So will I,' Ruby said fervently.

'And so will an awful lot of other people.' He looked at her directly. 'You didn't think of that, did you? My sister lost her only child. She wanted to grieve with his wife, with Heather, so that they could comfort each other. It would have helped, yet Ellie was left to find out by accident that Heather is bearing the only grandchild she and Albert will ever have.'

'I don't know what you mean!' She felt genuinely puzzled.

'You shut everyone out, Ruby,' he said gently, kindly. 'It didn't enter your head that other people were suffering as much as the girls.

You shut *me* out. I tried to offer comfort, but you didn't want it. You didn't want *me*. You pushed me away.'

'It wasn't deliberate,' she cried.

'I know, darling. I know you couldn't help it. But it wouldn't do, would it, to marry someone you can't turn to when something dreadful happens? I must mean very little to you.'

'You mean everything to me. *Everything*,' she added emphatically.

'It's felt more like nothing over the last few weeks,' he said ruefully. 'I doubt if it's possible to love a person too much, but you love your girls to the exclusion of everyone else. If we got married, I'd feel very much second best which, I'm afraid, just wouldn't do. I happen to feel that as your husband I should be the most important person in the world.'

'But you would be, you already are.' She wanted to run to him, throw herself on his knee, plead, but had the awful feeling that he would push her away, as he was claiming she'd pushed him.

'No, Ruby, I'm not. I only wish I were.'

'So, we're not getting married?' Her voice cracked.

'I don't think it's such a good idea.'

She got up, began to walk wildly to and fro across the room, then turned on him angrily. 'How can you do this to me, now, of all times?'

'Do you think I *want* to!' He beat the arm of the chair with his fist. It was the first angry gesture she'd ever known him make. 'It's the last thing I imagined doing. Oh, I don't expect our love for each other to be weighed on scales and your side must exactly match mine. But I need to feel *needed*, darling. The last weeks have shown how *unnecessary* I am to you.'

'Oh, Chris!' She began to cry and he took her in his arms.

'Don't, darling.' He was almost in tears himself. 'You'll get over me far quicker than I will you. I'll love you for as long as I live.'

'Is there no hope for us?' she sobbed.

'I'm sorry, Ruby.' He went over to the door. 'Can I see the girls before I go?

'Of course.'

He kissed her forehead, released her, and left the room. She heard him knock on the bedroom door, and sat with her head in her hands remembering, too late, the times she'd turned him away, rebuffed him. Once, he'd come to the flat and she wouldn't let him in. She'd thought he'd understand, but would she have understood given the same circumstances? It was her own fault that she'd lost him.

She had no idea how long he stayed in the bedroom. When he came out he said, 'They seem slightly better than I expected. Perhaps young hearts are tougher than old. Do you mind if I make a suggestion?'

'Of course not.'

'Ring Ellie and Moira, invite everyone round. I hope this doesn't sound brutal, but you've hurt them badly. You moved the girls back here and didn't tell a soul, as if the Whites and the Donovans didn't exist. If you value their friendship I suggest you try to make things up before it's too late. Don't forget, Greta and Heather are now part of their families too.'

A month later, Greta was found to be expecting twins. 'Larry was a twin,' she said sadly when they got home from the clinic. 'But his brother died in Moira's womb.'

'I didn't know that!' Ruby exclaimed.

'Nor did I.' Heather scowled. 'Why didn't you tell us before?'

'Because Larry didn't want anyone to know, that's why. It was a secret between us two.' She sighed and patted her stomach. 'He would have been so pleased.'

The lodgers all wanted to stay – at least she must be doing something right, Ruby thought drily. Mr Hamilton and Mr Oliver hadn't got round to looking for somewhere else, Mr Keppel had found a place, but withdrew when he discovered he could probably stay put. Mrs Mulligan claimed she had tried, but had been unable to find anywhere remotely suitable.

There'd been a time, not long ago, when Ruby would have been glad to see the back of Iris Mulligan, but Iris had proved worth her weight in gold over the last few months. During the weeks when Ruby couldn't have cared less whether the lodgers ate again or if the clothes rotted on their beds, Iris had taken charge. She saw to the meals, did the washing, kept everywhere tidy, answered the phone, collected the rents, and arranged for the shopping to be done.

'I made sure the men did their share,' she told Ruby. 'Mr Oliver did the ironing, Mr Keppel peeled the spuds and set the table, and me and Derek,' she blushed ever so slightly, 'I mean, Mr Hamilton, did the shopping.'

Derek Hamilton, a crusty bachelor in his fifties, formerly her greatest enemy because his television was always on too loud, now appeared to be her greatest friend. The television was still too loud, but now it didn't matter because Iris was usually in Mr Hamilton's room watching with him, which meant one good thing had come out of the tragedy.

Ruby warned everyone not to feel too settled. She'd written to the landlord explaining the changed circumstances and was still waiting to hear back. Matthew Doyle might not be prepared to let her stay.

'I've already applied for outline planning permission,' Matthew Doyle announced when he eventually turned up. It was a sultry, hot July day, and he wore cotton slacks and an Aertex short-sleeved shirt with the top buttons undone exposing his scrawny neck. His thin arms were very brown. 'An architect is drawing up the plans.'

'What for?' Ruby enquired coldly.

'A block of four terraced properties with garages at the back. They'd go for eighteen hundred each in an area like this.'

Ruby bit her lip and supposed she'd better be nice to him, though it would be awfully hard. 'Couldn't you delay it for a few years?' she suggested sweetly, then spoilt it by adding, 'You must be made of money. Another few thousand wouldn't make much difference to your bank balance, would it?'

To her annoyance, he laughed out loud. 'Another person would have grovelled, but not you, Ruby. Even when you need a favour, you can't help being nasty.'

'I wasn't being nasty, just pointing out the obvious.'

He raised a sarcastic eyebrow. 'You think that's a tactful thing to do?'

'What do you want me to do?' she demanded. 'Get down on my knees and beg?'

'Some people might.'

'Well, I'm not some people, I'm me!' She swallowed. She was going about things the wrong way. 'I told you in my letter what had happened.'

'I already knew. I sent a wreath to the funeral. You didn't say anything about a wedding in the letter. I thought you were getting married in a few weeks?'

She hadn't mentioned it because it was none of his business. 'It's been postponed,' she said shortly.

'I understand.' He nodded, a gesture she found irritating because he couldn't possibly have understood. 'How are Greta and Heather? Can I see them?'

'They've gone out for a walk. Heather's bearing up, but Greta . . .' she paused. 'Greta's still nowhere near her old self. She's expecting twins. She . . .' She paused again.

'What?' Matthew prompted.

'She talks to Larry in her sleep, as if he was still alive, and keeps looking at her watch when it's time for him to come home. There's other things.' Like wanting to know where Larry's shirts were so she could iron them, making sandwiches for him to take to work.

'I refused to believe it when me gran died. I used to close me eyes and try to imagine she was there.' He smiled, his dark eyes soft with the memory. 'Sometimes, I actually managed it – and then we'd talk.'

For a minute, Ruby didn't know what to say. She couldn't imagine him having done anything that wasn't hard and calculating. 'How old were you then?'

'Thirteen. I was completely on me own. Me mam scarpered straight after I was born and dumped me on gran. I must have had a dad, but no one knew who he was.'

'How did you manage?' she asked, genuinely wanting to know.

He leant his sharp elbows on the table. 'The war started – you'd gone from Foster Court by then. I tried to get a job, but anybody would have been mad to take me on. I could hardly read and write except for the bit Gran taught me, and I was nothing but skin and bone. I looked like death warmed up – people still say the same about me now. Then Charlie Murphy took pity on me.'

'The landlord?'

'S'right. He was our landlord too. He could get things for people. At first it was just food; sugar, tea, fruit, all nicked from the docks. I'd deliver the stuff for him, collect the money, take orders. Charlie gave me a cut of the proceeds. It was a bit like being the pawnshop runner,' he said with a grin.

'That was perfectly honest and above board,' Ruby said hotly. 'What you did was criminal.'

'I knew that would rile you.' He actually had the nerve to reach across the table and pat her hand. As flesh touched flesh, Ruby had the same disturbing sensation in her stomach that he so frequently caused. She snatched her hand away.

'I thought Charlie was killed in the raids?' she said.

'He was. By then, I knew his contacts and took over the business, though everyone called it the black market. It was either that or starving to death.' He shrugged. 'I went from strength to strength, but I knew it would all stop when the war was over, so I started buying property. It wasn't long afterwards that I met you.'

'And you're still going from strength to strength?'

'I've just got back from Australia. I'm going into swimming pools. I only saw your letter yesterday.'

And he'd come straight away! Ruby was beginning to wonder if she'd misjudged him, when the front door opened and the girls came in. To her surprise, they both looked extraordinarily pleased to find him there, particularly Greta, who inexplicably burst into tears. 'Oh, it's lovely to see you,' she cried.

Matthew gave her a hug and a kiss. He wiped the tears away with an impeccably ironed white hankie. 'And it's lovely to see you, both of you.'

He left soon afterwards, without saying if she could stay in the house. Ruby was left to assume that she could.

'He's a strange man,' she mused aloud to the girls. 'Fancy someone in his position collecting rents.'

'I don't see anything strange about him,' Heather said defensively. 'And it's only *our* rents he collects, because he likes us and wants to be friends.'

Greta chimed in. 'I think he's smashing. Larry and Rob thought he was the gear. He used to get them tickets for . . . oh!' She clapped her hand to her mouth and ran from the room.

'For what?' asked a mystified Ruby.

'Football matches,' Heather said briefly. 'He used to get them tickets for football matches, the best seats. I'll go and see to her.'

That night, while the girls were in the lounge watching the newly acquired television, Ruby sat at the kitchen table and wrote a short letter to her mother, informing her of the recent tragedy and that she was no longer getting married. They hadn't seen each other since the girls' wedding. She finished with, 'I'll let you know when Greta's babies arrive in case you would like to come to the christening.'

She addressed the envelope, stamped it, and opened the writing pad again. Now Beth, whom she should have telephoned weeks ago, but it was easier to describe the events of that dreadful day on paper. The other way, she would have broken down, wept herself silly.

'Well, that's a load off my mind,' she sighed when Beth's much longer letter was finished and ready to post tomorrow.

Ruby cupped her chin in her hands and stared into space. It wasn't long since she'd sat in this very spot thinking everything was about to change. The girls had just got married, she was getting married herself.

But now it seemed she was destined to remain in Mrs Hart's house, and hardly anything had changed at all.

Chapter 12

1963–1970

The woman was crying loudly outside the school gates, a small tubby woman of about thirty wearing blue and white striped cotton slacks and a bright red jumper. Her brown hair was cropped untidily short. Ruby stopped and enquired, 'Are you all right?'

'No, I'm not,' the woman sniffed and dabbed her eyes with a sodden handkerchief. 'I'm devastated if you must know. Me little boy's just started school and I don't know how I'm going to manage without him.'

'You will,' Ruby said with conviction.

'How would you know? Oh, of course. I just saw you taking three little girls into the classroom. They all seemed quite happy considering it's their first day. Which are yours? The twins or the red-haired one?'

'They're all mine in a way. I'm their gran.'

'Goodness me! You don't look nearly old enough to be a grandmother.'

Ruby was forty-four. She preened herself, being apt to take offence on the rare occasions she was assumed to be a grandparent. She and the woman began to walk together away from the school.

'Where are their mothers?' the woman enquired. 'That's if you don't mind me asking, like?'

'I don't mind at all. The twins' mother, Greta, hasn't been well for a while. She's at home. My other daughter, Heather, goes to work.' It had been necessary, not long after the babies were born, for the girls to have a room each to accommodate their offspring. Fortunately, Mr Oliver had announced he was leaving at about the same time, so Ruby had moved upstairs. It meant one less rent was coming in and although her daughters received an allowance from

236

the state, it wasn't enough. Heather had returned to work and was now a clerk in a solicitor's office, leaving red-haired Daisy in Ruby's capable hands.

'I'm Pixie Shaw, by the way,' the woman said. She had stopped crying, though her eyes were still bloodshot. 'Me real name's Patricia, but me husband claims I look like a pixie, so that's where the name comes from.'

There was no way on earth that Ruby would have allowed anyone to call her Pixie. 'It's very nice,' she said unconvincingly. 'My name's Ruby O'Hagan.'

'I'd ask you back for a cup of tea, Ruby, 'cause I feel like talking to someone, but me house is a tip.'

Ruby took the blatant hint. 'You can come back to ours if you like.' Her own house was a tip, but she didn't care. Nor did she feel like talking to anyone, but felt even less like entering a house bereft of children where Greta would still be asleep. She'd get used to the silence eventually, enjoy it, but it would take a while. It didn't help that it was such a horrible morning, dark and forbidding, with black clouds bunched threateningly overhead.

'That'd be nice, ta. I didn't have time to tidy up before I left. Me and our poor Clint were bawling our heads off. Neither of us wanted him to go to school.'

'Clint!'

'He's called after Clint Eastwood from *Rawhide*. It was my favourite programme on the telly. Did you ever see it?'

'No, but my daughters did.' By the time Ruby collapsed in front of the television, it was usually time for the national anthem.

'It's finished now, but I miss it still. What are your granddaughters called?'

'Daisy's the red-haired one. She's four months younger than the others, but the headmistress thought it'd be best if she started at the same time rather than after Christmas. The twins are Moira and Ellie.' Naming the twins after their maternal grandmothers had finally healed the rift that Ruby's thoughtlessness had caused, though it could create confusion at family gatherings.

'Daisy's a pretty name,' Pixie remarked, leaving Ruby to assume that she didn't think much of Moira and Ellie. 'Ooh! Is this where you live?' she gasped when Ruby turned into the drive of the house. 'It's ever so big. What does your husband do?'

'He died in the war.'

'Oh, I'm sorry to hear that. How long have you lived here?'

'Twenty-four years.' Ruby sighed. She led the way around the back rather than go in the front which might disturb Greta.

'Have you never thought of having the kitchen modernised?' her new friend enquired, staring aghast at the wooden draining board piled high with dirty dishes, the ancient wooden dresser, the floor with its chipped black and white tiles.

'I like it as it is.' Ruby tossed her head. 'Anyway, it's not my house. It's only rented.' She was wondering if she'd made a mistake in inviting Pixie Shaw for a cup of tea. She wasn't sure if she liked the woman whose only resemblance to a pixie was that she was very small. Otherwise, she was most unattractive, with pale, watery grey eyes, a flat nose, and a little prim mouth.

'My husband completely gutted our kitchen. We've got lovely new units; lime green laminated and an orange tiled floor. Mind you, we *own* the place, so it's worth our while to make improvements. Oh, you've got a cat? Or is it a dog?' She pointed to the earthenware bowl on the floor.

'It's a cat's bowl, but I'm afraid he's no longer with us. My daughter won't let me throw it away.' It had been a terrible year, 1958. So many deaths; Larry and Rob, then Martha Quinlan had died, shortly followed by Fred. One day, when Tiger didn't appear for his morning milk, she'd gone down into the cellar and found him curled in a ball in his wardrobe. His furry body was cold to the touch when she tried to wake him.

It had been Tiger's death that sent Greta completely over the edge. She'd wanted the twins to play with him, she sobbed.

'But, love, Tiger was already the oldest cat in the world.' Ruby had stroked her daughter's soft, fair hair. 'We were lucky to have had him for so long.'

'That only makes it worse. I'd known Tiger for nearly all me life, as well as Martha. Soon, everyone will die and I'll be the only one left.'

For a long while, she'd put milk out for Tiger every morning, called him in at night, looked for him in the wardrobe. Once, Ruby found her on the old settee they'd used during the raids. She was singing, 'We'll Meet Again', but stopped when her mother appeared. 'I just heard the siren go,' she said.

'She'll get over it,' the doctor said complacently. 'She's rather a fragile young woman who has had too much grief. Would you like her to go away for a while?'

'Where to?'

'A mental home, where she'll get treatment.'

'No, thanks. Tell me what sort of treatment and I'll give it to her here.'

'You must think of yourself, Mrs O'Hagan.' The doctor frowned. 'You're working yourself into the ground with three small children to look after, not to mention a sick daughter and the folks upstairs. You're not exactly young.'

'I'm not exactly old, either. I'll manage.'

Under no circumstances was Greta to be stressed. She took a tablet every morning to steady her nerves and another at night to make her sleep. The afternoons were her best time, when she usually played with the children. Ruby made sure she watched nothing on television that would upset her and limited her reading to women's magazines.

Greta, still in her dressing gown, came wandering into the kitchen while Ruby and Pixie were drinking the tea. She smiled dreamily at the stranger. 'Hello.'

'This is Pixie,' Ruby said. 'Pixie, this is my daughter, Greta.'

'Are you the one with the twins who's been ill?' Pixie enquired with a complete lack of tact.

Before Greta could answer, the telephone rang and Ruby went to answer it. It was Heather wanting to know if the children had settled in school and how was Greta? She rang every day to ask after her sister.

'The children seemed fine,' Ruby told her, 'And so does Greta as it happens. I brought some woman back and I can hear them in the kitchen chattering away like nobody's business.'

'What woman?'

'Her name's Pixie. She seems a bit silly to me, but Greta obviously likes her.'

'Make sure she doesn't upset her.'

'Of course, love.'

When Ruby returned to the kitchen, Pixie was saying, '*Three* widows, all living under the same roof! It sounds dead romantic, like a novel.'

Greta nodded. 'I suppose it does.'

Ruby regarded her daughter with shock and amazement. She couldn't recall the term 'widow' having been mentioned in the house before. Everyone was careful with their language when Greta was around.

'And your husband never got to see his kids!' Pixie gasped.

'No, nor did Heather's. She hadn't even told Rob she was pregnant with Daisy.'

'Oh! That's too sad for words. My husband, Brian, is thinking about buying a car but, meself, I've always considered them dangerous. He mightn't be so keen once I've told him about you and your sister.'

'Well,' Ruby said in a loud voice, 'It's about time I got on with some work.'

Pixie was better at dropping hints than taking them. Or perhaps the words hadn't registered. Greta picked up the cups which Ruby noticed had been refilled in her absence. 'Let's go in the other room. We can talk while Mam tidies up.'

'Have you got a picture of your wedding, Grete?'

'There's an album somewhere. Do you know where it is, Mam?'

'On the bottom shelf of the sideboard.' It hadn't been opened since the day Larry and Rob had died.

'Come on, Pix. I'll show you.'

Ruby sat down heavily when the pair disappeared into the lounge. For years, Greta had been treated with kid gloves, then along had come the tactless Pixie Shaw and her daughter had seemed more than willing to talk about Larry and the day that had forever changed all their lives. Perhaps Greta had been well for a long time, yet they'd all continued to walk on eggshells, treat her as an invalid. It had needed someone like the garrulous, nosy Pixie to show them she was better.

At midday, Pixie announced she had to leave to collect Clint from school. 'He wants to come home for his dinner.'

'Bring him round after school one day to play with the girls,' Greta suggested. 'Once he's made friends, he might stay for his dinner.'

'That's a good idea,' Pixie enthused. 'I fancied having him home for the company, but the morning's just whizzed by and I've hardly

240

thought about Clint at all. 'Fact, I'd have stayed longer if it weren't for him. 'Bye, Grete. See you tomorrow.'

Ruby closed the door on their guest. 'She's coming again?'

'You don't mind, do you, Mam? We're going to nightschool together. It starts next week. Pixie had already put her name down for leatherwork, but I thought I'd learn cake decorating, same as Martha. Pixie's decided to do it with me.'

'But Mam, that's not fair,' Heather complained that night after tea. She was drying the dishes while Ruby washed. Greta was watching television with the children who were tired after their first day at school. 'I've been asked loads of times at work to go to the pictures with the girls, but I always refuse because I'd sooner stay in with our Greta.'

'Surely you're glad she seems so much better?'

'Yes, but . . .' Heather made a face. 'Perhaps I could go to nightschool with her and this stupid Pixie.'

'Don't be silly, love. You'd be bored out of your mind decorating cakes.' Ruby sighed as she put a casserole dish on the draining board. Her own mind was numb with the effort of feeding nine people and keeping everywhere clean. Mr Keppel had left to get married years ago, and Iris Mulligan and Mr Hamilton had found a house of their own where they'd gone to live in sin, Ruby supposed. Three students from Liverpool University, young men, now lived upstairs and seemed determined to eat her out of house and home. No matter how much food she made, every scrap had gone by the end of the meal.

Clint Shaw came to play on Saturday morning. The weather had bucked up; the sky was blue and the sun was shining. By the end of the week, Ruby had had enough of Pixie who'd been every day. She was relieved to find Clint a blond angel of a child, very sensitive, with none of his mother's brashness.

She watched through the window as the children played in the garden. It seemed only yesterday that she'd watched her daughters play with Jake on the same lawn under the same trees.

'How time flies,' she murmured.

Now it was Ellie who was the leader, the one who determined what games were to be played. She was the younger of the twins by an hour, yet the most forceful as well as the tallest. But Moira wasn't prepared to be ordered about as Greta had been. There was rarely any argument; Moira just went her own sweet way no matter what Ellie said. They were obviously twins, alike in many ways, different in others. Apart from being fractionally smaller, Moira's rich brown hair was curly, her eyes a lovely light blue, her chin round, soft and dimpled. She was a self-contained little girl with a gentle, kindly smile, almost adult.

Ellie's hair was wavy and her expressive cobalt blue eyes were never still. She flashed like lightning around the garden, running the fastest, shouting the loudest, climbing the highest trees. Her pointed chin was always gritted, as if she had great problems to grapple with, and she suffered from a singular lack of patience, though having realised at a very early age it was a waste of time getting angry with her sister, she was inclined to turn on her cousin instead.

Daisy! Ruby's heart contracted when she looked at her third granddaughter, the solid, freckle-faced, red-haired Daisy, hanging timidly back from the others as usual. Such a pretty name for such a plain child – a woman had actually said that once in the clinic when Ruby had taken the girls for an injection.

No one knew where Daisy had got her looks from. The Whites had racked their brains, but neither could recall having had a relative with red hair, no matter how far back they went. Ruby had asked her mother, but Olivia couldn't help.

'There aren't any redheads in my family. As for your father, he had black hair, same as yours, but there could have been loads of ginger-haired O'Hagans in America. I wouldn't know.'

Ellie White, Rob's mother, probably didn't realise she made such an almighty fuss of her glowing, vivacious namesake, rather than her own son's child, the dull, slow-witted Daisy.

'How's Greta been today?' was the first thing Heather always asked when she came home from work, as if her sister was far more important than her daughter.

Ruby tried to make amends, make a fuss of the little girl who always seemed to be trying hard to look happy. But it was difficult. She didn't want it to appear too obvious to the twins – Moira wouldn't mind, she might even understand, but Ellie wouldn't be pleased if she thought her cousin was Ruby's favourite. Ellie could be spiteful at times.

Greta and Pixie came out of the lounge where they'd been talking animatedly. 'Is it all right if me and Pix go into town to do some shopping?' Greta asked.

'Me sister-in-law's getting married in November. I need an outfit for the wedding,' Pixie put in.

'We won't be long, Mam.'

'Why not ask Heather to come with you?' It was years since the girls had gone shopping together.

'She can shop in the lunch hour,' Greta said airily. 'Anyroad, she's in the bath.'

'All right, but don't you dare think about going out next Saturday. It's the twins' birthday party, there's twelve children coming, and I'll need all the help I can get.' She was already dreading it.

'Wouldn't dream of it, Mam.'

She must have been mad, inviting twelve strange children for four whole hours, when three hours would have done, or even two! The meal had been eaten in a flash and the kitchen floor was covered in jelly which the boys had flicked at the girls. There was also a scattering of crisps and crusts of bread. Two glasses had been broken and the tablecloth was soaked with ginger pop and lemonade.

Never again, Ruby vowed as she brushed the mess up, put the cloth in the laundry basket, and wiped the table, wincing at the screams coming from outside where the girls and Pixie were organising the games. Next party, she'd go out and leave them in complete charge.

For the next few hours, Ruby, never that keen on entertaining other people's children, cowered in the kitchen and listened to her garden being wrecked. Children came in frequently to demand a drink, something to eat, the lavatory, have a cut bathed, or to complain about something or other.

Pixie had brought a portable wireless which was being switched on and off. Ruby assumed they were playing musical chairs – without chairs – or statues or pass the parcel. She couldn't be bothered looking, just wanted everyone to go.

An unusually bright-eyed Daisy came running into the kitchen followed by Clint. 'Can I show him me colouring book, Gran?'

'Of course, love. Go in the bedroom, it's quieter there.'

She was pleased the two had paired off. Daisy needed a friend outside of the twins. When she looked in some time later, she and Clint were sprawled on the floor taking turns colouring in a picture.

Only another half an hour to go. Ruby sighed with relief as she filled a tray with glasses of lemonade and chocolate biscuits to take outside, where she was pleased to find a couple of mothers had arrived to collect their children – the sooner the better as far as she was concerned.

'I bet you've had a helluva day,' one of the women remarked. She looked about Ruby's age, very slim, with short brown curly hair and smiling eyes. 'I was dead relieved when my other kids grew out of birthday parties – I've a boy and girl in their twenties – but right out of the blue I had Will, and now I have to start all over again.' She groaned. 'He's five next week. The girls have been invited to his party.'

'Which is Will?'

'The blond one in the blue T-shirt. I won't ask if he's behaved himself, because I know for sure he won't have.' Ruby recognised the impish Will as the instigator of the jelly flicking. 'He hasn't been so bad.'

'You're only being nice. You're Ruby, aren't you? I'm Brenda Wilding. Oh! And this is my husband, Tony. He's been parking the car.' A good-looking man with Will's blond hair joined them. 'Tony, this is Ruby.'

'Pleased to meet you. Ruby.'

'Excuse me! There's a child stuck up a tree. I'd better rescue him before his mother comes.'

'I'll do the rescuing,' Tony Wilding offered, 'If you fetch Will's coat we'll take him off your hands. We're in a bit of a rush, we're going to the theatre tonight.'

'He didn't have a coat, just a jumper,' Brenda laughed. 'It was cream when he put it on, but it'll be black by now.'

Ruby found the jumper, still recognisably cream, on the hall floor. When she took it into the garden, Brenda Wilding was leaning back against her husband who had slid his arms around her waist and was nuzzling her neck. Ruby stopped in her tracks and a feeling of pure envy swept over her. They must have been married for a quarter of a century, yet were still obviously in love.

More parents arrived and the garden thankfully emptied. Pixie noticed Clint was missing. 'And where's Daisy?' enquired Heather.

'They're in the bedroom,' Ruby said.

Ellie ran into the house. 'That's not fair,' she cried. 'He should be playing with *me*.'

Ruby couldn't see anything unfair about it, but said nothing. She'd had enough. 'I'm going to lie down for a while,' she announced. The students had gone hiking and weren't coming back for tea, but tomorrow there would be a grown-up party to which the Whites and the Donovans had been invited, which meant she had another hectic day ahead.

She threw herself face down on to the bed and punched the pillow. 'I'm fed up,' she informed it. 'Fed up to the bloody teeth. Why aren't *I* going to the theatre with a dishy husband?'

The pillow remained mute. 'Stupid thing!' Ruby gave it another punch, then buried her head in the feathery mound with a deep, heartfelt sigh. She hadn't been out with a man since Chris Ryan. Her entire life, from the age of seventeen, seemed to have been centred around children, first her own, and now her daughters'. And housework, endless housework. She was sick to death of cooking, washing, ironing, cleaning. She'd never been to the theatre, the last dance she'd gone to was during the war, and she couldn't remember when she'd last been to the pictures or out for a meal.

There was a knock on the door. She folded the pillow over her ears so she wouldn't hear if the person knocked again and gave a little shriek when she felt a hand on her back.

'Ruby,' said Matthew Doyle.

She sat up, outraged. 'This is a *bedroom*,' she gasped.

'I thought I could hear you crying.'

'I wasn't crying, but if I had been, I'd've thought it a reason to stay out, not come in.'

He had the cheek to sit on the edge of the bed. It irritated her that he seemed to regard himself as a member of the family, though that was Greta and Heather's fault. They encouraged him, asked him round, invited him for meals – he was coming to tomorrow's party. The little girls adored him and called him 'Uncle Matt'.

'I brought some presents for the twins. I got something for Daisy too, in case she felt left out. What's the matter, Rube?'

'Nothing.' She resented him calling her 'Rube'. And why couldn't he have brought the presents tomorrow?

'You look down in the dumps.'

There seemed little point in denying it. 'So what?' she said churlishly. It had been a tiring, unpleasant day, and seeing Brenda and Tony Wilding together had been the last straw, though she wasn't going to tell him *that*.

'You need cheering up.'

'Do I?' She did. She definitely did.

'Let's go out somewhere. I need cheering up too.'

'Why?'

'Caroline's divorcing me.'

Ruby wasn't surprised. He must spend more time with the O'Hagans than he did with his wife. 'What have you done?'

He shrugged. 'It's what I won't do that's the problem. She's fed up with Liverpool. Daddy's retired to the South of France, to Monaco, and she'd prefer to live there. I flatly refused and she ses I'm being awkward.'

'So, she's divorcing you for being awkward?'

'Seems like it.'

He'd never said anything horrible about Caroline, but he'd never said anything nice either. She sensed he wasn't particularly upset, but the end of a marriage, even if it hadn't been blindingly happy, was always sad.

'What about us going out?' he said encouragingly. 'Last time I asked – it must be five or six years ago – you turned me down because I was married. Now that hardly applies. I'll be a bachelor again in no time.'

'A divorcee,' she reminded him. 'You'll never be a bachelor again.'

'Don't nitpick. Let's have a night on the town.'

Normally, Ruby wouldn't have walked to the end of the road with Matthew Doyle, but tonight she felt tempted. She would never cease to dislike him, but he seemed to like *her*, and was easy to talk to. She would express astonishent when her daughters said they considered him good-looking. 'He's too gaunt and hungry-looking,' she would protest yet wonder why he so often caused a riot in her stomach. Always impeccably dressed, today he was wearing grey trousers with a knife-edge crease, a navy-blue blazer with brass buttons, and an open-necked shirt. He looked as if he was about to leap on to his yacht. She was surprised he wasn't wearing a white peaked cap.

If she stayed in, what did the evening ahead have to offer? Lord knows what time Pixie would leave. She was another who was coming to regard the house as a second home. If Pixie stayed, Heather would have a face on because she didn't like the way she monopolised Greta and the children wouldn't go to bed while Clint was still there.

She shuddered. A night out with almost anyone was preferable. 'OK,' she said. 'But I'll need a while to get ready.' She must look a wreck.

He jumped off the bed with alacrity. 'I'll wait downstairs.'

Ruby looked in the wardrobe for a dress fit for a night on the town but, as expected, could find nothing. Along with all the other things she hadn't done in years, she hadn't bought much in the way of clothes. The only thing faintly suitable was the fuchsia dress she'd bought for the girls' weddings which was badly creased. She took it downstairs to the kitchen, set up the ironing board, and was just finishing when Heather came in looking sulky.

'When's *she* going?' She nodded towards the lounge from which Pixie's shrill voice could be heard above the even shriller chatter of the children.

'I don't know, love. Soon, I expect. Clint's bound to be tired.'

Heather frowned. 'Why are you ironing your frock?'

'Matthew's taking me out,' Ruby said with a happy grin. She couldn't wait to get away. Tonight, her daughters' needs seemed second to her own.

'And you're leaving us by ourselves?'

Ruby put the iron down with a crash. 'For goodness sake, Heather, you're twenty-six years old. Do you really expect your mother to stay in with you at your age? Greta's been so much better lately.'

'Oh, and I suppose that's all that matters!' Heather's sternly pretty face went red. 'Greta's better and there's no need to worry about me. Have you ever cared about how *I* feel? My husband died too, you know.' She burst into tears. 'The minute she's better, Greta doesn't want me any more.'

So *that's* what the tears were all about. Greta had been surprisingly thoughtless since Pixie had appeared on the scene. And it was an undoubted fact, Ruby thought guiltily, that no one had been overly concerned how Heather felt over the past five years. All their attention had been focused on Greta.

'I've always been sidelined,' Heather sobbed. 'Greta's everyone's pet.'

Ruby put her arms around her younger daughter. This was serious. Heather was a stalwart and hardly ever cried, not even when she was a child and had hurt herself. 'She wasn't Rob's, was she, love? Nor is she mine. It's just that she's always been so frail, she's needed more attention.'

'Just because I'm strong, it doesn't mean I don't want people to love me.'

Matthew appeared in the doorway. Ruby shook her head over her daughter's heaving shoulders and he gave a reluctant nod of understanding. The night on the town was off.

'There's something burning,' he remarked.

It was Ruby's frock, branded for ever with the shape of the iron and completely ruined.

A few weeks later, Heather asked her mother if she minded if she went abroad.

'Of course not, love,' Ruby said, pleased. 'A holiday would do you the world of good.'

'I didn't mean on holiday, Mam. I meant to work.'

Ruby didn't answer immediately. 'How long for?'

'I'm not sure. These two girls in the office are planning to hitch-hike around Europe getting jobs wherever they can. They might only be away weeks, but it could be months. They said I could go with them.'

'That sounds awfully dangerous, Heather.'

'It won't be, not with the three of us.'

'What about Daisy?' She already knew what the answer would be.

Heather squirmed uncomfortably. 'I can't take her, can I? Anyroad, she won't miss me. She's fonder of you than she is of me. Oh, Mam!' Her voice rose. 'The idea of getting away from everything seems like heaven. I can't stand it here any more. I had this stupid idea in me head that once Greta was herself again, it'd be like it was before, that we'd be best friends, go shopping together, to the pictures. But that's not going to happen, is it? Pixie's taken my place and things won't ever be the same again.'

★

Greta was entirely unrepentant when Ruby accused her of behaving disgracefully with her sister. 'You've driven her away from home. Heather's always thought the world of you, but all of a sudden you've dropped her like a hot brick.'

'Huh!' Greta snorted. 'Our Heather's always been far too possessive, so Pixie ses. She treats me like a child, not her older sister. In fact, *everyone* treats me like a child. No one seems to realise I'm a grown woman with two children.'

'You're not acting like a grown woman now. In fact, you never have.' It was the first time ever that Ruby had snapped at the daughter who'd always been such an agreeable little thing. 'I wouldn't expect the twins to come out with such a load of rubbish. What's got into you, Greta? You sound awfully hard.'

'I'm going to be hard from now on. Pixie ses being soft gets you nowhere.'

'Since when has Pixie been such a font of wisdom. Oh!' Ruby got up and left the room. What a stupid thing to say. What was the matter with everyone? Were her daughters having teenage tantrums ten years too late? Maybe it was time she indulged in a few tantrums herself.

Pixie Shaw turned out to be a fickle friend. Six months later Greta was dropped for someone else as unceremoniously as she'd dropped her sister. Ruby found it hard to be sympathetic. She would never forget the way Greta had behaved, and if she'd done it once, she could do it again.

Clint continued to come and play after school. Ruby was glad. Although Daisy didn't appear to be missing her mummy, she clung to her gran as if worried she might also go away. Clint and Daisy got on well, though Ellie did her best to pry them apart.

'Oh, Mam, when's our Heather coming back?' now became Greta's constant cry.

'Who knows!' Postcards arrived reguarly, there was the occasional letter. Heather was washing dishes in France, working as a chambermaid in an Italian hotel, cleaning lavatories in Germany, harvesting fruit in Spain. Over Christmas, she worked in a restaurant in a ski resort in Austria. 'It doesn't matter that I only speak English because almost everyone else is foreign.' The card was posted in Innsbruck.

Ruby followed her progress in the atlas that had once been Max Hart's. His name was printed childishly in red crayon inside the tattered cover. She thought about him whenever she opened it and wondered what had happened to the brave, young airman who'd made love to her so desperately that first Christmas of the war?

She'd never imagined that all these years later she'd still be living in his mother's old house, doing the same things that she'd resented doing then. She'd had dreams, once, of doing other things, but every time there'd seemed a chance the dreams would come true, something happened to prevent it. Perhaps it would have helped if she'd known what the dreams were, but all she'd ever had was vague, airy-fairy ideas about studying something or other, starting her own business – the first woman-only decorating company, she remembered with a smile.

Heather came home the following summer. She'd been away nine months. When she reached Lime Street station, she telephoned to say she was about to catch the bus.

It was the most perfect of August days, brilliantly sunny, the air scented with flowers. The children were halfway through the summer holidays. Ruby left the front door open and every now and then someone would look to see if Heather was coming. It was her intention to let Daisy go first to welcome her mummy home.

'She's here,' Moira shouted, but Ruby had scarcely turned round to look for Daisy, before Greta was running down the path, flinging her arms around her sister, kissing her, crying, 'Oh, it's so good to have you back.'

'It's good to *be* back, sis,' replied a surprised and extremely delighted Heather.

A fortnight later, Greta started work as a receptionist with a firm of accountants in Victoria Street, not far from the solicitors where Heather had returned to work. They met each other at lunchtime, went shopping together on Saturday afternoons. They put their names down at nightschool for shorthand and typing so that one day they would get better-paid jobs.

Ruby wrote a long letter to Beth and told her of the events of the last few months. 'Greta is her old self again and she and Heather are back in each others' pockets, the best of friends. I'm not sure if that's good or bad. They're not likely to meet another Larry and Rob, which means they're stuck with each other, and I'm stuck in this bloody house. Sometimes, I feel like doing a Heather and disappearing for nine months, but fat chance! What would happen to poor little Daisy? I'm the only one who seems to notice she's alive. There's *always* a reason to stay. *Always*.'

She put down the pen, then took it up again and added another paragraph. 'I shouldn't complain. Despite everything, I'm happy. It's a lovely house to be stuck in and I laugh far more than I cry. My granddaughters are a joy, my girls seem content, we're not exactly poor. On the whole, life is good.'

Beth was also content at last. Things had marginally improved in Little Rock. She'd joined a black – white integration group, and had been appointed secretary, 'Only because no one else wanted to do it.' A year ago, she'd gone to Washington and had shaken hands with President Jack Kennedy only weeks before he was tragically killed and all America had gone into mourning. Daniel disapproved of her activities. 'He wants black supremacy, not equality.' They argued all the time. 'But he respects me at last. He's suddenly realised I've got a brain, and my awful mother-in-law has now decided she quite likes me, after all.'

Jake was married and Beth would shortly become a grandmother. Ruby shivered. The years were racing by with frightening speed.

Olivia Appleby came in September, late one Monday morning when the children were at school and the girls at work. Ruby only saw her mother four or five times a year and then it was for just a few hours. Her children, her *other* children, she would stress, would want to know where she was if she stayed overnight.

'They don't know about you or your father. It's a secret I've always kept close to my heart. I couldn't bear to talk about him to anyone else, only you.'

It seemed to Ruby that, as the years took her further and further away from Tom O'Hagan, the more clearly Olivia remembered him. His face she described in specific detail, and she could repeat the conversations they had word for word. She was only now recalling long forgotten things, such as railway lines glinting, like silver wire in the moonlight', the strange smell – 'it was just the other day I realised what it was, a mixture of night flowers and burnt flesh'.

When she came, Olivia asked if they could go into the garden.

The day wasn't particularly warm, a weak sun appeared occasionally from behind pearly grey clouds. They sat in deck chairs under the trees that were just beginning to turn gold, Olivia a melancholy figure in her pale, linen suit and large framed hat, smoking the inevitable cigarette.

'I've brought you something,' she said in a whispery voice that Ruby could hardly hear. She seemed tired today, washed-out. 'It's in my bag in the house.'

'Oh, what?' Ruby tried to sound enthusiastic. She was unable to describe exactly how she felt about her mother's visits; a mixture of resentment, embarrassment, and guilt – mostly guilt. She didn't doubt that Olivia would prefer to have found a far more loving daughter than herself.

'It's a matinée jacket, the only item of baby clothes I kept. I didn't even buy it, Madge did, but I thought you'd like to have it as a memento.'

'I'll treasure it for ever.'

The colourless lips twisted in a smile. 'My dear Ruby, you try so hard, but you're not a good enough actress to deceive. You find me a pain, don't you?'

'Of course not!' Ruby protested.

'Yes, you do, dear. Not that I blame you. It was selfish of me to come bursting into your life nearly forty years too late, but once I'd discovered where you lived, I *had* to get to know Tom's daughter.' She looked curiously at Ruby. 'Don't you ever wonder how your life would have gone if he hadn't been killed?'

Ruby shook her head. 'It seems a waste of time.'

'I've wasted an awful lot of time thinking about what might have been,' Olivia said with a sigh. 'I wish I were strong like you.'

'It's not a question of being strong.' The circumstances of her birth had been entirely beyond her control. It was pointless trying to imagine how it would be had things gone differently. 'It would have been nice, living in America, being part of a big family,' she said, hoping this would please Olivia.

'It would have been more than nice. It would have been perfect. I used to think of contacting Tom's family, even going to see them. She smiled thinly. 'I was too nervous, though. I would have felt like an intruder. Then I met my husband and by the time he died it was too late.'

'Would you like more tea?'

'I'd love some, dear.'

'I won't be a minute.'

'Do you think you'll ever get married again?' Olivia enquired when Ruby returned.

'I don't know. It's something else I don't think about. I've got my hands full as it is.'

'I'd like to see you settled before . . .' she broke off. 'It's a pity that Chris turned out to be such a fool.'

'A fool?' Chris Ryan had always seemed eminently sensible.

'Fancy giving you up for loving your girls too much! Did he expect to have taken their place in your heart?' She angrily flicked the ash off her cigarette. 'What conceit some men have. Have you heard from him since?'

'I've seen him lots of times – he's Ellie White's brother. We've talked a bit, but never about anything intimate. He's getting married soon, but I haven't met the woman.'

'What about that Matthew I seem to meet whenever I come to your house?'

Ruby laughed. 'Why are you so anxious to see me married?'

'I told you, I'd like to see you settled. Matthew seems very nice. He's also very rich, so I've been given to understand.'

'Until recently, he was also very married. Now he's divorced and he sometimes asks me out, but I always refuse.'

'Why?'

'Because I don't like him,' Ruby said simply. 'We shared some of our past and I'm the only one he can talk to about it. That's why he comes. Now he seems to regard us as his substitute family.'

'It's not always possible to escape the past,' Olivia murmured.

'Anyway, Matthew's got a girlfriend, so I'm afraid, Olivia, there's no sign of a husband on the horizon at the moment. I'm not exactly worried.'

Olivia looked pleased, she always did when Ruby used her name. She crushed a cigarette beneath her heel and lit another. 'Tell me about your husband. You hardly ever talk about him.'

'Jacob? There's nothing much to tell.' Ruby racked her brains for things to say about Jacob without revealing what a disaster it had been. She described meeting Jacob on Humble's Farm, invented their wedding, smartened up Foster Court so it sounded quite respectable, avoided her cleaning career – Olivia already knew she'd been the pawnshop runner. After she'd finished, Olivia asked about the convent, about Emily, then Beth.

'She seemed so nice, Beth. It's a pity she went away.'

'It certainly is.' Ruby's voice was hoarse with answering so many questions. She'd been talking for hours. They'd spoken about the same things, the same people, before, but today Olivia wanted to know every trivial little detail. 'I have to collect the children from school soon. Would you like to come with me?'

'No, thank you. I'll just sit here till you come back. I'm rather tired.' There were dark circles under her eyes and her cheeks were hollow. 'That's a pretty dress, dear. I meant to say before,' she commented when Ruby stood up.

'I bought it the day the twins had their sixth birthday party. I left the girls to get on with it and went shopping by myself. It was such a treat. I'd almost forgotten what town looked like.' For years, her life had been confined to a small patch of Liverpool; the park, the school, the shops in Ullet Road. 'I might do it more often.'

'It's about time you spread your wings a bit. You suit that colour.'

The dress was wine corduroy, very fine, with a cowl neck and short sleeves. 'Emily used to say I had terrible taste in clothes.'

'Emily didn't know what she was talking about.'

When Ruby returned from school with her granddaughters, three large, beautifully-dressed dolls were perched on chairs around the kitchen table and Olivia was making a pot of tea.

'In order to avoid an argument, they're identical,' she said. 'Sorry I couldn't get them here in time for your birthday, girls. As you can see, I got one for Daisy too.'

The children fell upon the dolls with screams of delight. 'Why does Daisy get presents on our birthday, but we get none on hers?' Ellie wanted to know.

'So she won't feel left out,' said Ruby.

'What if me and Moira feel left out?'

'Do you?'

Ellie considered the question earnestly. 'No.'

'Well, there's your answer. Have you all thanked Olivia for the lovely present?'

'Thank you, Olivia,' they chorused. They hadn't seen enough of the woman who was their great-grandmother to grow fond of her, but were always pleased when she came, as were Greta and Heather who'd been told she was a 'friend from the past', someone Ruby had known when she'd lived in Brambles with Emily.

Olivia went with the children into the living room while Ruby made the tea and wondered why she hadn't gone by now – she rarely stayed more than a couple of hours. It was a long drive to Bath and she'd already said she was tired.

This was Ruby's busiest time. The children ate and returned to watch television and Olivia stayed in the kitchen and chain-smoked while her daughter prepared another meal.

'Are you sure you won't have anything?' Ruby asked.

'No, dear. I'm not at all hungry, though I wouldn't mind another cup of tea. I'll just wait and say hello to Greta and Heather, then I'll go.' She glanced at the heap of potatoes Ruby was peeling. 'What a brick you are, doing this every night of the week.'

'Except Sundays, when the students feed themselves and the girls do the cooking. During the war, I often made meals for a dozen people, sometimes more.'

'I helped the Red Cross in the last war, just dressing wounds, that sort of thing. Although I was qualified, I hadn't nursed for more than fifteen years.'

Ruby paused, a potato in one hand, the peeler in another. 'I'd be a hopeless nurse. I'd get impatient with people if they didn't get better.'

'You didn't get impatient with Greta when she was ill.'

'No, but she's family. I'm wonderful with family, horrible with everyone else.'

'Thank goodness I'm family,' Olivia gave one of her rare rusty laughs. 'Not that I think what you said is true. I'm sure you're not horrible to the students or the people you fed during the war.'

'Not openly, but I feel horrible inside.'

They smiled at each other, and Ruby thought it was rather nice to have her mother sitting companiably by the table while she worked. For the first time, she felt stirrings of what might turn into a relationship. 'You must come again soon,' she said.

Perhaps her mother sensed it too but, if so, why did she look so sad? 'I'll come as soon as I can,' Olivia said.

★

Beth rang on Christmas Day to say she'd become a grandmother and felt very odd.

'You'll soon get used to it,' Ruby assured her. 'What time is it there?'

'Eight o'clock. I'm not long up. It's a beautiful day.'

'We're just about to have our tea – the Donovans and the Whites are here. It's already pitch dark, freezing cold, and snowing.'

'It sounds mad, but I'd sooner be in Liverpool right now, particularly if it's snowing.'

'I'd sooner you were too, Beth.'

'Ah, well,' Beth sighed. 'Have you had a nice day so far?'

'Lovely. The children are over the moon with their presents.' Matthew had bought them a toy typewriter each and she'd felt obliged to invite him to dinner.

'We've come through, haven't we, Rube?'

'We have that, Beth. Merry Christmas.'

'And a Merry Christmas to you.'

It was four days after Christmas. Greta and Heather had returned to work and the children were playing snowballs in the garden. Ruby was making another batch of mince pies, everybody's favourite, when the telephone rang.

'Hello. Oh! Now there's pastry stuck to the damn thing.'

'I beg your pardon?' It was a woman at the other end, well-spoken, with a nothing sort of voice, expressionless.

'Sorry, it's just that I'm baking and I forgot to wipe my hands. Hello, again.'

'Is that Mrs O'Hagan?'

'Speaking.'

'We found a note on mother's pad to ring you if something happened. I'm sorry to say she died on Christmas morning.'

'Who is this? I'm afraid I don't understand.'

'I'm Irene Clark. My mother's Olivia Appleby. She's never mentioned you before. There was just this note on her pad . . .' The voice trailed away.

'Olivia's *dead*?' Ruby gasped incredulously.

'Were you a friend?'

'Yes.'

'Well, it can't have come as a surprise. She's known for months she was dying. All those cigarettes! Eighty a day for years. When did you last see her?'

'September.'

'Then you must have been one of her last visitors.'

'Actually, she came to see me.'

'How incredible. Where are you, by the way? Yours isn't a local number.'

'Liverpool.'

'Liverpool! Mother came all the way to Liverpool in September! Are you sure you're not confusing this year with last?'

'Perhaps I am,' Ruby couldn't be bothered arguing. She disliked the woman's dull, deadpan voice. She didn't sound the least upset that her mother had just died.

'Oh, well. I've let you know as she requested. The funeral's Monday if you want to come.'

'I'm afraid that won't be possible. I'm very sorry to hear about your mother. Thank you for ringing.' Ruby replaced the receiver and went back into the kitchen where she ferociously kneaded the pastry, then pounded it just as ferociously with the rolling pin. Too late – such thoughts always came too late – she realised she'd wasted the opportunity of getting to know her mother. Poor Olivia, with her sad, sweet smile, who'd lost her lover, then had her newborn baby snatched from her arms. Why wasn't I nicer, more friendly, more loving? Ruby asked herself in an agony of remorse, then chided herself for being a hypocrite. She'd had every opportunity of doing all those things, but she hadn't, and it was no use crying over spilt milk. Except she was. She wiped the tears away with the back of her floury hand and wondered if she should ring Olivia's house in case Irene Clark was there and apologise for being so unsympathetic. Fancy assuming the woman wasn't upset because she had a deadpan voice! Maybe her voice was like that *because* she was upset.

'Oh, what a horrible person I am!' Ruby wailed aloud. 'And I don't get better as I get older.'

The children came pouring in from the garden, mittens soaking wet, their noses cherry red, faces glowing with health. Daisy was sniffing audibly, close to reluctant tears, because Ellie had stuffed a snowball down her neck. For some reason, Ruby hugged the three of them extravagantly, even Ellie who'd been such an extremely naughty little girl.

★

257

By the end of the following year, Greta and Heather had become competent shorthand typists. Greta moved to a different firm, but Heather was promoted to secretary in the solicitors and began to study towards becoming a legal clerk.

In 1968, Beth's youngest child, Seymour, enrolled at Liverpool University and it seemed only natural for him to stay with the O'Hagans. He was eighteen, a stranger in a strange land, who'd abandoned his country to escape the draft. On the other side of the world a cruel and pitiless battle was being fought as America attempted to wrest North Vietnam from the control of the Communists. Daniel Lefarge wasn't prepared for his son to be sacrificed in what he considered was a white man's war. On this, he and Beth wholeheartedly agreed.

Seymour was a shy, withdrawn young man, not a bit like Jake, his half brother. He studied hard in his room upstairs, but always came down for the Nine O'clock News on television, when he would watch, making no comment, when students in his home country were shown demonstrating against the war, or when scenes of the fighting appeared on the screen and the numbers of dead were announced.

After the long, hot summer break, Seymour didn't return to university for his second year. Ruby found his room empty of most of his things and a note on the bed:

'I don't like being a coward. By the time you read this, I will have given myself up to the American Embassy in London. Please remind Pop that all my life he taught me to fight and I can't just stop when it pleases him. I need to fight for my country, otherwise I won't be able to live with myself for the rest of my life. Tell Mom I love her.'

In the first month of the new decade, January 1970, Private Seymour Lefarge lost his young life in the jungles of North Vietnam. For a long time, Beth was inconsolable, but eventually the memory of her son was tucked away in a corner of her mind to be brought out and cherished during times when she was alone. Daniel, though, never recovered. From the moment he heard about Seymour's death, he was a changed man.

Ruby had only witnessed the sixties from afar. She was too old to have gone to the Cavern, an open-air pop concert, worn flowers in her hair, and sung songs extolling love and peace. Carnaby Street could have been on the moon for all the chance she'd had of seeing it and, although the Liverpool Sound had spread throughout the world, she'd only heard it on 'Top of the Pops'.

Even so, she was aware that the sixties had mainly been a heady, idealistic decade when compared to the ugly violence of the seventies. In Vietnam, the conflict was escalating and, suddenly, there seemed to be wars all over the place. Politicians were kidnapped and murdered, planes hijacked. Even on mainland Britain, bombs were killing and maiming innocent people as a consequence of the troubles in Northern Ireland.

She remembered the day that war had been declared on Germany and she and Beth had taken the children to Princes Park. Jake was still in his pram. Then, she'd been terrified that her children would be hurt. More than thirty years later, Ruby wondered what sort of world awaited her granddaughters when they grew up?

Daisy and the twins

Chapter 13

1975–1981

Clint's problem was he was far too polite, Daisy thought wretchedly. It wouldn't enter his head to tell Ellie he was in a hurry. If they didn't leave soon, they'd be late for the film and she'd been looking forward to seeing *Godfather II* for ages and didn't want to miss a single minute. It meant they'd have to go to a different film and she hadn't a clue what else was on.

Was she the only person in the world who saw through her cousin and realised what a horrid person she was? Didn't Auntie Greta, or Moira, or even Daisy's own mother, consider it unreasonable for Ellie to ask Clint in her sweet, helpless way – though the real Ellie wasn't even vaguely sweet or the least bit helpless – if he wouldn't mind fixing her portable radio just when he and Daisy were about to go out? Gran might have said something, but she was in the kitchen washing up. Daisy had rushed into the bedroom – no one had noticed – to sulk and seethe and feel wretched on her own.

Of course, she could have said something herself, but was worried she'd show herself up in a bad light next to the sweet and helpless Ellie who was always as nice as pie when Clint was around. Daisy could hear her, giggling like a little girl, while he tried to fix her radio, which he knew as much about as Daisy did herself.

Gran stuck her head around the door. 'Haven't you gone yet, love? You're going to be late.'

'I'm waiting for Clint,' Daisy said in an agonised voice.

'I'll tell him to get a move on.'

Seconds later, Clint appeared, so heartbreakingly handsome that Daisy caught her breath. 'We'd better hurry,' he said, as if it had been *her* holding *him* up.

'It's too late to hurry,' she said mildly when she would have

263

preferred to scream. 'We'll never get there in time. The film starts at quarter past seven.'

'That's the programme, Daise. We'll miss the trailers and the adverts, that's all. The picture's not till half past.'

They arrived just in time, but it seemed as if everyone else in Liverpool had wanted to see *Godfather II*, and the Odeon was almost full. They had to sit in separate seats and Daisy didn't enjoy it nearly as much as she'd expected.

When they came out, they went to McDonald's for a chocolate milk shake. Daisy felt much better. When she and Clint were alone together, they got on perfectly. She'd liked him since the day they'd started school, drawn towards the little boy who looked as shy and awkward as herself. She was thrilled when they'd become friends, though Ellie had always been a thorn in her side, wanting to monopolise him, take him away, determined never to leave them by themselves.

Clint preferred to do quiet things with Daisy; mainly draw and paint, but seemed unable to resist when Ellie dragged him off to play leap-frog or climb trees. Now they were all seventeen and Ellie found different reasons for prying them apart, like fixing her stupid radio, which Daisy suspected hadn't been broken in the first place.

At some time over the last twelve years, she had fallen in love with Clint Shaw, but had no idea how he felt about her. He *liked* her, that was obvious, otherwise she wouldn't have become his regular girlfriend, but whether he wanted to spend the rest of his life with her, Daisy didn't know. She was always on tenterhooks, praying every night that he would suggest they get married or at least engaged but, so far, the prayer hadn't been answered. It worried her that one of these days the penny would drop and Clint would realise how attractive he was and she'd be jilted for a girl equally attractive. Like Ellie.

They began to discuss the picture which Clint considered even better than *Godfather* I. Daisy pretended to have enjoyed it because it seemed sour to say how she really felt.

'I thought Robert DiNiro was brilliant,' Clint enthused. He was a film buff and his ambition was to become a Hollywood director, though he never mentioned taking her with him.

'Me too, but I preferred the first film.'

'Why?' Clint wanted to know. He was always interested in her opinion.

'It was more suspenseful. I remember being on the edge of me seat the whole way through.'

'You might be right.' Clint nodded in agreement, but claimed he still thought the second *Godfather* superior to the first.

They had another milk shake, strawberry this time, then Clint took her home. At the gate, he kissed her chastely on the lips and squeezed her waist, which was the most he'd ever done, much to Daisy's disappointment. She sometimes had the horrible feeling in her agonised brain that he looked upon her as a sister and was never likely to do anything else.

Gran was the only one still up. She was on the settee watching an old film on the telly and patted the seat beside her.

'It's nearly finished,' she said. 'I saw this with Beth before the war.'

'What's it called?' Daisy asked so she could tell Clint.

'*Of Human Bondage*, with Bette Davis and Leslie Howard. Me and Beth cried our eyes out.'

There was a photo of Beth on the mantelpiece. She was in Washington holding a placard for the Third World Women's Alliance. Gran said she'd been such a meek and mild person and was amazed she'd become a political agitator, always on demonstrations and marches.

The picture finished, Gran sniffed a bit and turned the set off. 'Did you get to the Odeon on time?'

'Sort of. We had to sit in separate seats.'

'Oh, dear.' Gran squeezed her hand. 'Ellie doesn't mean anything, you know. She just likes to draw attention to herself, make her presence felt.'

'If *I* did that, no one would take any notice. Everyone notices Ellie.

'I don't think so. Clint is such a nice, obliging young man who hasn't learnt to say no. One of these days he'll get his priorities right, don't worry.' She yawned. 'I think I'll turn in. Would you like some cocoa?'

'I'll make it.' Gran worked herself to the bone every day looking after them and deserved being waited on when the opportunity arose.

To Daisy's surprise, Ellie was in the kitchen with one of the students, the Irish one called Liam. He'd probably been searching for something to eat. He was extremely good-looking and had red hair, sort of gold, much nicer than Daisy's carroty colour. Gran was threatening to take only women students next year in view of the amount of flirting that went on.

'They must think they've landed on a bed of roses, finding themselves in the same house as three pretty teenage girls.' Gran had said this in Daisy's presence and she was only being nice, because Daisy wasn't remotely pretty and as solid as a piece of rock. The students were forever asking Ellie and Moira to functions at the university; discos and concerts. Daisy wouldn't have gone, she had Clint, but it would be nice to be asked.

Liam smiled at her nicely when she went in. Ellie ignored her. While Daisy poured water in the kettle, Liam asked what A levels she was taking.

'None,' she replied. 'I go to work.'

'She had to leave school at sixteen because she didn't get a single O level,' Ellie informed him.

'I got one in Art,' Daisy argued, going red.

'Huh, *Art*!' Ellie said, as if Art was totally useless.

'Not everyone can be a genius,' Liam said reasonably.

Daisy's brain was in proportion to her looks, below average. She'd tried hard to study, but the words made no sense and danced all over the page. The headmistress had said it wasn't worth her while staying for A levels like the twins – it had once been suggested she go to a special school, but Gran had insisted she stay where she was. Uncle Matt had given her a job, but Daisy suspected he was only doing Gran a favour. She was as useless in an office as she'd been at school. Clint had also stayed to take three A levels and she felt very much out of things when everyone discussed the subjects they were taking. Clint and Ellie were in the same class for English.

Oh, God! Daisy clenched her teeth. Life was *torture*!

'Are you making cocoa?' Ellie enquired.

'Yes.'

'Make us a cup while you're at it. Would you like some, Liam?'

'I wouldn't say no.' He had a lovely, lilting Irish accent and at least had the grace to thank her when she sulkily shoved the mug in front of him. Ellie took hers without a word.

'Why were you so nasty with her?' Liam asked when Daisy had gone.

'Was I nasty?' Ellie looked at him in surprise. It was the way she'd always spoken to Daisy.

'You weren't exactly nice.'

'I suppose she gets on me nerves,' Ellie replied after a few moments' thought. 'I find her a drag, always have. She's so slow and witless. I think she must have sludge for brains.' She'd never understand in a million years what Clint Shaw saw in her.

'I wouldn't want to get on your wrong side.' He pretended to shudder.

'There's not much chance of that.' Ellie let her tongue roll provocatively over her pink lips. She allowed her knee to touch his under the table. The whole house would have been shocked to the core had they known she and Liam Conway made love regularly.

Another thing no one knew was that when Liam finished his degree in two months' time, Ellie was returning to Dublin with him. There was no suggestion of them getting married. Both agreed this was the last thing they wanted. Ellie intended to have all sorts of adventures and this was only the first. Liam didn't want to be hampered by a wife and family while he travelled around the world – he could speak French and Spanish fluently and had a smattering of German and Italian.

Liam wasn't the first man Ellie had slept with, though he was the oldest and the best-looking. There'd been two before, one a student, and the other a boy at school. She wasn't over keen on the sex part, though it was OK. What she enjoyed was the enormous feeling of excitement, knowing the risk she was taking, making love with a man when her grandmother was in the next room and the rest of the family were downstairs. There'd be hell to pay if she was discovered, but that made it even more daring.

Liam leaned over the table and kissed her. 'Will I see you later?'

Ellie giggled. 'You might.' Or he might not. The longer she avoided it, the more he would want her when next she condescended to visit his room. *That* was exciting too.

★

'Is our Daisy coming down with something, Mam?' Heather enquired over breakfast next morning.

'You should know, love. She's your daughter,' Ruby replied as she made mounds of toast in preparation for the students.

'She seemed very quiet earlier.' Daisy was the first to leave in the mornings. Matthew Doyle's head office was in Crosby and she had to catch a bus and a train. 'Perhaps she doesn't like that job.'

'Why not ask her tonight?' It could be work that was getting Daisy down. On the other hand, it might be Ellie, or possibly Clint, or a combination of all three.

'I can't tonight. Greta and I are going to the Playhouse.'

'Can't you go to the Playhouse another night?'

'But we've already got the tickets,' Greta wailed.

'Perhaps you could have a word with her, Mam,' Heather suggested. 'Are you ready, sis?'

'I'll just get me coat.'

'Before you go, Greta, would you kindly remind the twins that it's time they were up?' Ruby said with heavy sarcasm that went completely unnoticed.

'All right, Mam,' Greta said with the air of someone who was doing her a favour.

Her daughters seemed to regard their children as entirely the responsibility of their mother. Ruby sometimes wondered if she'd given birth to twins and a red-haired child without having noticed.

She'd once written to Beth to ask her opinion as to why they should think like this, and Beth had replied that the death of the boys had knocked the girls' lives out of kilter. 'They returned to being daughters when they could no longer be wives,' she wrote. 'Having children of their own doesn't fit in with this role. *You're* the mother, so you should take care of their children, just as you took care of everything when they were little. Daisy and the twins are your concern, not theirs.'

At first, Ruby thought this a load of rubbish but after a while conceded it made, sort of, sense, and was preferable to thinking it was all her own fault for being too domineering in the past.

She waved the girls goodbye, as she did every morning. They linked arms as they walked down the path. From the back Greta, in her pink fluffy coat and high heels, looked more like a teenager than almost forty, and Heather was very much the career woman in a black suit, hair pulled severely back in a bun, giving the appropriate gravitas to someone who was now a Legal Clerk specialising in Probate. Heather actually had her own secretary, something of which Ruby was immensely proud. Greta was still a shorthand typist and showed no wish to be anything else.

There was a noise, as if a herd of elephants were trampling down the stairs, and two of the students, Frank and Muff, arrived in search of breakfast. She wondered what their mothers would say if they could see them now; unshaven, hair uncombed, clothes filthy. It was her job to do their washing, but it hardly ever appeared and she had no intention of pressing them.

Once again, she wondered if she should ask for girls when the new term started in October. She preferred boys. They were no trouble, apart from consuming a horrendous amount of food. Lately though, she'd begun to feel uneasy.

The chief cause of her unease came into the kitchen and wished her a breezy, 'Good morning.'

Liam Conway, a brilliant language student, twenty-one, but with the confidence of a man twice his age, and the ability to charm the birds off the trees. She didn't like the way he looked at Ellie – or the way Ellie looked at him, come to that. Something was going on, Ruby felt convinced.

Perhaps it would be best in future if three virile young men and the same number of young women ceased to have temptation put in their way by being housed under the same roof.

'Hi, Gran.' Ellie parked herself at the table. Until Liam Conway had arrived, she'd always been late for breakfast. Nowadays, she was early. Ruby had felt obliged to lay down the law and insist she came fully dressed instead of in her dressing gown, putting the students off their food, though this morning Frank clearly found the white lace bra visible through her thin school blouse just as disconcerting, but Muff was too busy eating to look up.

Liam didn't even glance in her direction and Ruby sensed it was deliberate. Ellie made a great show of tossing her head and flashing her lovely blue eyes, accidentally on purpose reaching for the milk at the same time as he did so that their hands touched. Liam looked at her then and Ruby tried to fathom the expression on his face. His eyes had narrowed, he was looking at Ellie through lowered lids and biting his bottom lip.

Desire! He was looking at her seventeen-year old granddaughter with desire!

A little voice in Ruby's head shouted, 'Help', and she decided that later she would write to Beth.

The three-storey office block in Crosby overlooked the River Mersey. Daisy sat at her desk, unable to take her eyes off the water that shimmered in the gentle April sunshine. The sky was powdery blue with clouds like scraps of lace floating across.

It would make a stunning painting; ceruleun blue as a base for the sky, yellow ochre with white or chrome orange for the sand. The silvery water would present a challenge.

A few people were walking along the sands; a man with a dog, a woman pushing an empty pram, two small children running behind. The dog would run into the water, back to his owner, shake itself vigorously, then run off again. It was a collie and was obviously having a wonderful time, furiously waving its great flag of a tail.

The children kept stopping to pick up things from the sand which they would show to their mother, who put them in a shopping bag attached to the handle of the pram. Daisy imagined the bag being full of shells and stones and funny little scraps of seaweed which the children would play with when they got home.

She sighed enviously. She would give everything she owned – not that she owned much – to be one of the people on the sands, able to run into the water, collect shells.

It was hard to concentrate when paradise was only fifty or so yards away. And now a ship had appeared, a tanker. Daisy rested her head in her hands and wondered where it was going? Somewhere exotic, a foreign port, with foreign smells, where people wore strange clothes and rode on camels.

Daisy's longing to be anywhere else in the world rather than the place where she was now, was so strong, it felt like a sickly ball in her throat.

'Haven't you started on that filing yet?'

'I was just looking through it,' Daisy lied as she shuffled the pile of papers on her desk. She had been taken on to assist Uncle Matt's secretary whom he claimed was overworked. Theresa Frayn had treated her nicely at first, but had long ago become impatient with her slowness. She had never known anyone take so long to do filing or type a simple letter. If it hadn't been for Uncle Matt, Daisy suspected she'd have been shown the door months ago.

She began the painful task of sorting through the filing, putting the sheets in the alphabetical order, conscious of Theresa glowering at her from across the room. The incoming letters weren't so bad. They had bold letterheads and were easy to understand, but the carbon copy replies were difficult. As she tried to make sense of the words, Daisy had a familiar feeling of disorientation, as if the world had turned upside down.

'Morning, girls.' Uncle Matt came into the office. He was wearing jeans and an anorak which meant he would be visiting a site during the day.

'Good morning, Matthew,' Theresa said girlishly, fluttering her lashes.

'Good morning, Mr Doyle.' Gran had stressed she mustn't call him 'Uncle Matt' in the office.

'Tea!' He pretended to gag. 'I desperately need a cuppa.'

Theresa got to her feet, anxious to please her handsome boss, but Uncle Matt said, 'Let Daisy do it.' He grinned. 'She makes a lovely cup of tea does our Daise.' It was one of the few things Daisy could do efficiently.

The day wore on. Uncle Matt went out, more people appeared on the sands, more ships glided across the glistening water, in and out of the port of Liverpool. Daisy copy-typed a specification and made such a hash of it that Theresa Frayn ripped it to pieces in front of her eyes. 'I'll do it again meself,' she snapped.

While Daisy was struggling with the typewriter, Ellie and Moira were walking home from school arm in arm, a boy on each side and two trailing behind. The Donovan twins were the prettiest girls in the sixth form and the fact they were so alike gave an added flavour to their already plentiful charms. They were usually accompanied by a court of admirers.

'What'cha doing tonight?'

'Fancy going to a disco?'

'How about the pics? I'll buy you some chocolates.'

The boys didn't mind which twin responded, each being as appealing as the other.

Ellie giggled and Moira stuck her nose in the air. She wouldn't be seen dead with a boy her own age, preferring older, more sophisticated men. Apart from Uncle Matt who was fifty-one and *too* old, she hadn't so far met one that she liked, but she would, one day. It didn't matter when, she wasn't in any hurry. It was Moira's intention to gain three top grade A levels, go to university, and become a teacher. Once this ambition had been realised and she had worked for a few years, she might think about getting married and starting a family.

'Come on, Ellie,' a boy called slyly, 'have a heart. John Perry said you're an easy lay.'

Moira glanced at Ellie. 'Aren't you offended?' she asked, but her sister just shrugged. If a boy had said that to her, she'd have slapped his face. They walked in silence for a while until Moira said, 'Unless it's true.'

Still Ellie didn't answer, but smiled instead, as if she wasn't a bit perturbed by the suggestion.

'I know some nights you go upstairs to Liam Conway's room.' Moira was an exceptionally light sleeper. Ellie or Daisy only had to turn over for her to wake up. It was months now since she'd first heard her sister creep upstairs. Shortly afterwards, the bed in Liam's room which was directly overhead would creak. About an hour later, Ellie would return. Moira hadn't said anything, being a firm believer in letting the world go by with the minimum of interference. People, her sister included, were masters of their own destiny, and if Ellie wanted to sleep with Liam Conway, then it was up to her. She was, however, a little disturbed at the idea that Ellie was sleeping around.

'Are you going to clat on me?' Ellie said casually.

'You know I won't.' Moira had never told tales in her life.

'Not that I care, like. I just wondered. Another thing, don't tell anyone this either, but when Liam goes back to Dublin in June, I'm going with him.'

'They mightn't let you.'

'They can't stop me. Anyroad, so as to avoid a fuss, I might just run away.'

'That would be very inconsiderate, Ellie.' Despite not wanting to interfere, Moira was extremely shocked. She also believed people should have standards. 'Mum would be terribly upset and it would break Gran's heart.'

Ellie looked momentarily abashed. 'Oh, I'll come back, don't worry,' she assured her sister. 'Dublin will just be the first of my adventures. I shall have loads more.'

'Aren't you worried you'll get pregnant?'

'I can't. I'm on the pill.'

Moira could never quite understand her twin. Sometimes, she wondered if Ellie's heart beat twice as fast as other people's, if her blood raced around her body when everyone else's merely flowed. She was never still, always agitated, impatient, wanting to do things first, be the centre of attention, be the loudest, the brightest, the most daring of all. Ellie had to have everything.

Yet she wasn't happy. Moira was the only person who recognised the turbulent nature of her sister hid a dissatisfaction that would never be soothed by normal means. Ellie craved excitement, it was the reason why, years ago, she'd stolen things from school. Fortunately, the culprit had never been discovered. It was why she'd started sleeping with men, why she wanted to run away.

'Did you do it with John Perry?' she asked.

'Yes.'

'Where?'

'Behind the gym, after school.'

'Say if you'd been seen! You'd have been made to leave and couldn't have done your A levels.'

'Who cares!' Ellie laughed. 'Anyroad, I wasn't seen, was I?'

Sometimes, Ellie would watch through the bedroom window when Clint brought Daisy home. All he did was kiss her, and then only the once. He didn't realise what he was missing. Half the girls in the sixth form were crazy about him and would have gone much further than just a kiss.

Yet Clint stuck to Daisy, despite Ellie having made it obvious that she fancied him. She'd like to bet he was a virgin, which was no wonder, having the ugly, clodhopping Daisy for a girlfriend.

Before she went to Dublin, Ellie resolved she'd do her utmost to seduce Clint Shaw, show him what it was like to be with a real woman! It would be a problem finding the opportunity, they were hardly ever alone together, but that only made the task more exciting.

Ellie rubbed her hands together. She could hardly wait!

★

Ruby regarded the painting with dismay. 'It's very nice, love,' she said, trying to put some enthusiasm into her voice.

'It's the view from the office window,' Daisy explained. 'I had to do it from memory.'

'You're lucky, having such a lovely view.'

'I suppose,' Daisy sighed. 'Though I find it very distracting.'

Daisy was very easily distracted when she had to work. It had been the same at school when she'd always been bottom of the class, except for Art, which was surprising considering the dreadful paintings she turned out. The latest was particularly crudely done, the paint laid on thickly like tar. Instead of being smooth, the sky was full of ridges and for some reason the river was white and grey lumps. There was a strange figure standing in the water which Ruby eventually recognised as a dog and the other, even stranger figure, on the sand – more lumps – was presumably its owner.

'What's this, love?' she asked, pointing to what looked like litter on the beach.

'Children. They're collecting shells and stuff. And that's their mother with a pram.'

'As I said, it's very nice.'

'Where shall I hang it? It still needs hooks and some string. Ellie doesn't like my paintings in our bedroom. She said they're ugly.'

'I'll put it in my room, shall I?' Most of Daisy's unframed work went in Ruby's room. Even Heather refused to hang her daughter's paintings in a place where they could be seen. Ruby had put some in the students' rooms and none had so far complained. 'Leave it where it is for now, love,' she said.

'OK, Gran,' Daisy said happily. 'I'll go and tidy the shed.' She painted in the garden shed where Mrs Hart's garden tools were still stored, including a roller that couldn't be budged.

Mrs Kilfoyle, who taught Art, had suggested Daisy go to college for the subject, but Heather had put her foot down and refused. 'I wouldn't take any notice of Mrs Kilfoyle. She's as daft as a brush. Our Daisy lazed her way through school. It's about time she buckled down to some proper work.'

Daisy had meekly agreed. 'Anyroad,' she confided to Ruby, 'I don't want to leave one school for another.' It was obvious she'd had enough. Not long afterwards, she arrived home laden with boxes of paint and squares of hardboard and set up work in the shed, where it was either freezing cold or like an oven depending on the weather. Even Heather felt guilty for not having provided the materials before.

'Oh, Mam! She mustn't have liked asking us to buy them. She waited till she was earning money of her own. I thought that O level was just a fluke.'

The paintings that emerged from the shed only confirmed that Heather had been right. The O level had indeed been a fluke.

Ruby's heart bled for her unhappy granddaughter. How would poor Daisy cope as she grew older? She fervently hoped she and Clint would get married. A genuinely nice boy, he was clearly fond of her – and she of him, though it would mean his mother, the loathsome Pixie, would become a member of the family.

Everyone had eaten, the dishes had been washed and dried, the kitchen looked unusually clean – a sight that Ruby always found slightly disturbing it was so unnatural. Daisy was out with Clint, and the twins were in the bedroom doing their homework. An evening in front of the television with Heather and Greta stretched ahead seductively.

Ruby was about to switch on *Coronation Street*, when Heather said, 'Mam, I thought I'd better tell you, me and Greta booked a holiday in Corfu today. We're going for a fortnight in July.'

'How kind of you – to tell me that is,' she said icily. 'Well, at least I'll know where you are when you disappear for two whole weeks.'

Heather looked taken aback. 'We didn't think you'd mind.'

'I'd like to have been consulted first. I assume you're not taking your children with you, that they're being left with me?'

'We couldn't afford for the five of us to go.'

'Oh, dear! But thank goodness you can afford to pay for two. I hope you both have a lovely time.'

'We'll cancel it if you like,' Greta offered, sensing her mother wasn't exactly pleased at the news.

'Though we'll lose the deposit,' Heather warned.

'I wouldn't dream of putting you to any inconvenience. Fortunately, your holiday doesn't clash with mine.' Ruby had never made up her mind so quickly about anything before.

'You're going away?' the girls gasped, more or less together.

'I'm going to stay with Beth in Washington for a week in June.

It's International Women's Year and there's all sorts of things going on.'

'But how will we cope without you?' Greta wailed.

'Same way as I'll cope without you.'

'Have you booked the flight?' demanded Heather.

'No. I intended discussing it with you first,' Ruby lied shamelessly. She was fed up being taken for granted. 'All you have to do is get up early and make everyone's breakfast, then do the dinner when you come home. I'll change the beds before I go,' she said helpfully.

'Why couldn't you have gone later, like us, when the students will have gone?'

'You obviously haven't noticed, Heather, but we have foreign students in the summer. The upstairs rooms can't stay empty for three and a half months. We need the money.'

'Actually, Mam,' Greta grumbled, 'We could do with the whole house to ourselves. I wouldn't mind a room to meself, and neither would Heather, and the girls are too old for three to a room.'

'If you'd like to ask your boss for a two hundred per cent rise, then we can have the whole house to ourselves.'

'You're being dead sarcastic tonight, Mam. Why can't we get a cheaper house?'

Ruby guffawed. 'With a room each for the six of us! Which planet are you living on, Greta?'

'We could ask Uncle Matt to reduce the rent.'

'Don't you dare even *think* such a thing!' Ruby angrily thumped the arm of the settee and the girls jumped. 'We're fortunate to get it as cheap as we do. It's a lovely house and you're not exactly cramped sleeping two or three to a room. Nowadays, Matthew could sell this place for thousands and thousands of pounds. You should be thanking your lucky stars, not complaining. Now would someone mind switching on *Coronation Street*? I've already missed half.'

Ellie couldn't make head nor tail of Milton's *Paradise Lost*, which was part of the English A level. It was something to do with hell having been taken over by some guy called Beelzebub. When the class had finished, she asked Clint Shaw if he understood what it was about.

'Well, yes,' he stammered.

'Then help me with tonight's essay.' She fluttered her lashes and looked at him pleadingly. 'We could do it together.'

'I was going to do mine as soon as I got home. Me and Daisy are going out tonight.'

'Then I'll come with you,' Ellie said with alacrity. 'Your mum won't mind, will she?'

He didn't look terribly keen on the idea, but he'd never been able to refuse her anything. 'Mum won't be there. She goes to work.'

Ellie already knew that. Fate had provided the perfect opportunity to seduce Clint Shaw.

The Shaws lived in a street of substantial terraced houses off Wavertree Road, a street that Ruby had been very familiar with when she'd been the pawnshop runner, though the young people didn't know that. Ellie had been to the Shaws' house before. She thought it rather garish and over-furnished.

'I usually do me homework in the kitchen,' Clint mumbled.

'That's OK by me.'

They spread their books on the lime green table, sat on the lime green chairs, and he explained that *Paradise Lost* described the fall of man for having disobeyed God's laws. Satan was trying to exact revenge for being expelled from heaven.

'You make it sound so much clearer,' exclaimed Ellie, filling her eyes with admiration.

Clint blushed. Gosh, she marvelled as the blush spread over his smooth, fair skin, he was incredibly good-looking. How come he hadn't realised? Why didn't he play the field as boys did who were only half as attractive? His hair was thick and blonde and almost straight apart from the ends which flicked up slightly, not quite reaching the collar of his school blazer, but not short enough to look old-fashioned. Everything about his face was perfect, from the fine eyebrows, grey eyes with lashes that most women would give their eye teeth for — not Ellie, who had equally long lashes of her own — straight nose, and slightly full mouth.

Gran used to wonder aloud where Clint had got his looks from. 'Not his mother, that's for sure.' She'd never liked Pixie. 'They must have come from his dad.' Brian Shaw had turned out to be a rougher, tougher version of his son.

'Can I have a glass of water?'

'I'll make tea if you like?'

'Oh, *please*.' She got to her feet when he did. 'I'll help, shall I?' By the sink, she brushed against him so that her breast touched his arm.

Clint looked embarrassed and edged away. Ellie giggled, slid her hand inside his blazer, and tickled him. She lifted her head and bit his ear, then rubbed her lips against his cheek. 'You need a shave,' she whispered, before kissing him fully on the lips.

She would never forget his reaction. He shuddered violently, as if he'd just had an electric shock and pushed her away. '*Don't do that!*'

'Oh, come on, Clint. What harm would it do.' She approached him again and was about to put her arms around his neck, but he caught hold of her hands and held them tightly. 'That hurts,' she complained in a babyish voice.

'Leave me alone.' He flung her hands away, as if they were contaminated. There was a look on his face, as if he wanted to be sick.

'Why?' Ellie demanded.

'Because Daisy's me girlfriend. It wouldn't be fair on her.'

Neither spoke for quite some time, just stared at each other across the room. Then, with a shiver of comprehension, Ellie understood. She felt herself go very cold.

'No, that's not why,' she said slowly. 'It's nothing to do with Daisy. It's because you don't like women. You're a queer.'

'Just because I don't fancy you, it doesn't mean I'm a queer,' he blustered, looking even sicker.

'No, it doesn't,' Ellie conceded. 'But you'd have behaved the same with any woman. I just know.' She began to put the books back in her satchel.

Clint was trembling, leaning against the sink, supporting himself with his hands, as if his legs were about to give way. His face had lost all vestige of colour and his eyes were hot and feverish.

'Don't tell Daisy.' The hoarse voice was as agonised as his face. 'Don't tell anyone. *Please!*'

'Don't worry,' Ellie assured him. She felt scared and a little bit ashamed. 'I won't tell a soul.'

That night, Daisy came home early when everyone was still up. She burst into the living room, eyes shining. 'You'll never guess,' she cried.

'Guess what?' demanded a chorus of voices.

Ellie didn't speak. She sensed what her cousin was about to say.

'We didn't go to the pictures, but for a walk instead. Clint asked me to marry him. We're getting engaged. On Saturday, we're going to town to buy a ring. Only a cheap one,' she added quickly. 'He's only got a few pounds of pocket money saved.'

'Oh, that's wonderful, love.' Gran leapt to her feet and hugged Daisy warmly. 'What do you think, Heather?'

Heather frowned. 'You're awfully young, Daisy.'

'But Mum, we're not getting married for ages, not till Clint's at least twenty-one. We might go to live in London where it'll be easier for him to get the sort of job he wants, scriptwriting, or something.' She smiled blissfully.

'Congratulations, Daise!' Moira planted a kiss on Daisy's freckled cheek.

'I'll get the sherry and we'll drink a toast,' Gran cried. 'Someone fetch the glasses. What a pity Clint didn't come in so we could have congratulated him too.'

'You know Clint, he's terribly shy,' Daisy said with a proprietorial air. She examined the third finger of her left hand as if she could already see herself wearing the cheap ring.

'I hope you'll be very happy, Daisy.' Ellie gave her cousin a brief hug. She'd never had much time for Daisy, but she was family and meant more to her than Clint Shaw ever would. He saw nothing threatening about Daisy and was using her as a cover. Was she supposed to protect him at the expense of Daisy's happiness, let her go blithely ahead and *marry* the guy?

Yet she'd never seen Daisy as happy as she was now, as if a light had come on inside her. How could she spoil everything by telling the truth? Did Daisy know what a queer was? Would anyone, not just Daisy, believe her if she told them what she knew about Clint Shaw? Ellie doubted it.

Chapter 14

She wanted to see the White House, Georgetown, the Lincoln Memorial, sail along the Potomac to Mount Vernon, visit museums and art galleries, which she wouldn't have dreamt of doing at home, but was the sort of thing people did on holiday. She bought a guide book and made a list of sights to see.

Beth was delighted she was coming to Washington and had booked a room at her hotel. 'You'll love it, Rube. There'll be loads of exciting things to do, and you'll meet all my friends.'

As usual, Ruby's wardrobe was devoid of anything smart, but now she had a perfect excuse to renew it. Everyone in the house contributed in some way towards the holiday in Washington, even the students who clubbed together and bought a lovely black leather handbag to thank her for being such a great landlady. Before leaving, Ruby bade them a fond farewell. They would be gone by the time she came back.

Greta and Heather stayed in for three Saturdays in a row to see to things in the house, giving their mother time to roam the city shops and look for clothes. A delirious Ruby, drunk with excitement, purchased an elegant black linen suit, a blue frilly blouse and a plain white one to wear under it, two floaty, feminine Indian frocks in stunning jewel colours, a pair of daringly high-heeled shoes to go with the suit and gold sandals to go with the frocks.

Daisy bought her a pretty cotton nightdress – the ones she had were probably older than Daisy herself and only fit for ripping into dusters, and the twins took note of every single item in her filthy, ancient make-up bag. They replaced each thing with a new one; lipstick, powder, eye shadow, rouge. 'Cake mascara's dead old-fashioned, Gran,' Moira told her. 'Nowadays, it's in a wand. Oh, and we got you some kohl eye-liner.'

'I've never used eye-liner before, but I'll give it a go.' She'd try anything once.

'We bought a new make-up bag an' all and some perfume. It's only a little bottle,' said Ellie.

'I love *Je Reviens*. Oh! Aren't you lovely girls! I know I'll only be gone a week, but I'll miss everyone something rotten.'

'I'll miss *you*, Gran.' Ellie looked unusually tearful.

Now, here she was, on the plane, wearing the black suit, feeling like a member of the human race again.

The flight was enjoyable and she wasn't the least bit sick or frightened as Heather had warned she might. She drank two gins and orange after the meal, then lost herself in a novel she'd been meaning to read for ages, feeling ever so slightly tipsy.

It was five o'clock on Saturday afternoon American time when Beth met her at Washington National airport. The occasional photos Beth had sent hadn't shown how much she'd changed. She wore no make-up and her skin had acquired the texture of old, polished wood. It was hard to believe she'd once been so soft and plump when now she looked the opposite, hardy and tough. Her eyes held a glint, rather than a sparkle, and she even moved differently, in short, hurried spurts when she'd used to glide, driving Ruby mad with her refusal to hurry. She wore jeans, a T-shirt, and shabby sports shoes. Her short, wiry hair was almost completely grey.

'You make me feel over-dressed,' Ruby cried after they'd hugged each other affectionately.

'You make me feel like an old bag lady,' Beth responded with a grin.

'What's that?'

'A woman tramp.'

'We've always been honest with each other, Beth. You do look a bit like a tramp.'

'I can't be bothered with doing meself up nowadays.'

'I spent ages doing myself up for you. I've just learnt to use eyeliner and I had my hair tinted. I've got a few grey ones.'

'I've got rather more than a few and they can stay grey for all I care. Come on, I've a cab outside.'

She linked Ruby's arm and began to lead her towards the exit. Ruby thought it a shame that the girl who, during the war, had melted the remains of half a dozen lipsticks in an unsuccessful attempt to make a whole one, no longer cared how she looked. She recalled the unxious flattery they'd both heaped upon various American soldiers in the hope of acquiring nylons.

To her surprise, the cab driver turned out to be a woman.

'Ruby, this is Margot,' Beth said when they got in.

'Hi, Rube. Nice to meet 'cha.'

The three chatted amiably as the cab carried them through a warren of streets. Ruby's eyes were everywhere. It was hard to believe that she was in a foreign country. 'They're all straight,' she remarked.

'What was that, honey?' Margot asked.

'The streets, they're all straight. At home, they go all over the place.'

'We're more orderly this side of the Atlantic.'

'Where are we staying?' she asked Beth.

'Halfway between Old Downtown and the White House.'

'The White House is one of the first places I want to see.' If you went on a guided tour, it was possible to get a glimpse of President Ford going about his business.

'You'll see it tomorrow morning.'

'Goody!'

The hotel was clean and functional and seemed to be run and occupied entirely by women. Beth introduced Ruby to the desk clerk and virtually every other woman they met on the way up to the second floor.

'I always use this place when I stay in Washington,' she explained, opening the door on to a small, plain room, completely devoid of pictures or any sort of ornament. 'Would you like a rest?'

'No, thanks, though I wouldn't mind getting washed and changing into a frock.' The temperature felt at least ten degrees hotter than in England. 'Another thing, I'm starving.'

'We'll eat downstairs the minute you're ready.'

The restaurant was more like a school canteen, the tables big enough for eight. Ruby, freshly made-up and wearing a filmy green Indian frock and gold sandals, felt slightly over-dressed when she went in with Beth who was still in her bag lady outfit. The food was plain and nourishing and reminded her of the convent. More women joined their table as the room quickly became crowded and a floundering Ruby was asked loads of questions about her home country to which she didn't know a single answer.

No, she hadn't a clue how many women were members of the British parliament, or how many were senior civil servants, leaders of unions, announcers on television, chief executives of this or managing directors of that.

'Margaret Thatcher was elected leader of the Conservative party earlier this year,' she told them in a lame attempt to show she wasn't completely ignorant, but they already knew.

No, she'd never been a member of a union, she confessed. 'I've never had a proper job, so there's never been the need.'

'Isn't there a housewives' union?' one of the women queried. 'I remember reading about it once.'

Ruby had no idea. Beth took pity on her and changed the subject. 'You'll never guess what she did before the war. Tell them about the pawnshop runner, Rube.'

The women listened, fascinated, while she described going to and from the various pawnshops with Greta in her arms, then both children in a pram. She got quite carried away – or perhaps she wanted to impress after the abysmal ignorance she'd just shown – so told them about Foster Court, the cleaning jobs, and Jacob's extended stay in bed.

'Gee, honey, you sure showed some enterprise.'

'I guess you've seen poverty most of us have never known.'

'I suppose I must have,' Ruby said modestly.

Everyone remained seated while the tables were cleared. 'What's happening now?' she asked.

'There's a meeting,' Beth replied.

'What's it about?'

'The glass ceiling.'

'Oh, right.' Ruby had never heard of the glass ceiling, but soon discovered it was what women encountered when they tried to climb the hierarchy of an organisation. It wasn't visible, but it was there. Women were promoted so far, but all sorts of sneaky, underhand things were done to prevent them rising further.

Ruby couldn't find much sympathy for the speaker, an aggressive, well-spoken journalist who claimed she'd been thwarted on numerous occasions when she'd applied for promotion. 'I wouldn't like to work for *her*,' she whispered. Beth just smiled.

When the meeting was over, an all-women rock group appeared to entertain them. By the time they'd finished. Ruby was ready for bed.

Next morning, she put on her other frock – turquoise with little gold beads around the neck – and applied her make-up with extra care for the visit to the White House, hoping her hand wouldn't shake as she drew a fine black line around each eye – Moira and Ellie claimed eye-liner made her look exotic and glamorous.

'I'm not too old for it at fifty-seven?' Ruby had asked them anxiously. 'I don't want to look like mutton dressed up as lamb.'

'You always look gorgeous, Gran. Everyone at school thinks you're our mother.'

Last night at the meeting there'd hardly been anyone wearing make-up, or frocks, come to that. They'd mostly been like Beth, in jeans and T-shirts.

'Will you be comfortable like that?' Beth enquired at breakfast.

'Why shouldn't I be?'

Beth shrugged. 'No reason. Let's not dawdle over coffee. People are already beginning to collect outside.'

'What for?'

'The march to the White House.'

An hour later, Ruby found herself in the blazing sunshine marching up and down Pennsylvania Avenue in front of an impressive white building holding a placard bearing the message, 'Equal Pay for Equal Work', a concept with which she fully agreed, but she'd been expecting something other than a march. Not only that, the gold sandals had started to pinch, her feet hurt, she was perspiring from every pore, and her throat was as dry as a bone. She was beginning to wonder if there'd ever be time to go sightseeing or whether the week ahead was to be a long series of demonstrations and marches.

'Have you come far?'

She turned to find a young woman beside her. 'England,' she replied in a cracked voice.

'We're from New Zealand. I'm with my mum. She's back there somewhere.' The girl gestured vaguely. 'They weren't doing much to celebrate International Women's Year at home and mum was determined to experience at least a bit of it. It's wonderful, isn't it? The feeling of sisterhood, of women being in charge, able to do things that men have always insisted that they couldn't. I wonder if there'll ever be a woman President one day – of America, that is.'

'I don't see why not.'

'Well, there's not much sign of it yet,' the girl said, her face glowing with youthful indignation. 'Don't you feel as mad as hell when you see all the world leaders together on television and there's not a single woman amongst them?'

'I do. I feel outraged.'

'It's not fair, is it? Why should it only be men who have a say in how the world is run when more than half the population are women?'

'You're right. It's not a bit fair.'

'Oh, my mum's calling me. Well, it was nice talking to you. Perhaps we'll come across each other again some time.'

'I hope so.' Ruby smiled. For the first time, she was aware she was taking part in a great event. The women began to sing 'We Shall Overcome', and she joined in, moved and uplifted in a way she'd never felt before. Later, she'd buy jeans, a couple of T-shirts, and some comfortable shoes, and leave the pretty, entirely unsuitable frocks for when she got home. It seemed unlikely she'd sail along the Potomac, visit a single museum or gallery, and this was as near as she would get to the White House. Still, it was International Women's Year and she was determined to enjoy the experience to the full.

After a rally and numerous speeches, they returned to the hotel for dinner which was followed by a black factory worker describing how the female workforce had been sexually harrassed, then sacked when they'd demanded to be represented by a union. Three years later, after a vigorous campaign, they'd been reinstated and the union recognised. The entire room erupted in cheers when the woman finished.

Later, Ruby, Beth, and half a dozen other women went to a nearby basement club and drank too much wine. Ruby wondered aloud why every single person there was female. 'Are men banned?' she enquired.

'No, but they're not exactly welcome,' she was told.

'Why not?'

'It's a lesbian bar, honey.'

Had Beth become a lesbian? Ruby asked her when they got back to the hotel. They stopped in the foyer to buy coffee from the machine and went to sit in the lounge.

'Of course not, idiot.' Beth laughed. 'But we have to show solidarity with all our sisters, Rube, whatever their colour, race, or sexual disposition. Women should stick together.'

'That woman last night, the one on about the glass ceiling, she was pushy and aggressive and would make a terrible boss. I don't see why I should show solidarity with someone like her.'

'Why should only men be allowed to become terrible bosses?' Beth said reasonably. 'No one's saying all women are nice, but being nasty doesn't stop men from getting on.'

'Gosh, Beth, you've changed.' Ruby stared at her friend's gritty, determined face. 'There was a time when you never had a sensible idea in your head. Now you're full of them.'

'If my marriage had been different, I'd be at home baking cookies and keeping the house nice, bemoaning the fact that one of my kids was dead and the others were married. But I was forced to do something or go under. The more I did, the more I became involved and the more I changed. Things mattered that I'd never thought about before.'

Ruby nodded. 'And now it's Daniel stuck at home. Is he happy?'

'Not really. He can't stop mourning Seymour. I don't like leaving him, but he left me when *I* was unhappy. I suppose that sounds selfish, but I don't care.'

'You still loved Jacob, though he did much worse than that.'

'I still love Daniel. I'm just putting myself first.'

'I've never been able to do that,' Ruby said with a sigh. 'The girls have always come first with me, then *their* girls. They'd never manage without me.'

'Are you quite sure about that, Rube?' Beth's eyes narrowed. 'Are you honestly saying Greta and Heather wouldn't have somehow coped if you hadn't been around? People usually do. You know the old dictum, "No one's indispensable."'

'Are *you* saying I've wasted my life?' Ruby replied hotly.

'No, but you've done exactly what you wanted to do, Ruby. Don't get angry.' She put her hand on Ruby's arm. 'You'd make a lousy employee. If the boss looked at you sidewise, you'd bawl him out. You can't stand criticism. You need to be top dog, to be in charge. So, you created your own little world and crowned yourself its queen. Don't tell me you haven't been contented with your lot, for most of the time, that is.'

'I suppose I have, but what if Larry and Rob hadn't been killed and the girls hadn't come back home? What would I have done then?'

'Married Chris, trained for a career, ended up as someone important. You have to be *important*, Rube. Remember how much we all needed you during the war? You revelled in it.'

'Did I?'

'You certainly did.'

Ruby would have liked to continue the conversation, but more women came into the lounge and joined them, and a different conversation ensued well into the early hours.

The rest of the week flew by. By the time it ended, Ruby had learned more about herself and the rest of the world than she had during her entire lifetime. In the past, she'd watched television or read the paper and complained loudly to whoever would listen about the injustices in the world, but apart from the years in Foster Court, she'd never had to struggle. She'd worked hard, but had never fought for anything in her life. Compared to many of the women she'd met that week, she'd had things easy. When she got home, she was determined do something, join something, read the books she'd bought from the numerous stalls and broaden her education. Most of her life had been spent in a rather comfortable rut – with the help of Matthew Doyle, she realised thirty years too late.

On her final afternoon, Beth took her on the metro to City Place, a bargain mall, where Ruby bought a long cream jacket to wear with the jeans she'd got earlier in the week – she'd travel home in the new outfit, give everyone a surprise. She chose little gifts, mainly ethnic jewellery, for the girls, and hesitated a while over a navy silk tie with a tiny embroidered White House on the front before deciding to buy it.

'Who's that for?' Beth asked.

'Matthew Doyle.' It wasn't much, but it was a gesture.

Ruby wasn't the only one leaving next morning. The night was spent wishing a tearful farewell to women with whom she'd become instant friends and was unlikely ever to see again. It finished with drinks and a singsong in the hotel where the warm, comradely atmosphere was thick with emotion and virtually the whole room was in tears.

Nothing would ever be the same again, Ruby thought dismally. Life would be unbearably dull back in Liverpool.

Saying goodbye to Beth next morning was the worst thing of all. They could hardly speak, just clung to each other at the airport until Beth pushed her away, saying gruffly, 'You'll miss the plane.'

'Bye, Beth.'

'Tara, Rube,' Beth said, lapsing into a Liverpool accent for the first time. Ruby burst into tears.

It had been an exhausting seven days. For most of the flight, she slept soundly, but woke up feeling not even faintly refreshed. Her legs could barely carry her when she walked down the steps and her feet touched the tarmac in Manchester airport.

She caught a taxi home; hang the expense. All she wanted was to see her family, give them their presents, then go to bed, where she would probably sleep for a week.

Mrs Hart's house looked smaller than she remembered and much shabbier. The front door opened when she was paying the taxi driver and Greta came out. Ruby thought she'd come to help carry her bag as she didn't think she had the strength left to lift it.

Instead, Greta said in a tragic voice, 'Oh, Mam! Our Ellie's disappeared. According to Moira, she's run away to Dublin with that student, Liam Conway. Oh, Mam! What are we going to do?'

At that particular moment, Ruby had no idea.

It wasn't the only thing that had happened, just the worst. Three fifteen-year-old French students were arriving on Monday.

'Some woman rang to ask if it was all right,' Heather told her. 'I said it was.'

'But I wasn't expecting them until the week after!' Ruby cried. She'd like to bet no one had cleared up after Frank, Muff and Liam. From previous experience, the rooms were usually a tip, full of rubbish and unwanted belongings, when their occupants left for good.

Ellie wasn't the only one in disgrace. Daisy had given up her office job and was working as an usherette in the Forum.

'An usherette!' Ruby said faintly. 'Is that where she is now?'

'Yes.' Heather pursed her angry lips. 'She didn't discuss it with me first, just gave in her notice weeks ago and swore Matthew to secrecy. I'd have given him a piece of my mind, except he's already got troubles of his own.'

'What sort of troubles?' Had she really only been away a week? It felt more like a month, or six months.

The news about Matthew Doyle had been in the *Echo*. The dampcourses were faulty on an estate of 250 houses that his firm had built and the sub-contractors responsible had declared themselves bankrupt.

'Uncle Matt's got to put them right, but it's not covered by the insurance. It'll cost the earth,' Moira told her. Moira was also in disgrace, having known all along what her sister was planning to do, yet had kept it to herself.

'Sly little monkey,' Greta snapped during the argument that followed.

'Not as sly as our Daisy,' Heather countered.

'I promised to keep it a secret,' Moira said, unperturbed. 'I wasn't prepared to break me promise. What do you think, Gran?'

'Don't ask me,' replied a distraught Ruby. 'I'm incapable of thought at the moment.'

'The holiday doesn't seem to have done you much good,' Greta said huffily.

'The holiday did me a world of good, but coming home's done me no good at all. I was only tired before. Now, I feel as if the world's collapsed around my ears.'

And no one had noticed she was wearing jeans.

Perhaps the events in Washington had made Ruby more tolerant. When she thought about it the next day, she couldn't see much harm in what her granddaughters had done. Ellie had acted very irresponsibly, but she would be eighteen in September, an adult. At the same age, Ruby had had two children and was living in Foster Court.

As for Moira, the girl had made a promise and felt morally obliged to keep it. Her loyalty was to her twin, not to her mother. And what would Greta have done if she'd been told of Ellie's plans – tied her headstrong daughter to the bed for the rest of her life?

Furthermore, it was entirely understandable that Daisy hasn't told anyone except Matthew she was leaving. Heather would have tried to stop her, yet the girl clearly wasn't cut out for office work. Ruby admired her enormously for having taken charge of her young life.

Daisy came with her to midday Mass. She loved her new job, she declared. 'All you have to do is show people to their seats, and you can tell by the colour of the tickets what section they should be in. Of course,' she went on importantly, 'you have to be careful not to shine the torch in anyone's eyes.'

'Doesn't it get a bit boring?' Ruby asked.

'Not really, Gran. I watched *The Sting* twice because Robert Redford's so gorgeous, but once the picture starts, you can stand outside the door and talk to the other usherettes. I don't feel even the littlest bit stupid and some of them are dead envious I'm engaged to Clint. He came one night to see *The Sting* – we let him in for nothing,' she added in a whisper, as if the manager of the Forum was within earshot.

'I'm glad you're happy, love. Did Matthew mind you going?'

'No. He wished me luck and said to take as long as I liked to find another job. Oh, Gran, I don't half feel sorry for him. He's in terrible trouble.'

'I know. I'll give him a ring when we get home.'

'All the houses are occupied and the downstairs rooms will have to be re-decorated,' Matthew said despondently when Ruby phoned to ask exactly how much trouble he was in. 'Apart from putting right the dampcourse, floorboards have to be replaced, carpets have been ruined. It's going to cost millions to put right.'

'I'm so sorry, Matthew. Look, I was just about to start dinner. You're welcome to come if you want. I've brought you a little present back from Washington.'

'Have you?' He sounded pathetically pleased. 'I can't manage dinner. I'm due at the office any minute to go through figures with the accountants. The workforce have seen this as an ideal opportunity to demand a pay rise. I'll try and make it later.'

'I look forward to seeing you, Matt.'

He made a little harrumping noise. 'I doubt that very much, Ruby. You're just being polite.'

Ruby replaced the receiver and went into the kitchen where she

290

began to peel potatoes. Her thoughts went back to the day she'd first met the gangling, would–be property developer, with his misspelt visiting card and cheap suit. Over the years, she'd been horrible to him, ignoring his kindness, his wish to become friends, resenting the way he had attached himself to her family, bought the girl presents, invited himself around. But now she was deeply sorry he was in trouble and would do all she could to help.

Ruby had only been home a few days when she called the hotel in Washington for a moan. 'I almost wish,' she groaned, 'that I'd never gone away. If I'd stayed, nothing bad might have happened; Ellie would still be here, Daisy wouldn't have changed her job, Matthew's business would be all right.'

'I'd've thought you'd be pleased about Daisy?'

'I am.' Ruby sighed. 'But our Heather isn't.'

'You're nothing but a soft girl, Ruby O'Hagan,' Beth said scathingly. 'You're not *that* important. The entire household doesn't fall to pieces just because you're not there.'

'I know.' Ruby sighed again. 'One thing though, the French students wouldn't have come for another week. I could do without them at the moment. The boy's all right, Louis, except he expects me to teach him English. He follows me everywhere, making notes. One of the girls is terribly homesick, poor thing, and cries all the time. The other one keeps picking up boys and bringing them home. She'd have them in her room if I'd let her.'

'Never mind, Rube. It won't be for ever.'

Right then, Ruby found that difficult to believe. 'Another thing, Greta's driving us mad. She wants to go to Dublin to look for Ellie, but she's nervous about travelling on her own. Heather's too busy to go with her, Moira flatly refuses, and now she's badgering me.' There was a note of hysteria in her rising voice. 'As if I could possibly drop everything and go on what's bound to be a wild goose chase.'

'Calm down, Rube. Take a deep breath or something.'

'Whereabouts are you in the hotel?'

'In a booth in the foyer. The desk clerk said there was a call just as I was leaving. You only just caught me.'

'What are you doing this afternoon?'

'It's morning, actually. I'm going to an anti-apartheid rally in support of black families in South Africa.'

'I wish I were there,' Ruby said wistfully. 'I miss it something awful. That's really why I called, to hear what Washington sounds like, if only for a minute or two.'

'I'm leaving tomorrow, Saturday. Nearly everyone is. This time next week, we'll all be back in our dull little houses or tedious jobs, and we'll be feeling exactly the same as you, Rube.'

On top of everything else, Ruby was worried about Matthew Doyle. He looked ill, not a bit like his usual dashing, confident self. The owners of the affected houses had called a meeting and asked him to attend.

'I can't think why,' he said ruefully. 'They were so angry, they'd hardly let me speak. I was shouted down every time I opened me mouth. Everyone considers it *my* fault.'

'Write to them,' Ruby urged after a few moments' thought. 'Find out their names and send a letter to every single house. Explain what happened, that the sub-contractor responsible has made himself bankrupt and the onus of putting things right has fallen on you. Say you'll do it as quickly as possible, but ask for their patience. Appeal to their better natures.'

'I don't suppose it would do much harm,' he conceded. 'Mind you, that's not the only thing on me mind. I've got two big contracts that should have been started by now, but I can't spare the manpower. They've both got penalty clauses if they're not finished on time. At the rate things are going, they won't be finished at all. I need the entire workforce for that bloody estate.'

'Have you advertised for more tradesmen?'

'Yes, but the response was pretty poor. Word gets around. These days, Doyle Construction's considered a dodgy outfit to work for.'

'But that's not fair!' she gasped, outraged.

He suddenly grinned. 'I'm glad I've got you on my side. I should have taken you with me to the meeting. You'd have shouted the lot of them down.'

'I'd have tried,' Ruby said stoutly. 'What happened to the business in Australia, the swimming pools?'

'It went to Caroline when we got divorced.' He pretended to

shudder. 'I'd sooner not think about Caroline. I've got enough on me plate. By the way, I meant to say before, you suit jeans.'

'Well, I'm glad someone's noticed.'

The French students left after a fornight and another three took their place, all girls, who couldn't stand English food. Ruby didn't care. She made salads and gave them an apple for afters. It was much easier.

She flatly refused to iron the frocks Greta and Heather were taking to Corfu the following week. 'You can iron them yourselves when you come home from work. All you do is watch television.'

'You've been dead funny since you got back from Washington, Mam,' Greta complained.

Ruby haughtily tossed her head. 'I'm making a statement.' She'd meant to do all sorts of things, but had been submerged by events. She hadn't touched any of the books she'd brought back – she didn't even know where they were.

'What's the statement about?'

'I'm not sure.' She was fed up being a maid-of-all-work. She wanted a life of her own, though what she intended doing with it, she had no idea. Something important.

Two weeks later, the girls returned from Corfu, both with an enviable tan. It quickly became obvious that they weren't speaking to each other.

It was about time the pair of them grew up, thought an impatient Ruby. 'What's wrong?' she enquired as soon as she got one of them on their own. It happened to be Heather.

'She only clicked with some chap, didn't she, our Greta?' Heather said indignantly. 'I was dropped like a hot brick. A few days later, I met this man – I didn't mean to, we just bumped into each other in a shop and started talking and he asked me for a drink. Then Greta's chap went home the first Saturday, and *I* was expected to drop mine, which I flatly refused to do. She had a lousy time the second week and seems to think it's all *my* fault.'

'Well, I hope you make things up pretty soon. I don't like an atmosphere in the house.' Ruby was surprised. It wasn't like Heather not to put Greta first. She thought her daughter looked rather sad. 'What was your chap like?' she asked.

293

'Actually, Mam, he was awfully nice. His name's Gerald Johnson. He lives in Northampton and works in a bank. He's got two kids and his wife was killed in a road accident, so straight away we had something in common. We got on ever so well, but neither of us felt the least bit romantic towards each other. I can't imagine getting involved with another man and Gerald feels the same about women.'

'Oh, well. I'm glad *you* had a nice time.'

Heather's stern face melted. 'Oh, I did, Mam! Gerald was lovely to talk to. We're going to write to each other. He might come and see us one weekend.'

'I thought neither of you wanted to get involved?'

'We don't, but it doesn't mean we can't be friends. Talking of friends, I'll go and have a word with our Greta. I don't like us not speaking. Mind you, it's entirely her own fault.'

'I love Dublin,' Ellie sang, flinging back the curtains of the tiny bedsit that had a distant view of the River Liffey. Fortunately, the room wasn't overlooked, so no curious observer could see she had nothing on.

'Jaysus! The sun's bright.' Liam pulled the bedclothes over his head. 'Why do I feel so hungover? Did I drink much last night?'

'Only gallons and gallons of Guinness.' Ellie, her eyes on the glittering river in the distance, began to sing raucously, 'Bridge Over Troubled Water'.

'Do you *have* to sound so happy? And so fucking loud?'

'Don't swear,' she said automatically.

'I'll swear as much as I fucking want.'

'I might leave you.'

'I don't care.'

Ellie ran across the room, threw herself on top of him, and yanked the sheet away. Liam shrieked. His eyes were full of sleep and he looked dreadful.

'Do you really mean that? About not caring if I left?' she demanded, tickling his chest.

'You know I don't.' He rolled over so that she was beneath him and pushed himself inside her. He was ready to make love at any time, whether it be morning, noon, night or day.

'That was nice,' he said, rolling off her.

'Only nice!' Ellie pouted.

'I've known it better.'

'With me or someone else?' she enquired, making a face.

'With you, of course, me darling girl.'

Ellie was about to wrap herself around him, but changed her mind when her nose came in contact with his smelly armpit. 'I'll have to get ready for work in a minute.'

'Me too.'

He worked in a supermarket stacking shelves and collecting trolleys. After a lifetime spent studying, he wanted a job that didn't tax his brain. It would only be for a few months. Once he got the result of his degree, he'd leave Dublin, go abroad. 'The world will be my oyster,' he boasted.

What would she do then? Ellie didn't know and didn't care. He was only the first of her adventures. She had a job in a restaurant which she quite enjoyed and Dublin was full of attractive men. Among Liam's many friends were students from Trinity College and he and Ellie were invited to parties almost every night. An American student, Dean, lived in the room above, and there were two girls on the floor below. If there wasn't a party, they'd all end up in someone's room and get drunk.

The university term had ended, but there were still loads of young men around that Liam had been to school or played rugby with, as well as girls he used to date. Whenever they went to a pub there was always a crowd Liam – and now Ellie – knew.

Sunday afternoons, they went for a drive in Liam's car, a yellow Hillman Imp, which he'd bought on his eighteenth birthday. It had been left with his brother, Felix, in the family home in Craigmoss, a village about ten miles from Dublin. When Liam's father died, his mother had gone to live with her sister in Limerick, and Liam's own sister, Monica, lived in London.

They'd caught the bus to Craigmoss to collect the car soon after they'd arrived in Ireland. 'Next Sunday, we'll go to Sandymount Strand – there's a beach,' Liam said as the bus lumbered through the pretty Irish countryside. 'James Joyce used to go for walks there.'

'Did he, now!' said Ellie, who'd never heard of James Joyce, despite having taken an A level in English.

The Conway house was depressing, both inside and out, she thought when they arrived. It was called Fern Hall and was very large, very tall, and situated on its own just outside the village, reminding her of the house in *Psycho*, a film she'd recently watched on television and hated – she'd had nightmares about it ever since.

Felix Conway lived alone in Fern Hall. He was five years older than Liam, a slighter, paler version of his handsome brother. His eyes were a lighter green, his receding hair not quite so red. He had a faint, whispery voice and wore round glasses with pearly white frames that Ellie thought made him look slightly sinister, like the house.

Even the meal was depressing, served in a miserable, musty smelling dining room; cress sandwiches made from stale bread, digestive biscuits served in the packet, and weak tea.

Ellie didn't like the way Felix watched her from behind his round glasses, still and contemplative, as if he was trying to look into her soul. 'Why isn't he married?' she asked Liam on the way back to Dublin in the Hillman Imp.

'Don't ask me. He's been courting Neila Kenny ever since me horrible old daddy died. I don't know what they're waiting for. Their old age pensions perhaps.'

'Let's not go again, Liam. I didn't enjoy meself a bit.'

'You needn't go again, me darling Ellie, but I certainly shall. Felix is me brother and I quite like the guy.'

'Please yourself,' Ellie sniffed.

'I always do,' Liam replied with a smile she thought unnecessarily grim.

Since then, he'd only been to see Felix the once, on another Sunday afternoon, leaving Ellie on her own, but not for long. Dean was still upstairs, waiting for his family to arrive when they would go on a tour of Europe. He had come down to borrow something and was still there when Liam returned. 'I hope you two haven't been up to anything,' he said with a leery grin.

Ellie was a bit put out that it didn't seem to bother him if she and Dean had spent the time making mad, passionate love. But would she care if she found *him* with a girl under the same circumstances? She decided that she wouldn't. They were using each other, that's all. It made her feel sophisticated and very grown-up.

They had been in Dublin almost two months when Ellie discovered she had run out of contraceptive pills.

'Fuck!' Liam said when she told him in bed that night.

'There's no need to swear. I can easily get more. I'll look up a birth control clinic in the telephone directory tomorrow.'

'Are you mad or what?' He roared with laughter. 'This is Ireland, girl. It'd be easier finding a brothel than a clinic dishing out contraceptives.'

'Why's that?' enquired an astonished Ellie.

He laughed again. 'Some Catholic you are! Don't you know the Church is totally opposed to birth control? In Ireland, what the Church says goes.'

'That seems very unreasonable.'

'Unreasonable or not, that's the situation. Is there anyone in Liverpool who can send you more pills?'

'God, no!'

'I'll ask around at work. If necessary, we can drive across the border, get them there. Otherwise, I'll have to find meself another bed partner. The last thing I want to hear is the patter of little feet.'

Ellie hit him with a pillow. 'Neither do I. So remember, until I get more pills, you'd better be careful.'

Liam brought the pills home a few days later. They were in a little brown bottle.

'Are you sure they're the right ones?' There wasn't a name on the bottle when Ellie examined it.

'I should hope so. They cost five quid.'

'These are white, the others are blue.' She popped one in her mouth all the same.

'They're a different brand, that's all,' Liam said easily, more concerned with opening the letter with a Liverpool postmark that had arrived for him that morning, almost certainly the result of his degree. He gave a joyful shout. 'I got a First and was top of my year. I think this calls for a drink – Champagne, the very best. Put your glad rags on, me darling girl. Tonight we're celebrating. Tomorrow, I'll buy the newspaper and start writing after jobs.'

As usual, there were plenty of people they knew in the pub. They got in with a crowd celebrating a wedding anniversary, and pretty soon they were all celebrating together.

Someone started to sing an Irish folk song accompanied by the plaintive strains of a fiddle. It was all terribly Bohemian. Nothing like this ever happens in Liverpool, Ellie thought, entirely forgetting she'd never been inside a Liverpool pub, so wouldn't know.

Chapter 15

Daisy shone the torch discreetly along the back row of the Forum. It was filled with couples snogging madly, not even faintly interested in what was happening on the screen, despite *The Conversation* with Gene Hackman being such an excellent film. Clint had already seen it three times for free. In his expert opinion, it was one of the best ever made.

Every seat was occupied. Daisy transferred the torch beam to the right aisle. 'There's two empty seats in the middle,' she said to the young couple who'd only just arrived and asked to be seated at the back. *The Conversation* had started fifteen minutes ago, but watching a film was clearly the last thing on their minds.

She switched the torch off and went outside where her fellow usherette, Paula, was having a smoke.

'That pair were probably the last,' Paula said. She was a lovely, cheerful woman, with dyed blonde hair and purple lips. 'I think I'll take the weight off me feet and sit down.'

Daisy sat on the padded seat beside her. 'They went in the back row. I don't understand why people come to the pictures just to neck. It's nothing but a waste of money.'

'Perhaps they've got nowhere else warm to go, luv. I don't think me and Chas saw a picture properly the whole two years we were courting.' She tittered. 'There was one on telly the other night, *My Sister Eileen* with Janet Leigh. I know me and Chas went to see it, but all we could remember was the name.' She gave Daisy a painful nudge with her elbow. 'Don't tell me you and your Clint always sit with your eyes glued to the screen when you're at the pics?'

'We do, actually,' Daisy said primly. 'He's a film fanatic. He watches every single minute, even if it's not very good.'

'Then you've obviously got somewhere else to neck.'

'Not really,' Daisy was about to say, but limited herself instead to a telling laugh. She and Clint had never necked or snogged or whatever you called it, but she wasn't prepared to reveal that to Paula.

'Anyroad, Daisy, luv,' Paula said, 'I've got something to tell you. That painting you gave me, I wasn't sure about it at first, but Chas, he really liked it. Anyroad, he hung it over the mantelpiece. "I never thought we'd ever have our own, original masterpiece," he said. Meself, I thought that was going a bit far.'

'You've told me all this before,' Daisy reminded her.

'I know, luv. I'm leading up to something else, aren't I? Our Brigid's boyfriend's sister goes to art college. Her name's Mary, and when she came the other night she was dead impressed with your picture. She wants to meet you, and I wondered, luv, would you like to come to tea on Sunday?'

'I'd love to. Can I bring Clint? We don't have much time together since I came to work here.'

'I took it for granted you'd bring him, Daise. What it must be like to be in love, eh?' She nudged Daisy again. 'Mind you, me and Chas still have our moments.'

As she journeyed home on the bus, Daisy thanked her lucky stars she'd exchanged her office job for that of an usherette. Not only could she do it as well as anyone else, but she'd made loads of friends. As far as work was concerned, nowadays she was dead happy.

She was happier at home too since Ellie had run off to Dublin with Liam Conway. It meant she had Clint all to herself. But life still wasn't perfect – would it ever be? Daisy wondered desperately, thinking about the conversation with Paula, the bit about the back row.

It was two months since she and Clint had got engaged and still all he did was kiss her by the gate. Lately, she'd starting kissing him back with all her might, pressing her lips against his as hard as she could, hoping he'd put his arms around her, groan a bit, the way the boys did in the back row when they started kissing the girls.

But the pressing had had no effect. She'd seen enough films to know that engaged couples did rather more than give each other a brief kiss whenever they had the opportunity, and it was usually the man who was keener than the woman. She'd like to bet that Ellie and Liam had *gone all the way*! Just the thought of it made Daisy go all funny. Perhaps *that* was why Clint had never properly kissed her. He was holding himself back, worried he'd lose control, and *they* would go all the way, which Daisy would have found quite scary, even though she loved him with all her heart and soul.

On reflection, it was probably best that things remain as they were. She'd stop kissing him back, just in case he lost control and it would all be highly embarrassing. There was probably a happy medium which she would have very much preferred, but it seemed that wasn't possible, men being what they were.

Ruby prepared the tiny fifth bedroom – it had hardly been used since the war – for when Gerald Johnson came to stay the weekend. It was only a month since he had met Heather in Corfu.

'I don't want anyone thinking it's serious,' Heather warned. 'We're friends, good friends, that's all.'

'Are you sure?' Greta asked suspiciously.

'Quite sure, sis.'

Gerald was an extremely pleasant young man. Lord, I'm growing old, Ruby thought with a groan. He's forty if he's a day, yet I look upon him as young.

He showed them photos of his children and his late wife and Heather showed him a photo of Rob.

As if to emphasise the relationship was purely platonic, they insisted on taking a petulant Greta with them to the pictures on Saturday night – they went to the Forum, where Daisy proudly showed them to their seats.

The A level results arrived and Moira was thrilled to find she'd got three B's. She'd been provisionally accepted by two universities, one in Canterbury, the other in Norwich, depending on her grades. Now it was up to her to choose.

Greta was dismayed. 'You're not leaving home too!'

'You know I've always wanted to go to university, Mam,' Moira said with her usual calm reasonableness. 'I've discussed it with you loads of times.'

'Yes, but I never thought it'd *happen*.'

'I wish the twins had been thick, like Daisy,' Greta said tearfully to her mother. Ellie hadn't done all that badly considering her mind had been taken up with other things; two C's and a D.

'Daisy's not thick.' Ruby sprang to the defence of her other granddaughter. 'She's just got an unusual mind.'

'Whatever! She's not thinking of leaving home, is she? Come October, I won't have any daughters left, not like our Heather. I might go to Dublin and fetch Ellie back, even if I do have to go on me own.'

Clint's results were the best in the school; three straight A's. Daisy was terrified he'd also decide to go to university where he'd come into contact with girls as brilliant as himself and far better looking than she was. She was pleased and flattered when he declared he couldn't bear to leave her.

'I think I'd go mad without you, Daise.'

Mad! It seemed an extreme word for someone only eighteen to use. He had a retiring disposition, not full of himself like most boys with only half his looks, but he'd always seemed entirely sane. He actually hugged her for quite a long time, and Daisy had the strangest thought, that he was scared to go to university. She tenderly stroked his cheek. 'Don't worry, Clint. I'll always be here for you.'

She rather hoped he'd tell her he loved her, or call her 'darling', both of which she longed for, but he just stiffened slightly and began to discuss the film they'd just seen.

Mam said she was daft. Didn't she realise Dublin was a huge place, a city? Finding Ellie would be next to impossible. Where would she look? Who would she ask? Heather agreed it was a mad idea.

Greta sighed and gave up. No one seemed to realise how miserable she felt, losing both her daughters. For the first time in her life, she felt very alone and very small, merely the tiniest of specks in the vastness of the universe. Say if Ellie never came back! Moira would be gone and Heather could well marry that revolting Gerald Johnson. Greta couldn't stand him and didn't believe they were just friends. One of these days, Mam would die, then she'd have no one, not a soul in the world. She'd be truly alone, not just temporarily, like now.

'Oh, God!' It was a horrifying thought, unbearable. She'd sooner be dead.

She'd just have to get married again. But who to? Someone who'd look after her because, Greta thought fretfully, she wasn't able to manage by herself. She remembered there was a man who'd played a significant part in her life, who never forgot her birthday, bought presents at Christmas, made a fuss of her whenever he came to the house.

Matthew Doyle had always been a father figure in a way, yet he was only twelve years older than she was. She was as fond of him as he was of her. He was having financial problems at the moment, but she felt sure they would be overcome.

Greta decided Matthew would make a very satisfactory husband. Somehow, she'd have to put the idea in his head that she would make a satisfactory wife.

The wedding ring was the thinnest in the jeweller's shop and the cheapest. It was secondhand, almost certainly off the finger of a dead woman, and it fitted Ellie perfectly.

'Remember, Felix is the only person who knows we're not married,' Liam said on the way to Craigmoss in the Hillman Imp. It was a horrible day, quite different to the first time she'd gone, when the flowers had been out and the air smelt fresh. Today, the sky looked like grey soup, the trees were bare, everywhere felt damp. 'Everyone else thinks you're Mrs Liam Conway, I've got a job abroad, and you'll join me when you're ready. This being Ireland, an unmarried woman in the family way could have a pretty hard time. It's all right to have affairs, but it's not done to get pregnant.'

'If it wasn't for bloody Ireland, I wouldn't be pregnant,' Ellie reminded him in a hard voice. 'What were they, aspirin?'

'I wouldn't know.' Liam's voice was equally hard. 'I was told they were contraceptive pills. I paid a good price.'

'I'm paying an even higher price.'

'I'm sorry, Ellie, but I'm trying to do the right thing, aren't I?' he said reasonably, as if he thought she'd listen to reason when she felt completely at the end of her tether. 'If you'd gone back to England in the first place and got rid of the damn thing, there'd have been no need for these shenanigans.'

Ellie placed her hands over her swelling tummy. 'I couldn't have got rid of it,' she whispered. 'It would have been murder. He or she would have come back to haunt me.'

Liam laughed. 'You're a rum girl, Ellie; screwing like a rabbit one minute, back in the Dark Ages the next.'

He zoomed around a bend. They were getting nearer to Craigmoss, to Fern Hall, to Felix. Ellie shivered, remembering the way he'd looked at her with his pale green eyes. If only she hadn't been too scared to have an abortion, or felt too proud to go back to Liverpool. But she had planned to return when she'd had all sorts of adventures to boast about, not expecting an illegitimate baby.

'I'm surprised,' Liam said, 'That you didn't press me to marry you.'

'I'm not. It so happens I don't want to get married, and certainly not to you.'

'Oh, well.' He laughed. 'Then I won't propose.'

'Just in case you do, the answer's "No". One thing though, I think you might have stayed a bit longer, not landed me on Felix right before Christmas. It'll be dead horrible.' It was true he'd got a job abroad, as a translator with the United Nations in Geneva.

'They wanted me by mid-December, Ellie.'

She didn't believe him. He just wanted to get rid of her so he could have a good time, go to parties and stuff. The United Nations wouldn't need much in the way of translating done over the Christmas period.

The car turned into the drive of Fern Hall, stopped. Ellie got out. Liam fetched her suitcase from the boot. He'd given her the money to buy some pretty maternity frocks.

Felix came to the door, the pale ghost of his brother. He looked as damp as the weather. The outside walls of the house were wet, as if they were weeping, and she felt like weeping with them. She went inside and Felix prepared a meal; tinned soup with bread and margarine, and for afters, tinned fruit, followed by weak tea.

Then Liam said he had to be going, and she and Felix went with him to the door.

'I'll give you a ring over Christmas,' Liam promised.

Ellie didn't want him to stay – she'd gone off him completely – but even less did she want him to go. At least he had some life in him, unlike his brother. He pressed an envelope in her hand. 'That's my last week's wages, fifty quid. It should keep you going for a while. Look after yourself, Ellie. Don't forget, you're pregnant.'

As if she could!

★

303

Ellie's absence wasn't allowed to spoil the festive spirit in Mrs Hart's house. The living room was drenched with paper chains and tinsel and the tree was so big it would only fit in the hall. Heather spent an entire evening decorating it. Gerald Johnson was coming with his children – Lloren, ten, and Rufus, two years older – and she wanted it to look extra special. The students had gone home so accommodation wasn't a problem. Clint was invited to Christmas dinner along with his parents, the revolting Pixie Shaw and her husband, Brian.

'Flippin' hell, Ruby,' Pixie exclaimed when she came in, her eyes everywhere, 'This place hasn't changed a jot since I was last here. You've still got the same wallpaper and how you can stand working in that old-fashioned kitchen, I'll never know.'

'I like it,' Clint put in, unusually for him. 'It's got character.'

'So do I,' remarked Gerald. 'It's got charm as well.' He smiled at Heather, who blushed slightly and smiled back.

'*I* wouldn't want it any different.' Greta had never forgiven Pixie for severing their friendship many years before.

Even the normally unruffled Moira, home from university in Norwich, looked indignant. 'Me neither.'

'Oh, well, there's no accounting for taste,' said Pixie, entirely unabashed.

'The place *is* looking a bit shabby, Ruby.' Matthew glanced around the living room, as if he'd never looked it properly before.

'I sometimes touch the paintwork up or emulsion over the wallpaper.' Ruby didn't give a damn what anyone thought. Like her, the house was showing its age and could do with patching up a bit. 'Who'd like a drink before dinner?'

'I'd quite like a cocktail.'

'I'm afraid I haven't any cocktails, Pixie. There's red or white wine, sherry, or beer. Take your pick.'

'Oh, that's a shame. Brian bought us a cocktail shaker for Chrimbo, didn't you, luv? If I'd known, I'd have brought it with me. I'll have a sherry. Sweet, if you've got it.'

'I've only got medium.'

'I'd love a beer,' said Brian.

Greta jumped to her feet. 'I'll get the drinks, Mam, while you get on with the dinner.'

'Would you like a hand, Ruby?'

'No thanks, Pixie. I can manage on my own.' Pixie was bound to notice she was still using the same saucepans and she might feel tempted to hit her with one.

Mid-afternoon, Pixie and Brian Shaw went home to their cocktail shaker. Not long afterwards the Whites and the Donovans arrived for tea. Ellie White tried not to look upset when she was introduced to Gerald Johnson and his children. Having lost her only son, perhaps she sensed she was about to lose his wife. Heather might claim she and Gerald were merely friends, but it was obvious to everyone else it was rather more than that.

'I suppose they'll move to Northampton when they get married,' she said privately to Ruby.

'There's been no mention of them getting married yet.'

'I wonder if Daisy will go with them? She's our Rob's daughter. Pretty soon, she'll be all I'll have left of him.'

'Daisy would never leave Clint. Did you know he's got a job with the Liverpool Playhouse? Only as a stage hand, helping to paint scenery, that sort of thing. He thinks it's all grist to the mill for when he goes to Hollywood to direct films – movies, he calls them.'

'Daisy told me.' Ellie smiled wanly. 'I wonder what Rob would have thought of Clint? It's hard to imagine him as a forty-year-old father making judgements on his little girl's boyfriend. In my mind, he's still only twenty-three.' She sighed, her eyes full of pain. 'Poor Rob, he never had the chance to grow old, did he? Nor Larry.'

Ruby was reminded of Ellie's words when they arrived at the White's house for tea the following day, minus Heather, who had gone with Gerald and the children to the pantomime at the Empire.

'I should have stopped her,' she thought uncomfortably. 'Not today, it was too late, the children were looking forward to it, but weeks ago, when she first came up with the idea of buying tickets. She should be here. Oh, Lord! I'm the most insensitive person who ever lived'

Chris Ryan was there to remind her of her insensitivity to other people's feelings. He was with his wife who wasn't much older than Ruby's girls, and their son, a delicate little boy of ten who had severe asthma.

Before, at similar gatherings, Chris and Ruby had done no more than smile at each other, perhaps exchange a few polite words.

Today, however, Chris followed her into the kitchen when she went for a glass of water after a hectic game of Charades.

'I was thinking about us the other week,' he said.

'Us!' Ruby replied, taken aback.

'You, me – us. Did you know we had a terrible scare with Timmy? It was about a month ago. We thought he was going to die.'

'Oh, Chris! I'm so sorry. I knew he had asthma, that's all.'

'He had a particularly bad attack. We didn't think he was going to make it.' His eyes clouded over. 'I can't think of a worse torture than watching the child you love suffer. You'd give everything you possessed if you could take the pain away, suffer it yourself. Nothing, no one else in the world matters. I guess that's how you felt about your girls when Rob and Larry died.'

'I guess it was,' Ruby said slowly.

Chris smiled drily. 'It's taken me all this time to understand. I was a bit of a prig, wasn't I?'

'I wouldn't say that.'

He leaned against the wall, hands in pockets. When she'd been in love with him, Ruby had thought him very attractive with enormous charm. In her eyes, he probably wouldn't have changed had they stayed together Now he was just an ageing man, almost sixty, with thinning hair. There was nothing exceptional about him.

'I wanted to see you for two reasons,' he said. 'One was to confess I'd been a prig, the other to say goodbye. The three of us are off to New Zealand in February. We might not see each other again. The Liverpool air's no good for Timmy, it's too damp, and I've been at a bit of a loose end since I stopped being a copper. I'm going to start my own security firm.'

'Good luck. I hope Timmy's health improves and you do well.' She held out her hand and Chris took it.

'I often think about the year we were engaged, how it would have been if we'd got married.' He held on to her hand and squeezed it. 'I wish I hadn't been such a fool, Ruby. I'll always regret it.'

Ruby pulled her hand away. 'Well, you shouldn't,' she said brusquely. 'It was over and done with a long time ago. You should look to the future, not the past. *I* always do.'

Not long after Christmas, Matthew Doyle put his big house in

Ormskirk on the market – he urgently needed the cash – and came to stay with Ruby while he looked for somewhere cheaper.

'I thought you owned loads of houses and flats,' Ruby exclaimed when the idea was first muted.

'I got rid of them years ago. They were hardly worth the trouble,' he said.

'You didn't get rid of this one.'

'Because it's different, that's why. This is my second home, the place where, lately, I come and shelter when I'm in trouble.'

Ruby bit her lip. 'There's only the little bedroom where there's hardly room to swing a cat. The others have all got students.' It didn't seem right that the owner of the house should have the smallest room.

'The little bedroom will do me nicely, Rube. It shouldn't be for long.'

Ruby prepared the room for her temporary guest, painting the woodwork glossy white and the walls a pretty eggshell blue. She bought new bedding - brushed nylon that didn't need ironing - and a rug for beside the bed. She realised she was quite looking forward to having Matthew stay – if she hadn't been so horrible, they could have been friends years ago. There were times when she wondered if she was her own worst enemy.

'Very nice,' Matthew said approvingly the day he arrived, not long after breakfast when everyone had gone. It was the first of February, bitterly cold, despite the clear blue sky and the distant sun, not nearly strong enough to melt the layer of glittering ice that covered their part of the earth. The garden was a frosty wonderland and the bare trees looked eerily pretty in their cloak of white. It was a day Ruby would never forget and always regret, despite her frequently expressed belief that one should never look back and regret anything.

She took Matthew upstairs. 'I hope the bed's long enough.'

'Beds usually are.'

'Lately, you seem to be growing taller,' she remarked.

'I'm growing thinner, that's what. It's probably an optical illusion.'

'I'll feed you up. I hope you like plain cooking. I can't be bothered with anything fancy. I'll make us some tea.' She turned to leave, but he caught her arm.

307

'I appreciate this, Rube.'

'It's not much, considering all you've done for us.'

'Have you ever wondered why?'

'Sometimes.' Ruby shrugged carelessly. 'I assumed it was because I reminded you of Foster Court, of your gran. Me and the girls were your substitute family.'

'Is that really what you think?' He was frowning slightly and his eyes looked very dark. She could feel the tension in the long thin fingers on her arm.

'What else is there to think?'

'There could be another reason.' The fingers were trembling now.

'And what would that be?'

He released her arm and sat on the bed. 'I've always found it hard to talk to you. Because I wasn't short of a few bob, you thought I was being patronising. You like to be on equal terms with people or, better still, on top. Well, now it's different.' He looked at her directly and Ruby was reminded of the first time they'd met, when he'd been so unsure of himself. It was an expression she'd never seen since. 'By the end of the year, I'm likely to be skint, so now I can tell you how I feel – how I've felt, ever since you came through the door downstairs covered in paint. I . . .'

The phone rang. 'Just a minute,' Ruby said, and ran down to answer it.

It was Clint, wanting Daisy. 'She's at the dentist,' Ruby informed him. 'Didn't she tell you?'

'Oh, yes. I forgot.' He began a rambling explanation. They were meeting for lunch, but he'd be late. He'd see her in McDonald's instead of by the theatre. 'If I don't turn up at all, I'll drop in the Forum sometime this afternoon and say hello.'

There was a mirror by the telephone. Ruby stared at her reflection. She saw a woman who didn't look her fifty-seven years, a woman who nowadays would be described as handsome, as good-looking women were when they grew older. Her black hair was sprinkled with grey – the tint she'd had for Christmas had almost washed out. Her neck was lined, getting scraggy, she thought. Perhaps she'd better start wearing polo necks. After a while, as Clint's voice droned on about something or other, the reflection grew blurred, while at the same time the meaning of Matthew's words, of what he'd been about to say, became clear. He'd been about to tell her that he loved her! He'd almost got the words out, but she'd thought it more important to answer the phone.

There were footsteps on the stairs, brisk and fast. Matthew was coming down, his face stony. He was wearing a padded jacket, obviously on his way out.

'Clint,' she said hurriedly. 'I have to ring off.'

'Don't forget to tell Daisy.'

'No.' She slammed down the receiver just as Matthew opened the front door. 'What was it you wanted to tell me?' she called, surprised to find that she was trembling and her heart had leapt to her throat. It was vital that she hear the words he'd been about to say before she'd interrupted him so rudely.

'It doesn't matter now.' His voice was bitter. 'Anyroad, it was nothing important.'

The door slammed. Ruby groaned and sank on to the stairs, head in her hands. She'd made many mistakes in her life, but now she'd just made the biggest mistake of all.

Ellie hadn't thought it possible for Christmas to be so dead miserable. She'd gone with Felix to the little village church for Midnight Mass and woke up late next morning.

Christmas morning, she thought gloomily, and imagined waking up at home where there'd be loads of presents under the tree which would be opened after breakfast – Gran always made a lavish breakfast on such a special day and everyone would eat it together for a change. The telly would be on, even if no one was watching, and carols could be heard all over the house.

She supposed she'd better get up. Ellie put one foot on the floor, winced, and put it back under the covers. The linoleum was freezing and she didn't have any slippers. She managed to get dressed without getting off the bed. Her tummy was getting quite big, she noted, although the baby wasn't due till May, and she was already wearing maternity frocks. She threw back her shoulders, took a deep breath, and went downstairs.

'Good morning, Ellie.' Felix was in the parlour, a small, dark room at the back of the house, where a fire struggled to burn in the black grate and half a dozen Christmas cards stood on the mantelpiece. Liam hadn't sent one, nor had he, so far, made the promised telephone call. Ellie had no wish to speak to him if he did. 'Would you like some tea?' Felix enquired courteously.

'Please.' He treated her like an invalid, which she didn't mind, preferring to be waited on rather than the other way round.

He went to fetch the tea and Ellie sat in one of the old-fashioned armchairs and held out her hands to the fire. The armchair felt damp. Everything in the house felt damp; the walls, the floors, the furniture, her bed. It was no wonder Liam and his sister had left. Even their mother had gone the minute her husband died. He'd been a miser, according to Mrs McTaggart who came in three times a week to do the washing and clean. Eammon Conway had owned the village chemist which was a little gold mine, being the only one for miles, but had refused to spend a penny on his family or the house. Instead, the money had gone on the horses, so there was nothing for his wife and children when the fatal heart attack struck.

Now Felix ran the chemist's shop, but it was no longer a gold mine, Mrs McTaggart said sadly. A supermarket had since opened in the village, only small, but called a supermarket all the same. It sold aspirin and cough linctus, cold cures and corn plasters, all much cheaper than the chemist's, so people only called on Felix when they needed a prescription or had ailments that required medicine the supermarket didn't stock.

Felix brought her a cup of weak tea. 'What would you like for breakfast?' He stared at her intently from behind his pale-framed spectacles.

'Just some toast,' Ellie sighed. The look no longer bothered her. It was the way Felix looked at everyone, as if he was trying to see behind their eyes to some deep, inner part of them.

'We're having chicken for dinner,' he said proudly. 'Neila will be along in a minute to roast it.'

The chicken would be no bigger than a pigeon. Felix was finding it hard to survive on the profits from the chemist. There were times when Ellie felt quite sorry for him, which was odd, as she was inclined to regard inadequate people with contempt. But Felix never complained, never lost his temper, and had the patience of Job, as Gran would have said. She actually felt a sneaking liking for him. He wouldn't be nearly so hard up, she thought darkly, if he got rid of Neila Kenny, who'd been his father's assistant. Perhaps he didn't like to sack her because she was his girlfriend.

It was a strange relationship. She'd never seen them touch, let alone kiss. At first, she'd assumed they did those sort of things during the dinner hour when the chemist closed, but Mrs McTaggart said Neila went home for dinner and Felix treated himself to half a pint of Guinness in one of the local pubs.

Neila Kenny was older than Felix, a large, raw-boned woman of about thirty-five, with scrappy hair and a face that the most charitable person in the world would have to admit was ugly. The shabby, shapeless clothes she wore looked as if they'd come from a jumble sale. Her stony grey eyes regarded the newcomer with hostility and Ellie found her just a bit scary.

Her favourite person was Mrs McTaggart, who brought her home-made scones and girdle cakes, otherwise she would have starved – even the toast when Felix brought it would be horrid, either underdone or burnt. Craigmoss didn't have a gas supply and the ancient electric cooker was unpredictable.

There was no knowing whose fault it was – Neila's or the cooker's – that Christmas dinner turned out such a disaster; the chicken almost raw, the potatoes hard, the Brussels sprouts soggy.

Throughout the meal, Neila subjected her to the third degree, asking questions about Liam that she'd asked before, as if trying to catch her out in a lie. Where had they got married? she asked suspiciously. Was it a white wedding? Did they have a honeymoon? Why hadn't she gone with him to Geneva?

'I'm expecting a baby in case you haven't noticed,' Ellie replied in answer to the last.

'Your wedding ring's awfully thin. Is it secondhand?'

'Yes, it's all we could afford.'

Ellie stayed put while Neila cleared the table. From the lack of spoons, she assumed there wasn't to be a pudding and, so far, there'd been no sign of anything alcoholic to drink.

Neila retured with a tray containing three cups of tea and three mince pies. 'I hope these are all right. I got them from the supermarket. They've been warmed up a bit in the oven.'

Ellie burnt her tongue on the mincemeat filling. She yelped and left hurriedly to get a glass of water from the nineteenth-century kitchen which led to a miserable, barren garden. She stood by the sink, dangled her tongue in the icy water, and thought how stupid she must look, how dreadful everything was, and how incredibly unhappy she felt.

'Are you all right, Ellie?' Felix enquired from the door.

'Yes. Look, could we go to a pub for a drink? It'll be my treat.' She hadn't used any of the money Liam had given her and was desperate to get out of the house.

'The pubs are closed today. Anyway, the Craigmoss pubs don't welcome women, so you couldn't go if they were open.'

Time had never passed so slowly. There was nothing to do, nowhere to go except the village. After a couple of forays, Ellie decided never to go again. There was only a handful of shops; the supermarket which was pathetic, the chemist's, a tiny post office, a shop that sold wool, sewing things, babyclothes, and adult fashions she wouldn't have been seen dead in. People were quite friendly and stopped in the street to chat but, even so, Ellie had a feeling they didn't believe she'd married Liam and hoped to trip her up. What would they do if they discovered the truth, she wondered? Stone her to death, beat her with sticks and drive her from the village, ban her from Mass?

A library van visited Craigmoss once a week and Ellie spent most of the time with her head buried in a book. Felix insisted she visit the local doctor who examined her and advised she was putting on too much weight.

'You need more exercise,' Dr O'Hara said sternly. He made a note in his diary of when the baby was due – he would deliver it himself.

In order to keep sane, remind herself that a world existed outside the confines of Craigmoss, every few weeks Ellie caught the bus to Dublin, where she wandered round the shops, buying nothing, because it was important she keep Liam's money for when the baby arrived and she could leave Fern Hall. Her only extravagance was a cup of coffee. She would sit in the restaurant, savouring the rich aroma, and try to plan ahead, impossible in Fern Hall where her brain felt as damp as the house itself.

But even with a clear head, it was hard to imagine what she would do once she had a child. Best not to think about it, see how she felt when the time came. If it was well-behaved, she'd buy a sling and carry it on her back and it wouldn't stop her from having the adventures she had planned.

★

The weather improved and so did Ellie. The garden she'd thought barren suddenly sprang into life and the trees gradually became covered in pink and white blossom. She took a chair outside and read her book in the warm, spring sunshine. When Mrs McTaggart finished her work, they would have a cup of tea and a gossip.

Mrs McTaggart was a widow, comfortably plump, with red apple cheeks and three grown-up sons; two worked on farms nearby, and Brendan, the youngest, was in prison in Belfast.

'He's a terrorist,' his mother said proudly. 'He threw a bomb at someone. They still sent him to prison, even though it missed.'

'I like the name Brendan,' Ellie opined.

'You'd like Brendan himself. He's a lovely lad. He went to school with your Liam. They were a pair of imps, always in trouble.'

'What was Felix like when he was young?' She couldn't imagine Felix being young.

'Clever, far cleverer than Liam, if you don't mind me saying. It was always planned he'd go to university, but when the time came, he couldn't bring himself to leave, apart from which there wasn't the money. Liam was only thirteen, Monica a year older, and his poor mam was being driven silly by his philandering dad. So, Felix stayed. All them brains, but what does he do but get a job in The Rose as a barman.' Mrs McTaggart's normally cheery face was sober.

'That's a shame,' Ellie said encouragingly. It showed how bored she was that she found this stuff of interest.

'It is indeed! Maybe he'll get his reward in heaven, because he certainly hasn't had it on earth. Five years later, didn't his daddy go and die! By then, Monica had already left for London, Liam was ready for university himself, and Eammon Conway hadn't been in his grave for more than half an hour, before his wife ups and parks herself on her sister, leaving Felix with the chemists and a house no one in the world would want to buy. Not to mention,' Mrs McTaggart added darkly, 'Neila Kenny.'

'What's Neila Kenny got to do with things?' demanded Ellie. 'And what did you mean by his philandering dad?'

'I shouldn't really tell you.'

'Oh, go on. I won't repeat it. I'll not be here much longer, will I? It doesn't matter what I know.'

'It's not that. It doesn't seem right to spread gossip.' She gave Ellie a reproachful look, as if spreading gossip was the last thing on earth she'd do. 'As to repeating it, I doubt if a soul in Craigmoss doesn't already know.'

'If everyone already knows, then it's not gossip.'

'Do you think not? Ah, well, I don't suppose it'd hurt.' She was obviously dying to spill the beans. The truth is,' her voice dropped to a whisper though the garden was empty except for themselves and a couple of birds, 'Neila Kenny was Eammon Conway's bit on the side for nigh on ten years.'

'Never!' Ellie was genuinely shocked. 'You mean they slept together?'

'I doubt if they slept much, but they definitely did the other,' the woman said smugly.

'For ten years! But this is Ireland! I thought you couldn't get contraceptives. How could they have made love for ten years without having babies all over the place?' Ellie was annoyed. She'd only made love for five minutes with the son of Eammon Conway before she was up the stick.

Mrs McTggart dropped her voice even lower. 'Neila's never had periods, so she can't have babies.'

'How the hell do you know *that*?'

'Everyone knows everything about everyone in Craigmoss,' said her informant, tightlipped, as if she disapproved. 'But you see what's happened, Ellie? Felix has taken over his father's woman, just as he took over his shop and his house. Now he's stuck with her. One of these fine days they'll probably get married, or so everyone expects. There's some people, and Felix Conway is one, who are far too good for this world. That man's a saint.'

Chapter 16

LOCAL BUILDING FIRM GETS MUCH NEEDED HELPING HAND, ran the headline in the *Echo*.

'Crisis-hit Doyle Construction has been taken over by Medallion, the company responsible for some of the most impressive buildings recently erected in London and other major British cities. A spokesman for Medallian said all outstanding contracts would be honoured and completed on time. Matthew Doyle, founder of Doyle Construction, is being retained as Managing Director of the Liverpool arm of this prestigious company, though he will not have a seat on the board . . .'

Ruby laid the paper down with a sigh. Matthew hadn't thought to tell her the good news himself – she assumed the news was good – he'd left her to find out for herself.

She sighed again because she knew this wasn't true. Matthew hadn't *wanted* to tell her himself. It wasn't thoughtlessness on his part. He hardly came to the house nowadays, and then only when he knew there'd be other people there, at evenings and weekends. He'd stayed upstairs only for a few weeks before purchasing a one-bedroom flat in a modern block in Gateacre. Greta had helped put up curtains.

How she must have hurt him! Ruby cringed. But then all she'd done was hurt him since they'd met. He must love her very much, she thought, to have put up with it, with her, for so long.

But did he still love her now, she wondered? Perhaps he'd given up. He'd been about to open his heart and in return had received the equivalent of a slap in the face. She wouldn't be surprised if he hated her.

Ever since, on the few times they'd met, she'd looked at him in a different light, not as a friend, not as the man she'd once found so very irritating, but as a lover. She realised she would quite like to go to bed with Matthew Doyle, lie in his arms, marry him if he asked. The excited thrill she'd had when they first met, which had never completely gone away, returned with a vengeance. The half-spoken acknowledgment of his feelings had unlocked the key to her own heart, sadly too late.

One of these days, Ruby vowed, she'd get Matthew by himself and *force* him to say the words he'd been about to say on that brilliant February morning. He may have given up on her, but she hadn't even started on him.

'Forty-one!' Greta grimaced at her reflection in the mirror. 'I don't *feel* forty-one. Do I look it?'

'No way, sis.' Heather was sitting on the bed, conscious that it was twenty years almost to the minute that she'd been in exactly the same position, doing the same thing, watching her sister get made-up on her birthday. Then, Greta had been twenty-one. 'Do I look forty?' she asked. It would be her own birthday in two weeks' time.

'Hardly thirty. Is this lippy all right?'

'It's a bit dark. You've got a thing about dark lippies. With your colouring, you need something lighter.'

'You always say that.'

'You shouldn't ask my opinion if you don't want it.'

Greta rubbed the lipstick off with a tissue and applied a paler one. 'Does that look OK?'

'Much better.'

'What shall I wear?' Greta got up and examined her half of the wardrobe.

Heather shrugged. 'Anything'll do. It's only the two of us going for a meal.'

'We should have had a party.'

'Who would we have invited?'

'Oh, I dunno. People from work?'

'They're all married,' Heather said. 'We'd have been the only single ones there.'

Greta took out a frilly chiffon frock and examined it critically. It would look good with her black velvet jacket. 'I'm surprised Gerald isn't coming for Easter,' she remarked. 'It's only next week. Moira will be home from Norwich, and there's Matthew, Daisy and Clint. We could have had a family party then. Mam would have been pleased.'

'I'm not seeing Gerald any more.'

'Why not?' Greta span round so fast she nearly fell over. She looked at her sister with amazement. 'I know you only started off as friends, but I thought it had got serious.'

'It had,' Heather said calmly. 'He asked me to marry him.'

'What did you say?'

'At first, I didn't know what to say. I thought about living in a strange town, leaving this house.' Heather glanced around the familiar room. 'I tried to imagine what it would be like, not seeing Mam every day, you, our Daisy. I wondered if Gerald's children would grow to love me, and would I ever love them?'

'And what did you decide?' Greta sat on her bed and the sisters looked at each other across the small space between, as they'd done thousands of times in the past.

'I decided I could do all those things.' She gave herself an approving nod. 'I said, "yes", to Gerald.'

'But I thought you weren't seeing him any more!'

'I'm not.' A wry smile drifted across Heather's stern features. 'I didn't tell anyone about getting married. I was waiting for the right opportunity, I suppose. One night, not long after he proposed, Gerald rang. We were discussing things, the future. He told me how much he earns in the bank. It was a lot less than I do, so I suggested it would be best if I got a job as a legal clerk in Northampton and he looked after the children.'

'What did he say?'

'He nearly hit the roof.' Her eyes rolled, as if she still felt shocked by the memory. 'He said it was the daftest idea he'd ever heard and he was surprised at me. Men went to work, women stayed at home and did the housework. Apparently, any other way and civilisation would crumble.'

'Cheek!' Greta gasped.

'Isn't it?' Heather said indignantly. 'I said it wouldn't hurt to discuss the matter and he lost his temper. That was how he felt and there was to be no discussion, so I told him I didn't want to marry a man whose mind was so made up he wouldn't talk about things.

Then I put the phone down and we haven't spoken to each other since.'

'He's bound to call again, apologise.'

'Then he needn't bother. I've finished with him.'

'Oh, sis! And it happened just like that?'

'Just like that.' Heather snapped her fingers. 'One minute I loved him, next I never wanted to see him again for as long as I live.'

'That's amazing.'

'I know, and it's also a bit scary.' Heather's eyes grew round. 'Say I'd married him, and *then* discovered what he was like.' She jumped to her feet. 'C'mon, Grete, else it'll be too late to go out. I hope you're not intending to wear that frock, it's awfully thin, and it's cold outside.'

Greta couldn't be bothered arguing. She put the chiffon frock back in the wardrobe, and took out another, warmer one. 'I was rather hoping you'd get married,' she said.

'Why?'

'Then I wouldn't feel so bad if I got married meself.'

From past experience, Heather knew Greta would always do exactly as she wanted, including getting married. It had hurt, being used, then ditched when someone more appealing appeared on the scene like the time in Corfu, but it didn't stop her from loving her sister. The thought of life without Greta, living in this room on her own, was horrible, but it seemed Greta didn't feel the same.

'Have you got some chap up your sleeve?' she asked. Greta had gone out a few times recently and refused to say who with.

'Sort of.'

'What does that mean?'

Greta giggled. 'It means I've got some chap up me sleeve.'

Three months later, on a melting July day, Greta's missing daughter returned to the house by Princes Park with her beautiful two-month-old son whose name was Brendan.

'You're just in time for the wedding.' Moira had opened the door. She'd only been home from university a few days herself.

'Whose wedding?'

'Our Mum's. She's getting married to Matthew Doyle next Tuesday.'

★

318

The birth had been extraordinarily easy and quite painless. Ever since it had been imminent, Mrs McTaggart had been coming every morning, just in case, and Neila Kenny deserted the chemist's and came afternoons.

One morning, just after eleven, Ellie felt a twinge and phoned Dr O'Hara who came straight away. Two hours later she was the mother of a perfect baby boy. It was that easy.

'Why do some women make such a fuss?' she wanted to know when the doctor placed her newly-born son in her arms.

'Because some women have a much harder time than you. Ask Mrs McTaggart here what she went through. I was there.'

'Agony,' Mrs McTaggart said dramatically. 'Hours and hours of sheer agony, and each time was worse than the time before. What are you going to call him, Ellie?'

'Brendan,' Ellie said promptly.

The older woman went pink with delight. 'I hope he gives you as much pleasure as my Brendan gave me.'

Dr O'Hara raised his eyebrows. 'Does that include landing up in a Belfast jail?'

'It does indeed, Doctor. I'm proud of him, and so would his daddy be if he was alive.'

'I like the idea of having a son named after an Irish terrorist,' Ellie said with a gleeful smile. She looked down at the baby. He had a fluff of reddish hair, large blue eyes, a plump face and plump, pink hands. The blue eyes were fixed intently on her face. 'He's staring straight at me. He knows I'm his mother.'

The doctor gave Mrs McTaggart a knowing smile. 'Babies can't see properly for the first few weeks, Ellie.'

'I thought that was kittens.'

'It's babies too.'

The front door slammed, there were heavy footsteps on the stairs, and a red-faced, strangely bright-eyed Neila Kenny came rushing into the room. She looked just a little bit mad.

'I saw Doctor O'Hara's car outside. Oh, the baby's come! Is it a boy or a girl?'

'A boy,' Ellie said proudly. 'I'm calling him Brendan.'

'Let me look at him. Can I hold him? I wish he'd come this afternoon when I was here.'

'You can hold him some other time, Neila,' Dr O'Hara said. 'I'd like to see him at his mother's breast right now. She and Brendan need to get used to each other.'

Ellie felt a tiny bit embarrassed, undoing her nightie, and exposing her breasts in front of three people, one of whom she wholeheartedly detested. She wished Neila would go away, not stare at Brendan as if she'd like to eat him.

Her son attached himself to her left breast and began to suck loudly.

'Very good,' the doctor said approvingly.

'It hurts,' Ellie complained. 'Me breasts feel dead tender.'

'That's quite normal. Let him try the other breast once he's had his fill.'

'How will I know?'

'Brendan will let you know, don't worry.'

A few minutes later, Brendan set up an angry wail and was transferred to the right breast. To Ellie's intense irritation, Neila seemed to think it necessary to lend a hand. 'I can manage meself, thanks,' she snapped.

Mrs McTaggart offered to make a cup of tea, but the doctor refused and said he had to go. 'I'll come back tomorrow, make sure everything's all right, but don't hesitate to give me a call if there's a problem.'

'I'll be looking after her, Doctor,' said Neila, 'don't worry. I'll ring Felix in a minute, tell him to bring more nappies and one or two other things. He'll be thrilled to bits it's a boy.'

'You're all heart, Neila. Ellie's lucky to have you.'

Ellie didn't think so.

Before, time had crawled by. Now it flew. Brendan, already a big baby according to Dr O'Hara, seemed to grow bigger by the day, not surprising considering the amount of milk he consumed. Ellie's breasts were sore, and she had to grudgingly concede she couldn't have coped without Neila Kenny, who abandoned the chemist's altogether and came to Fern Hall every day. Ellie had assumed bathing a baby, changing nappies, were the sort of things that would come naturally to a mother, but they seemed to require a knack she didn't have. Brendan was terrifyingly slippery when he was wet, and it was impossible to hold a squirming baby with one hand and wash him with the other. Nappies got in a terrible tuck and came off faster than she put them on. Neila could do all these things with incredible efficiency having had five younger brothers and sisters to learn on.

Brendan was demanding, but a good baby, according to Mrs McTaggart, far better behaved than Brendan the First, who'd screamed his bad-tempered little head off for three whole months, so much so that Mr McTaggart, bless his heart, had threatened to throw his latest son out of the window.

The new Brendan slept in a cot beside Ellie's bed and required feeding twice, sometimes three times, a night, followed by the inevitable burping. Ellie would scarcely have closed her eyes, when she would be alerted by an urgent cry. '*I'm hungry again,*' Brendan would yell. Next morning, she would hand him over to an eager Neila before going back to bed for a few hours of much needed sleep.

The amount of washing was horrendous. So many babyclothes, bedclothes, dozens and dozens of nappies; dirty nappies, soaking nappies, nappies drying on the line, nappies dried and aired and ready for use. Mrs McTaggart helped when she could, but she had other tasks to do and only came three times a week.

Despite her utter weariness, there were some mornings Ellie went back to bed and couldn't sleep. Although she knew the cot was empty and Brendan was safely downstairs, her mind remained alert and expectant, as if any minute there would be a desperate appeal for food. After a few hours, she would give up trying to sleep and go downstairs where there was always work to do.

It was on such a morning, when Brendan was six weeks old, that Ellie came down, aching for a cup of tea, to find the front door open and Neila coming in with the baby in his carrycot on wheels.

'Have you been out for a walk?' she asked.

'I go most mornings, didn't you know?'

'You never said before. Did you go to the village?'

'We needed shopping done.' Neila removed a nylon shopping bag from the tray under the pram and stared at her aggressively. 'Do you mind?'

Ellie minded very much her baby being examined by the entire village and his likeness to Liam – very strong – commented on.

'Everyone's surprised,' Neila remarked, 'That you're not getting yourself ready to go to Geneva.'

'What's in Geneva?', Ellie nearly said, then remembered Liam was, and he was supposed to be her husband and she was supposed to be joining him when the baby was born. 'Do I look as if I'm ready to go Geneva?' she said irritably instead. The furthest she got was the garden. Her hair was lucky if it got combed once a week, she'd forgotten what make-up looked like, and was wearing a maternity frock because she'd put on so much weight none of her old clothes would fit.

'*I'm* surprised Liam hasn't rung, or you haven't rung him, or that you haven't written to him or he to you.' Neila lifted Brendan from the pram, put her large, red hand on his fluffy head and pressed it tenderly into the curve beneath her chin.

Ellie resented her baby being touched by the hateful Neila Kenny. 'You're surprised at an awful lot of things. If you must know, I've written to Liam twice since I had Brendan.'

'You didn't ask me or Felix to post the letter.'

'That's because I asked Mrs McTaggart.'

'Liam hasn't answered.'

'Do you examine the post?'

'I pick it up off the mat when I come in, don't I?'

'I wouldn't know. I'm not a spy like you.'

Neila's big hand spread over the baby's back, the other supported his bottom. She said angrily, 'I'm not a spy. I can't help but notice things, that's all.'

Unable to think of a reason why Liam hadn't replied to her imaginary letters, Ellie turned on her heel and went into the kitchen to put the kettle on. Neila followed, Brendan clinging to her the way a monkey clings to a tree, as if *she* were his mother.

'You never married him, did you, Ellie?' Neila spat from the kitchen door. 'He ran off and left you. He doesn't give a damn about you or Brendan.'

'Say that were true,' Ellie said tiredly, 'What business is it of yours?'

'I'm worried about Brendan, that's all.' The horrible woman kissed Brendan's rosy cheek. 'He needs his father.'

'*I* didn't have a father,' a seething Ellie pointed out. 'He died before me and me sister were born. Neither of us seem to have come to any harm.'

'Ah, but you had a proper home, a family. What sort of life will

Brendan have with you on your own? No husband, no job, nowhere to live.'

Ellie realised with a shock that Neila was after her baby. She shivered. Although common sense told her the woman could do nothing harmful, she felt the need to get away from Fern Hall with all possible speed; tomorrow or the day after. The longer she stayed, the more possessive Neila would become. She held out her arms, forgetting the tea. 'He's due for a feed. I'll do it in the garden.'

It was June and the garden looked especially lovely. The crumbling walls were covered with trailing flowers, the trees with budding fruit. Ellie sat in a deckchair, opened her frock, and began to feed her always-hungry son. She wasn't sure if she loved Brendan, but he was *hers*, grown and nurtured in her womb. He was part of her, and she'd no more intention of letting him go than of getting rid of one of her limbs.

Next morning, Ellie was making her breakfast when Neila Kenny arrived, having washed her hair and made up her face for the first time in weeks. She'd also managed to struggle into a pair of jeans – all the hard work had made her lose some of the extra weight.

'You're up early,' Neila said, surprised, when they encountered each other in the kitchen. 'Where's Brendan?'

'Asleep in the garden. He only woke up once last night.' Perhaps he realised it was time he gave his mother a break. 'By the way, I'm going to Dublin tomorrow to see a friend, Amy. She lived in the same house as me and Liam.' She'd sooner not say she was leaving forever and provoke a scene.

'And taking Brendan with you?'

'Naturally, Amy would love to see him.'

Neila frowned and looked as if she'd like to object. 'Will you be able to manage on your own? I'll come with you if you like. I wouldn't mind a stroll around the shops.'

'I wouldn't dream of it. You've already done enough. I'll always be very grateful to you and Felix,' Ellie said falsely. She would have to put the planned adventures on hold for a while. Neila was right about one thing. It would be impossible to get a job when she had a small baby and where would she live? Well, Ellie could think of one place where she would be welcomed with open arms – home. It was one thing crawling back after a few months with her pregnancy a

323

badge of shame, but another altogether returning with her head held high, proudly, bearing the world's most beautiful baby, and pretending she'd had a super time over the last year. She would think of a reason for having left Liam so it didn't reflect badly on her – say he was dead, for example.

That night, after Neila had gone, she sat with Felix in the garden, nursing a sleepy Brendan in her arms. It was very peaceful, very still. The flowers shimmered in the golden light of the evening sun which was slowly setting into a mishmash of red, green and purple stripes, casting a dark, moving shadow across the grass, slowly stripping the blooms of their vivid colour. The air was heavily scented – Gran had flowers in the garden at home, Ellie remembered, that smelt wonderful at night. It was the first time in her life she had appreciated the beauty of nature and she thought it strange this should happen when she was on the point of leaving Fern Hall.

'You should get central heating,' she said.

'Eh!' Felix looked understandably taken aback by this strange remark.

'Central heating. It would make the house much warmer in the winter, get rid of the damp.' Now she thought about it, it was quite a pleasant house, gracious.

Felix's face softened into a gentle smile. 'I couldn't afford it, Ellie. It takes me all my time to pay the bills I have now.'

Ellie felt guilty, something else that was a first. He'd paid for Brendan's pram, his cot, mountains of babyclothes and nappies, and all the other things that were needed for a baby. It hadn't crossed her mind to say, 'thank you', yet it wasn't Felix's job to provide for his brother's child – a child he adored, always remarking how like Liam he was.

'Can't you turn the chemist's into something else?' she suggested. 'A tea room, for instance.' Lots of cars passed through Craigmoss on their way to and from Dublin or Dun Laoghaire, from where the ferry sailed to England – from where she and Brendan would sail tomorrow.

'People need a chemist for their prescriptions. It would be irresponsible to close it down.'

She wanted to shake some sense into him. It was time he put himself first, not conduct his life for the convenience of all and sundry. 'Fern Hall could provide bed and breakfasts,' she said. 'It's conveniently situated on the main road.'

'I'm not very good when it comes to business,' Felix said simply. 'It takes me all my time to run the chemist's.'

He needed a wife behind him, a pushy, determined wife, not the oaf-like Neila Kenny, who'd been his father's mistress and was someone else he felt responsible for. She was about to suggest other things he could sell from the chemist's, flowers for instance from the garden that could be put in buckets outside, but knew it was a waste of time. Life had beaten Felix and he'd lost the will to fight.

'I'll miss you and Brendan when the time comes for you to go,' he said in his husky whisper.

'I'll come and see you sometime.' Ellie genuinely meant it. 'At least, I'll try.'

'You'll always be welcome.'

It was a good job she didn't tell people at home that Liam was dead – she'd said they were 'incompatible' – because she'd only been in Liverpool two days when he rang to say Felix had tracked him down in Geneva, worried where Ellie was.

'He said you went to Dublin for the day and didn't come back,' Liam said accusingly. 'Did you *have* to walk out without a word? I told him it was just like you and I wasn't a bit surprised. He only wants to know if you're safe.'

'I'm quite safe, thanks, and I only left without saying anything because I was worried Neila Kenny would make a big fuss.'

'And why should Neila Kenny make any sort of fuss?'

'She was after Brendan, that's why, because she can't have children of her own. I think you should rescue your brother from Neila Kenny, Liam. Did you know she was your father's mistress for nearly ten years?'

'Y'what?' Liam gasped.

'You heard. He inherited her along with Fern Hall and the chemist's. Another thing, Felix bought all Brendan's stuff, so you owe him loads of money. *I* can't pay him back.'

There was silence for a moment while Liam digested these startling facts. 'What's he like, Brendan?' he eventually asked.

'Gorgeous. Everyone here loves him to death.'

'I might come and see him some time?'

'If you do, you're likely to get some dirty looks from me family.' Ellie gave the receiver a dirty look before slamming it down.

She couldn't have arrived home at a better time, amid preparations for her mother's wedding, with people too busy to question what she'd been up to, lecture her for turning up with Liam Conway's baby and brazenly announcing she wasn't married. Mum was pleased she'd got back in time to be a bridesmaid and was more concerned with getting her a frock the same as Moira and Daisy's than anything. And it was true what she'd said to Liam; everyone loved Brendan to death, particularly Gran. An old cot had been unearthed from the cellar, a new mattress hurriedly bought, and mother and son were installed in an upstairs room, empty now that the students had gone for the summer. Unlike with Neila, Ellie didn't mind a bit when Gran took Brendan off her hands every morning, allowing her to have a long sleep in.

Ruby felt as if Brendan had been sent by heaven to take her mind off the fact that the man she loved was about to marry another woman. If the other woman hadn't been her daughter, she might have put up a fight, told him that she loved him, forced him to admit he loved her back, insisted he was making a mistake.

She had no idea what had prompted Matthew to ask Greta to be his wife, but he had, and there was no going back, mistake or no mistake. She'd made a mess of things with Jacob, then with Chris Ryan, and the worst mess of all with Matthew Doyle. 'You're a soft girl, Ruby O'Hagan,' Beth used to tell her, and Beth was right.

Greta and Matthew made a perfect couple. They had known each other for the best part of their lives. Greta had liked him from the start, in the days when Ruby had called him every name under the sun. Even Heather approved of the match, though Ruby knew it would break her heart to lose her sister now that the relationship with Gerald Johnson had fizzled out.

The sole topic of conversation became the wedding, which couldn't take place in church because Matthew was divorced. Greta didn't mind and although there was a time when Ruby would have minded very much, things had changed. Nowadays, all sorts of people got divorced and couldn't be expected to remain alone for the rest of their lives, particularly if they were the innocent party, like Matthew.

Now that he was on his feet again, Matthew was paying for everything. A hotel had been booked for the reception – a new one in Paradise Street, very expensive. The menu was discussed endlessly, how many guests should be invited. Flowers were ordered, cars booked. Daisy knew of a pop group if they wanted music. Heather was to be Matron of Honour, Daisy and Moira bridesmaids. Moira was ordered home from Norwich for the weekend so she could be bought a dress – pale blue voile with a pleated bodice and a gathered skirt. Appointments were made at the hairdresser's – there would be plenty of time for shampoos and sets because Greta wanted an afternoon wedding.

Ruby was dragged into town to help choose the bride's outfit. Greta still had a weakness for frills and flounces and ended up with a cream lace, knee-length frock that made her look like a Barbie doll, and a mixture of feathers and flowers pretending to be a hat. Ruby bought her own outfit at the same time; a simple mid-blue sheath with a short boxy jacket. Looking in the mirror, she thought Matthew was right to have chosen the daughter not the mother, because the mother looked a sight; old, grey, with drooping eyes and a neck like a piece of old rope. She threw back her shoulders. She was even getting a hump.

Matthew was buying a lovely house in Calderstones. The solicitors were doing their utmost to exchange final contracts before the newly wed couple returned from their honeymoon in the South of France. So far, everything was going smoothly, but for Ruby nothing was going smoothly at all.

Beth couldn't come to the wedding. 'I'm speaking at a conference,' she wrote. 'I'd feel awful, cancelling, though if it were *you* getting married, Rube, I'd be there if it meant snubbing President Carter himself.'

She hadn't seen Connie and Charles for ages and hoped an invitation to a wedding might tempt them back to Liverpool, if only for the day, but Connie rang to say Charles was too ill to travel. 'It's his heart, Ruby. He's not allowed to drive any more and he's not up to the train journey. Give Greta our love and tell her we're sending a present.'

If that wasn't bad enough, a few days later she saw in the *Echo* that Jim Quinlan had died. Over the years, she'd felt glad that he hadn't been attracted to her as she had been to him. There'd been a time when she would have married him like a shot – perhaps because he was so different to Jacob. Or maybe, without realising it, she'd just been casting round for someone to love and Jim had fitted the bill.

Why do people have to grow old, die? she wondered, and for the first time in her life, Ruby was overwhelmed by an all-consuming sadness, feeling as if her own life was hanging by a thread, and asking herself the inevitable question, 'What is it all for?'

Then Ellie returned from Dublin with Brendan, her first great-grandchild and, although Ruby never received an answer to her question, the sadness lifted, and she took the baby boy to her heart.

It was a daft idea, thought Heather, to have a Matron of Honour and three bridesmaids when you were only getting married in a registry office. For once, she'd kept her opinions to herself. After all, it was Greta's wedding, not hers. As for that dress, it was far too short, and you'd think Mam would have talked her into something at least ballerina length.

And there was something strange, not quite right, about being joined together in Holy Matrimony in an ordinary room by a man in a suit – there were actually women registrars, which would be even stranger.

'Do you take this woman . . .?'

'Do you take this man . . .?'

'I do,' Greta murmured in the girlish voice that had hardly changed since she was a child. Heather felt her eyes prickle with tears, not because she was losing her sister, but she knew that, unlike Greta, she would never say those words again. She couldn't have brought herself to say them to Gerald, nor to any other man on earth. She had said, 'I do' just once, to Rob, and she'd meant it for ever. Heather knew that she would remain Rob White's widow for the rest of her days.

There was a dreadful smell coming from Brendan. The little monkey had dirtied in his nappy, and in the middle of a wedding too. He was perched in the crook of Ruby's arm making cooing noises. She worried that she hadn't brought enough spare nappies, only three, and it would be hours before they could go home.

Considering it was a wedding, the atmosphere was rather flat. She missed the grandeur and dignity of a church, and wondered if second marriages always lacked the excitement of the first. The groom hadn't smiled once and Heather looked as if the world was about to end. At least Greta seemed pleased she was about to become Mrs Matthew Doyle.

Ruby glanced across at the Donovans and the Whites. Their faces were sober, no doubt remembering the day they'd attended a different wedding which they had thought would be a beginning, but had turned out to be the end.

Thank the Lord she'd come home when she did, Ellie thought as she danced with a dead gorgeous chap called Gary who was a sculptor, or something arty. She was having a great time. The reception had been a bit boring, especially the speeches, but Grannie and Grandad Donovan had been so pleased to see her and had made a desperate fuss of Brendan. Ellie had felt very proud, as if she'd performed a miracle.

'He's our Larry's *grandson*,' Grannie Donovan said tearfully. 'Is he like him or not?'

'The spitting image,' Grandad Donovan confirmed, making four different people Brendan had been declared the spitting image of that day.

At seven o'clock, the pop group arrived along with loads more people and the reception turned into a party. The Gigolos made up for in noise what they lacked in talent, but were easy to dance to – how come Daisy knew a pop group?

Not long afterwards, the bride and groom left for their honeymoon and the dancing stopped for the guests to cheer them on their way. Moira came over and whispered to her twin, 'I'll never get used to Mum being married. It seems really weird. Just look, Matthew's got his *arm* around her.'

'I suppose it is a bit weird,' Ellie agreed. She hadn't been home long enough to give the matter much thought, though the news had initially come as a shock. 'It means Matthew's our step-father.'

'Mum wants us to go and live with her in Calderstones. I don't know about you, but I said "no". I'd sooner stay in our old house with Gran. I think Mum's a bit annoyed.'

'She hasn't asked me yet, but I feel the same as you.' Ellie couldn't imagine her mother looking after Brendan while she had a long lie in, unlike Gran.

The music started again. Unable to resist, the twins grinned at each other and began to dance on the spot, twisting and turning in rhythm with the loud, throbbing beat. In no time, two young men appeared; Gary the sculptor, and a pony-tailed individual wearing shredded jeans who paired off with Moira.

Ellie prepared to dance the night away, entirely forgetting she was a mother with a hungry baby to feed. She was annoyed, even if it was hours later, when Gran tugged at her sleeve and announced Brendan was screaming fit to bust. 'Why can't he have a bottle?' she asked irritably.

'He's drunk both his bottles, love.'

'Does that mean I'll have to go *home*?' Ellie was outraged.

'I can't feed him, can I? Anyway, his nappy's soaking. That's the fifth today. I sent out for some of them disposable ones, but I don't like changing it again. The poor little chap needs a bath by now, else he'll get a rash. I'll ring for a taxi.'

'Where is Brendan?'

'With your other gran. He's wet her lovely new costume.' Ruby hurried away.

'Have you got a *baby*?' Gary looked at Ellie askance.

'Yes.'

'Oh! Excuse us a mo, there's a mate over there I want to talk to.'

Gary vanished into the crowd, without mentioning the party he'd invited her to on Saturday night, and Ellie knew it would always be like this. Her time was no longer her own now that she was responsible for another person's life. She couldn't go out whenever she felt like it, do whatever she pleased, and men would keep their distance if they knew about Brendan, worried they'd be landed with another man's child.

Ellie hardly spoke to her grandmother on the way home in the taxi, though it was hardly Gran's fault she'd had a baby. Mind you, Gran hardly spoke to *her*, which was odd because she was usually so cheerful. In fact, she'd seemed a bit down all day. Ellie didn't care, although she thought the world of her grandmother. She was too fed up to care about anything.

When Ellie woke, it was still dark and someone was sitting on the bed trying to shush a bawling Brendan. She sat up and switched on the bedside lamp. 'What time is it?'

'Three o'clock.' The someone was Daisy, still in her blue bridesmaid's frock. 'Me and Clint went back to Mary's house and I've only just got in. I heard Brendan cry and thought I might stop him before he woke you, but he must need feeding.'

'The bloody little sod always needs feeding.' Ellie opened her nightdress and Daisy put Brendan in her arms. 'I only fed him five hours ago.'

'You must be awfully tired not to have heard him.'

'I'm more than tired. I'm totally exhausted,' Ellie replied piteously.

'Why don't you put him on the bottle permanently and we can take turns looking after him during the night? I wouldn't mind, and nor would Gran. You can get tablets from the doctor to dry your milk up.'

'Can you?' It seemed a marvellous idea. Ellie decided to see the doctor first thing in the morning.

'Would you like us to make you some cocoa?'

'Please. Can I have a biscuit too? I'm starving.'

By the time her cousin came back, Brendon was halfway through his mother's second breast.

'What does it feel like?' Daisy asked.

'It either hurts or tickles, one or the other.'

'Me and Clint are going to have loads of children.'

'Are you now! Is that Clint's idea or yours?' Ellie suspected Clint was keeping well out of her way. They hadn't come face to face since she'd got back.

'Mine, I suppose. You know Clint, how shy he is. He doesn't like talking about certain things.'

Having babies being one of them, Ellie thought cynically. 'Are you two still getting married?'

'Yes, a year next January, 1979. You can be a bridesmaid with your Moira if you like,' Daisy offered generously.

'That'd be nice, ta.' Ellie looked at Daisy's innocent, wholesome face. She'd changed a lot in the last year, was far more confident, and had loads of friends, though was as dumpy and plain as she'd always been. The friends were artists, Moira said, and considered Daisy to be a fantastic painter. They'd held an exhibition and some of Daisy's paintings had actually been *sold*.

'You mean people gave money for them?' Ellie gasped.

'Yes, isn't it amazing?'

'Truly amazing.'

Brendon detached himself and smacked his lips with satisfaction. Ellie hoisted him on to her shoulder to bring up his wind.

'Shall I do that while you have your cocoa and biscuit?'

'Thanks, Daise.' Ellie gratefully handed her son across.

'I like the feel of him, the way he fits against me like the piece of a jigsaw puzzle.' She began gently to pat Brendan's back. 'He's a very masculine baby. He doesn't suit nightgowns. Do you mind if I buy him one of those all-in-one stretchy things?'

'I don't mind a bit.'

'I'll get one in Mothercare tomorrow.'

It was rather nice, leaning against the pillows, sipping the cocoa, and watching someone else burp her child.

'Were you pleased about your A levels?' Daisy asked.

'I did much better than expected.' Ellie had been astonished to find she'd done so well considering she hadn't revised a single subject.

'Are you going to look for a job?'

'I hadn't thought about it. What about Brendan?'

'Gran will look after him, won't she? She looked after us when your mum was ill and mine went to work.'

'I suppose she would,' Ellie said thoughtfully. After Daisy had gone and Brendan was back in his cot, snoring softly, Ellie snuggled under the clothes and considered what had just been said. She didn't want an ordinary job, like in an office or a bank, but fancied working in a night club or an advertising agency, becoming a model or an actress, travelling the world. She'd thought having Brendan had put a stop to these dreams, but if Gran was prepared to have Brendan while she went to work, she might be prepared to have him if she went away!

Only might! Ellie had a feeling that if she put this proposal to her grandmother, she would object. After all, looking after a baby for a few hours a day wasn't the same as looking after one the whole time. And Gran might insist Brendan needed his mother, even if it was only at night.

In that case, Ellie would just have to leave the way she'd left before, the way she'd left Felix and Fern Hall, without telling a soul, knowing her son was in safe hands. This time, she wouldn't even say anything to Moira who'd only disapprove.

And so it was that, two months later, in the middle of September, when Ruby crept into the room to collect Brendan and give him his bottle, Ellie's bed was empty. She wasn't in the bathroom, either, nor downstairs. A few hours later, when there was still no sign, Ruby came to the inevitable conclusion that, not for the first time, her granddaughter had run away.

Chapter 17

So much money, enough to buy all the clothes she wanted, anything for the house, yet Greta felt bored. And it was such a beautiful house, mock Tudor, with five bedrooms, living, dining and breakfast rooms, and a kitchen with every conceivable modern device. The garden was a picture, neatly perfect, and a man came twice a week to weed and prune and cut the grass.

Matthew had had the place re-decorated from top to bottom; new carpets everywhere. She had rarely enjoyed herself so much, choosing the colours, the curtains, wandering around the most expensive shops picking any item of furniture that took her fancy.

Now it was all done, the limewood wardrobe and the matching chests of drawers were full of new clothes, and suddenly there was nothing else to do. They had a cleaner as well as a gardener, and all Greta did was put the washing in the automatic machine, transfer it to the dryer, and make an evening meal for Matthew.

She wondered if she should have kept her job, but it hadn't seemed right, being married to a hugely successful businessman, living in such an impressive house, yet working as a shorthand-typist. If she'd had a profession, like Heather, it would have been different. Anyroad, she'd never liked work. Mam always said she was lazy, that she preferred her bed, which Greta had to concede was true.

It was upsetting that neither of her girls had wanted to live with her – four of the five bedrooms hadn't been used. It didn't matter that Moira was at university or Ellie had taken it into her head to run away again. At least she could have got their rooms ready for when they came back, furnished them in a way she knew they would have liked.

Matthew worked harder now that the company belonged to

someone else. Some nights, it was ten o'clock by the time he got home and the meal was spoilt. Greta felt lonely on her own, which was ironic in a way, as she'd only married him so she *wouldn't* feel lonely. More and more, she found herself going round to see Mam. She hadn't realised when she'd lived there just how shabby and run down Mam's house was, and it made her more cross that the twins hadn't wanted to leave. It was Mam, not her, talking about Moira coming home from university for Christmas.

Now Heather was studying for a law degree through the Open University, getting up at unearthly hours of the morning to watch programmes on television. Evenings, when Greta went into her old room and sat on her old bed wanting to chat to her sister, Heather was usually studying or writing essays and made it obvious she didn't appreciate being interrupted.

During the day, Mam was usually busy with Brendan, nearly eight months old, a delightful baby, but a terrible handful. Poor Mam was up to her eyes with work, what with Brendan, three students, and Heather and Daisy to look after.

'Why don't I take Brendan off your hands?' Greta suggested one afternoon when Brendan was being given his tea and turning it into a game, holding the food in his mouth for ages, before slyly letting it dribble out so that Mam had to catch it with the spoon and put it back. His green eyes sparkled with mischief, and he kept slamming the tray on his high chair with his big hands and thumping it with his fat knees at the same time. He was a handsome child, perfectly built, with Liam Conway's eyes and hair a lovely golden red. Brendan would keep her busy during the day and she was sure Matthew would love a baby. They could get an au pair to look after him during the night and do things like change his nappies.

'I don't need him taking off my hands, love,' Ruby said mildly.

'But you've so much to do, Mam!'

'If you feel liking helping, Greta, you can make the students' tea.'

Greta pouted. It wasn't the same. After all, Brendan was Ellie's son and Ellie was her daughter, which made her Brendan's Grandma. She had far more right to him than Mam. 'But that's not fair,' she said. 'We've got a much nicer house, a lovely garden. We could buy him far more things, toys and stuff, clothes.' Brendan's stretchy suit was so small, the feet had been cut off to accommodate his legs and he was wearing a pair of frilly girl's socks that she remembered had belonged to one of the twins.

'I'm sorry, love,' Ruby said, very slowly and deliberately, but when you said you'd take him off my hands, did you mean permanently?'

'Yes.'

'And why, all of a sudden, do you want a baby? Is it because you're bored all day in your much nicer house?'

'Yes, no. No, of course not,' Greta stammered, and all of a sudden she and Mam were having a terrible row, which they'd never done before. At least Greta was having a row, Mam didn't say much. She accused her mother of having stolen her children so that she'd hardly seen anything of them when they were little, and now she was stealing her grandson. She ended up storming out, screaming something about going to court, getting her grandson back, when she'd never had him in the first place.

When she got home, the house was in darkness and felt cold. She turned up the central heating, threw herself on to the bed, and burst into tears. Why wasn't she happy? She'd always been happy apart from the few years after Larry died, and she'd thought she'd be happier still in a smart house with pots of money. Although it hadn't been her intention to go one up on her sister, nevertheless she'd thought Heather would be envious of her new position in life, but nowadays Heather appeared serenely contented as she studied for her law degree.

Matthew didn't help much, though it wasn't deliberate. He was incredibly kind and thoughtful, took her out at weekends, was buying her a fur coat for Christmas, and complimented her on her cooking. Making love was oddly thrilling. Matthew had been part of her life for almost as long as she could remember and although she'd always considered him attractive, she'd never remotely thought of him as a lover. But now he was her husband, she went to bed with him every night, and felt instantly aroused by his touch, yet sensed that Matthew was only doing what was expected of him, that he was detached from the whole thing. Sometimes, even when he was being his kindest, she felt as if he was detached from the marriage itself.

Ruby was still shaking when her other daughter came home. She'd burnt the students' tea, but fortunately she'd taken boys again and they didn't seem to care what the food was like as long as it arrived in heaps – girls, she'd decided, were far too much trouble, always complaining about something or other.

'Where's Brendan?' Heather enquired.

'Asleep, for once. Look, love, d'you mind having an omelette? There's nothing else ready. I'm way behind today.'

'An omelette's fine. What's the matter, Mam?' Heather had noticed her mother's trembling hands.

Ruby sat down, close to tears. 'I had a terrible row with our Greta.' She explained what had happened. 'I don't know what's got into her. She's not been the same since she got married.'

Heather reached for her mother's hands. 'I'm sorry, Mam, but none of us really know what our Greta's like. Oh, she's as nice as pie while she's being spoilt and made a fuss of, loved by one and all, but she's got a selfish streak. She's always put herself first – it's what she was doing today, no matter how much it upset you. It's obvious she's not happy in that big house on her own and she sees Brendan as a way of filling the time, making her feel as if she's somebody again.'

'Oh, I don't hold with all this psychological claptrap, Heather. Beth's always coming out with stuff like that.'

'Can you think of another reason why Greta behaved the way she did?'

'No,' Ruby sighed after a few moments' pause.

'Ellie's the same,' Heather continued. 'She does her own thing and to hell with the consequences.'

'Your dad was a bit like that. He had no conscience. He'd sooner walk away than face up to things.' Ruby frowned. 'I hope Matthew's being all right with our Greta.'

'I'm sure Matthew's being fine, but he's not there all the time, is he? He's got other things to think of, and Greta's not the centre of the universe any more, like she was here – with you and me, at least.'

'Perhaps I should go and see her.'

'No,' Heather said in a hard voice. 'Let her stew in her own juice for a while, she'll soon be back. You see,. Mam, Greta needs us far more than we need her.'

'That only seems more reason why I should go and see her.'

'She's forty-one, Mam. She's got to learn to stand on her own two feet. You've got enough to do with Brendan.'

A week later, Greta returned, by which time Moira was home and the Christmas decorations were up. She felt a twinge when she saw the worn paper chains, the balls and bells that opened and closed like concertinas, the elderly fairy on top of the tree, things she'd helped put up in the past, but this time it had been done without her.

Moira was lying on the living room floor playing with Brendan, teaching him how to put one block on top of another, but he clearly preferred flinging them as far as they'd go.

'Hi, Mum,' Moira sang, but didn't get up and kiss her.

Greta had come all set to apologise to her mother, but felt annoyed at the signs that life was continuing smoothly without her in the place she still regarded as home. She found Ruby in the kitchen emptying flour into a plastic bowl.

'Oh, hello, love.' She smiled, as if their last meeting had never happened. 'Does that look like a pound to you? I thought I'd make the mince pies early for a change, rather than in a rush on Christmas Eve.'

'I wouldn't know, Mam. I thought you were supposed to weigh it first.'

'I usually do, but Brendan's broken the scales.'

'Actually, Mam,' Greta said on an impulse. 'Me and Matthew thought you'd like to come to us for Christmas dinner. We've bought this huge turkey,' she lied, and imagined herself the star of the show, everyone saying what a wonderful job she'd done, admiring the house which they'd hardly seen.

'Greta, love, it's a bit late to ask now. I was expecting you and Matthew to come to us. Clint's coming, and I've already invited his mum and dad, and Jonathan will be here.'

'Who's Jonathan?'

'One of the students. He's from India, Karachi. It's too far for him to go home, so he's staying here.'

'Why is he called Jonathan if he's Indian?'

'Because he's a Christian. He'll be coming with us to Midnight Mass.'

'Matthew and I can't come to dinner on Christmas Day,' Greta said bluntly.

Her mother looked perplexed. 'But you just asked us!'

'If me family can't come, we'll go somewhere else. We've been asked to loads of places for dinner.' Greta knew she was cutting off her nose to spite her face, but felt deeply hurt that her invitation had been refused, unreasonable though it was at such a late date. She felt as if she didn't matter any more.

The dining room in the house in Calderstones had never been used since they moved in. She and Matthew usually ate in the little breakfast room which was much cosier. Perhaps it was a mistake to serve dinner on the vast table on Christmas Day, just the two of them, Matthew clearly puzzled that they hadn't been asked home.

They didn't say much during the meal. Afterwards, Greta cleared the table and watched the portable television in the kitchen, and Matthew watched the one in the lounge. It stayed that way until six o'clock, when it was time to get ready for the party in Southport being held by one of the executives from Medallion, the company who'd taken over Doyle Construction.

Greta put on a red crêpe frock with shoelace straps and a frilly hem, a bit like the sort Spanish dancers wore. Without Heather there to advise her, she painted her lips bright red to go with the frock and applied a little too much rouge and mascara. Matthew looked a bit surprised when she appeared, but didn't say anything, just helped her on with her new fur coat which was sealskin with a mink collar and cuffs, terribly glamorous.

At the party, quite a few men wanted to talk to her, tell her what a stunner she was, how much she suited red and, Greta, always used to being the centre of attention, felt like a star after all. She even gave one chap, an American whose name was Charlie Mayhew, her telephone number, and he promised to call and take her to lunch. She was sure Matthew wouldn't mind, but didn't tell him.

'She seemed such a sweet little thing,' Matthew muttered.

'Are you saying she isn't?' snapped Ruby.

'Not any more,' said Matthew.

It was two weeks after Christmas, and Matthew Doyle had appeared unexpectedly in the middle of the afternoon. Moira had gone for a walk with Brendan in his pram, and Ruby had taken the opportunity to wash the students' bedding. They were due back in a few days and she hadn't had the chance before.

'We've only been married six months and I've a horrible feeling it's already a failure,' Matthew said miserably.

'Why are you telling me this?' She wondered why she sounded so abrupt when she was so pleased to see him, even if the news he'd brought was distressing. Her heart had turned a somersault when she'd opened the door and found him outside.

'Because I've got to talk to someone and you're the only one I can.'

'Would you like a cup of tea?'

'I was hoping you'd ask.' He sat his long body on a kitchen chair, shoulders drooping.

Ruby ran water in the kettle and gave the washing machine a kick when it stopped. It was on its last legs and needed encouragement. 'What's wrong, Matthew?' she asked, kinder now.

'I dunno, Rube.' She felt warmed by the 'Rube'. It meant they were at least friends again. 'I don't know what I'm doing wrong. I don't know what's right any more. She's moody all the time, bad-tempered, bored. There was a time when I couldn't have visualised Greta being bad-tempered, but I've witnessed it quite a few times lately.'

'I've witnessed it myself. It shook me too.'

'Have you?' He didn't look surprised. 'She hasn't a good word to say for you or Heather, or Moira come to that. She seems to think you're all against her for some reason.'

'We're not.' Ruby said fervently. 'I'm worried sick about her. Heather seems to think she'll come round in her own time. I don't think Moira's noticed anything amiss.'

'She's got a thing about Brendan. She wants him.'

'Brendan's not a parcel to be handed round at whim. He's already had two different people looking after him.'

'That's what I more or less told her meself.'

'Are you sorry you asked her to marry you?'

'I didn't ask her. Rube. She asked me.'

'*What*!' Ruby was pouring boiling water into the teapot. It splashed on to her hand and she gave a little scream. 'Ouch!'

'Are you all right?' Matthew leapt to his feet, grabbed her hand, and put it under the cold tap. 'Does that feel better?'

'Much better, thanks. Why did you accept?' He was patting her hand gently with the teatowel. They were standing very close, touching. His breath was warm on her cheek.

'Because I'm a soft lad, because I was flattered, because I was feeling particularly low and vulnerable at the time.'

'Why were you feeling low and vulnerable?'

'You know the answer to that, Ruby.'

She turned away and faced the sink, unable to meet his eyes. 'I'm sorry, Matthew. I was stupid, rude. I was every horrible name you can think of. I've always been slow-witted. It didn't enter my head what you were trying to say until I was on the phone. I called you, but you didn't come back.'

'I was too bloody mad to come back.' There was a long pause during which both were very still. Then Matthew whispered softly, 'What would you have said if I had?'

'It's too late for that now, Matthew.' Ruby moved away. 'You can see that, can't you?'

He sighed. 'I'm not sure if I want to.'

'Then you must,' she said with a briskness she didn't feel. She would have preferred to weep, throw herself into his arms, make up for the hurt she'd caused him, but he was her daughter's husband, and it was much, much too late. Had he been married to anyone else, she would probably have felt pleased his marriage had failed. 'Oh, this damn washing machine!' It had stopped again. She gave it another kick. 'I'll never get this lot done in time.'

'For Christ's sake, Ruby, buy a new one.' Matthew was himself again. The conversation they'd just had might never have occurred. He returned to the table and she gave him a mug of tea.

Ruby laughed sardonically. 'What with?' Greta no longer contributed towards the household finances and Brendan was an extra expense, if a welcome one.

'I'll get you one for Christmas.'

'I couldn't possibly accept such an expensive present. Anyway, you already gave me some scent.'

'Climb down off your high horse, Rube. We're family now. You're my . . .' He paused.

'Mother-in-law?'

'My mother-in-law.' They grinned at each other and she was aware of an intimacy between them that had never been there

341

before, though there was nothing sexual about it. 'As such,' Matthew went on, 'I'd prefer you forgot about the rent for this place from now on. I mean it, Ruby,' he said flatly when she opened her mouth to protest. 'If you send a cheque, I'll only tear it up.'

'If you insist,' Ruby said stiffly.

'I do. Oh, and don't thank me. Rube. I might have a heart attack.'

'All right, I won't.'

The following afternoon, Ruby left Brendan with an adoring Moira, and went to see her daughter, but found no one in. She telephoned that night and was pleased when Greta sounded quite her old self again.

'I was having lunch in town with a friend,' she said. 'Her name's Shirley and she lives next door. We're going again on Monday.'

'I'm pleased you've made a friend, love. When can we expect to see you again?'

'Oh, I dunno, Mam. Soon, I suppose.'

Charlie had taken her through the Mersey tunnel in his red sports car, then deep into the Cheshire countryside, to a little thatched pub where they'd had scampi and chips and two bottles of wine. Medallion were planning to set up business in the States, he told her. He had already spent six months with the head office in London, and was staying another six in Liverpool, the latest jewel in the Medallion crown, familiarising himself with the way things were run.

'And I'm sure you'll make my stay very pleasant,' he twinkled. He was very handsome, very charming, very sure of himself, with broad, athletic shoulders and an engaging smile.

Greta felt drunk and giggled a lot. She liked being the object of Charlie's undivided attention, which she never was with Matthew, whose mind always seemed to be elsewhere.

On Monday, they returned to the same pub, had a different meal accompanied by the same amount of wine. Charlie leaned over and played with a lock of her fair hair.

'How about coming upstairs with me, gorgeous? All I have to do is book a room.'

She knew instinctively that he wouldn't ask her out again if she refused. It was what he'd been after all along. 'A roll in the hay,' Americans called it. Greta didn't answer straight away. It wasn't the sort of thing that she would have dreamt of doing once, but since she'd re-married, she no longer felt like her old self. Now she was bolder, more demanding, as if it had taken all this time to properly grow up. She enjoyed Charlie's company, the way he made her feel extra-special. What's more, she *wanted* them to make love as much as he did. Matthew would never know.

'Why not?' Greta giggled. And so Charlie booked a room and they went upstairs.

In June, Moira came home, having completed her second year at university and Brendan celebrated his first year on earth. Daisy swapped her day off with someone else so she could be there for his birthday tea and Heather came home early from work. Greta had been invited, but Ruby saw her daughter only rarely these days, and wasn't sure if she would come.

Brendan ruled the roost in the house, with every single person there attentive to his slightest whim. Moira often rang up from Norwich solely to ask how her nephew was, and Daisy and Heather were his slaves. Clint thought the world of him and Matthew considered the sun shone out of his little fat behind.

'He's being spoilt rotten,' Ruby would frequently cry, and although she loved him the most of all, she did her best to be firm with the little boy when he was naughty. But it was difficult – Brendan was even more adorable and funny and kissable when he was naughty than when he was good. Anyway, finding him on the floor with the shoe-cleaning box, having scrubbed himself all over with black polish, wasn't exactly *naughty*. It showed the child was clever and was trying to clean himself, even if the result was the reverse. When Brendan planted the clothes pegs around the edge of the lawn, it was because he'd thought they'd grow, and merely another sign of how brilliant he was. He could walk at ten months and had a vocabulary of half a dozen words, of which 'Bee', his name for Ruby, had been the first.

Ruby lived with the constant fear that he would be taken away. Greta's threats had frightened her, though there'd been no repeat since. Say if Ellie came home and, quite reasonably, wanted her son back? Ruby couldn't possibly refuse. She tried to prepare herself in advance for when this happened so it wouldn't come as a devastating shock. It was hard to imagine that each day spent with Brendan might be the last, but it was what Ruby did. It made the time they spent together very precious.

For his birthday, she had bought him denim overalls with red patches on the knees, a red T-shirt to go with the patches, and training shoes. Thus attired, Brendan presided over the table in his high chair, while the guests paid court and presented him with their gifts.

Halfway through the meal, Clint appeared, panting slightly, bearing a giant beach ball. 'I've got an hour off. I'll have to go back in a minute.' He beamed at the little boy. 'Happy birthday, Brendan.'

Brendan decided he preferred to play with the ball rather than finish his tea and the party transferred to the garden, where Daisy had to chase him with the birthday cake and implore him to blow out the single blue candle, which eventually went out of its own accord.

It was a fresh June day, slightly colder than it should be, and the sun and the sky were exceptionally bright. The flowers in the garden were fully in bloom, the trees dressed with leaves of every possible shade of green.

Ruby sat on the grass and wondered how many children's parties had there been since she'd moved into the house? Then, Greta had only been three, Heather two, and Jake just a baby. She'd had birthday teas for the children she'd looked after during the war – Mollie, she remembered, had turned four only a few weeks before a bomb had demolished her house. The little girl had never had the chance to become five. The twins' parties had always been chaotic affairs with loads of friends invited. Daisy had preferred to have just her family present – and Clint, of course.

Clint was about to leave. He kissed Daisy chastely on the cheek. There wasn't much passion between them. Perhaps they knew each other too well, like brother and sister. Neither had had a relationship with another member of the opposite sex. Ruby wasn't sure if this was a good thing or a bad.

Just as Clint left, Matthew appeared carrying a tiny, three-wheeler bike. He waved to her, and Brendon immediately abandoned the ball and made for the bike. Matthew sat him on the seat and Moira and Daisy showed him how to turn the pedals with his feet. Heather shouted she was going to make some tea, and Matthew came and flopped down beside Ruby on the grass.

'I thought you were madly busy,' she said.

'I am. I pretended I was going somewhere vital and came here instead. It's too nice to be stuck in an office. These days, I spend too much time indoors. It goes with the job.' He removed his dark jacket and loosened his tie. His white shirt was beautifully ironed. At first, she'd been impressed, thinking it was Greta's work, but it turned out they went to the laundry. She asked if Greta was coming.

'She didn't mention it this morning, just that she was going to lunch with that friend of hers, Shirley.'

'What's she like, this Shirley?'

'Dunno, Rube.' He shrugged. 'I've never met her.'

'I thought she only lived next door?'

'No, Woolton somewhere. Greta met her in the hairdresser's.'

'But . . . oh, never mind. I must have got it wrong.' She hadn't though. Ruby distinctly remembered Greta saying that Shirley lived next door, but it wasn't worth an argument. It was a relief to know that Greta was all right again, had been so for months, though it would have been nice to see more of her.

'You look nice,' Matthew remarked. 'Is that a new frock?'

'No, I bought it for Washington. There's scarcely been an opportunity to wear it since.' It was the turquoise Indian cotton with beads around the neck.

He lay back on the grass and rested his head in his hands. 'Have the students gone?'

'The last one left at the weekend. It feels odd, knowing I won't be having more. Normally, I'd be expecting the foreign students to arrive any minute.' Months ago, they'd held a family conference and had decided the students could be dispensed with at the end of term now that the house was rent free. On Monday, Moira was starting a summer job as a waitress so she could contribute towards her keep, and Daisy had reminded them she was getting married in less than a year and her contribution could only be relied on until Christmas – she and Clint were going to live in London, the only place for a person with a film career in mind.

Brendan had hurt his foot on the pedals of his bike. He gave a little whimper and trotted over to Ruby who rubbed it until it was better. 'Is that OK?'

'Yeth, Bee.' He returned to the bike, giving the ball a kick on the way as if to confirm the foot was in perfect condition.

Heather came out with a tray of tea and chocolate biscuits and handed them around.

'I wish you could do that to me, Rube,' Matthew said gloomily.

'Do what?'

'Make me better.'

She glanced at him sharply. 'Are you ill?'

'No, but I'm bloody fed up.'

'What with?' She hoped he wasn't going to say, 'Greta'.

'Me job. It's not my company any more. I'm just an employee like everyone else, responsible to those on high.'

'You should be thanking your lucky stars, not complaining. Sit up and drink your tea.'

He eased himself to a sitting position. 'Thanks for the sympathy. I knew you'd understand.'

'What is there to understand?' Ruby said cuttingly. 'Most people would give anything to be in your position.'

'Yes, but Rube, it's not *exciting* any more. I know exactly what I'll be doing from one day to the next.' He turned towards her, brown eyes wistful. 'You know what I'd like? To start again, by meself, like I did before, except this time I'd have more than a few bob in me pocket.'

'Why not do it, Matthew. There's nothing stopping you.'

'Isn't there?' His laugh came out like a bark. 'D'you think Greta would be pleased if the money suddenly dried up? Her favourite occupation is shopping. She's got enough clothes to sink a ship.'

'*I'd* help,' Ruby offered. 'I could type letters for you.'

'You can't type.'

'I can learn.'

'Oh, Rube, I don't half wish . . .' He paused and said no more. Ruby didn't ask what the wish was because she already knew. She wished the same herself.

When Greta let herself in – she still had a key – the house appeared to be empty, but there were voices in the garden. Everyone had gone outside. Instead of joining them, she went into her old bedroom, sat on the bed, removed her sunglasses, and looked in the mirror at her red, swollen eyes. It was obvious she'd been crying and the tears had made little shiny rivulets on her powdered cheeks. Heather's compact was on the dressing table. Greta picked it up and the shiny marks were quickly obliterated, but there was nothing she could do about her eyes. She'd have to keep the sunglasses on.

An hour ago, she'd said goodbye to Charlie Mayhew for the last time. At that very moment, he was on his way to London. This time tomorrow he would be back in America. She would never see him again.

Charlie had been as upset as she was. They'd grown fond of each other over the last six months – well, more than fond. They were a little bit in love, but he had a wife and three young children and she had a husband and twin daughters but, Greta thought darkly, she may well have been childless for all she saw of them.

Making love for the final time had been bitter-sweet; both wonderful and terribly sad. She had sobbed in his arms that she didn't want him to go and he had cried a little too.

But he'd gone. He had to, and that Greta understood. It meant she had no choice but to return to her empty life. What was she to do with herself from now on? She lay on the bed, her head sinking into the soft pillow, and hoped someone would come in, ask what was the matter, make a fuss of her. She would say she didn't feel well to account for the red eyes.

No one came and there was laughter in the garden. She recognised Heather's low-pitched chuckle. She must have stayed off work for Brendan's party. Had Greta been living there, she would have stayed off too. They'd have had great fun getting everything ready. For the briefest of moments, Greta considered leaving Matthew and coming home. In no time at all, things would return to how they'd always been. The thought was tempting, except she'd have to go back to work and there'd only be the usual few pounds a week to spend. Greta felt torn between the idea of being a wealthy lady of leisure, albeit an unhappy one, and resuming her old, hard-up life, with Mam fighting a continual battle to make ends meet.

The lady of leisure easily won and Greta felt slightly better. She'd made a choice and it showed she had some control over her life. And it helped, knowing she could always come home if she felt *too* unhappy. Mam would welcome her with open arms.

Greta sat up and combed her hair. Her eyes already looked better. She went into the kitchen, where the door was wide open, and the first person she saw was Matthew, lying on the grass beside her mother. When had he ever come home during the day for *her*? Never! And there was something familiar about the way the pair were chatting so easily, as if Mam was his wife, not her.

As if that wasn't bad enough, Heather and Moira had their heads together, giggling helplessly over something. Her sister and her daughter, obviously the best of friends.

Brendan must have been given a bike for his birthday and Daisy was following him around, arms stretched protectively over his head in case he fell off.

Everyone was having a fine time without her, they probably hadn't noticed she wasn't there. She no longer meant anything to her family.

She turned on her heel and left. No one had seen her come, no one had seen her go. She wouldn't be missed.

Chapter 18

At Daisy's request, it was the simplest of weddings. Her frock was cream jersey, calf length, without a single adornment, worn under a sky-blue velvet fitted jacket. For the first time, she wore lipstick, and carried a posy of white Christmas roses tied with blue ribbon. The only bridesmaid, Moira, carried a similar posy tied with pink to match her own plain frock. Clint had bought his first formal suit, dark grey, and throughout the ceremony, his handsome face was sombre.

Matthew, the sole male member of the O'Hagan clan – not counting Brendan – gave the bride away. There were only twenty guests, including the young couple's immediate families and a collection of friends.

The January day was icy cold. Heavy grey clouds lumbered slowly across the dull sky and several people remarked it looked as if it might snow. The guests were dressed appropriately for a winter wedding. Ruby had treated herself to a new coat, bright scarlet, and was relieved it wasn't the sort of wedding that required a hat, though neither Greta or the loathsome Pixie Shaw seemed to think so. Pixie's great fur contraption looked as if it was designed to be worn on the Russian Steppes, and Greta's face could hardly be seen behind a jungle of green feathers.

She found it all very moving. Daisy and Clint looked so unworldly. They didn't know much about anything and she wondered how they would cope in a big city on their own. One of their artist friends had arranged for them to live in a cheap bedsit in a place called Hackney. As a sort of honeymoon, they were spending their first two nights in a hotel by Piccadilly Circus.

Snow had started to fall by the time the short service was over,

349

and everyone returned to the house for the buffet meal that Pixie had insisted on helping to prepare, giving her the opportunity to remark that everything reminded her of her grandma's house before the war.

The newly-married couple only stayed a short while. After barely an hour, Daisy appeared in the living room, still in her wedding dress, with her best coat on top, and wearing a woolly hat and gloves to match. The lipstick had worn off and she hadn't bothered to renew it. Clint stood awkwardly behind with a suitcase.

'We're off now, Gran. The taxi's waiting.'

'Already, love?'

'The train takes four hours and we've got to find the hotel. The underground looks very complicated.'

'Have you said goodbye to your mother?'

'Yes, Gran. She's in the bedroom.'

'Have a lovely time now.' Her heart ached unbearably as she kissed them both. They were scarcely more than children. 'Don't forget, Matthew's arranged for all your things to be delivered on Monday. Make sure you're in or you won't have any bedding to sleep on.' The bedding, wedding presents. Daisy's painting gear, clothes, all the other things necessary for a place that contained nothing except furniture, had been packed in a crate to be collected early Monday morning by one of Medallion's lorries.

'Don't worry, Gran. We'll be there.'

''Bye, love. Bye, Clint. Look after her now.'

The guests crowded into the hall and watched the sturdy young woman and the slender young man go through the snow and climb into a taxi.

Ruby looked around for Heather, but she was nowhere to be seen. She found her in the bedroom, face down on the bed, sobbing her heart out. 'Oh, love!' She sat on the edge of the bed and laid her head against Heather's dark hair. 'I know how you feel. I feel the same myself.'

'She looked so *young*, Mam,' Heather wept. 'And she's not a bit hard, like some people. You can tell from her eyes. She's always been so good. Daisy's never given me a moment of trouble. Oh, I know she was useless at school, but at least she tried.'

'She'll be all right, love. She's probably tougher than we think.'

'You know, Mam, I could kill Ellie. She knew when the wedding would be. Daisy asked her to be bridesmaid and was dead upset when she didn't even send a card.'

'She didn't send a card for Christmas either.'

The door opened. 'So, this is where you are!' Greta cried. 'I thought you might have decided to go to London with Daisy.'

'Heather's a bit upset,' Ruby explained.

'I'm not surprised. I'll cry buckets when my two get married. Mind you, for all I know, Ellie's already married. She might even have another child.' Greta smiled. 'It doesn't upset me any more. I've too much to do. I'm going to Grenoble skiing next week with the girls.'

Not only had Greta learnt to ski, she'd learnt to drive and play bridge. The 'girls' were a group of fortyish women with nothing else to do with their time except play cards, attend coffee mornings, and hold dinner parties. Ruby considered them an idle, useless lot.

She'd changed a lot had Greta since she married Matthew, not just her personality, but also her looks. She was becoming prettier as she grew older. Gone were the childish, frilly clothes she'd always been so fond of. Now she wore chic, expensive outfits that clung to her shapely figure, and her hair was expertly cared for by one of the best hairdressers in Liverpool. Regular visits to a beauty parlour had taught her the most flattering way to apply make-up, so that she was always impeccably and beautifully turned out. Today, she wore an oatmeal tweed suit over a green silk blouse that matched the feathered hat she'd taken off when she got in.

'Would you like a nice, stiff whisky, Heather?' Greta asked.

'No, thanks.'

But Ruby insisted it would do her good. 'Fetch one for me while you're at it. Then I'd better see to the guests.'

Daisy and Clint sat opposite each other on the London train. Clint had found a newspaper and was doing the crossword.

'Two across, four letters, O.T. prophet.' He groaned. 'What does that mean?'

'Old Testament. Does Esau fit?'

'Isn't Esau a donkey?'

'No, that's Eeyore.' Daisy giggled.

'I'll leave it for now. Here's a ten letter one, three down. Author of *The Forsyte Saga*.' He frowned. 'I should know that. I've got an A level in English.'

'Galsworthy,' Daisy said promptly.

He looked at her curiously. 'For someone who has such a hard job reading, you're pretty smart, Daise.'

Daisy went pink. 'It was on television. I remember things.' She could also remember the names of all the actors and the parts they'd played, as well as every detail of the plot.

'European capital, seven letters, second letter's "i".'

'Vienna?'

'Eighteen down, a hermit.'

'Recluse?'

'Right. I'm impressed, Daise.'

'You've married a genius, Clint Shaw.'

'Seems like it.' His face closed up. He threw down the pen and turned to look out of the window. It was dark, and the snow was throwing itself against the glass. Lights could be seen twinkling in the towns and villages the train passed through on its way to London. The outlines of the buildings were blurred, merging into the black sky.

Today was a day she'd been looking forward to for most of her life, Daisy thought as she watched the lights flash by but, lately, it had become a day to dread. She felt confident she wasn't the only young woman in the world who'd been courting for five whole years yet was still a virgin. There must be others, even if they were rare. Even so, Daisy had a feeling there was something terribly wrong.

It would have been nice to discuss her worries with her mother or Gran but, not only would it have been embarrasing, she couldn't expect them to be shocked that she and Clint hadn't made love. They'd probably approve. And if she'd expressed the fear that she wasn't even prepared to admit to herself, they would have tried to dissuade her from marrying him. They would never understand that she was prepared to take Clint for better or for worse because she loved him so completely.

She wasn't quite as innocent as people thought. It was three years since she'd gone to tea at Paula's and met Mary Casey, then at art school. Mary had been impressed with her painting and they'd become great friends. Through Mary, she'd got to know other young people who were artists of some kind and admired her work.

Daisy and Clint quickly became one of the crowd. They went to parties where things went on and things were said that would have horrified her family, where joints were passed around – she'd taken a puff on more than one occasion, but it always made her sick. Daisy probably knew more about life than her mother and Gran put together.

Gran had booked the hotel by Piccadilly Circus. It was her wedding present. Naturally, she'd asked for a double bed.

The bed looked very large and a bit ominous – Daisy pretended to ignore it as she busily unpacked the clothes and put them away. 'Oh, look!' she cried. 'There's a kettle and tea things. Would you like a drink?'

'Yes, please.' Clint was in an armchair, watching her. She was surprised he hadn't switched the television on.

'Let's look for a restaurant when we've finished. I'm starving. It's only half past eight. There might be one in Soho, it's no distance away.'

She was setting out the cups, pouring milk from the tiny containers, when Clint said, 'I need you, Daise. I can't tell you how much.' His eyes were very bright, as if he was about to cry.

'There's no need to tell me. I know.' She longed to take him in her arms, but the first move must come from him.

They held hands while they wandered around Soho, where every other building appeared to be a restaurant serving food from all over the world. They had spaghetti bolognaise and a glass of red wine in a trattoria and, after another wander around, returned to the hotel.

Daisy's trousseau consisted of a single nightie; white cotton with puffed sleeves and embroidery on the yoke. She took it into the bathroom, cleaned her teeth, washed her face, combed her hair, wishing it had a shape and wasn't just a halo of red fuzz. Then she put the nightie on.

The mirror revealed a most unglamorous bride, modestly attired, shapeless hair, face shining like a beacon and covered in freckles. Still, that was how she was.

Clint was sitting up in bed, clad in tartan pyjamas and watching television. Daisy's heart thumped madly as she lifted the covers and got in beside him. 'What's on?' she enquired.

'An old James Cagney movie, *Angels With Dirty Faces*.'

353

'I don't think I've seen it.'

'It's only just started.'

'Would you like some tea? Or there's coffee for a change.'

'Coffee would be fine.'

Had it not been their wedding night, Daisy would have quite enjoyed sitting companionably up in bed with Clint, drinking coffee and watching a film. As it was, she couldn't concentrate. What would happen when the film finished?

When 'The End' came on the screen, Clint got out of bed, switched the television off, got back in again, kissed her cheek, slid under the clothes, and said, 'Goodnight, Daise.'

'Goodnight.'

And that was that.

Daisy had done her best to make the room in Hackney look cosy, spreading their things around so it looked lived in. It was a vast, high-ceilinged room, and the dusty curtains on the tall windows had clearly been made for somewhere else as they were at least a foot too short. None of the ancient furniture matched and the top hinge was missing off one of the wardrobe doors so it had to be held when it was opened in case it fell off. A long time ago, the floor had been painted chocolate brown. Now most of the paint had worn away, and the minuscule rug may once have had a pattern, but if so it was no longer obvious.

She'd actually felt relieved to find there were twin beds. It was easier to sleep, not having Clint lying next to her, worrying what was wrong, *suspecting* what was wrong, but not being prepared to face it. The same thoughts haunted her all day long, but at least she could sleep.

Clint had an interview already arranged when they came to London and was now working for a company that made short promotional films. He wrote the scripts which boasted how successful a firm had been selling their goods abroad, describing how washing machines were put together, or how glass was blown. It was another step on the way towards him becoming a Hollywood director.

Daisy would have liked to be an usherette again, particularly in a West End cinema, but it would have meant they'd hardly see each other. She was a salesgirl in a little, exclusive shoe shop off Oxford Street.

'I really wanted someone a bit smarter,' the manageress said rudely at the interview, 'But I suppose you'll just have to do. The job's been vacant for ages. I just can't get anyone.'

It didn't seem possible for shoes to cost so much when there was so little of them. The heels were thin as cigarettes and the tops merely a few straps – Auntie Greta would love them. One day, when the manageress had gone to lunch, Daisy tried on a pair and immediately fell over.

She quite liked her job. At least she didn't have to read anything and although some of the women customers were ruder than the manageress, others were very nice. A few faces she recognised from television and it was lovely writing home to say she'd sold a pair of shoes to a well-known actress.

A couple of times a week, after they'd eaten, they went to the cinema. Clint enjoyed seeing films the minute they came out – it was usually weeks, sometimes months, before they were shown in Liverpool. Most nights they stayed in and watched television – Uncle Matt had given them a coloured portable for a wedding present – or Daisy painted at the easel she'd set up in front of the window, while Clint worked on his latest script. He had changed since coming to London, was more outgoing, obviously happier living there. Perhaps he was even happy being married.

One night when he came home, he told her he'd been asked out for a drink by one of the chaps from work. 'But I said, no, my wife was expecting me home.'

'I wouldn't have minded,' she exclaimed. 'You must go if you're asked again.'

His face fell. 'I thought you'd be worried if I was late.'

'You could have rung the phone downstairs in the hall. I can hear it from here.'

'Hmm.'

He seemed upset she didn't mind if he deserted her for a few hours, arrived home late. She realised he needed to be needed, to belong. He referred to her as 'my wife' whenever he had the opportunity; in shops, at the pictures, on the buses or the tube, as if he wanted to stress he was part of a couple.

The awkwardness of the first few nights was long over and they were the best and closest of friends – as they had always been, but now possibly closer. She loved him, he needed her. They shared the same opinions on most things, but enjoyed the arguments when they didn't.

Life would have been perfect, almost was, except for that one thing, which neither of them ever mentioned.

After two months in London, they went back to Liverpool for the weekend to find everything exactly the same as when they'd left.

But it will always be the same, Daisy thought. Nothing ever changes. People come and people go, but Gran will always be here, bossing everyone around, loving them. She had missed her gran more than anyone during the time in London.

On Sunday afternoon, they went to dinner with Clint's parents. During the meal, Pixie gave her a painful nudge. 'I thought you'd come because you had something nice to tell me!'

It took a few seconds for the penny to drop. Pixie had thought she might be pregnant. Daisy waited for Clint to supply an answer. When he didn't, she said seriously, 'We thought it was time we came to see everyone, that's all.'

They didn't stay long. They had a train to catch and the journey took longer on Sundays. Neither spoke on the way back to Gran's. Daisy was thinking about babies. She'd always wanted at least two. For the very first time, she felt angry with Clint, walking silently at her side. What was he thinking? Did he expect her to forget the idea of having babies? One of these days she'd have things out with him, but it was awfully difficult. She loved him so much and didn't want him to be hurt.

Moira had just sat the final paper for her English Literature degree. She put down her pen and, along with every other student in the room, uttered an audible sigh of relief. The invigilator began to collect the papers. She'd done well in all the exams, her thesis on Mary Shelley had been thoroughly researched, and she was confident she'd get a First. In October, she was starting a teacher training course. Once she'd qualified, she'd stay with Gran, teach in Liverpool for a year, then apply for a post further afield. It might be nice to work in London near Daisy, or go abroad. For Moira, the future stretched tidily ahead. She was looking forward to it.

As she shuffled out of the room, her thoughts turned to the summer ahead. She'd rest for a few days, then look for temporary work as a waitress during the holiday, as she'd done last year. The suitcase in her room was already packed. All she had to do was collect it and catch the train from Norwich to Liverpool. Her years at university were over and she couldn't wait to get away.

She turned a corner, lost in thought, and collided head on with a figure coming in the opposite direction. 'Look where you're going!' a male voice said indignantly. 'Now there's papers everywhere.'

'Sorry.' Moira returned from the future to the present. She knelt and began to gather up the scattered papers. 'This wouldn't have happened if you'd used a paper clip or kept them in a folder.'

'Perhaps I should be apologising to you,' the man growled as he knelt on the ground beside her.

'Don't be childish. I hope these pages are numbered or it'll take ages to sort them out.'

'I'll try not to think about you while I'm doing it.'

Moira got to her feet. 'Oh, pick them up yourself. You're very rude. I was only trying to help.'

The man stood at the same time and they glared at each other. Moira had had few boyfriends over the last three years – they would only have interfered with her studies – and this was the type she avoided like the plague. A few years older than herself, he had long, untidy hair, a Zapata moustache, and wore a flowered Indian shirt, cotton trousers, an earring, and plaited sandals on his otherwise bare – and dirty – feet. She'd never seen him before, which wasn't surprising, as the incomprehensible symbols and columns of figures on the fallen papers indicated he was a science student. Moira willingly conceded that she was useless at anything to do with science.

In view of his disgusting appearance, his earrings, and the fact he was clearly a bad-tempered individual, she wondered why their eyes held for such a very long time – it seemed like for ever – and why her heart was beating extremely fast and why her knees suddenly felt weak. It may have been because, despite everything, he was devastatingly attractive.

The man's eyes were glued on hers and he didn't seem to care that the remainder of his papers were being trampled on or blown to the wind. 'Sorry about before,' he said eventually in an odd, choked voice. 'I've just sat my final paper and I don't think I did all that well. We bumped into each other at the worst possible time.' He gulped. 'My name's Sam Quigley. Would you like a coffee?'

'I'm Moira Donovan, and I'd love a coffee.' Was it only minutes ago she couldn't wait to get away?

It was nice to have a wedding completely devoid of tension; the young couple so obviously mad about each other, money no object – Matthew Doyle, step-father of the bride, was paying for everything – and the groom with a First Class degree and a Master's degree in Applied Mathematics and already employed as a junior lecturer at Cambridge University.

Greta was upset that her daughter's own First Class degree had been a complete waste of time. Moira was engaged to be married when the result came through.

'Don't be daft, Mum,' Moira sang. 'I'm still going to be a teacher, aren't I?'

Ruby had worried that Sam, an otherwise commendable young man, might turn up for his wedding looking like an unwashed hippy, but as the weeks and months passed his appearance gradually improved. He discovered soap and water, socks, wore clean jeans, shaved off his moustache, had his hair trimmed to shoulder length, and remembered to comb it.

When Sam married Moira, flushed and beautiful in ivory lace, he looked a perfectly respectable member of society. Once again, Matthew was prevailed upon to give the bride away. 'Two granddaughters down, one to go,' Ruby murmured when the newly married pair came out of the church and posed for photographs. She wondered where Ellie was, what she was doing, why she didn't get in touch. She could at least write, let everyone know she was all right so they wouldn't worry.

Daisy certainly wasn't all right, though she was pretending to be, smiling stoically at everyone in sight. She'd lost weight and the creamy yellow bridesmaid's dress made her look pale. Like her mother, Daisy had always been a stoic, never showing her feelings when she was hurt. She was hurting now, Ruby could tell and wondered why. It might be because Clint hadn't come with her, he was too busy with his job, or it might be that was merely an excuse and it was for quite another reason that Clint hadn't come.

'Oh, you children are a worry,' she complained to Brendan who was doing his best to break free from her restraining hand and create havoc among the guests – Sam's widowed mother looked a nervous soul. 'In another twenty years, I could be standing here and it's *you* getting married. Mind you, by then I'll be going on for eighty and might not live that long.'

No one noticed Daisy creep out of the reception. She caught a bus to the house she still thought of as home and let herself in. It was the first time she'd been in the place alone and the familar objects looked different, almost threatening, without Gran or her mother there, or one of her cousins. It was hard to imagine a door wouldn't open any minute and someone would yell, 'Daisy!' or some other name. When she went to put the kettle on, the kitchen clock ticked more loudly than she remembered, and it was scary how the stairs creaked on her way upstairs to the lavatory.

Later, the tea made, Daisy sat in Gran's spot on the settee, switching the television on for company, but without the sound. Everyone seemed to have accepted her explanation for Clint's absence from the wedding. He was busy at work she'd told them. He'd written to Moira to apologise for not coming. Daisy was supposed to be seeing his mum and dad tomorrow. She hated letting people down, but had no intention of going; she wasn't in the mood for Pixie Shaw and her probing questions.

It was exactly a week ago that Clint had gone to America. It was her decision, not his, that she didn't go with him. He'd written the script for a film promoting an electronics company that made those new-fangled video recorders. The film had been shown in California where the light, amusing tone of the narration had been much admired by a man called Theo Gregory who prepared videos for circulation. He'd managed to track Clint down. So far, they'd only spoken on the phone.

'Theo said my script wasn't pedantic and boring like these things usually are,' Clint told her excitedly. 'He wants me to write trailers. Just think, Daise, I'll have to watch the movies first! And Santa Barbara's not far from Los Angeles – *Hollywood*, Daisy.'

'That's wonderful, Clint.' At first, she was just as excited as he was. 'When will we go?'

'Soon. Don't tell anyone yet. I've got to sign a contract.' He looked sheepish. 'I've never signed a contract before. It's the sort of thing they do in America. The salary's amazing, about four times what I get now. You won't need to work, just paint.'

'It sounds marvellous!'

Two days later, Jason Wright, who lived downstairs, came to ask if he could borrow some milk. Jason was a sculptor who welded old bits of metal together with remarkable results. Daisy had seen his work as he was inclined to leave his door wide open when he was welding because of the dreadful smell.

'Just half a cup will do, Daisy,' he said at the door. 'I'm dying for some coffee and I can't stand it black. Oh, is that your painting? Do you mind if I have a look?'

'Come in.' She never felt shy or uncomfortable with fellow artists who were only interested in her work, not her appearance. 'Would you like some coffee now? You can have the milk as well. I'm just about to make a meal. My husband will be home in a minute.' Clint and Jason had never met.

'You're a mate, Daisy.' He came into the room and went over to the easel. He was a magnificently built young man, dark like a gypsy, with broad muscled arms and shoulders of which he was obviously proud as he always wore sleeveless T-shirts, even when it was cold. Today he was all in black, and his peeling leather trousers were tight on his bulging thighs. She admired the way the muscles rippled as he walked. One of these days, she might paint him.

'This looks interesting,' he said in front of the painting she'd only started a few days before. 'What's it going to be?'

'A womb,' she explained. 'My home, the house where I was brought up, was like a womb. I can't say I was all that happy there, but I felt dead safe, as if nothing could touch me. The outside world seemed very far away and it didn't affect us. Things that happened, the tragedies and the wars, could have been happening on a different planet. Our house was warm and comfortable, full of people. It was the best place on earth to come home to, the only place.' Somewhat inexplicably, Daisy felt close to tears.

'Wow!' Jason looked impressed. 'Did you go to art school?'

'No. I'm not being conceited or anything, but I paint for meself. It's the way I see things and I don't want to be taught any different.'

'What do you do with your paintings when they're finished?'

'They're over there.' She pointed to the stack of canvases on top of the wardrobe.

'Can I look at them too?'

'Of course.' Daisy went to get a chair.

'I'll get them down. Don't worry, I'll be careful.'

Jason was reaching up for the paintings when Clint came in. 'Oh, here's my husband. Clint, this is Jason from downstairs. He's a sculptor.'

'Hello,' Clint muttered.

The two young men stared at each other across the room. For several seconds, there was a surprising silence and Daisy was trying to think of something to say to break it, when she noticed Jason was looking at her husband with undisguised admiration in his dark eyes. Her gaze swiftly turned to Clint, and a feeling of horror swept over her when she realised that, caught unawares, he was returning the look.

The two young men were attracted to each other. Her worst suspicions had been confirmed.

Jason left without the milk he'd come for. That night, Daisy didn't talk about what had occurred. She didn't ask Clint why he was so edgy, just made the tea, watched the news on television, then got on with her painting.

When the contract from Theo Gregory arrived, Clint signed it immediately, put it in an envelope, and said he'd post it in the morning. 'If I'm to start work on the first of October, we need to see the landlord soon, give him a month's notice on this place.' He glanced around the tall, miserable room. 'I can't say I'll be sorry to see the back of it. It means we can't go to Moira's wedding. Do you mind?'

'There's no need to see the landlord,' Daisy said in a quiet voice. 'And I'll be going to Moira's wedding. I'm a bridesmaid and I can't let her down.' She paused. 'But I'm not going to America with you, Clint. I'm staying here.'

'*What*' He looked at her in astonishment. 'What on earth do you mean, Daisy?'

'What I said, that I'm not coming with you.'

'But I *need* you, Daise,' he said frantically. His face had gone pale

361

and he looked sick. 'I'll not go if you don't come. I'll tear the contract up.'

'Why do you need me? As a shield to hide behind, so people won't know the truth?' It struck her that he'd been extremely selfish. He'd taken advantage of her love, used it, expected her to live a life of lies, pretending a marriage that would never be real, where there would never be children.

'A shield?' By now, he was visibly shaking. 'I don't know what you're talking about, Daisy.'

'Yes, you do, Clint. Don't pretend you don't know what I'm trying to say. I think you should go to America, find yourself, admit what you are.'

He shrank into the chair, seemed to grow smaller in front of her eyes. 'What I am?'

'It's nothing to be ashamed of.' Daisy felt very wise and calm and sensible. 'I'll always be proud to call you my friend, but not my husband, Clint. It was wrong of you to marry me. Perhaps you thought I was so plain and unattractive that I'd never find a husband, that I'd be happy to make do with one who wouldn't want to sleep with me, kiss me properly, do all the things a proper husband does.'

'Oh, *God*!' He dropped his head into his hands and neither spoke for a long time. The only sound was the traffic outside which never stopped, not even at night. Then Clint pushed himself to his feet and came and knelt beside Daisy's chair, laid his head on her lap. 'Daisy, you're the loveliest girl I've ever known. I *wanted* to love you, I *do* love you.'

'But not in the right way, Clint. Oh!' She put her hand on his neck and stroked it. 'I wish you could, because I love you more than anyone on earth'. Even now, she felt tempted to stay with him, but he had to learn to stand on his own two feet. In the long run, they'd be better off without each other.

'I'm sorry, Daise.' His voice was muffled. She could feel his breath on her skirt. 'I've been terrified all me life that someone would find out. Someone did once,' he paused and made a face. 'They didn't tell anyone. But me dad would have killed me, and I daren't think what Mum would have said. It would have been torture at school. I tried not to admit it, even to meself. Even now I can't say the word that describes what I am.'

'There's no need to say it, we both know. From now on, you

362

must be proud of what you are, not ashamed.' Daisy began to cry. 'Be happy in America, Clint. I'll be thinking of you all the time.'

Daisy cried again, sitting in Gran's place on the settee, watching people do meaningless things on television, not making a sound. At the wedding earlier, she'd felt envious of Moira, so clearly head over heels in love with Sam and he with her.

'Why don't you go back to your womb?' Clint had said, only days before he'd left. The painting had remained untouched since the night she'd forced him to admit the truth.

'Go home? Oh, no, I couldn't. I'd never be able to keep up the lies. Anyroad, it's going back and I'd sooner go forward.' Somehow. She'd asked him not tell anyone about America until Moira's wedding was over. There'd have been too many questions otherwise.

'You'll come and see me, won't you?' he said anxiously. 'Say at Christmas. The weather's fantastic in California.'

'I'll try.' Daisy knew she would probably never see him again.

'Don't forget, I'll send money. You can't afford to live in London on your own.'

'Thank you, Clint.'

'Oh, Daisy!' He cupped her face in his hands – he'd touched her more in the last few weeks than in all the years that had gone before. It was as if he could be himself at last. 'Don't thank me. You'd still be back in your womb if it weren't for me. I've messed up your life and I'm sorry.'

The key sounded in the door and Daisy went into the hall. Gran came in carrying a deceptively angelic Brendan who was fast asleep.

'He's out like a light,' she whispered. 'He must have run a hundred miles today. I don't know why it is kids have to go mad at weddings. I remember your mam and Greta going beserk at a wedding we had here during the war.'

'Here, let me take him.' Daisy held out her arms.

'Be careful, he weighs a ton.'

'Is his bed made?'

'I've no idea, but he's not likely to notice if it isn't. Just take his top clothes off. The little imp can sleep in his underwear.' Gran looked at her keenly. 'I didn't notice you leave the reception. Have you been crying, love?'

'There was just this sad film on the telly.' If only she could tell Gran everything! A trouble shared is a trouble halved, so people said. But Daisy had the feeling she would only cry again – and this time she would never stop.

When Daisy came home on Christmas Eve, she brought with her a large painting which she stood on the mantelpiece. 'This is for you. Gran.'

'Thank you, love.' Ruby was taken aback. 'What is it?' she asked politely.

'Home.'

'Home?' The painting consisted of a large circle – not a very good circle at that – filled with splodges. 'It's lovely, Daisy. Thank you very much. I don't suppose you'll be staying long, not with having to get back to work.'

'I've left the shop. Next week, I'm starting as an usherette in the Odeon in Leicester Square, so I've got seven whole days.' It meant the manageress of the shoe shop had been left in the lurch, what with the winter sales starting directly after Christmas, but the woman hadn't a polite bone in her body and didn't deserve any better.

'I'm surprised you didn't go to America for Christmas, stay with Clint.'

'Can't afford it, Gran. Anyroad, he shares a flat with a pile of other people. He couldn't have put me up.' The lies had already begun.

'That's a shame, love. You've hardly been married five minutes and already you're living apart.'

Daisy decided that after Christmas, as soon as the celebrations were over, she'd tell Gran and her mother the truth.

Matthew came later with presents for under the tree. Daisy had gone to bed. 'I can see what she's getting at,' he said when he saw the painting.

'Then explain it to me,' Ruby demanded. 'It makes no sense at all as far as I can see.'

He shook his head. 'One of these days the penny will drop and you'll understand.' He glanced from the painting to Ruby, then back again. 'You're very lucky, all of you. I wish I were in Daisy's painting, but there was never a chance of that and now it's too late.'

Ruby hadn't the faintest notion what he was talking about.

★

It was almost midnight when Moira and Sam arrived. Moira's career as a teacher hadn't got off the mark. She was three months' pregnant and thrilled to bits. The baby was expected in June.

Nowadays, Pixie Shaw took it for granted she and her husband would be invited to Christmas dinner. Throughout the meal, Daisy was subjected to the third degree. 'Clint hardly tells us anything in his letters,' Pixie complained. She was annoyed Moira was having a baby and Daisy wasn't. 'And you got married so much earlier.'

'It's not a race, Pixie,' Ruby said tartly. 'Daisy and Clint will have children when it suits them, not you.'

'Hear, hear,' Heather echoed. There was no love lost between her and Pixie Shaw. 'I wouldn't dream of pressing Daisy to have a baby just so I can be a grandmother. It seems most unfair.'

For the first time ever, Ruby was glad when dinner was over. The meal had been full of tension. Next year, she'd tell Pixie they'd been invited out, though the strained mood hadn't only been Pixie's fault; Daisy was clearly upset, Greta was sulking about something, and Matthew hardly spoke. Even Brendan didn't help, he was aching to get back to his presents. She thanked the Lord that Moira and Sam were there, providing at least two happy faces.

Greta and Matthew must have had another row, which was all they seemed to do these days. Perhaps Greta had been spending too much money again. 'She'll have me bankrupt, so she will,' Matthew had groaned only a few weeks ago. 'She's only gone and bought a gazebo for the garden – in the middle of winter too!' Ruby had never dreamed her nice, agreeable daughter could be so thoughtlessly extravagant.

It was unreasonable to feel so cross when Moira and Sam decided to go for a walk, depriving the house of their cheerful company. She marched into the living room, determined to make everyone play a game and elicit a laugh or two, but Greta had already turned on the television and they sat like lumps for the rest of the afternoon watching *The Sound of Music*, a film Ruby had seen before and hadn't liked – and liked even less the second time around.

It was a lousy Christmas. Ruby was glad when it was over and things returned to normal. But not for long, because Daisy revealed the reason why Clint had gone to America on his own and completely spoilt New Year.

★

Matthew rang one afternoon in March when a brisk, urgent wind was playing havoc with the house, rattling the windows and whistling through the cracks around the doors.

'Ruby, something terrible's happened.' His voice shook.

'Oh, yes?' Ruby said coolly.

He mustn't have noticed her frosty tone. 'I got home from work early, about an hour ago. I was feeling dead rotten, I think I must be coming down with flu.'

'Dearie me.'

'I thought Greta was out – until I went upstairs and found me fucking wife in bed with another man. Oh, Rube!' he said hoarsely. 'I don't know what to do. I've got to talk to someone. Can I come round?'

'Not now, Matthew, Greta's here. My God!' Ruby gasped. 'I didn't realise . . . She's in a terrible state. She said you just turned on her for no reason at all.'

'And you believed her?' His bitter laugh tore at her heart. 'You mustn't have much of an opinion of me. No wonder that other fellow wouldn't marry you, Ruby. You put your family before every other bloody thing on earth, no matter what they do. Tell my wife to stay where she is. You're welcome to each other.'

'Matthew!' Ruby cried frantically. 'I'll come and see you straight away.' But she was talking to herself. Matthew had slammed down the receiver.

She went into the garden and screamed for Brendan. He was halfway up a tree he'd been forbidden to climb and made his way down, looking guilty, expecting to be told off. 'Come on,' Ruby said brusquely. 'We're going for a ride in a car.' She pulled him into the house, 'Get your coat,' she commanded.

'Yes, Bee.' Brendan said obediently. He was nearly four and aware something was wrong.

Ruby turned her attention to her daughter. Earlier, Greta had thrown herself on to the settee, sobbing her heart out. Matthew was an awful person, truly horrible. That afternoon, he'd flown into a rage, she'd no idea why.

'Greta,' Ruby said from the door. 'Get up immediately. I want you to take me to your house in the car.'

'What, Mam?' Greta raised her tear-streaked face, surprised.

'I said, drive me to your house. That was Matthew on the phone.

366

You stupid girl, you've hurt him badly. You didn't tell me he'd found you in bed with another man. That's not the way you were brought up. Oh, I'm so ashamed!' Ruby stamped her foot in rage. She'd be sixty next month and it was about time she had a bit of peace. 'Who was he, the man?'

There was a pause.

'The husband of one of me friends.'

'Well, you won't be friends much longer once she finds out. If you don't get off that settee this very minute, I'll drag you outside. I'll have a go at driving the car myself if you won't do it.'

Greta got sullenly to her feet. 'I don't know why you're so concerned about Matthew.'

'Get a move on, girl,' Ruby snapped. 'I'm concerned about Matthew because he's been the best friend this family could have had. Are you coming or do I have to drive myself?'

No one spoke on the way to Calderstones, not even Brendan who was unusually subdued. When they reached the house, Ruby turned to her daughter. 'Give me the key.'

'I haven't got it. It's in me handbag at home.'

'*This* is your home,' Ruby said tartly. 'Or at least it was. I'll just have to knock and hope he answers.'

'He won't answer, 'cause he's not there. His car's gone.'

'Damn!' She'd let him down again.

Matthew still wasn't home by midnight. Next day, when Ruby rang Medallion and asked to speak to Mr Doyle, she was told he was on holiday.

'When will he be back?'

'He didn't say when he would return.'

'When he does, please tell him Mrs O'Hagan would like to speak to him urgently.'

'I'll relay that message to his secretary.'

The day after, Greta drove round to Calderstones to collect her things, after phoning first to make sure Matthew wasn't there. She returned, the car full of clothes, and tearfully reported that the house was up for sale.

'Oh, Mam, I've been such a fool,' she sobbed.

'You certainly have. Oh, come here, love.' Ruby held out her arms. It was impossible to stop loving someone because they'd been

367

a fool – well, a bit more than a fool where Greta was concerned. But it would be a long time before she would forgive her for what she'd done.

Heather no longer wanted to share a room with her sister. She had bought a portable television so she could watch Open University programmes and study in bed. Greta would be in the way.

'Can I sleep with you, Mam?' Greta sniffed pathetically after a few nights on her own. 'I've never slept by meself before. It feels dead peculiar.'

'You certainly can't. I like my privacy too.'

'What about Brendan? Can I sleep with him?'

'Not when there's two empty bedrooms upstairs, no. By the way, have you done anything about getting a job?'

Greta sighed. 'Not yet.'

'Then I'd appreciate you doing it soon.'

'I'll look in the *Echo* tonight.'

'If nothing's there, try the Labour Exchange tomorrow.'

'All right, Mam,' Greta said with a martyred air, but Ruby was having none of it.

'It's entirely your own fault you're in this situation, so I want none of your pained looks. Heather's the only one in the house earning a wage. It's not up to her to keep you.'

A fortnight passed and Matthew still hadn't acknowledged her phone call. Ruby called Medallion again.

'Mr Doyle was made aware of your message,' she was told. 'He said to tell you he'll be in touch next time he's in Liverpool.'

'When will that be? Where is he now?'

'I'm afraid I've no idea when it will be, Mrs O'Hagan. Our firm has just been awarded a contract for three hospitals in Saudi Arabia. Mr Doyle will be overseeing the work.'

'Thank you.' Ruby rang off. Saudi Arabia! If Greta had been there just then, she would have strangled her.

Six months later, a letter from a solicitor dropped on the mat addressed to Mrs Greta Doyle. Matthew wanted a divorce on the grounds of adultery.

'He can't divorce me for adultery,' Greta pouted. 'He hasn't any proof. I'm going to write back and contest it.'

'He might try and get proof,' Ruby pointed out. 'He's sure to know the name of the chap he found you in bed with if he was a friend's husband and involve him, then the wife would be round here, making a scene. It'd be in the *Echo*, and your name would be mud. Not only that, the legal costs would be horrendous. You'd end up in debt for the rest of your life.' She had no idea what she was talking about. Every word she'd just said could be a lie. But Greta *had* committed adultery and no longer deserved to be married to Matthew.

'So what should I do?' Greta cried piteously.

'Just write to the solicitor and agree the divorce can go ahead as it stands.' There were times when honour demanded *not* putting your family first.

The following year, 1981, as soon as her divorce from Matthew was finalised, Greta got married for the third time. She was forty-five. Frank Fletcher was a sweet, if rather dull little man, a widower, with two grown-up sons, both married. He was a clerk in the shipping company where Greta worked, and owned a semi-detached house on the estate where she would have lived with Larry had life gone differently.

The wedding was held in a Register Office. There were just six guests; Ruby, Heather, and Frank's sons and their wives – none seemed too pleased that he was marrying again. Brendan had just started school and was otherwise occupied.

After the soulless ceremony, everyone went to Ruby's for something to eat. The Fletchers refused the wine and beer she'd bought, saying they preferred tea. After politely eating a few sandwiches, they went home, leaving only the enamoured Frank who could hardly believe his luck in landing such a pretty bride. The newly-married couple left for their honeymoon in Scarborough in the afternoon.

Greta was still on honeymoon when Ruby tidied her room and was surprised to find the wardrobe full of her smart clothes. She mentioned the fact to Heather when she came home.

'She doesn't want them any more,' Heather told her. 'She said there'd be no need for stuff like that when she's married to Frank.'

'I wonder if any of them will fit us?'

When tea was over, they went upstairs to try on the clothes, accompanied by Brendan, who seized the hat Greta had worn to Daisy's wedding and put it on, grinning at them through the green feathers. The women went through the wardrobe and wished Greta was taller.

'I wonder if I could have a false hem put on this?' Ruby held up a blue crêpe frock.

'I could wear this jacket, but not the skirt. Look at this sweater! I bet it cost the earth. Oh, I can't do this!' Heather threw the sweater on to the floor and burst into tears.

'Neither can I.' Ruby dropped the blue frock as if it was too hot to touch. 'I feel like a grave robber.'

'I don't think she'll be happy married to Frank, Mam.'

'She might, love,' Ruby said sadly. 'You know, I should have been nicer to her when she came home, but I was so annoyed . . .'

'Our Greta's never been any good on her own. I should have let her back in our room. We drove her away, Mam.'

'I wouldn't put it quite as strongly as that, love.' Ruby put her arm around her weeping daughter. 'She behaved disgracefully with Matthew. It would have been wrong to welcome her home and act as if nothing had happened.'

'It *wouldn't* have happened if Rob and Larry hadn't died.'

'That's something we'll never know, Heather. If it hadn't been Matthew, it might have been something else.' Ruby sighed. 'Brendan! Give us that hat before you wreck it. One of these days Greta might want to wear the damn thing.'

370

Brendan

Chapter 19

1985

She was in a hotel room, an expensive hotel, not her own, and she was lying in a double bed, feeling like death. The other half of the bed had been occupied. She could see the indent of where a head had lain on the pillow and the bedclothes had been thrown back when the person had got out.

Who, Ellie wondered? Last night there'd been a party and she could recall getting plastered, but from then on her mind was a blank. She looked at her watch; half past nine.

It wasn't the first time this had happened. Ellie worked for a London-based agency that provided pretty girls for all sorts of occasions; company dinners to which wives hadn't been invited, business exhibitions, sporting events. At the moment she was in Madrid with six other girls for a motor show – sports cars – and it was their job to drape themselves provocatively over the bonnets as an incentive to prospective purchasers to part with monumental amounts of cash. Last week it had been a computer exhibition in Sweden where they'd been expected to look charming and wise. Next month it was office equipment in Rome, though the work was mainly based in the British Isles.

The agency adopted a high moral tone. It had its reputation to consider and the girls were forbidden to have sexual relationships while employed on a job. Ellie only occasionally broke the rule, and always when she'd had too much to drink, like last night.

She sat up, clutched her reeling head, and noticed her clothes were on the floor beside the bed. The net curtains on the open window billowed outwards and she saw a stone balcony outside. The sun was shining brilliantly and it was already warm considering it was only May – she dreaded to think what Spain would be like in summer. People could be heard splashing about in a pool.

The room had two doors, one of which was ajar, revealing a bathroom. Ellie climbed out of bed and got washed, then put on the tight white skirt and red blouse, the uniform for the motor show. They were badly creased and there was a wine stain on the skirt. She'd prefer to be gone when the owner of the room came back. *If* he came back. There was no sign of anyone staying there; no suitcase, clothes, toilet gear. Maybe he'd already checked out.

When she opened her bag to get her make-up she found it stuffed with notes; Spanish pesetas. She had no idea what the exchange rate was, but there was plenty of them. The guy, whoever he was, must have thought she was on the game.

Ellie sat on the bed, feeling slightly ashamed. Still, she hadn't come to any harm. The cash was a plus and maybe the guy was just showing his appreciation. It was scary, though, to think she'd spent the night with a man she couldn't remember. He might have looked like King Kong for all she knew or he could have been a pervert.

There was a knock on the door and she stiffened. 'Who is it?' she called.

'It's Barry, darling.'

The girls jokingly referred to sixty-year old Barry as their chaperone. He booked hotels, made travel arrangements, saw that they were properly fed, and got to the various events on time. He was a little, roly poly man, almost completely bald, with a warm smile that never reached his eyes. Ellie considered him two-faced, but so were most of the people she met these days – she probably was herself.

'How did you know where I was?' Ellie asked when she let him in.

'You and Bruno Pinelli seemed very much an item last night. This being his room, it seemed the first place to look. Bruno Pinello,' he went on in response to Ellie's puzzled look, 'was at the show yesterday signing autographs. He's a racing driver, Italian, very good-looking. He invited a few of us back to the bar downstairs for a drink and it turned into quite a party. Then Bruno disappeared at exactly the same time as you did. It didn't take much in the way of brains to put two and two together.'

Ellie dredged up a vague memory of dark, flashing eyes and an

374

exceptionally virile lover. 'I had a bit too much to drink,' she muttered.

'More than a bit, darling. You want to be careful. Next thing you know, you'll be an alcoholic.'

'Don't talk daft, Barry.' She laughed. 'I'm a social drinker. I never drink during the day.'

'Maybe not, but when you get near a bar, you can put a fish to shame. What's this?' He picked up the ashtray and frowned at the contents. 'Have you been smoking grass?'

Ellie couldn't remember. 'We must have done.'

'And you've left the evidence for anyone to find!' He looked grim when he took the ashtray into the bathroom. The lavatory flushed. He returned and said harshly, 'If humping guys and getting sloshed wasn't bad enough, now I find you've been smoking an illegal substance. If you don't pull your socks up, darling, I'll have to advise the agency to let you go.'

'That's decent of you – darling, ' she said icily.

'I don't have to give you a warning,' he replied, just as coldly. 'I could advise the agency today.'

'I've got the message, Barry.'

'Glad to hear it, Ellie.' He smiled, but his eyes didn't. 'You've got two hours before the show opens and you look like shit. I'll get room service to bring you something to eat and some black coffee. While you're waiting, put your war paint on, and I'll arrange to have a change of clothes brought over. Fact, I'll do both things right now.' He picked up the phone.

'What about this Bruno guy? Is he likely to come back?'

'No, he checked out early this morning.'

'Thanks, Barry – for everything.' She didn't like having to be grateful, but he could have her fired.

Not that it would matter all that much Ellie thought when Barry had gone. It was a lousy job which had seemed exciting at first. Now she found it boring. Most jobs turned out boring in the end.

She sat in front of the dressing table and began to apply her make-up, difficult when her hands were shaking so badly. Barry was right, she looked like shit. Halfway through, a waiter arrived with the coffee and some rolls.

'You pay for this now, please,' the man said courteously handing her a bill. 'Señor Pinelli, he already settled his account.'

'How much is this in English money?'

'About ten pounds.'

Just for coffee and rolls! Ellie blanched. She didn't even want the rolls and dreaded to think what it would cost to stay in the place. The waiter appeared satisfied with two of the notes Bruno Pinelli had given her and left. Ellie finished her make-up, then sat at the small table in front of the window to drink the coffee. The room was on the first floor at the rear of the hotel. Outside, a shimmering blue pool looked a mile long and was set within an avenue of shady trees. A man was teaching a little boy to swim and, at the far end, a youth was poised on the edge of the diving board. He raised his arms, jumped, and soared downwards, hardly raising a splash, to the cheers of a group of watching teenagers and the few people so far occupying the loungers and umbrella-covered tables surrounding the majestic pool.

Ellie felt a pang of envy. These people didn't have to spend the rest of the day inside a stinking hot marquee, pretending to be nice to people, not caring whether they bought a car or not. Why hadn't she the money to stay at a place like this? What had gone wrong with her life?

She was twenty-six, getting on, getting nowhere. After she'd left home the second time, Ellie had hung around the pop scene for a while, hoping for a job in a promotional capacity, as an assistant of some sort, or in advertising. But nothing had happened. Nor had anything happened during the time spent working in the office of a fashion magazine. No one had suggested she become a model, though she was prettier than most of the successful ones. She'd remained unnoticed as a film extra and during the year with the television company where she'd never risen above making tea and doing the filing – an office girl. When she'd joined the agency two years ago, it had seemed a step up. At least she'd been taken on for her looks and her figure, her personality. But it was a dead end job without any chance of promotion.

Barry was wrong to say she'd become an alcoholic, though she wouldn't mind a good, stiff drink right now, help buck her up a bit. Trouble was, it didn't always work, and she'd have another stiff drink, then another, and end up drinking herself into oblivion.

There was another knock on the door. This time it was one of the girls, Trisha, with a fresh outfit.

'Barry sent this. Did you have a good time last night?' Trisha hadn't been to the party. She was eighteen, a lovely, fresh-faced girl who, right now, made Ellie feel old and rather grubby.

'Great.'

'Oh, well. I'll love you and leave you. See you later, Ellie.'

'See you.'

Ellie changed her clothes and brushed her hair. She was beginning to feel better and decided to eat one of the rolls, seeing as how it had cost an arm and a leg. She poured more coffee and took it on to the balcony. There were more people in the pool since she'd last looked and she regarded them jealously. A woman with ghastly red hair, a toad-like figure, and legs like duffle bags, was waddling her way towards a thickly cushioned chair under an umbrella. She wore a sack-like gingham frock and sat down with a thump that Ellie sensed rather than heard.

'I'd sooner be as poor as a church mouse than have a shape like that,' she said to herself.

The woman took a good look around before putting on a pair of large sunglasses and settling back against the cushions. There was something about the way she moved, the red of her hair, that was very familiar and a few seconds later an astonished Ellie realised it was her cousin, Daisy.

She crammed the remainder of the roll in her mouth and washed it down with coffee, then checked her reflection in the mirror. She looked svelte and smart, her long, brown hair gleamed, her make-up was perfect. Picking up her bag, she ran downstairs, found the way to the pool, and approached her cousin. Daisy had always made her aware of how lucky she really was.

'Hi, Daise!'

'Ellie!' Daisy gasped, removing the sunglasses. Her freckled face had gone fat and podgy and was covered in perspiration. 'What a lovely surprise. What on earth are you doing here?'

'I'm working in Madrid. I'm a model. I get sent all over Europe.'

'How wonderful!' Daisy looked incredibly impressed. 'Are you a fashion model? Have you come on a shoot or something?'

'Yes,' Ellie lied. 'How's things at home? It's ages since I wrote. I keep meaning to . . .' Her voice trailed away.

'All sorts of exciting things have happened since you left, Ellie.' Daisy wiped her face with a tissue – how awful to be so fat in hot weather. It was no wonder she was sheltering under the umbrella, she always turned as bright red as her hair in the sun. 'Your Moira's married for one. Sam, her husband, is terribly nice and terribly clever. He's a lecturer and they live in Cambridge and have two children, a girl and a boy.'

Ellie felt uneasily that Moira had got one up on her. Her twin had wanted to be a teacher, which she considered the dullest occupation in the world. But marrying a lecturer and living in Cambridge sounded the opposite of dull.

'Oh, and you've got a sister.'

'I know, you've just told me about her.' Had Daisy lost her mind as well as her figure? It hadn't been up to much in the first place.

'I mean, a *new* sister. I don't suppose you know, I mean, it's years since you were home, but Aunt Greta and Matthew Doyle got divorced and she married a chap called Frank Fletcher. To everyone's surprise – including your mum's – she had a baby at forty-six, a little girl called Saffron. She's three now. Isn't that a lovely name?'

'Lovely,' Ellie said faintly. 'How's Gran?'

'She's absolutely fine.' Daisy looked at her strangely. 'And so's Brendan. He'll be eight next month and he's the image of Liam Conway, ever so handsome.'

Ellie hadn't forgotten about her son. He just didn't seem all that important.

'Let's see, what else has happened?' Daisy put her finger to her podgy chin. 'My mum's now a qualified solicitor.'

'You don't say!' Ellie rolled her eyes impatiently.

'Matthew Doyle's been in Saudi Arabia for ages. I think I've covered the lot. What have you been doing with yourself all this time, Ellie?'

'All sorts of exciting things.' Ellie shrugged modestly. 'I was in the music industry for a while, then worked for a magazine and a television company. I made a few films – I only had little parts,' she said hastily, in case Daisy asked for details. 'Then I decided to become a model which is why I'm here. What about you, Daise? Did you marry Clint?' It was the question Ellie had been wanting to ask all along. She'd often wondered about Daisy and Clint.

'Yes.' Daisy smiled. 'But we got divorced a year afterwards. Clint is gay, Ellie, but he was too scared to admit it. Now he's come out, he's much happier. He's living in California, writing scripts – you know how he was about films – movies, he called them. His main ambition has always been to direct. There's plenty of time, he's still young. We write to each other regularly.'

Poor, pathetic Daisy had been left to come on holiday on her own! She'd never get another man looking as she did. Ellie felt sorry for her cousin and at the same time immensely superior. She resisted the temptation to say she already knew about Clint.

'I'm so sorry, Daise. Do you still paint?'

'No. I haven't painted in years. I only did it because I was unhappy.'

'And you're not unhappy now?' It was hard to keep the surprise out of her voice.

'Well, no.' Daisy laughed contentedly. 'I don't suppose I *look* happy in this state, but I'm perfectly happy inside. I'll be happier still when the baby's born.' She patted her swollen stomach. 'It's due in less than four weeks. I'm full of water. We thought we'd grab a quick break, else Lord knows when we'd get away.'

'We?' Ellie said faintly. Daisy was *pregnant*!

'Michael, Harry and me. That's them over there,' she pointed to the pool. 'Michael's teaching Harry to swim.'

Ellie's eyes swivelled towards the man she'd noticed earlier with the little boy. Daisy was married with a child and another on the way. Already hot, Ellie felt herself grow hotter. She wouldn't have cared what had happened to her sister and cousin if her own life had gone the way she'd planned. But it hadn't. Instead, the last eight years had been wasted in a vain search for excitement and adventure, while Moira and Daisy had been successfully getting on with their lives.

'Harry's three,' Daisy was saying, waving furiously in the direction of the pool. 'Here they are now.'

Daisy's husband had hoisted the little boy on to his shoulders and was wading towards them. He wasn't a handsome man, but had a pleasant, quirky face and a charismatic smile. Ellie thought him rather appealing.

'Sweetheart! I didn't notice you there. You should have stayed in bed and rested. Have you taken your water tablet?'

'We're on holiday, Michael. I can rest perfectly well in the fresh air, and yes, I've taken my water tablet. Michael, this is my cousin,

Ellie. She's a model and in Madrid for a fashion shoot. Isn't it a coincidence that we met? It's ages since we've seen each other. Harry, this is Auntie Moira's twin sister, so she's another sort of aunt.'

Michael shook hands, apologising for it being wet. Harry merely glanced at Ellie, climbed out of the pool, and laid his head on his mother's stomach.

'Is it awake yet?'

Daisy and Michael exchanged complacent smiles and Ellie felt she could easily be sick at this vision of domestic bliss. She was about to jump to her feet, leave, when Michael said. 'He's been pleading for an ice cream. Would you like a cold drink, darling?'

'I'd love one. Something with lime in.'

'And how about you, Ellie?'

'No, thanks. I'll have to be going in a minute.'

'Come on, tough guy. Let's go find the ice cream man.' He ruffled Daisy's hair as he went past, and a feeling of raw jealousy swept like a pain through Ellie's body. She wanted to be loved like that, to have the same warm intimacy with a man that Daisy had with her husband, instead of feeling excluded, apart, alone.

'Where do you live, Daisy?' she asked, breaking the short silence that followed.

'London, a place called Crouch End. Michael's a doctor, he works terribly hard.'

How on earth had someone like Daisy managed to hook a doctor, such an attractive one at that. 'How did you two meet?'

Daisy wiped her red, melting face. 'We met at a clinic. Michael's dyslexic, same as me.'

'What?'

'Dyslexic. Remember I never learnt to read? Everyone thought I was daft.'

'No they didn't,' Ellie said falsely.

'Yes, they did, Ellie.' Daisy shook her head. 'I thought so meself. Anyroad, when me and Clint got married, we went to live in London, and I stayed after he'd gone to California. Oh, Ellie, I was dead miserable, working as an usherette, painting like a mad woman, hardly knowing a soul, and wondering what the hell I was doing with my life.' Despite the heat, Daisy shivered. 'Then Gran rang about this article she'd read on something called dyslexia. It explained why some perfectly intelligent people have trouble reading – they think in pictures, not words, though it's more complicated than that. The article gave the name of a clinic in London where you could go to be assessed. It turned out I was a perfect example of a dyslexic.'

'How come Michael managed to become a doctor if he couldn't read?'

Daisy laughed. 'He's got this dead pushy mother, Angela. She refused to accept he was as stupid as the teachers claimed. She coached him, taught him to read herself. It was Angela who wrote the article and started the clinic. The first time I went, Michael was there. You've no idea how wonderful it was knowing someone else had experienced the same problems as meself. Suddenly, everything fell into place and I didn't feel daft any more.' She sighed blissfully, remembering. 'Then Michael asked me out and things just went on from there. I never thought it was possible to be so happy. Oh!' she cried. 'Isn't it marvellous that the three of us have done so well; you, me, and your Moira!'

'Marvellous,' Ellie said thinly. 'Look, Michael's coming back. I'll just say goodbye, then I'll have to go.'

'It's been lovely meeting you, Ellie.' Daisy looked at her pleadingly. 'Write home soon, won't you? Your mum's always wondering where you are, Gran too. They worry themselves sick about you. Better still, when you're back in England, go and see them. They'd love to see you.'

Ellie dreamed that night about the house where she was born. It was Christmas, she was a little girl, and the walls inside had been painted silver. It was like a grotto and the tree was so big it filled the hall with its feathery branches. The girls' presents had been hidden all over the house. After breakfast there was a Treasure Hunt and they ran up and down the stairs, Ellie, her sister and her cousin, in and out of the rooms, screaming with joy when they found another mysteriously wrapped parcel. Ellie opened one and found the prettiest frock she had ever seen; pale blue silk with a lace collar, an old-fashioned, Victorian frock. She tried it on in front of the mirror in Gran's bedroom and sighed with pleasure; she was the most beautiful little girl in the world. When she grew up she would become something quite exceptional; a famous film star, an opera singer, a queen.

When Ellie woke, she found herself in the shabby hotel Barry had booked, with another long, hot day ahead in the marquee selling cars. She would have given anything for a drink to get her started.

Back in London in her tiny flat, Ellie looked through the red leather address book with a gold clasp that Daisy had given her as a birthday present when they were teenagers. It had seemed a stupid present at the time, but over the years it had gradually been filled. She opened the book at 'C', and his number was there, as she'd thought – Felix Conway.

She'd done a lot of thinking on the plane home from Spain. Her life was a mess, she was drinking too much, and it was important she do something about it. The time had come to settle down, in which case it was necessary to find a husband. She'd known many men over the years, but there'd only been one with whom she'd shared a sort of intimacy, not sexual, and not as close as that between Daisy and Michael, naturally, but she'd felt at ease with Felix Conway. She recalled the last night in the garden of Fern Hall when he'd evoked emotions she'd never had before or again. Felix, with his gentle voice and gentle smile, made her feel a nicer person, softer.

By now, he might have been long-married to Neila Kenny or some other woman, but a phone call wouldn't hurt. She couldn't imagine anything much having changed in Fern Hall and Felix would still be running the chemist's at a loss. What was needed was a guiding hand, someone who recognised the potential of the house and the shop. In other words, herself. It would be a challenge.

She collected together all her small change and took it downstairs to the communal phone, then dialled the number of the house in Craigmoss. Felix should be home by now. He answered almost immediately.

'Felix, it's Ellie. Do you remember me?'

'Of course.' His voice was faint, but he sounded pleased. 'I often think about you – and Brendan. He'll be eight soon. How are you both?'

'We're very well and Brendan's getting on famously at school. I wondered, Felix, if I could come and stay for a while? Would Neila mind?' she added cautiously.

'Neila? She left Craigmoss years ago. She's living somewhere in England with her brother.' He gave a whispery sigh. 'There's only me and I'd love to see you. When will you be coming?'

'In a couple of weeks or so.'

'Will you be bringing Brendan?'

'Yes,' said Ellie after a pause.

Brendan came home from school and threw his satchel on to the kitchen table. 'Where is she?'

'If you mean Ellie, love, she's gone to town to do some shopping.'

Ruby saw him visibly relax. She poured a glass of lemonade and he drank it thirstily. They'd both felt on edge since Ellie had arrived a week ago. The girl was completely devoid of tact, expecting her son to fall into her arms, treat her as a mother, when she was a total stranger as far as Brendan was concerned.

Over the years, Ruby had tried to talk to him about Ellie, show him her photograph, but Brendan wasn't interested. He was a well-adjusted, self-confident child, quite sure of his place in the world, and had never shown any sign of missing his parents. Old for his years, he made friends easily, and frequently brought home some of his mates from school, though not since Ellie had arrived. She made him embarrassed, tousling his hair, kissing him, buying him sweets he didn't like, calling him, 'kiddo', as if trying to make up for the fact that she was a mother who'd so far played no part in his young life.

It was rare Brendan looked miserable, but he did now, hunched at the table, nursing the empty glass. Ruby sat beside him. 'Would you like a scone?'

'With jam on?'

'Of course. We've got strawberry.'

'Then I'd like a scone, Bee.'

'I think I'll have one too, keep you company.' She did him two scones and one for herself. At the table again, they sat shoulder to shoulder, loving each other so much it hurt, and terrified that very soon they might be parted.

Ellie hadn't said anything, but Ruby could sense it in the air and could tell Brendan did too. They didn't discuss it, because putting their fear into words would only make it seem more real. Ellie hadn't given a reason for coming home, hadn't said if she was staying or going, and there was something about the calculating way she watched her son, asked repeated questions, as if trying to catch up on the time she'd lost, familiarise herself with his habits, his likes and dislikes, become his mother within a week.

In a little corner of her mind, Ruby had always feared something like this would happen. In a fatalistic sort of way, she had been prepared for it. But Brendan wasn't. It would be cruel beyond belief for Ellie, whom he didn't like, to suddenly remove him from the only home he'd ever known and the people who loved him.

Ruby knew she could point this out till the cows came home, but in the end she had no rights. Brendan belonged to Ellie. It was an irrefutable fact, and Ellie was selfish, she thought of no one but herself. If it suited her to reclaim her child, she would do it, regardless of the hurt it would cause. In her own way, Greta was the same. It seemed the worst of Jacob's genes, the ones that made a person selfish and uncaring, had been passed to his eldest daughter and then on to that daughter's child.

Ruby and Brendan were on the settee, watching *Blue Peter*, when Ellie and Heather came in together, having met on the bus on the way home. There was a stiffness between them. A grim-faced Heather went straight to her room. She'd always been dutiful and conscientious and disapproved of the way her niece behaved. In a few days' time, she was going to stay with her own daughter. Daisy's baby was expected soon and she was looking after Harry while his mother was in hospital. Everyone had got over the surprising revelation about Clint, apart from Pixie, and were thrilled that Daisy and Michael had found each other and were so obviously happy.

'See what I bought you, kiddo!' Ellie was laden with carrier bags. She opened one and produced a garish, flowered shirt.

Brendan blushed scarlet. 'I'm not wearing that!'

'Don't be rude, Brendan. It's lovely, very fashionable.'

'He prefers T-shirts, Ellie,' Ruby said mildly.

'Not for best, surely. Anyroad, he wears shirts for school.'

'Only reluctantly, and then they're grey.'

'I thought he could wear it when we go to Ireland.'

There was a long silence. Ellie pretended to sort through the shopping and didn't look at them.

'Ireland?' Ruby was aware her voice sounded querulous and old.

'Not far from Dublin, to be precise. I'm going to stay with a friend, Felix Conway, Liam's brother, and taking Brendan with me.'

'You can't just take him out of school!'

'I can do anything I like, Gran.' Ellie arrogantly tossed her long brown hair.

'How long will you be going to Dublin for?'

'I'm not sure, a while.'

'I don't want to go to Dublin,' Brendan said mutinously. He rarely cried, but his eyes were dangerously full of tears.

'It's only for a little holiday, kiddo.'

'You just said you weren't sure when you'd be back,' Ruby pointed out. 'I tell you what, let's talk about this some other time.' Tonight, for example, when Brendan was in bed and she could speak her mind. But Ellie wasn't willing to give an inch.

'No, Gran, let's talk about it now,' she said, her eyes steely hard. 'Brendan is my son and I want him. Oh, I know I've not been much of a mother, but I will be from now on. I'm taking him with me to Dublin and, if you want the truth, I might not come back. It's time I settled down and I quite fancy doing it in Craigmoss with Felix Conway.'

'And you don't give a damn what Brendan thinks, how he feels?'

'He's only eight. He'll soon get used to things.'

Brendan threw himself at the woman who claimed to be his mother and began to beat her with his fists. 'I'm *not* eight,' he screamed. 'I'm only seven. You don't even know me *birthday*. I'm not going to Ireland with you.' He stamped his foot. 'I *won't*.'

Ruby lost her temper. 'Now see what you've done, you foolish girl. You must have been at the back of the queue, Ellie Donovan, when the Lord handed out good sense.' She pulled Brendan away, clasped the heaving figure in her arms, and could feel his heart beating madly against her own. It was a long time since she could remember being so angry, but if she let rip to her feelings, it would only distress Brendan more.

Ellie had the grace to look uncomfortable at the upset she had caused. She laid her hand on Ruby's arm. 'I'm sorry, Gran. I didn't want to hurt anyone, but he *is* mine. You must have realised this might happen one day. I've got plane tickets for tomorrow. I thought it best not to say anything before. He'll soon grow to love me, won't you, kiddo?' She ruffled Brendan's hair, but he tore himself away.

'I'll never love you,' he hissed. 'Never, never, never.'

The most mind-shattering things in life always happened suddenly, without warning. One minute everything was normal, next minute things had changed and would never be the same again. Jacob had deserted his family to join the Army, Arthur Cummings had died, the lads had been killed. Yet still life continued, sometimes better than before, sometimes worse.

During the sleepless night that followed, Ruby discovered she wasn't as hard as she used to be, not quite so confident. The thought of life without Brendan was scarcely bearable. Nothing and no one would ever take his place. Even so, had the circumstances been different, had she known he would be happy with his mother, she would have resigned herself to his going. But what made it even more unbearable, was knowing he would be desperately unhappy with Ellie. He would never grow to love her as she hoped.

Next morning, she went downstairs, her head thumping with tiredness. To her surprise, Heather was already up and looked at her with concern.

'I heard you tossing and turning all night, Mam. How do you feel?'

'How d'you think, love?'

'I wish there was something we could do to stop this.'

'There's nothing, Heather,' Ruby said wearily. 'You're a solicitor, you should know. Everything Ellie said was right.'

'Legally right, but morally wrong. Does our Greta know she's going?'

'Greta's coming later to say goodbye.'

When Brendan appeared, he was accompanied by Ellie and rather surprisingly wearing the new shirt. 'He put it on without a murmur,' Ellie said jubilantly.

'That's because he's a good boy.' Ruby held out her hand, praying she wouldn't cry. Brendan took it without a word.

Greta arrived alone. Saffron was at playgroup, she explained. Four generations of O'Hagans sat in the living room making stilted conversation, waiting for the taxi to take Ellie and her son to Lime Street station to catch the Manchester train, from where they would fly to Dublin. Brendan's clothes and toys had been packed the night before.

At exactly one minute past eleven, the taxi sounded its horn . . .

Brendan hardly spoke on the way to Manchester. His mother kept pointing things out through the window, as if she thought it was the sort of thing mothers were supposed to do. He acknowledged her comments with a brief nod of his head. She offered to buy him a can of drink when a trolley of food was pushed through the carriage, but he refused.

All Brendan could think of was Bee. Bee's face when he'd left her, Bee stroking his head when he felt sick, Bee singing him to sleep, reading to him, playing cards, watching football on the telly and screaming encouragement for the wrong side, then Bee's face when he'd left her yet again. Bee was his world. He didn't like his mother and never would.

The journey to Manchester didn't take long. They were catching a coach to the airport.

'I want to go to the lavvy,' he said when they went through the barrier.

'Say lavatory, kiddo. Or toilet's even better. You should have gone on the train.'

Brendan made a face behind his mother's back. 'I want to go to the toilet.'

'That's better. There's a Gents over there.'

'I'd like a drink now, please.'

'What sort?'

'Any sort.'

'They sell them in the newsagents. I'll meet you there. Don't get lost now.'

'No.' Brendan trotted into the Gents and re-emerged almost immediately. He saw his mother disappear into a shop and sped towards the platform where they'd just got off the train. A man in uniform caught his collar as he went through the barrier.

'And where d'you think you're off to, sonny?'

'I'm going to Liverpool with me mam,' Brendan explained nicely. 'I've lost her.'

'Well, you won't find her on this train. The next train to Liverpool's on platform 2. Where's your ticket?'

'Me mam's got it.'

'You'd better get a move on, or you'll lose her altogether. It's leaving in a minute.'

Brendan found platform 2 and ducked under the barrier when no one was looking. The train was only half full and he easily found a seat from where he could see the platform, ready to hide if his mother came looking for him.

It took twice as long to return to Liverpool as it had to go the other way, or so it seemed to Brendan, whose heart was in his mouth for the entire journey. He kept changing his seat, dodging into the lavatory whenever anyone in uniform appeared.

At last the train drew into Lime Street station where, to his utter astonishment, he found an anxious Bee waiting for him by the barrier. He'd thought he'd have to walk all the way home.

'Brendan!' She held out her arms. Her grey hair was waving all over her face and she had on the frayed jeans she wore to do the housework and a giant T-shirt that almost reached her knees, but in Brendan's eyes she had never looked so beautiful.

'Bee!' He flung himself at her. 'How did you know . . .' He couldn't find the words he wanted. How did she know to meet the train, that he'd be on it? But Bee knew what he meant.

'Your mother rang, love. She was terribly worried, but she guessed you were on your way home.'

Brendan's heart returned to his mouth. 'Is she coming after me?'

'No, love.' Bee took his hand. 'Seeing as we're in town, would you like to go to McDonald's for a hamburger? It's a lovely day.'

'No, ta, Bee. I'd sooner go home.' He didn't want to be seen for longer than necessary in the dead horrible shirt.

'So would I,' Bee said comfortably.

The phone call had come about an hour ago. Ellie had sounded frantic. 'Gran! Brendan's disappeared. He went to the Gents and was supposed to meet me in the newsagents, but he never came.'

'Did you send someone into the Gents to look for him?' Ruby said sharply.

'Yes, but he wasn't there. One of the ticket inspectors or something said a boy sounding like Brendan tried to get on the wrong train. He directed him towards the right one. He must be coming home.'

'What time does the train get in and I'll meet it?'

'Two thirty.'

'And what happens then, Ellie, when I've met the train?'

Ellie sighed. 'Nothing, I suppose. It doesn't seem such a good idea, taking Brendan to Dublin. I'll have his luggage sent back. Felix is going to be disappointed. He thought the world of him when he was a baby.'

'If it's your intention to make a life with Felix Conway, Ellie,' Ruby said gently, 'then it shouldn't matter whether you take Brendan with you or not.'

'Oh, Gran!' Ellie wailed. 'I desperately want to be happy.'

'Don't we all, love. Don't we all.'

Within a week, Brendan was his old self again, full of life, and inviting his mates home to play in the garden. Dublin and his mother had been forgotten.

But the incident had shaken Ruby. For some reason, she felt fearful, jumping at the least sound, always expecting something terrible to happen. She felt like a creature that had lost its outer shell and was now vulnerable to dangers never known before. Whenever the telephone rang, she'd get a sickly sensation in her stomach. It could only be bad news, though it never was.

Daisy had her baby, another boy. 'He's beautiful,' Heather reported from London. 'And she's going to call him Robert, after her father.'

Moira rang to say she and Sam were expecting another baby at Christmas. 'Me and Daisy are having a race, Gran. I've bet her I'll be the first to have five.'

Ruby was beginning to feel better, when something else happened, trivial when compared to losing Brendan but, for a while, she thought she was losing her mind.

It was August, sizzlingly hot, and she and Brendan had had a wonderful day in Southport, where they'd built castles in the sand, spent a fortune in the fairground, wandered along gracious Lord Street, and had tea in a glass-roofed arcade. While they ate, she told Brendan about Emily, who'd brought her to the very same place more than fifty years before. 'We could even have sat here, in this same spot.'

'And you were young, like me?' Brendan asked through a mouth full of cream cake, as if he couldn't conceive of such a thing.

'Older than you, fourteen.'

'What did you look like then?'

'Pretty. Everyone said I was pretty.'

'You're still pretty,' Brendan said loyally.

Ruby laughed. 'Thank you, love. During the war, me and Beth were evacuated to Southport, though we only stayed a few days. Your mam was three – I mean your gran.' The two small children she'd brought to Southport were now grandmothers! Despite all that had happened since, it seemed little more than yesterday that, on a similarly hot day, she'd waited by the station for Beth and Jake. She shrugged herself back to the present. 'I feel like buying things,' she said. 'A nice new summer frock for me. What do you fancy?'

'A goal,' Brendan said promptly.

'A goal?'

'You get them from Argos. A boy at school's got one. I went to his house once and it's the gear.'

'Will it be heavy to carry?' Ruby looked doubtful.

'I'll carry it, Gran. Don't worry,' Brendan said stoutly.

They returned happily to Liverpool; Brendan with his goal in a cardboard box and Ruby with a crush-proof two-piece from Marks & Spencers that would never need ironing, to find the house had been burgled.

Not much had been taken; Heather's portable television, the chopper bike Brendan had got for his birthday, Ruby's jewellery box which contained little of value, a few ornaments that had been gifts from people over the years. The burglar or burglars had left a mess behind – perhaps annoyed to have found so little of value in such a large house. The contents of drawers had been thrown on to the floors, dishes had been broken, a mirror smashed, chairs upturned, cupboards emptied.

The police were very sympathetic, but didn't hold out much hope of the goods being recovered. Ruby was advised to fit deadlocks on the doors and windows and have a burglar alarm installed.

'This place was a cinch to break into. Once they'd established no one was in, they merely kicked in the back door.'

For the first two days, Ruby was very calm. She concentrated on putting everything back where it belonged. The bike and the television were covered by insurance and would be replaced. Heather was arranging for the deadlocks and burglar alarm to be fitted.

It was when she began to list the contents of her jewellery box that something broke inside her. The police wanted details, 'In case an item's offered for sale. We provide jewellers with a list of stolen property.'

'But it was hardly worth anything,' Ruby cried. She'd never possessed a precious stone in her life.

'It could have been kids who burgled your home, Mrs O'Hagan, and they could still try and sell it. All we're asking for is a list. The stuff might even turn up at a car boot sale.'

Most of her jewellery had been presents from the girls; a tiny amethyst pendant on a silver chain with earrings to match were the first things that came to mind, bought when the girls had not long started work and couldn't have afforded more than a few pounds; gold stud earrings, very small; a silver cross and chain; a silver and amber bracelet brought back from Corfu. There was a brooch from Beth, a cheap thing that had gone dull with age.

As she wrote the things down, each brought back its own particular memory, when it had been given, why – a birthday, Christmas, or for no special reason at all. There was a scarf ring, she remembered, with a huge green stone which would have been worth thousands had it been real. Greta and Heather had bought it the day they'd met the lads. 'For being such a lovely mam,' Greta had said at the time.

Ruby felt as if the memories had been taken away and soiled. Her house had been soiled, her life had been invaded. A stranger or strangers had walked through the rooms touching her things, Heather's things, Brendan's.

Then she recalled the jewellery box had contained the ring Olivia had given her, the ring that had belonged to her father. 'It's my grandpop's wedding ring,' he'd said when he gave it to Olivia – she remembered the words exactly, she told Ruby. 'And the way he said it. I remember every single thing about that night.'

'Ruby to Eamon. 1857,' Ruby said aloud, and began to cry. She'd always meant to buy a gold chain and wear the ring around her neck, but had never got round to it. And now she didn't have the ring. It had been stolen.

She would never feel safe in the house again. What's more, she'd never be able to *leave* the house again. The thought of finding the rooms in turmoil a second time, their possessions strewn on the floor, made her feel physically sick. She was frightened to stay in, frightened to go out.

Ruby went into the kitchen and began to clean the room from top to bottom, wiping every surface, including the walls, so there would be no trace left of the intruders. Every single inch would have to be cleansed of their touch and the places where they'd breathed. There was a robotic urgency about her movements, and a slightly mad look in her eyes.

She worked herself to a standstill, but forced herself to start on the living room. As soon as she'd finished cleaning, she would wash everything; their clothes, the bedding, the curtains, all the things that had been contaminated by the thieves.

That night, she hardly slept, thinking of all the work that had to be done, listening to the creaks and groans of the old house, familiar noises that had once been comforting, but which she now found sinister. She got up twice to make sure Brendan was safely asleep in his bed and hadn't been murdered.

'Have you decided to spring clean in August, Mam?' Heather enquired a few days later when she came home from work and found Ruby up a ladder in her room cleaning the picture rail.

'I suddenly realised what a state the place was in. It needs a thorough going over.'

'It looks all right to me. Anyroad, since when have you cared what state the place was in? You look worn out. Would you like a cup of tea?'

'Please, love.' Heather didn't realise how hard she'd been working. Ruby hadn't told anyone how she felt. 'The meal's in the oven, it'll be ready soon. Brendan's round at a friend's house.'

Heather returned a few minutes later to report there was no tea. 'I'll just nip round to the shops and get some.'

'I could have sworn there was a packet in the cupboard,' Ruby said vaguely.

'Well, there isn't. I won't be long.'

'While you're there, will you get some sugar? We're nearly out of that too.' They were running out of all sorts of things. She usually bought the groceries on Thursdays, but was waiting until the weekend when Heather was home and the house wouldn't be left empty.

When she climbed down the ladder, her legs were shaking. She felt exhausted, yet there was so much to be done. Upstairs still hadn't been touched. She was working herself into the ground, hardly sleeping, all on account of a burglary in which not much had been taken. Far worse things happened to people on a daily basis – they'd happened to her – I but she'd never felt like this before, completely gutted.

The phone went. It was Angela Burns, Daisy's mother-in-law, a pleasantly brisk woman with a finger in all sorts of pies. They'd met just once at the wedding. Angela wanted Heather. The two got on like a house on fire, although Angela was nearer Ruby's age. After a brief chat, she said she'd call back later when told Heather wasn't in.

Later, when Angela rang, Ruby shamelessly eavesdropped during the conversation with her daughter. It seemed Heather was being offered a job in London, a good one. She sounded excited, but then her voice dropped and Ruby had to strain to hear.

'I couldn't possibly leave just yet. I told you we'd had a burglary, didn't I? Well, it's badly affected my mother. She's in a bit of a state, though she pretends not to be, and I pretend not to notice. She hates to be thought weak.' There was a pause, then, 'Yes, yes. As soon as I can. I'm looking forward to it.'

When Heather returned, Ruby was innocently watching *Top of the Pops* with Brendan.

'Angela said Rob's thriving. You two must meet up again one day, Mam. You've never been to London, have you?'

'No, love.' And she never would. She couldn't possibly leave the house.

Later still, when Brendan and Heather were in bed, Ruby stayed up and watched an old film, knowing she'd never sleep. Would she ever sleep peacefully again? The film finished and for some reason, her eyes were drawn to Daisy's painting which still hung over the mantelpiece, though she'd been intending to move it for ages.

What did it mean? She'd often wondered. Perhaps that's why she kept it there, in the hope that one day she would understand. A wobbly circle with six splodgy figures inside, one much bigger than the others. If you stared hard enough, the figures seemed to move.

She went and made a cup of hot milk and returned to stare at the painting again. Six figures. Why six?

Matthew Doyle had understood. 'I can see what she's getting at,' he'd said. 'You're very lucky, all of you. I wish I were in Daisy's painting, but there was never a chance of that.'

Could the figures be herself, her daughters, and her granddaughters? Six people. Why were they lucky, these six people, sheltering with a circle, nothing touching them?

And *then* Ruby understood. This was Daisy's childhood world, the way she'd seen it before she married Clint and discovered how painful it could be. Greta, Ellie and Moira had also gone to experience the world outside for themselves. Soon Heather would also go and, of the six people, only Ruby would be left behind.

No wonder she'd been so upset by the burglary. It had shattered the circle. She was the large figure in the painting, cosseting and caring for her family, protecting them from harm. Perhaps it was a relic of Foster Court, the need to keep her children, and their children, safe.

'You created your own little world and crowned yourself its queen,' Beth told her that time in Washington.

But now Daisy's circle had been broken and couldn't be mended. Things would never be safe again. What's more, Ruby would just have to get used to it, not stay cowering in the house, scared out of her wits.

On impulse, she went into the hall and telephoned Beth. She spent most of her time in Washington these days, working for the Democratic party. It was a long time since they'd spoken.

'Beth Lefarge's office,' said a male voice, only young.

'Is Beth there? It's Ruby O'Hagan speaking, her friend from Liverpool.'

'Hi, Ruby. Hold on, I'll see if she's free.'

Beth came on almost immediately. 'Ruby! It's ages since we spoke.'

'I was just thinking the same thing. Who's the young man? Or do you have a male secretary these days?'

'My secretary went home at five o'clock. Hank's my grandson. We were just wondering how to get more black voters involved in the next election. How's things, Rube?'

'Up and down. I was thinking about going to Dublin before the school holidays are over. Ellie lives there, Brendan's mother. It's about time they got to know each other properly. I'll see what Brendan has to say about it.' An astonished Ruby had been thinking no such thing. The words had just come out, perhaps because they were the right words. Brendan would be far better off with his mother than a woman of sixty-six. He had to learn to love Ellie before it was too late, as it had been too late with Ruby's own mother.

'And our Heather's got a job in London,' she went on. 'I'm not sure of the details, but she'll be leaving soon. She's been a good daughter. Heather, and I'm very pleased for her.' As it was, she was holding Heather back, when she should be offering encouragement.

'You'll be left in that big house all on your own,' Beth pointed out.

'It will be a while before Brendan will come to realise he'd be happier with Ellie. When he does – well, we'll just have to see.'

By then, it would be time to leave the house by Princes Park for ever.

The week in Dublin went unexpectedly well. Ellie was living in a pretty village, Craigmoss, several miles from the city. She already seemed less frenetic, more content, her turbulent brain at rest. Felix Conway was a lovely man, very kind, and a good influence on her wayward granddaughter. He brought out the best in her. Brendan had taken to him immediately and had seemed happy to stay with him and Ellie when Ruby had gone to Dublin for the day, a deliberate ploy on her part.

She had felt lonely, wandering around the strange city on her own, wondering what the future had in store. So many times in the past she had wanted to *do* something, though she'd never known what. Very shortly, for the first time in her life, she would be free to do anything she wanted and she still didn't know what.

Late September, and Ruby was in the garden, sitting in a deckchair under a tree, watching the occasional bronze leaf float to the ground.

'Catch a leaf and make a wish.' The girls had done it in the convent, but Ruby couldn't remember a single wish she'd made. What was she likely to have wished for in those days? Probably *not* to become a housemaid or a cook, in which case it hadn't come true. She'd been cooking and doing housework all her life.

A cloud drifted across the warm sun and she shivered. In a minute, she'd get on with her painting in case it rained. Daisy had left a load of hardboard pieces behind and some half-used tubes of paint and Ruby was painting a picture of the back of the house. It was a foolish idea that had come to her out of the blue. No one knew, not even Brendan who was at school. She was too embarrassed to let people know.

At first, she'd got more paint on her clothes than on the board, but now the painting was almost finished. But she'd been thinking that for weeks. Every time she thought the picture was complete, she'd feel impelled to include another tiny figure; a disjointed, unrecognisable figure, sitting, lying, or standing on the grass. A figure playing with a ball or a skipping rope, or sitting on the back step with a dab of white paint that was supposed to be a cup in what was supposed to be a hand. After a while, Ruby had realised she was painting the story of the early years in the house. The figures were her children, Beth and Jake, Connie and Charles, Martha Quinlan, Max Hart, the kids she'd looked after during the war, like little ghosts amidst the trees. The person on the step was herself.

There was one person missing from the painting and she wasn't sure where to fit him in; right in the middle where he truly belonged, or on the periphery where he'd always been.

She closed her eyes and saw the painting in her mind's eye. Right in the middle, she decided. She'd put him beside herself, outside the back door. Over the last tumultuous weeks, she'd wished he'd been around, if only as a friend, someone to talk to. She'd always been able to talk to Matthew Doyle.

When she opened her eyes, she became aware a man had come round the side of the house and was regarding her gravely. He was a striking man, very tall and very thin. His once black hair was almost completely grey and his face had been burnt deep golden brown by the sun. He was impeccably dressed, as always, in khaki cotton slacks and a green anorak.

For a moment, Ruby felt totally disorientated. Had her painting come to life, her wish come true?

'Matthew!' she mumbled. She tried to struggle to her feet, but gave up when it appeared she'd lost the use of her limbs.

He came towards her and sat on the grass, still grave. 'I understand you left a message at the office for me to call.'

'That was five years ago,' she gasped.

'Sorry about the delay, but I've been busy.'

She patted her hair and realised it hadn't been combed and she wasn't wearing a scrap of make up to disguise the multitude of wrinkles. She had on the old jeans she wore to paint in. 'Why didn't you let me know you were coming. I'd have got ready, properly dressed.'

He smiled at last and her heart turned over. 'The first time I saw you in this very house, you were covered in paint. It's how I always think of you.'

A little excited shiver ran down her spine, as it had done they day they'd met. 'You suit grey hair,' she said.

'I think that's the first compliment you've ever paid me.' He looked pleased. Close up, she saw he had enough wrinkles of his own around his brown eyes. His cheeks were gaunt and heavily lined. She thought he didn't look well.

'Are you home for good?' Ruby held her breath, waiting for the answer, and thinking what a silly way it was for an old woman to behave.

'I've retired, so yes, I'm home for good.'

'Where are you going to live?'

'That depends on you, Rube.' He looked at her directly, his expression serious, then turned to watch a leaf detach itself from a tree and land softly on the grass. 'Have you missed me?'

'Yes, Matthew, I've missed you. I've always hoped you'd come back.'

He nodded, satisfied. 'How's everyone?'

'Fine. Even Ellie seems to have settled down.' She told him about Greta's baby, all the other babies, Brendan coming back from Manchester alone on the train, the burglary. 'I thought I'd lost it for a while, but I managed to recover.'

'You're strong, that's why.'

Ruby shuddered. 'I didn't feel strong then. Would you like some tea, Matthew?'

'I was hoping you'd ask.'

She tried again to struggle out of the deckchair and he reached for her hand and pulled her to her feet.

They stayed holding hands as they strolled across the grass towards the house. It would be just like old times, him sprawled on a chair while she made the tea. Ruby felt a pang, thinking of what she'd missed because she'd ignored her true feelings.

But, she thought impatiently, she'd never believed in dwelling on the past. The present was more important. All of a sudden, she saw with vivid clarity what the future had in store, what she would *do*.

She would marry Matthew Doyle.

Matthew

Epilogue

Millennium Eve

They sat on a balcony overlooking the River Mersey, an elderly couple, warmly wrapped up against the cold. It had just gone half past eleven. Only twenty-nine minutes remained of the twentieth century.

Daisy and Moira were having parties, but it was impossible to go to both. To avoid hurt feelings, they had decided to spend Millennium Eve at home, just the two of them, together.

'Are you warm enough, love?' Ruby said anxiously. Matthew was very frail these days. He hadn't known his lungs had been permanently damaged by the tuberculosis all those years ago until he found difficulty breathing.

'I'm fine, Rube.' His voice was slightly hoarse. 'I wouldn't miss this for anything.'

The river stretched in front of them, a black, satin ribbon, reflecting the bright lights of Wallasey and Birkenhead. The lights wobbled slightly in the gentle waves. It was a spectacular sight. Matthew loved it. In the summer, he would sit on the balcony of their riverside flat until long after it had gone dark.

The telephone rang for the umpteenth time – the sliding door had been left open so they could hear the phone and listen to the television. Ruby went to answer it. 'That was Beth,' she said when she came back. 'She's in Little Rock with the family. They're having a big do, but it's not midnight over there for hours yet. By the way, she's invited us to stay in Washington next summer.'

'I like Washington,' Matthew said. They'd been several times before. 'I'm already looking forward to it.'

Ruby prayed with all her heart he'd be fit enough to travel when the time came. She sat beside him on the wrought iron bench, feeling fidgety. 'Would you like some tea?'

'For God's sake, Ruby,' he said irritably, 'can't you sit still a minute and look at the view?'

'Nothing's happening,' she complained.

'It will, soon, when the fireworks start.'

'I'll make myself a cup of tea in the meantime.' Ruby got to her feet and gave a little shriek when a pain shot through her leg.

'What's the matter?'

'It's my damn arthritis.' She was eighty-one and hated growing old – all the mysterious pains that appeared from nowhere, then disappeared as quickly as they'd come when she thought she was about to die.

She hobbled into the kitchen which couldn't have been more different than the one in the house by Princes Park; all stainless steel, efficient, functional, and easy to clean, which was the way kitchens ought to be. The contrast between the two rarely crossed her mind nowadays, though had been a constant wonder when they'd first moved in. It was in 1988, when Brendan was eleven, that he'd gone to live in Dublin with Ellie and Felix, perhaps persuaded by the arrival of a baby sister and the need to belong to a proper family. Now he was managing the restaurant in Fern Hall that Ellie had started and which had proved such a great success. He had married an Irish girl, Katy, and would become a father very soon.

The house had been sold and Ruby had never gone back. She had no idea who lived there now. Leaving the place had hurt more than she'd ever imagined. The old walls held many memories, most of them good, and she preferred not to rake over them, though there were times when they unexpectedly returned, without warning, tugging at her heartstrings. Tonight, for instance, when Beth had rung, she'd put a face to the voice with its slight transatlantic twang, and found herself talking to the pretty, dewy-eyed girl she'd met in Arthur Cumming's house, not the gnarled old lady Beth was now.

The phone rang again. It was Robert, Daisy's son, on his mobile. 'We're on the Embankment, Bee.' Brendan's name for her had stuck with all the young people. 'The television camera's pointing straight at us. We're waving like mad, can you see us?'

'Just a minute, love. It's on the wrong channel. Yes, I can see you,' Ruby screamed, though without her glasses she could see only a crowd of blurred figures. 'Is Harry with you?'

'Yes, he's calling Mum on *his* mobile. We're going home as soon as the fireworks are over.'

'Have a nice time. Be careful now, and give Harry my love.'

'We'll ring again later, Bee.'

It would be nice, Ruby thought, when the camera moved to another location, to be on the banks of the Thames in the middle of all the excitement. Mind you, she could feel the excitement here. Buildings always seemed to know when something remarkable was about to happen. The air seemed to tingle.

'Who was that?' Matthew called.

'Robert. He's on the Embankment with Harry I just saw them on television.'

'I wondered what the screaming was about. What are you doing in there? I'm feeling lonely.'

'Making myself a cup of tea, but I think I'll have something stronger, a Martini, to toast the New Year – the new century. Would you like some whisky?'

'Can't, Rube,' he answered gloomily. 'Not while I'm taking those tablets. You have one for me.'

'I'll fetch orange juice, you can make a toast with that.'

She'd hardly been on the balcony a minute, when the phone rang yet again. Matthew groaned. This time it was an ecstatic Ellie. 'Katy's just had the baby, Gran, by express delivery. It's a little girl. Brendan asked me to ring you first. They're going to call her Ruby.'

'Tell Brendan I'm very flattered.' Ruby sniffed. She quite fancied a little cry.

'Now I'm a grandmother!' Ellie sounded slightly shocked, as if she'd only just realised. 'It makes me feel dead ancient.'

'Wait till your grandchildren have grandchildren, Ellie. *Then* you'll feel ancient.'

'I'd better go now and give Mum a ring. She's at our Moira's. You'll come and stay soon, won't you, Gran, meet your namesake?'

'As soon as we can, love.' She was glad Greta was staying in Cambridge with Moira and Sam and their five children. New Year's Eve wasn't a good time for widows. Frank Fletcher had died five years ago and Saffron, their beloved little girl, now eighteen, had been in and out of a series of unstable relationships. She was at the moment living with a dodgy character who sold used cars – a distraught Greta suspected they were stolen.

Life was so unpredictable. Just as one daughter had lost a husband, the other had acquired one. Heather, at the age of fifty-six, had married a fellow solicitor, and was living close to Daisy in Crouch End. The sisters, once so close, hardly saw each other nowadays.

'Who was *that?*' Matthew sounded cross.

'Ellie. Katy's just had the baby, a little girl. They're going to call her Ruby.'

'Good. Are you coming out again?'

'In a minute.' Ruby was staring at Daisy's painting which hung over the mantelpiece. It went perfectly in the ultra-modern high-ceilinged room that had once been the top floor of a grain warehouse. She and Matthew were the only residents over fifty in the development – she liked living in a place designed for young people.

Visitors often admired Daisy's painting. Some asked what the artist was trying to convey, but Ruby never told them.

There were too many O'Hagans now to fit in the circle, too many for her to watch over, keep safe. She began to worry about Harry and Robert on the Embankment – things could get out of hand on a night like tonight.

'Am I going to see the New Millennium in on me own?' Matthew called plaintively.

'Coming.' She stepped out on to the balcony and closed the sliding door.

'We won't hear Big Ben.'

'It doesn't matter. It's getting cold inside with it open. We'll know when it's twelve o'clock, don't worry.' She leant her head on his shoulder and he immediately put his arm around her.

'I'm glad I'm with you,' he whispered.

'And I'm glad I'm with you.'

'Honest?'

Ruby sighed contentedly. 'Honest.'

They sat in silence for a while, the only sound the distant hum of the city, each pre-occupied with their own thoughts. The past fifteen years with Matthew had been good years, almost perfect. They had travelled a lot, not only to Washington to see Beth, or to stay with relatives, but to places all over Europe. She had imagined this day, this very special New Year's Eve, many times in the past, wondering if she would still be alive to see it, where she would be, who with, and there wasn't a person in the world she'd sooner be with than Matthew. She said a prayer, thanking God for letting them both live long enough to welcome in the New Millennium, unlike the Donovans and the Whites, all dead now, along with Connie and Charles, and Daniel Lefarge, Beth's husband.

'It shouldn't be long now,' Matthew murmured.

As if on cue, the world suddenly erupted in a mighty cheer. In the distance, church bells chimed, a glorious sound, accompanied by the mournful wail of ships's hooters. Across the water, and on Kings Dock to their right, a thousand fireworks shot into the sky, exploding into a million stars. There were shouts and laughter from the balcony below. Somewhere close, a dog barked hysterically.

'Happy New Year, Matthew.'

'Happy New Century, Ruby.'

They kissed, a sweet, gentle kiss. There wasn't much passion left nowadays.

The noise went on, the fireworks, the cheering, the singing, as their small part of the world celebrated the advent of the twenty-first century.

After a while, Matthew began to shiver, so they went indoors and found the telephone ringing.

It was Greta. 'Happy New Year, Mam,' she sang.

'The same to you, love.' Ruby was glad she sounded happy. Moira came on, then Sam, followed, one by one, by the children, all five of them, anxious to wish Bee and Uncle Matt a Happy New Year.

Then Heather rang, Daisy and Michael, Brendan, the new father, as drunk as a lord. Harry called again from the Embankment. He and Robert were on their way home with a couple of girls they'd met. 'They're Swedish and drop dead gorgeous.'

Matthew had been watching television all this time. 'I think I'll turn in,' he said when Ruby judged there were unlikely to be any more calls.

'Would you like some hot milk to take with you?'

'No, ta, Rube. I'm dead beat.'

But Ruby had never felt more wide awake. 'Goodnight, love. I'll join you in a minute.' She kissed him, then watched him go, stooped and feeble, and remembered the tall, dark young man in the cheap suit she'd met the day the war ended. She sighed, went into the kitchen, but instead of milk, poured another Martini, then put her coat back on and returned to the balcony to watch the fireworks and listen to the bells and the sound of people enjoying themselves. All of a sudden, she ached to be part of the crowd, to dance and sing, celebrate this unique night. She was reluctant to go to bed, curl up beside Matthew's warm body, while the rest of the world was wide awake and having a wonderful time.

She went over to the bedroom door and listened. He was already asleep, snoring softly. It wouldn't hurt to go out, just for half an hour, mingle with the crowds, shake a few hands. She might well be a silver-haired old lady with arthritis, but she still didn't want to miss anything.